Amir Gutfreund

OUR
HOLOCAUST

TRANSLATED BY

Jessica Cohen

The Toby Press

First English Language Edition 2006
The Toby Press LLC

POB 8531, New Milford, CT 06776-8531, USA
& POB 2455, London WIA 5WY, England
www.tobypress.com

First published in Hebrew as *Shoah Shelanu*
Copyright © Amir Gutfreund and Kinneret, Zmora-
Bitan, Dvir – Publishing House Ltd, Tel Aviv, 2001

All rights reserved
Translation copyright © Jessica Cohen, 2006

ISBN I 59264 139 3, *hardcover*

A CIP catalogue record for this title is
available from the British Library

Typeset in Garamond by Jerusalem Typesetting

Printed and bound in the United States
by Thomson-Shore Inc., Michigan

1993: Our Laws

Grandpa used to say, "People have to die of something," and refused to donate to the war against cancer, the war against traffic accidents, or any other war. To avoid being considered stingy, he would occasionally burst into exemplary displays of tremendous generosity. He put on these shows with such proficiency that if not for us, his relatives, no one would have known the simple truth: he was a miser.

In his home, parsimony was the law of the land. He zealously collected empty bottles for their deposits, and when one of them broke he glued it back together with great artistry. Like a cuckoo, he tossed his shirts into other people's laundry hampers, staging stains when necessary. A wonderful ability to catch colds in tandem with us enabled him to use our cough syrup and conserve his own. He would declare the colds over prematurely, proclaiming, "We're better now!" and stockpile the remaining antibiotics. A bottle of liquid soap stood in his bathroom, and whenever the soap level dropped below a finger's width he watered it down in an endless process that ultimately produced a bottle of water convinced it was soap. But his most wonderful ruse involved a magical power over tea bags. Each bag, even upon its tenth descent into boiling water, yielded something of itself—the merest vapor of tea, just verging on physically tangible material. The hoisting of the bag out of the water was accompanied by an expertly suspicious look at the bag hanging off the teaspoon by its string. Based on signs perceptible only to himself, he would estimate the bag's vitality and decree its fate. *Selektion*, he called this ceremony when he wanted to be cruel to Grandpa Yosef. We suspected that even when the bags were exhausted he did not throw them away, but rather hoarded them in a secret location so that he could one day make them into a new mattress. We spent our childhood hunting for them, but even in our nosiest searches, when we exposed his letters to Joyce the dancer and his debt to the late Jew Finkelstein, we never found a single tea bag.

We were happy, at times, to remind ourselves that he wasn't even our real grandfather.

We called him Grandpa—Grandpa Lolek—due to our family's Law of Compression, a wonderful invention of our parents, the first generation of the Holocaust. Lacking brothers, uncles, fathers and mothers, they had done away with the requirement for precision. Anyone belonging to our parents' generation was simply called "Uncle." Their offspring were our cousins. Not that everyone was up for grabs. There were certainly rules. There had to be a corresponding sense of closeness among all the generations, so that the stitches holding us all together could heal and all individuals could find their relatives. A fond relationship among the parents' generation meant that we could acquire their offspring as our cousins. Introvert "uncles" who tended not to take an interest in family affairs denied us entire clusters of willing cousins. Denied. End of story. The Law of Compression left no room for compromise.

Our greatest need was for grandparents, and so we ploughed our way through the restrictions and gathered as many of them as we could. I never knew my father's father, Zev-Wolf. (In Dad's photo album, I was drawn to a small picture of his grave.) We chose his cousins, Grandpa Lolek and Grandpa Hainek, to be our grandfathers. On Mom's side we devised a similar ploy. Her father, sick Grandpa Shalom—who had yet to emerge from the Holocaust—was locked in the depths of a terminal illness brought on by Gestapo tortures, and so we annexed a distant relative of his as an official grandfather, Grandpa Menashe. At other opportunities we acquired Grandpa Ernst, Grandma Eva and Grandpa Weil.

How pitifully small was my real family, the one we covered up with camouflage relatives:

Grandpa Shalom, 1912–1980.

One aunt.

Her son, one real cousin.

And yes, there was actually another uncle, my mother's half-brother.

"You don't need a psychologist to understand that," Effi responded when I told her once how I yearn to sleep with Anat every time we come home from one of her family weddings. Still in the car, both tired, I reach out to unbutton her dress and she barely has time to take her shoes off. From the back seat come the grumblings of Yariv, our five-year-old prince.

Grandpa Lolek, the tea artiste, was not the first of the grandpas. We got hold of him fairly late in the day. But he was a powerful axis in our lives, a figure who showered sparks onto our daily routines. He usually burst into our world in his 1970 Vauxhall, a moribund chassis of protestations upon which only he could impose life. Always wearing a tie, always smoking and dressed in colorful grandeur, he would emerge from the Vauxhall as if he were Kaiser Franz Josef out to wave at the masses from his balcony. Within minutes he would be sitting at the table drinking tea, eating whatever cake he was served, and smoking a cigarette.

Grandpa Lolek, the clear anomaly in our environment, was not a Holocaust survivor at all. World War II had caught him serving in the Polish cavalry, one of those wretched madmen who stormed German tanks yelling "Hurrah!" and waving swords. When his unit fell apart, Grandpa Lolek fled to Russia, where he joined the volunteer army of the Polish General Anders. With Anders, he set off on a voyage through Persia and Palestine to England, to reenter the war. Anders' soldiers, with Grandpa Lolek among them, were thrown into some of the toughest battles and suffered the most terrible losses.

These dime-a-dozen soldiers who were sent into battle every time a general in some war-room mumbled "let's give them a try," sustained heavy losses that filtered and distilled them until all that remained were Grandpa-Lolek-types, people coated with a layer of pure luck, fearless in the face of their old friend Death. They faced it every day, watched it go about its business, and grew accustomed to acknowledging it with a polite nod or a tip of the hat. They did not meddle in Death's business, nor Death in theirs.

When World War II was over, the members of Anders' Army, the remnants of the remnants, were rewarded for their service with British citizenship. But Grandpa Lolek was in love with an American dancer from Kentucky by the name of Joyce, and besides which, he needed to return to Poland to find out what remained of his family. Joyce was lost on the way, abdicating her chance to become Grandma Joyce (to be precise, she replaced Grandpa Lolek with a Viennese pianist). Lolek's family had perished in the gas chambers. Only his younger brother Hainek remained, and together they immigrated to Palestine, where Lolek renewed his war against all the wretches who lamented their fates, whispering tales of Auschwitz and Buchenwald.

Grandpa Lolek would rebuke the survivors. "You had terrible *Selektion*? One out of three, they took from you? Ten hours, naked in snow in *Appellplatz*? Well, what coddling! With us, against the Germans at Monte Cassino, if only it was being one out of three! Two nights and two days, person that rests a little, they die. Come on, let's move, no rest. Well, such trouble for you..."

His Hebrew was a tale of one-thousand Hebraic mistakes, an octagon of errors rolling through almost every sentence. He used to raise his glass and proclaim, "Life is good, Jews!" A bit of an anti-Semite. Drank a lot. Smoked. Always upright with a straight spine, despite his backache.

He owned a piece of land near Gedera, which he had been led to understand by certain-officials-in-the-right-places would soon be rezoned for construction. From time to time, over the course of thirty years, he went off to examine his treasure, which was agricultural for the time being, covered with heads of lettuce and strawberries like baby teeth, soon to be shed to make way for the main event. The officials, over the course of thirty years, were replaced, but Grandpa Lolek did not lose faith. He had complete confidence in the reliability of corruption and refused to sell his land to some bothersome farmer from Moshav Kidron. The farmer made repeated offers, all rejected by Grandpa Lolek.

"On my land no vegetable will to be grown!" he declared with ideological fervor. He would not stand for land being humiliated by such ridiculous things as kohlrabi. His land would be a piece of pure real estate.

Every time Grandpa Lolek came back from Gedera, he drove directly to Green the Mechanic, because the Vauxhall could not travel all those miles without a resuscitation service. There, sitting among the Arab laborers while the car was serviced, he was immediately provided with a chair and a glass of bitter coffee, for which he paid with war stories. The laborers loved him: a Jew who could tell of victories, but not over Arabs. They could relax around him, listen without pangs of guilt to stories of battles and ruses. For a wax-and-polish they were even treated to a good word about Salah a-Din.

The 1970 Vauxhall was a rare hothouse of now-extinct spare parts. The car, which had long ago driven off the standard path of licenses-insurance-tests, was patched up with any spare part that came cheaply. "The cheapest are chosen and the fittest survive," was the modus operandi in the Vauxhall, to the point where all other garage owners had washed their hands of it. Only Green the Mechanic, a pure soul, agreed to touch the Vauxhall. He offered no warranties, no reports, no nothing. There was a mutual understanding between the two men, and Green the Mechanic had Grandpa Lolek's blessing to explore every solution. He gave the Vauxhall a radiator from an old Volvo and a pump from a Saab. Screws that were no longer manufactured anywhere in the world found their way into the Vauxhall, as well as Fiat, Renault and DAF windows. The awe-inspiring jewel in the crown was concealed within the Vauxhall's maze of pipes: a Chevrolet carburetor, the last of its kind.

Green the Mechanic did these favors for no one but Grandpa Lolek. He looked surprised when I took him my Subaru for repairs one day, and reminded me that his was a Volkswagen garage—How, in my opinion, was he supposed to repair my Subaru? He wanted to know when I would start driving a Volkswagen, at which point I explained that I was opposed to German cars on principle.

"Because of the price?"

"Because of the Holocaust."

Green the Mechanic was very understanding. There are people who don't buy Japanese because of their metal, on principle. The Holocaust was a principle too, but in that case, he said, I had to go to a Subaru garage. Grandpa Lolek and his Vauxhall were a special case.

Grandpa Lolek loved the Vauxhall dearly, and he always paid Green the Mechanic on time. Elsewhere he was stingy, refusing to follow through with the activity known as payment. He continually enhanced his debtism until the accumulation of debt became an art form. His debts were his fountain of youth. They gave him strength and energized his spirit. We could imagine no finer event than Grandpa Lolek setting off to discuss a debt. He met his creditors proudly, presented his demands, occasionally listened. The tougher and more well-to-do creditors who could back their demands more concretely only increased Grandpa Lolek's grandeur. Sometimes he would orchestrate our attendance at the discussions, sitting us down in a corner of the room. The sweet presence of a child takes the sting out of many hostilities, he reasoned. We sat silently, somewhat aware of our function, watching as Grandpa Lolek pulled out thick binders full of papers and bills. He would leaf through them, examining them, and suddenly his eyes would light up. Looking up at the creditor, he would exclaim, "Here! We've found you!" He would display the papers, glowing with satisfaction, as if half the problem had already been solved. With quick fingers that were speckled with a few brown old-age stains, he would draw some papers from the thick pile and spread them on the table. "Here!" He would slap his hand on them. And the interlocutor was expected to ease up his demands a little. Not all the creditors were gullible. Some tended to be violent. But the hero of Anders' Army would pierce them with his icy blue eyes and plunge them into a river of agreements, words, choices, debts, arrangements, restrictions and guarantees. Grandpa Lolek was a juggler. Dates were set, systems drafted, on occasion a payment date was even considered. Sometimes another loan would spontaneously materialize from the very force of the new agreement. Some of the creditors took Grandpa Lolek to court, where justice entered a dizzying series of wonders. Grandpa Lolek's cases dragged on through delays and mistakes. The court reversed its opinions again and again. It set dates and then canceled them, summoned meetings and withdrew from them. The court's transformation was incomprehensible, as if Doubt had sat down in the central office to translate pangs of conscience into cancelled hearings. Or else it was because Grandpa Lolek had found an old court clerk who admired his past in Anders' Army. Not because of Grandpa Lolek's own service, but out of reverence for another of General Anders' soldiers, the late Prime Minister Menachem Begin. Admittedly, Begin, like many other Jews, had defected even before the battles began, when Anders' Army passed through Palestine en route from Russia to England, and had joined the Zionist fight here. Nonetheless, Begin had been affected by his days in Anders' Army, and in return for Grandpa Lolek's recollections of him, the clerk would do his best with the court dates, arranging delays and postponements. Grandpa Lolek, regretfully, had not known Menachem Begin at all in those days, but as far as he was concerned a soldier was a soldier. And so he told stories upon stories, sometimes carelessly sweeping Begin along with Anders' Army to Europe instead of leaving him here to lead the Etzel underground movement. He took him to the battles of Monte Cassino, Loretto, Ancona, to the river fordings in Italy. His interlocutor, rather than protesting, enthused, "And all this, while the Zionist struggle was raging here!"

Alongside his debtism, Grandpa Lolek perfected the art of opportunity. Whenever time, usually a galloper, made the mistake of slowing down to a trot, Grandpa Lolek immediately swatted it. His newspapers were always spread out, open to the classifieds and the obituary pages. He rapidly connected this notice with that announcement, put on his most appropriate tie, and set off in the Vauxhall to hunt down an opportunity. Grandpa Lolek, a foot soldier, did not discount minor gains. He nurtured small accounts, sometimes tiny, in every bank. He transferred pennies from one account to the other, bearing the pain of commissions, and waited for a surprising event on a cosmic scale that would hit the pennies en route and turn them into billions. His life was guided by special offers. He would purchase sixty packets of spaghetti on sale without a qualm and lie patiently in wait for ketchup prices to go down. He smoked remorselessly, with the enjoyment of those who know that cancer will not kill them. This was one area in which he was never thrifty. He bought fine imported cigarettes even in the hardest economic times, and smoked them lovingly without fear. He would not take a cigarette from anyone and he gave them freely to others. One cigarette, two. And once, right in front of my eyes, he gave a whole pack to a panhandler on the street.

His debtism, miserliness and frugality, coupled with his lust for business, gave rise to a large amount of property. We reminded him of the possibility that someone might someday inherit all of this. Grandpa Lolek avoided heirs like the plague. He thwarted any attempts at producing offspring, who were nothing but temporarily disguised successors. He was not of the opinion that "after his passing" would be an appropriate time to allow someone to enjoy his money. When the subject came up he became aggravated, waving his fist at non-existent sons to ward them off. He went to bed every night alive, and in the morning inherited his own property.

This was a flawless arrangement. Ostensibly. For alongside the strait of his life another channel rolled along, an ever-multiplying serpent of offspring in the form of a gang of boys entitled to address him as "Uncle." They had been produced in quick succession by Grandpa Lolek's only brother, Grandpa Hainek.

Our anointing of Grandpa Hainek as a grandfather was solely due to Grandpa Lolek. He himself was not of much use, but when we adopted Grandpa Lolek we simply reached out and added Grandpa Hainek, just in case. He was distinguished by his blue eyes and blond hair, which had turned white over the long and torpid snowy years. His body was heavy and solid, almost dwarfish, and his face was handsome. At the beginning of the war, aged eleven, he had been given to a Polish family. His Aryan looks and his youth enabled him to fit in easily with the farmer's children. For five years he ran barefoot with the peasant children, earned his keep, learned about life. When Grandpa Lolek came for him at the end of the war, Grandpa Hainek did not recognize this man who was trying to separate him from his parents. The Polish family wanted to adopt him: He didn't look like a Yid anyway, and soon they would need more hands for the harvest. But Grandpa Lolek, hero of Anders' Army, persisted in his mission, and led Grandpa Hainek all the way to a cot in the youth hut of a kibbutz in the Naftali Mountains.

On the kibbutz, they took one look at Grandpa Hainek, wearing a black coachman's cap and boots in the middle of August, and sent him to work in the hay. He slowly grew accustomed to the Yids surrounding him, but was barely able to pick up their language and their ideas remained incomprehensible. Why was it bad to accumulate property on the kibbutz? He stole eggs, bread and knives from the kitchen, which he buried who-knew-where, the-devil-knows-why. He did find a common language with the local Arabs, those who hung around the edges of the fields, keenly interested in wagon shafts, tractor parts, anything Grandpa Hainek brought them in return for sheep skins and good pitchforks.

It was with the Arabs that he arrived in Tiberias. He found himself a pair of strong horses and started working as a porter and hauler of goods. Wearing heavy boots and a redolent sheep skin slung over his shoulders year-round, with what little broken Hebrew he spoke, Grandpa Hainek continued his life in the land of the Yids. He ate a lot of beets and a lot of cabbage. He distilled his own vodka from potatoes, and from the Christians in the Galilee he bought huge cuts of pork which he hung in his room alongside his coachman's overcoat, whip and sheep skin.

In one of the Yids' villages he found a wife, Tamar, and they had three sons together before she died of a nameless disease, most likely typhoid fever. Apart from his sons, she also left him her Shabbat candlesticks, an assortment of feminine items bundled together in a purse, and a book of Psalms that she was extremely fond of, and which Grandpa Hainek nailed to the wall above his bed as a talisman against witches. When he returned to the kibbutz for a short while to deposit his sons and make sure his treasures were still well hidden, he met Naomi. She was the educational coordinator on the kibbutz, and he was referred to her to take in his sons. After she had performed her job impeccably, she followed him, to live with him wherever he should choose. They bought a plot of land on an old moshav and lived off the fruits of their labors. They had no real connection with the State of Israel and were cut off from its institutions. Naomi would chat a little with the neighbors, Grandpa Hainek would not. He had heard of the Israel Defense Forces (he found the concept of a Yid army impressive) but not of the Sick Fund. He traded in straw, sowed oats, beets and potatoes. He fattened calves and pigs. He wanted to have children with Naomi but could not. He took her to Arab witch-doctors, to a rabbi in Tiberias, to anyone who offered a cure, but none was found.

He did not maintain contact with our family. Yids. Grandpa Lolek always knew where he was and how many children he had—that was enough. As long as there were no monetary demands he took no interest in Grandpa Hainek's affairs, not even when he left the moshav and settled on the outskirts of the abandoned Arab villages, Ikrit and Biram. Grandpa Hainek, roaming the Galilee, had found the villages deserted and free for the taking. He was immediately drawn to a church with a ruined bell tower at its peak, and to the expansive wilderness enveloped in low-growing weeds, where the only sound was the screeching of crows. He spent long days on the barren hilltops and in the *wadi* beds, where gray rivers groaned in wintertime. On snowy nights, when black rain threatened to wash everything into the rivers, Grandpa Hainek liked to roam about, battling the winds, in fear that the darkness descending from the woods of Mount Meron would settle on him. He scanned each and every ruin in the villages, examining the opportunities afforded by this Eden.

One day he took Naomi and housed her in one of the ruins. He gathered new bricks and built walls, a fireplace and chimneys. With his own two hands he installed a kitchen and cabinets, a wash-basin and house wares. He brought her feathers to make down comforters. He brought her windows that he stole from the Arab villages, and even sewed curtains for the windows. Adjacent to the house he turned a few ruins into covered barns. He fenced in some yards and raised goats. With the displaced villagers of Ikrit and Biram, who returned from time to time to examine their villages, he did not have many dealings. He respected them, and forced them to respect him. He usually made them leave. Sometimes he bought jewelry for Naomi from them, and in return sold them aspirins stolen from kibbutzim.

By a circuitous route, Naomi found religion. She suddenly began to observe the mitzvahs, pray, light Shabbat candles. Grandpa Hainek had to go with her to Tzfat to buy kosher meat, wait for her to bathe in the ritual *mikvah*, sit with her with rabbis, in congregants' houses, in synagogues.

He bore her barrenness silently. He was not angry at having to hire laborers to gather the potatoes instead of using his own sons. He built her a life of royalty and did not resent her tendency to visit with her family members, the Yids, to escape once in a while who knows where.

Naomi and Grandpa Hainek lived on the edge of the abandoned villages, childless, far from the family. Even when she persuaded him to take in the late Tamar's three children so she could bring them up properly at their father's side, and even when she dragged him to meet a few people—her family, Jewish friends from Tzfat, friends from the kibbutz—it never occurred to Grandpa Hainek to establish contact with us.

It is said that his first appearance in our family was at my *briss*, which happened to be held on the *Tisha B'Av* fast of 1963. He turned up for some reason, dressed festively in a white shirt. His yellowish hair was neatly combed and he had wiped the grease stains off his cap. No one looked at him much, and they ignored him when he ungrammatically and unabashedly wondered, "And the food, where is? And drinks, where are?" even though it was a fast day. Dumbstruck, they all gaped at Naomi with her light blue eyes and grey hair, her aquiline nose and high cheekbones. An angelic vine, a beautiful, noble icon with a white peasant's dress and a shy look. We immediately wanted her to give us children. To breathe life into our family. That tall, serene body was made for our offspring. We wanted to drink from this well of life, even at the cost of mingling with Grandpa Hainek.

The family members greeted her warmly, connected with her.

13

They asked—where had she left the children? Whispers traveled through the room: she was barren. Acting on a vague instinct, they brought her to my cradle, a fertility charm concocted on the spot.

Many more prayers were whispered for her, countless blessings were showered upon her, and finally they also thought to ask—it turned out that she had no Sick Fund membership and had not tried any doctors. Only witches and a soothsayer and one medic. Naomi was sent to the doctors and a year later she began to have children. Despite having been the source of the charm, I myself was somewhat forgotten, and her children—whom she bore at the ages of thirty-five, thirty-six and thirty-seven, until the midwife was unable to stop the bleeding when she gave birth to Oz, her fourth son—are not attributed to me.

Naomi had been loved and was deeply mourned. The family could not accept her death—we had touched the well of life itself. How could it be that instead of Aunt Ecka or Aunt Frieda, Naomi had suddenly been taken? Nor did Grandpa Hainek come to terms with her death. Perhaps he blamed himself. On the night when she gave birth to Oz, prematurely, he had run twelve miles in the snow after his horses had veered off the path, frightened by bright lights. But by the time he came back with the midwife, an old woman from one of the villages, it was too late to save Naomi. He went back to the kibbutz with his sons.

At the end of that year, the Yom Kippur War broke out. After the war, Grandpa Hainek's oldest son with Tamar, Ze'ev (1953–1975), left the kibbutz. He went to Canada to work in the oil fields, where he was killed in a glacier accident. Grandpa Hainek mourned the loss of his eldest son heavily, but there were those who subtly claimed that his expression gave off a hint of satisfaction—after all, this was death by drowning in a freezing lake, just like in the old days, in the Wisła near Krakow.

A year later, Dov (1954–1976) was killed. Dov was the second son. Some say he was a Mossad agent, some say something even more secretive. In Europe, on a mission, two bullets. Three people, one dressed as a priest.

In 1978, a hay wagon ran over Sagi, Naomi's second son.

Grandpa Hainek took his remaining sons and began an endless journey through the little Land of Israel, to get away from his Polish legacy and from the fate of the peasant coachman. He went from town to town, from vocation to vocation. He was an agricultural laborer in the Sharon region, a porter in Petach Tikva, a print worker in Haifa. He got as far south as Beersheba, far from the snow, and found work as a taxi driver. He changed his clothes, learned Hebrew, even voted in the elections. (Once. He stole an identity card and voted as Ernst Rabinowitz.) But all the roles he played, all the vocations, the attempts, the distance from the snow, none of these could rescue him from the claws of his true identity, the only possible one: a Polish coachman in the town of Kielce, wearing coachman's boots and a black cap.

Still, despite long snowy years under scorching *khamsin* heat waves, despite sauerkraut and vodka that destroyed his teeth, despite his dead wives and tragically killed sons, at the age of fifty-two, thanks to an argument over change at the grocery store, Grandpa Hainek met his third wife, Atalia. She quickly gave him three children from her young body. To protect her and her children, he took them even further south, to Machtesh Ramon. He went north only when snow capped the high mountains, after which he would return to Beersheba, startled, to a heat that had no snow and no woods and no slowly descending darkness. He went back to making a living driving a taxi, with the windows rolled up even in the heaviest *khamsin*, ignoring his passengers' pleas, sweating, his skin turning red. In Beersheba he had another child with Atalia.

Grandpa Hainek was the fertile opposite of our family: a Polish peasant, ignorant and uncomplicated. We never found any interest or use in him apart from his butterfly collection, which included an impossibly purple cabbage butterfly, and apart from his third son, Eitan, who was the first to show me pictures of naked ladies who were more developed than Effi was on the day she showed me her body.

Atalia was a different matter.

Aristocratic, tender and radiant, as were all of Grandpa Hainek's known women, she was a tall, slender Yemenite. She was always barefoot and her fingers were adorned with rings of white copper. She was twenty-three when she married Grandpa Hainek, only a few years older than us, and boundlessly in love with her white-haired partner. Atalia's sons ("the Lubliner Yemenites," Effi called them), shared the appearance Grandpa Hainek gave all his sons regardless of the ethnicity of his partner. Each of his eleven sons had an identical hardened look. They could never be seen in one full group (Grandpa Hainek's eldest were killed before Atalia's children were born), but partial gatherings were sometimes convened for Grandpa Lolek's ceremonious camera. These grandchildren of the headmaster of Kielce's Hebrew Gymnasium, the pedagogue and man of letters Dr. Feuer, appear in pictures surrounding their father. Their calves wrapped in leg-warmers, they wear clothes that look heavy and sour. Spanning all ages, their countenances are identical. A dark, boorish crew of mute masculinity, a gang fifty years too late to join the ranks of Alexander Zaid's nascent Shomer movement.

From a very young age, they paved their ways to living on moshavim or military academies. They were bulky and lonely. Their hair turned grey before they reached eighteen. In the army, they served in tight-lipped units. They had girlfriends, always moshav girls, always fair-haired. In time they each found an exciting line of work, but even their intriguing professions—hunters, spies, commandos, coal-miners—never gave them an aura of interest. They were ascetic, hardened types, who connected with the world only infrequently, to sleep with its girls or buy its spare tractor parts. Grandpa Lolek photographed them often. He enjoyed gathering them in front of his camera to immortalize his younger brother and nephews.

In the family, it was usually Grandpa Lolek who took pictures. He generously erected his Leica camera, a black metal monster with personality disorders, everywhere he went. It was no simple matter to produce a good picture with the Leica. Its internal mechanisms were controlled with one seemingly simple button that required no more than a click. But inside, the camera teemed with a religion of restrictions and mishaps. While the Leica produced attempts, failures and repeated adjustments, the audience opposite it grew increasingly impatient. Finally, the button. Pressing it produced an impressive sound and sometimes a picture.

(Effi: "If you press twice, you get an X-ray.")

Grandpa Hainek and his sons usually agreed to pose. The pictures always captured them eyeing the lens suspiciously with a cautionary look, as if to say, "No tricks, I'm warning you." They never asked for the pictures afterwards, uninterested in what had happened to the moment frozen by the Leica. Grandpa Lolek enjoyed photographing them and uncharacteristically overcame his sorrow at the lack of payment. He amassed the photos of his nephews, who had been imposed upon him as a calamity of potential heirs, and collected payment indirectly from other photography subjects.

The family members usually liked to be photographed, eternalized. The relatives, the friends, the acquaintances—all the survivors from *there*. After the Holocaust, eternity was as vital to them as oxygen, food, and good health. Even before they arrived in Israel, they photographed themselves with heavy black cameras at all sorts of events, proving that they existed, that they were real, a mathematical truth, a concept supported by science. They existed. They were photographed at resorts, on holidays, on afternoons of idle laziness, forgotten moments that they wished to immortalize so that future generations could not claim these people were never idle. The pictures were rarely gathered into albums. They generally bustled by the dozen, disorganized, in a chaos we spent evenings poring over, makings sudden discoveries of Mrs. Tsanz in a bathing suit, Uncle Antek embracing two young women. Smiling. Mrs. Tsanz too. There she was at the center of a merry group on a waterfront bench, a snowy background and a road-sign suggesting a season, a place. An unnamed park, perhaps in Krakow, chestnut trees overhead, and the people in the photograph are smiling. The awkward smile of a young girl, our Grandpa Yosef with his arm around her waist as if there were no prohibitions and no sins in this world. A snowman with a carrot nose, three anonymous people and Uncle Mendel kneeling at its feet, smiling. Springtime in a field divided by a walking path, a gang of people lingering briefly for the camera, smiling. Their clothes are heavy in summer too, their faces grave—here we are, living the good life. Recovering. Sated. Satisfied. Grumbling about this and that. And the park benches and the sidewalks and the doorways are full of them, gathered, smiling, the camera casting their images onto the negative. One click, and eternity.

Grandpa Lolek enjoyed taking photographs, but developing them for free was too much. He demanded money and made no superfluous niceties about it. He set a regular price for "regular" photos and a special price for "special" photos. What constituted "special"? Unclear. But Grandpa Lolek determined, "This one is special," and demanded a special price. Quarrels erupted. The relatives were furious. The Leica contained a precious moment of their new lives and in order to bring it out into the light they were being robbed. The impertinence of it. They would pay, of course they would, but so much? Goldberg on HaChalutz Street, the finest in Haifa, charges less. Why so much? The disputes thickened. Grandpa Lolek was not one to allow battles to simply die down. From the summits of Monte Cassino he taunted his adversaries.

The only person capable of moderating and untying these knots, sometimes by force of personality, sometimes with a little something from his wallet, was Grandpa Yosef. There should be no fighting among Jews, he believed.

Our kaleidoscope of memories, which turned everything upside-down, always contained a thousand colorful, crumbling versions of Grandpa Lolek arguing. Complaints from the audience, harsh words from Grandpa Lolek, back and forth. And everyone waited: When would Grandpa Yosef finally intervene? The kaleidoscope holds endless versions of one single dispute, until Grandpa Yosef arrives. He had been busy, someone needed his assistance, but now he was here. Why were they fighting?

Grandpa Yosef. The polar opposite of Grandpa Lolek. Our parents' generation found him and declared without hesitation: a grandfather. A short man with a yarmulke, his face was always locked with sorrow, his strides always small. A champion of the needy, always helping, rescuing, supporting. From morning to evening he was busy doing mitzvahs. He rode his bicycle everywhere. Always modest, always in the shadows. The needy knew how to find him. Not only the truly needy, but the family too. Every time we had to temporarily pass through the straits of religion, Grandpa Yosef the kindly ferry man was summoned. At funerals, memorials, sitting *shiva*, marriage ceremonies, bar-mitzvah lessons. In each of these, Grandpa Yosef played the role so needed by the secular heart: a man intimately familiar with the ceremonial, a purveyor of benevolent versions to those who could not make head or tail of it all. Beneath his tender face burned a blaze of faith that could have scorched the entire world if Grandpa Yosef had not trimmed it down to the measurements of a quiet, retiring man.

Grandpa Yosef knew hundreds of Jewish precepts by heart, as well as the length of the Orinoco River. We could find out from him how the price of milk had increased, month by month, starting at any year we requested. He could recite the Book of Esther, the names of the Shetland Islands, and the birthplaces of Galician rabbis lost in the Holocaust. He was a stormy genius, very quiet, always soft-spoken, with a tired gaze, his face lined with furrows of wisdom and tiny white specks of unshaveable stubble on his yellowish cheeks. He had a soft French accent; no one knew why. But his compassionate voice sounded wonderful with its French enunciation. Because of his accent, people believed he had a refined approach to food and that he was knowledgeable about wine. In truth, he rarely encountered wine, and only then by force of mitzvahs. At family meals he gargled peach-flavored sparkling wine and mumbled something about its "delicate savor," believing he was giving his audience what it wanted. In matters of food he was even less fussy. When he ate, his throat grew a pelican's crop, into which he rolled any kind of food without needless enquiries. He ate to his fill at every meal and accepted offers of coffee and dessert. He had no potbelly, thanks to the bicycle and the mitzvahs and due to a metabolic problem which allowed food to pass through his body like a roller-coaster. Precious little of his meals remained for him to grow strong on.

He lived in a small neighborhood where almost all the residents were Holocaust survivors, at the edge of the Haifa suburb of Kiryat Haim. Little houses, little yards. We went to visit him almost every Saturday, desecrating the Sabbath by driving, but not to worry. We spent whole weeks with him during summers. We attached ourselves to him like tropical ferns to the juicy core of an enormous trunk.

At his home, in the little room *they* called the "hall," which increased the value of the apartment, Grandpa Yosef had an old heavy desk made of brown wood, the only notable piece of furniture in his entire modest home. Behind it, on the wall, were book-lined shelves. First, gold-embossed volumes of the Scriptures, the six sections of the Mishna, the Babylonian Talmud, Rashi and Rambam. Then there were "liberal" books, which Grandpa Yosef knew by heart—Sholem Aleichem and Berdyczewski, Burla and Frischmann, Haim Nachman Bialik and Tchernichowsky. There was also an *Encyclopedia Hebraica*, which Grandpa Yosef did not know entirely by heart (he half apologized, explaining that it was wrong to know everything by heart as it only took up space in one's mind), and Eben-Shoshan's Hebrew dictionary (on occasion, he could be caught not knowing the definition of a word like 'batten' or 'burette'). The desk itself was usually scattered with volumes of the Scriptures, textbooks and fine literature. Also a glimpse of a little dish of pickled herring, which Grandpa Yosef preserved himself, and the pit of a fruit. Grandpa Yosef would be sitting hunched over, studying. A small lamp illuminated his face.

Despite the yellowing cheeks, the stubble and the folds of skin, the image of Grandpa Yosef the righteous scholar was forever a cornerstone in our lives. In the Garden of Eden that was our childhood, he was the Tree of Knowledge, just as Grandpa Lolek was the Tree of Life. To this very day, although we have grown up, Grandpa Yosef is still the Tree of Knowledge. He always wore loose slacks and white dress shirts tucked in tightly, with large cumbersome jackets that conquered his body and covered up the fine shirts. Grandpa Yosef tried to dress carefully, but the flap of something always peeked out from something else.

He came from the same little town as Dad, Bochnia, and although he was not related to my father's family, he knew them well. He would say things like, "He was a little rascal, your father, but a good boy. Got hold of lots of stamps for me," (a slightly enigmatic compliment, which I sanctified without further contemplation). In his distant way he was a disciple of the Admor of Belz, and he feebly fumed when Effi referred to him under her breath as "the Admor of Belzec." In our family's underground cell of Bochnia ghetto graduates, it was a known fact that before the Admor of Belz boarded the train from Hungary to Switzerland, leaving his disciples behind to perish in Auschwitz, he had spent time in the Bochnia ghetto until the collaborator Landau was able to transfer him to Hungary, then a safe-haven, leaving his believers to contend with the nuisance of the gas chambers at Belzec. Grandpa Yosef did not reach Belzec or Auschwitz, but his Holocaust trail was the longest and most intricate of all the survivors we knew. Over the course of the war he passed through no less than twelve concentration camps, ghettos and extermination camps. He never explained why. He did not dwell much on depictions of those days, but often tied the present to the past.

"It was in the Bochnia ghetto that I met Attorney Perl, and then we met again in Haifa."

"Mr. Hirsch was very helpful to me in the Lodz ghetto. If not for him, who knows…"

"I was at the men's camp in Ravensbrück and then I was transferred to Stutthof, but in any case Ravensbrück was officially affiliated with Stutthof. Officially, I stayed in the same place. In the train car, it took three days."

"The Death March? No, I wasn't there. Fortunately, I was transferred from Gross-Rosen to Waldenburg, so I was saved."

"Buchenwald uprising? Haven't heard of it. Perhaps it was after I was transferred from Buchenwald to Gross-Rosen."

The Shoah raged through the world, and Grandpa Yosef traveled to and fro on trains. We sometimes wondered why.

"He wasn't a good social fit at Buchenwald, so they transferred him to Gross-Rosen," Effi suggested.

Fifty years later, Grandpa Yosef himself explained. "It was not the Nazis who moved me from one place to the other, it was my heart that moved worlds until I found her, Feiga."

Feiga was his wife, the princess of his youth, his queen, who lay eternally ill in her room. When he stepped off the last train into a world turned upside-down at the end of the World War, he found his fiancée from before the war, Feiga, and married her, as their parents had agreed six years earlier in the spring of 1939. They were engaged at nineteen, married at twenty-five, and gave birth to Moshe.

Moshe was Grandpa Yosef and Feiga's only child, and from the moment he was born, it seemed, the angels had showered him with a host of disasters. He was mentally retarded, but not profoundly enough so that he could exist in a dulled serenity. He had slight brain damage, which tormented his movements, pulled his limbs as taught as springs and did not let go, only twisted them in pain. And adenopathy, a disease of the lymph nodes which caused internal sorrow to hide beneath his sealed face. "He has pain, sometimes. Try not to let him eat food that's too spicy or too sweet," said Doctor Gnessin. And there was something else. Not exactly autism, but a nameless disjointedness that thwarted all known methods for treating autism, prevented him from being taken in at autistic homes, and finally left him in his place under the sun on the low fence opposite his house, where he sat upright all day long.

Between sick Feiga and Moshe, Grandpa Yosef was in constant motion: Gemara, mitzvahs, preparing food, washing dishes, biking here and there. Medication for Feiga. Medication for Moshe. Even so, we were not amazed when Grandpa Yosef announced one day that he had decided to take some courses at the Open University. Why not? After all, Grandpa Yosef was a prodigy whose rabbinical dreams had been cut short by the Holocaust, and in any case he always had fifteen minutes to spare here and there. He would get his bachelor's degree and then see.

He signed up. Disappointed by the slow pace and the meager load of material, he decided to register at a regular university. He took the entrance exams and was accepted. He was even interviewed by the student newspaper; the university was happy to publicize their elderly student. But their delight was somewhat marred when, six months later, Grandpa Yosef applied for permission to take all the required exams for the bachelor's degree. His request was rejected, of course, and Grandpa Yosef dared not appeal ("Do not presume to defy the rulership," he had learned). The one thing Grandpa Yosef did accomplish with his request was to be taken under the wing of Professor Shiloni, a kindly renaissance man who was impressed by this elderly beacon of knowledge and arranged a customized course of study for him. And so on Chanukah of 1985, Grandpa Yosef was awarded an MA in Jewish History.

The Masters degree did not quench the predator's thirst. Grandpa Yosef decided he wanted a doctorate, claiming this had been his goal from the first. It was his life's duty to earn a doctorate on the topic of Jewish heroism in the Middle Ages—this and no other. We were surprised by his narrow focus: Why would Grandpa Yosef be interested in Jewish heroism in the Middle Ages? But under the guidance of Professor Shiloni, during Grandpa Yosef's plentiful quarter-hour openings, a foundation for the dissertation was laid. To this very day, the end of 1993, Grandpa Yosef can still be found scratching away at drafts he is never pleased with.

The years of our childhood solidified our belief that Grandpa Yosef knew everything, and this estimation was not diminished when we grew older. The main tenets of his knowledge—Talmud and Jewish history—were barely tested by us. Astronomy, meteorology, zoology—absolutely. When Brandy the dog gave birth to six piebald puppies underneath his brown desk, Grandpa Yosef was forced to elucidate for us the riddle of procreation. Even in the strangest corners of human knowledge, Grandpa Yosef was never without a response.

"Grandpa Yosef, when was the kite invented?"

"Grandpa Yosef, are giraffes kosher?"

He was our resource for settling any argument. The matter would be brought before him and the loser would reap consolation thanks to Grandpa Yosef's slight bending of the facts, allowing him or her to squeeze in next to the winner at the last minute.

"The longest river in the world? The Amazon."

Effi loses.

"But the Mississippi is the longest of the North American rivers."

Effi takes her place alongside the winner.

We would lie on our backs in the garden at our place, beneath the trees, and let our thoughts fly, contemplating the farthest or the strangest, to the very edge of our wits. Even before the era of Brandy the dog, we learned to love a good game of fetch. We would toss our questions as far as we possibly could, and wait for Grandpa Yosef to return with a proud answer in his mouth.

"Grandpa Yosef, what else can you grit, other than teeth?"

"Grandpa Yosef, why doesn't a spider float in grape juice?" (A failed experiment.)

Our memories were crumbled into the flakes of a kaleidoscope, and the answers are difficult to see. Things get forgotten, scattered, but Grandpa Yosef's gravity is remembered well. He would never belittle our questions.

"Grandpa Yosef, who would win: a thousand scorpions or a bear?"

"Grandpa Yosef, which prison is the hardest to escape from in the world?"

Grandpa Yosef considered. Were we counting the camps in Siberia as prisons? Would we count prisons that have been closed down? Like Alcatraz? Instead of a simple answer, Grandpa Yosef told us about the most terrifying prisons, lying with us on a blanket with blades of grass crumpled beneath our backs, roots crushed. We listened with eyes closed, pondered prisons, and enjoyed the strength infused in us by their force.

Wherever religious ceremonies were concerned, Grandpa Yosef's advantages were enjoyed by all. He was handed the field marshal's baton and asked to lead the way. He always positioned himself on the front, at the edge of the rabbi's beard, where he could hum with him, emphasize and echo certain syllables of his prayers, and cover for our awkward silences. And when necessary, with a reassuring look, he would urge orphans to recite *kaddish*, fathers to sign documents for their children's nuptials, bar-mitzvah boys to squeak out the readings he himself had taught them with the utmost patience and grace. Salvation and redemption were for him simple tokens to be distributed for the asking. He was summoned to every ceremony to stand as advocate between us and God, or at least between us and Uncle Mendel.

Uncle Mendel, a member of Grandpa Yosef's generation, was never even honored with candidacy for grandfatherhood. We had no choice but to tolerate his presence at funerals and *brisses*, where he would rapidly ignite with holy furor and terrible wrath against us idol worshippers. His eyes dispersed threats against the family and the officiating rabbi. His hints were clear: the slightest deviation from tradition, and heads would roll. The presence of Grandpa Yosef was able to slightly dilute the anxiety. "Shhh…Shhh…," he would calm Uncle Mendel with an enchanting whisper, unburdening the holy man of his anger and extracting from him a momentarily turned blind eye.

Uncle Mendel was invited to the celebratory events because it would have been unbefitting not to. And anyway, it was difficult to get around Uncle Mendel. He had managed to position himself both as a relative of some sort and as Grandpa Yosef's neighbor, and he lay in wait for any family gathering, so that circumventing him was both unpleasant and impossible. At family meals he took his place at the edge of the room in an observation armchair, vigilantly watching for any transgression. People examined their words carefully, omitted details that might set off Uncle Mendel, and gingerly approached the buffet table to take their fill. Sin could be lurking anywhere, you never knew. When Uncle Mendel himself finally drew near the buffet, he acted like a man preparing to dismantle an explosive device. He walked from his holy throne of an armchair to the table, rolling his sleeves up to his elbows. Mumbled assurances of "It's all kosher, it's all kosher," would be uttered righteously all around him when the crowd saw the patron of Godliness going to sample the food. Uncle Mendel, sternly dismissing these heretics' oral oaths, stood breathlessly surveying the bounty. This Buchenwald survivor, in whose hut people driven mad by starvation had gnawed on the dead as they lay on their bunks, stood within arm's reach of sin: golden-brown chicken thighs, cuts of beef, dumplings. Pink radishes, mounds of peas and bowls of sautéed cabbage winked at him from the side. Potatoes up to their chins in sauce, squares of quiche notched with a knife. Uncle Mendel stood there, temptation enveloping him like a prayer shawl.

The bridge of mercy, more often than not, was Grandpa Yosef. Somewhat embarrassed, his fork busy with a full plate, he would remark in Uncle Mendel's direction, "The cholent is excellent." Beneath this culinary judgment ran a subterranean confirmation of *kashrut*, and Uncle Mendel would begin to forgive the world. First a mound of cholent. Then a second helping. He shovels the piles into his mouth and helps himself to more. Walking this way and that in front of the table, heaped dishes set out before him, rich and dark as a Dutch still-life, he perspires. His jaws move too quickly. He coughs. Holds a pickle and clears his throat. Other people approach the buffet to demand their rights. Uncle Mendel bumps, clashes. His plate wobbles. People pass him left and right, rushing, the signs of his authority blurring. A mass of camp prisoners carries quivering plates piled with knolls of food, exhaling hot ashes and smoke through their nostrils. Grandpa Lolek uproots mountains of dumplings with his fork. Grandma Eva's strength is restored, her face glimmers with a copper tone as she clenches her jaw to defeat a stubborn bone. And Uncle Mendel, still there, waves a red napkin like a matador and burdens his plate further. Elbows jostle around the table, retiringly, politely. They will not let anyone beat them to it—not today, not here too. Conversations. Public opinion on the kreplach. One man talks, the crowd listens with joyful apprehension and a hesitant heart. They listen and pile on food. The brisket elicits cries for help. The plates are already dizzy. They rub against each other, shoving. No thoughts except seconds, the next course, and dessert.

Dessert was always compote, and it brought with it a quiet time when all was comfortable, shallow, at the end of the ends—the river's estuary. The compote had a ritual structure that permitted no deviations. Swollen cheeks of sugared apples drowning in compote syrup. Purple plums with stems removed, looking as if their flesh has been shredded by a Doberman. Grapes floating palely like skulls at the bottom of the bowl. That was the compote and there was no other. Afterwards, there was coffee for those who were allowed. The guests were exhausted by this time, their faces expressionless. A slight sense of suffering. And inside they would embark on glorious journeys, Mongolian horsemen whipping time away in their memories.

Eventually we would detect the softened look and slight quickness of breath that signaled the awakening of their nostalgic yearning for jam. They would open the cabinet, lips puckered, and take out sickening plum or blueberry preserves, holding them out for us to taste. We would flee in horror.

The family meals wandered from one house to the other by order of a secret code of generosity. But usually we met at Grandpa Yosef's. He was the uncontested focus, a patient host who served tea and home-made cakes—huge rounds of dough from which we pulled out raisins in disgust. At his home the Sabbath was desecrated almost every Saturday. Four generations happily watched soccer on TV, but Grandpa Yosef did not protest. He disappeared once in a while to take care of Feiga, Moshe, or a neighbor. At noon he went to synagogue. But in between business and caretaking he was an exemplary host. He bought the television himself, so the Sabbath desecrators would not be bored while he was busy. Television was permitted, he explained. They show educational programs and documentaries. But we caught him watching current affairs and the evening news. "Well, news is important," he responded.

When the anarchy increased, the television found its way to Feiga's bedroom. She tolerated only afternoon soaps and children's programs, which were important. And once we caught her cheering on Maccabi Tel Aviv, blessing the star player Miki Berkowitz and his family for generations to come. Grandpa Yosef bought another television to put in the living room for the Sabbath desecrators.

Grandpa Yosef was no saint. As proof, there was his support of the Maccabi Haifa soccer team. The family tradition was one of illogical support for HaPoel Haifa, a support that nurtured in us all the appropriate character traits. We learned how to lose honorably— it became our specialization. We learned to bear disappointment, to settle for less. We acquired modesty. And against these virtues, earned through our unwavering support of HaPoel Haifa, Grandpa Yosef infuriatingly fell under the spell of Maccabi Haifa. It was all those Saturdays when he let us turn on the TV at his home, desecrating the Sabbath with live soccer broadcasts, that gave rise to the calamity. He himself, of course, never participated openly in this public sin. But here and there his gaze lingered on the screen for just a moment. Unable to reveal that we had noticed his interest, we left him without guidance, without instruction. And so Grandpa Yosef, as a soccer fan, grew into a savage. The one man who might have been able to turn God's favor toward HaPoel accidentally became a fan of Maccabi. He won the championship with them, and the state cup final. He cheered and glowed, disinherited from all the characteristics we had attained through our love of the underdog.

Over the years, the rift grew. In Grandpa Yosef's heart, the halfback king Reuven Atar battled the Shabbat Queen. When we watched the Saturday match on TV, he lurked between the couches. When Maccabi Haifa worked its magic against helpless opponents, he could no longer pretend. The King had outdone the Queen. We were good to him. In the early summer days of soccer, when Grandpa Yosef was buried in prayer in the synagogue or on his veranda, we would pass by with a transistor radio playing the weekly soccer broadcast and yell out to an anonymous listener, "Maccabi Haifa still leading, three minutes to match time!" A holy rustle would sweep through the congregation. Grandpa Yosef was not the only one who secretly furrowed his brow. Three minutes! They have to make it! May the Lord be with them.

Grandpa Lolek would sit with us at Grandpa Yosef's on Saturdays, smoking, perplexed by this interest in soccer. He found it inconceivable that anyone could be excited over a profit divided among eleven men. And he had other criticisms of Grandpa Yosef's preferences: "How is it that with all those brains in his noggin, he married that woman?"

That woman. Feiga.

Feiga was, simply stated, a princess. The world had mixed things up and sent her to Kiryat Haim by mistake. World War II had shuffled the deck of history cards and Feiga had been uprooted from the life she was supposed to lead, but she let it slide. True, she had been destined to inherit kingdoms—the Sheba Kingdom, the ancient city of Cadiz, the Inca Palaces—but, exiled in Kiryat Haim, she established a little court and spread her monarchy over one subject, Grandpa Yosef. He was her foremost knight, her royal counselor and her stable boy. He slaved away without a grumble, tending to her and to the affairs of the kingdom—Moshe, the kitchen sink, the bills, the medications.

Ever since we could remember, Feiga had lain ill in her room. She was always cold, a stable condition unchanged by *khamsin* days or by the bundles of clothes in which she wrapped herself. A mixture of dresses, robes and sweaters arranged itself on her body in lumps and bulges, layer upon layer, until she looked like a bunch of grapes covered up beneath the blankets. Caretakers and cleaners were forbidden to enter Feiga's palace and any attempts they made, for Grandpa Yosef's sake, she torpedoed. She set extremely rigid terms. Feiga demanded perfection—an utter absence of errors. When this was achieved she had no complaints, but she rarely permitted Grandpa Yosef to attain this state for long. His failures were many and they begat one another, branching and mingling into a suffocating network of omissions. Had Feiga not been a princess, she surely would not have tolerated it all. She would have taken harsh steps. But as it was, she made do with complaining. Her complaints were a constant echo in the house, lacking any logic comprehensible to an outsider. Like the call of a mating bird in a forest that would mean nothing to a weekend hiker, Feiga's cuckoo call set the pace of time, changed the clocks.

Between her engagement to Grandpa Yosef and the end of the war, Feiga had found herself embroiled in a mysterious marriage to a young rabbi. It was not through any passion that suddenly overcame the man in the shadow of the *Aktionen* and the annihilation, but a desperate magical attempt to put creation right, or something of the sort. A few weeks after the mystical ceremony, the rabbi was shot on the street in down-to-earth simplicity, his attempt to change the world ending in nothing but Feiga's widowhood.

As soon as we found out about this, we confronted Grandpa Yosef with his embarrassing deputyship.

"So you were her second," Effi determined.

The silver medal winner graciously granted an interview. "Well, yes, the second," he said consolingly.

Grandpa Yosef worshipped Feiga.

We, conversely, found it difficult to take an interest in her.

In the face of her first husband, a spiritual giant, her intellectual prowess had been cowed. The few weeks spent between the holy rabbi's sheets had absolved her from the need to prove anything at all. Grandpa Yosef could make his own efforts, study Talmud, do righteous deeds—she had done her bit.

She did marry Grandpa Yosef when the opportunity arose, but her first marriage was the pillar of fire in her life. After being within a hair's breadth from the Lord of Creation, she was less than eager to relocate to suburban Haifa. And since she had been fortunate enough to serve as a holy vessel, Feiga had no choice but to continue her stormy life beneath the covers. In her own eyes, she was akin to the lantern of the temple, plundered by the evil Titus, cast upon her bed beside a window that, curiously, looked out onto the Acre-Haifa train tracks.

She generally spoke with the grammar of diseases, a language in which the subject and predicate of the sentence were diminished in the face of its object, where the true essence of the sentence occurred. Sometimes the subject and predicate were completely dropped in favor of a daring voyage into tempestuous auxiliary clauses:

"Pain in my forehead because the crows did not rest the tree will fall."

"When no blood in the feet, like a wild animal from the stomach down."

"Rain, *tsk, tsk*, no energy to the bones, all day, amen, Doctor Brattlebaum."

The Oracle of Kiryat Haim also gave blessings to the needy. People came to her and, by virtue of the late rabbi's holy sheets, she blessed them. Her days in the presence of the deceased had imbued her with a vast reserve of holiness. On her finger, she wore two wedding bands. This was not sanctioned by Jewish law, but it was by Feiga.

What Grandpa Yosef saw in her was unclear. How he withstood it—unknown. We could not understand how he was able to perform all his jobs and study a page of Gemara every day, and keep up his prayers and run around doing good deeds—his *tzedakah*—and study at the university. Genius could not explain everything, and so we had to add the factor of love to the equation. Grandpa Yosef broke the record of Jacob our Father, who worked for seven whole years to win Rachel, and then another seven. Grandpa Yosef worked for Feiga for forty-five years, well on his way to the perfectly biblical sum of seven times seven years. Inside his home, Grandpa Yosef was tantamount to a slave, while outside, in the neighborhood, he was the king of kings, the beacon of salvation. He was a patron for the needy, a solver of problems. As he walked or rode his bike, people stopped him to present a new problem, report on an old one, or remind him of problems long solved but still bothersome. Those who were unable to get out of bed to present their claims to Grandpa Yosef were treated to personal visits.

In that neighborhood, the Holocaust—the Shoah—had never ended. People had settled there after the war with their memories, their stories, their grudges. Like a huge flock of storks, they came all at once and landed near the woods on the edge of Kiryat Haim, and there they remained. Sick people, confined by their memories. After the war they had families, they existed, they made a living. They took cautious little steps. Every day they dragged themselves around anew, tied to the rotating minute hand of a clock. Distorted, bound, hauled. Date after date fell away on the calendar. The windows of their homes were closed, a slit in the blinds sufficed to see everything. Most stayed at home, where they sat by large radios that broadcast news in *their* languages. They sat quietly. Illegal-immigrants-for-ever-and-ever. If the day came to a close and nothing had happened—so much the better. Sometimes their heavyset bespectacled sons came to visit. Not often.

Everyone in the neighborhood had two types of past: there was "what you did during the war" and "where you came from before the war." The present and the future languished insignificantly in the distance. Everyone knew everyone else's stories, and bit by bit they were elucidated until thoroughly comprehended. The tales accompanied people's lives, never lost, never growing old. When the owner of a story died, the story went on without him, leaning on other stories on either side, plodding along in a row. Like in the camps, in rows of five, the weak leaning on the strong, the rows proceeded.

The place had a complex arc of supervisors and supervised, patients and caregivers, with no clear partition between the two. Helpless bedridden dependents would suddenly rise in afternoon miracles and go to care for a needy friend. Each of them jealously guarded *their* story, *their* troubles, *their* business, a possessiveness that led to a lot of sighs. They were always sighing. They gathered together to sigh, as if something too large was sitting inside of them and could not be released all at once for fear of explosion. And so they had meetings where they sat and sighed, let it all out in little pieces, looking for opportunities to sigh. And they cheated the rules by speaking in Yiddish, which allows for the release of larger portions.

We liked to listen to them, although in our presence (by Grandpa Yosef's orders) they did not delve too deeply into the Shoah itself. We sat at their feet, an inner ring inside the circle of tea-drinkers, enjoying a wonderful childhood in the shadow of their terrors. When Grandpa Lolek was not around they could compare stories, rate their suffering, measure their sorrow. And they could quarrel, declaring things like, "*Nu*, you, let's see you in Stutthof! Let's see you survive just two days there..." As if the possibility existed—a simple matter of addressing the package correctly, and the man would be sent off to Stutthof for two days.

Behind them, on invisible benches, sat their actions. Thanks to those actions they were here. They had survived.

Sometimes Dad would come to the neighborhood after work, at Grandpa Yosef's behest, to fix a closet for one poor man, do some electrical work for another. Dad's magic hands enabled Grandpa Yosef to implement righteous intentions, since he himself did not get along with things like soldering irons and screws. He paid Dad with his own pickled herring, a good cup of tea and a vague assurance of a place in heaven, to which he sometimes alluded as if he himself went up there once in a while to oversee construction.

There were a few rays of light in the neighborhood too. For example, Yehoshua's barbershop, where Dad stopped in when he visited the neighborhood to get haircuts for himself and for me. The barbershop was not exactly in the neighborhood, but across the way. Still, the whole neighborhood went to cut their hair at Yehoshua's. His name was known far and wide because he had once cut the hair of the Queen of Belgium (so they said), and also because he gave haircuts to the elderly in their homes. That was the greatness of Yehoshua:

anyone who could no longer leave their home and was lying ill in bed, earned a visit from him. He gave haircuts to the needy for free until their final days, never shirking, working diligently to fulfill his clients' requests. The caveat in this act of righteousness was his rule that the elderly person had to be a loyal client, to keep getting his hair cut at Yehoshua's as long as he could make it there. Under no circumstances could he get his hair cut at any other barber. And the temptation was there. On trips to Haifa, after errands and the market, after the plumber and the bank. On Herzl Street, for example, there were little shop windows that revealed barbers with white cloaks chatting inside. Behind them, on chairs, rows of people waited. You could go in and have a chat while you waited. *And where are you from? Ohanov? Nu, myself too, not far. Rawa-Ruska. Kapler was our name.* And the talk would go on.

But all that was forbidden. With Yehoshua the barber there were no compromises. Having no choice, in return for service during their old age, they enslaved themselves to him and took pains not to be absent, not to wait too long between cuts, certainly never to try a competitor. The touch of a foreign hand, even covered by months of growth, was immediately exposed, including the barber's name.

"So, you went to Pollack in town, eh?"

And the traitor was out of the charity program.

"Just thought we'd give Antek a try, eh? On HaNevi'im Street, yes? Thought Yehoshua wouldn't notice his livelihood was being robbed?"

And gone was the chance for free haircuts by Yehoshua during old age.

There was no forgiveness from Yehoshua-who-cut-the-queen-of-Belgium's-hair. Except for Gershon Klima, who did as he wished and Yehoshua did not protest. No one messed with Gershon Klima.

The main feature in Yehoshua's barbershop was a wall of mirrors across from the barber chairs. The entire barbershop was reflected in these mirrors, all the way to the opposite wall, where people sat waiting. You could see their closed eyes, their tired thoughts, and the magazines they glanced at once in a while, just scanning the letters. Nothing could be hidden from the mirrors, but even so, I sometimes found magazines with pages secretly cut out, only a woman's foot remaining on the page, or a crown of hair and the edge of an opulent bed. The mirrors were large; from my height they reflected the white ventilator, spider webs, the lamp. Old photographs were taped on the corners: two soccer players in black and white, shaking hands and exchanging little flags, and a scene in front of a goal with a soccer player jumping up for a never-to-be-materialized head-butt. I never asked who the player was. It seemed wrong.

Beneath the pictures on the counter were dozens of knives and other weapons of destruction, little bottles and containers with tubes protruding at odd angles. Yehoshua cut my hair using only scissors and a little tap water. Before the cut he rubbed the water into my scalp mercilessly with his thick fingers. (The Queen of Belgium?) I was even dispossessed of the little mirror that displayed the backs of the customers' heads for them afterwards. Deprived, I looked on as the adult customers were treated to shears and files, clippers and tweezers. At the end of his work, and sometimes during, he even squirted them with a toxic cloud of eau de cologne. Not sufficing with heads alone, the shrapnel of scent moved through the air like a little fish, floated across the mirror and made its way to the storefront window, where it sat down in little beads on top of the words, "Barber Yehoshua Elegant—Appointments Needed," (you came in and sat down—that was how you made an appointment), its glistening turning Yehoshua's barbershop into a feast of light. On the high wall above the lamps were pictures of all the Chiefs of Staff, apart from Moshe Dayan, who, in the Yom Kippur War, had killed Yehoshua's son. I memorized their faces, their names, the years they served in office.

Once, after much whispering in Dad's ear, on the special occasion of my birthday, Yehoshua consented to give me one squirt of eau de cologne. The burning sensation, the fire in my nostrils, the oddness of the occasion, all paled in comparison with the peaks on which my soul rested for a brief moment, a shepherd in the Garden of Eden. I felt as though I might burst. Through the tears, the excitement, and the mirrors, I could see the ancient picture of the soccer player rising up to butt the ball.

"Who is that?" I finally dared to ask, pointing. (After all, today I had entered the secret world of grownups.)

Dad and Yehoshua adopted solemn expressions and grew sad. Many years of stone bleachers and *Totto* betting forms, listening to little radios on Saturday nights, and memories of stadiums in Poland, all solidified in Dad's response: "That's Duncan Edwards from Manchester United."

"May God avenge his blood," Yehoshua added, but he looked at the row of Chiefs of Staff.

It turns out that Duncan Edwards had not been murdered at all, but had perished in February 1958, in a plane crash in which the entire Manchester United team was killed. And so I learned of new ways to love, to set one's heart on a single thing, to defeat logic in the face of the soul's devotion. Manchester United was engraved on my father's heart and on Yehoshua's heart, and on the hearts of those waiting their turn at Yehoshua's. And now it was engraved on mine too. The Mancunian induction was a gateway into the world of true love.

Anat.

We married a year after we met. The first time I heard her speak, she was uttering a lament: "But sir, eighteen thousand cases just this year. Doesn't that seem important to you?"

Desperately enveloped in the thread of an argument, trapped in Grandpa Lolek's net, she was not able to concede. He faced her as she stood in his doorway, stubbornly refusing to donate money, but more than willing to donate an opinion or two.

People soliciting for donations knocked on his door all the time. Pairs of children, slippery professionals, innocent young women like Anat. They were all treated alike. When knuckles rapped on the door, it was not enough for him to wait in tense silence for the nuisance to go away. Nor did he use any of the wonderfully odd phrases that thrive in the world of supplicants and their resisters: "No one's home," "We gave yesterday," "Mom's sleeping" (in a masculine, childish low voice). Grandpa Lolek's door was open to all—he was an equal-opportunity resister. Usually the supplicant would leave and turn to nearby doors, waiting for some reason for the resister's door to close. Sometimes things developed into a casual conversation or a lively debate. Bitterness fueled by tired feet often inflamed hostility and led to implied ill-wishes. Grandpa Lolek enjoyed the conversations. "Is important to stay in touch with young generation," he said.

When I met Anat, they were already in the depths of an argument. Anat, justice at her feet as always, like a faithful puppy, was pleading with Grandpa Lolek. She wanted to show him diagrams and reports. Perhaps he would like to visit their headquarters one day? A lovely, red-faced Andromeda, with no way out. Grandpa Lolek was unperturbed. When he saw me coming, he asked if I had had any luck with the blender.

Anat turned to me. She, a righteous soul, and me with the blender.

"Your grandfather is against donations on principle!" She exposed Grandpa Lolek's terrible secret.

"My grandfather is against lots of things," I said, slightly taken aback. Why had she assumed we were grandfather and grandson? I could have been a technician. We could have been, as indeed we were, extremely distant relatives, were it not for the Law of Compression.

"Are you in favor of donations?"

We looked at each other. Anat was the first to recover.

"You can donate five, ten or twenty shekels," she said.

I bought two vouchers for ten and one for twenty. Grandpa Lolek grunted contemptuously. "How's the blender?" he asked.

Electrical appliances went to die in his home. Pushing a button was, for him, only one of a dozen options, an unimaginative way to give life to an appliance. Knocking, shaking, rattling and all their various permutations were more correct methods, expressive of the relationship between man and his property. And when an appliance broke, he would find an opportunity to give it to me so I could get it fixed for cheap by my friend. There was no friend—just a repairman. Nor was he cheap, his prices were the same as everyone else's. But Grandpa Lolek insisted that I had a friend who fixed things practically for free. So he allowed himself to saddle me with the bills.

Long afterwards, Grandpa Lolek reconstructs the course of that fateful day. "For you, I did it all. To keep Anati at mine house. I knew you were to be coming, and she, what sweetheart." Happily hugging Yariv, he perceives his own role in my son's existence. He worries a little—Yariv is five now, already going to kindergarten, where they teach him all sorts of nonsense about Chanukah *gelt* and such.

Yariv is also worried. Grandpa Lolek has started teaching him to clean out the ashtrays in the Vauxhall, buy cigarettes, polish shoes. Grandpa Yosef is easier for Yariv to handle. Theirs is a boundless love. Grandpa Yosef was Yariv's godfather at his *briss*, where the flames of his pride threatened to burn down the hall. Every encounter between them involves trade in chewing gum and kisses. Grandpa Yosef rocks Yariv on his slightly rheumatic knee, switches him to his arthritic knee, and back again. "Grandpa, horsey!" Yariv commands. And to hear the word "Grandpa," Grandpa Yosef is willing to work hard.

Effi looks at righteous Grandpa Yosef playing with Yariv and says, "God aims and misses…" And our thoughts go to Moshe.

We wanted Grandpa Yosef to have a consolation son, something to give meaning to his difficult life. We wanted Moshe to get up one day, take the mask off his face, and explain that the whole thing had been a test—some sort of Jobian trial. We looked at Moshe, wondering if the moment was approaching. We glanced at Grandpa Yosef looking at his son. But we never saw complaint in his eyes. Only once in a while, it seemed, there was a glimpse. A thought exposed: "It's because of our seed, we who came from *there*." But the words never left his lips.

Moshe lived most of his life sitting on the low fence across from the apartment building. That was where a long life spent in institutions in which he did not fit and in futile attempts to improve his condition culminated. In his thirtieth year, he sat down on the fence and got on with his life. Year after year after year. Morning to evening, the hours anchored Moshe's life. Like moored ferries, swaying slightly, they lapped at each other with a gentle sound. A ritual strand of saliva hung from his lips. Expressions appeared on his face and dropped away, not belonging to him, just passing as if he were a bustling train station. His limbs lacked coordination. Enormous, doleful powers stood him tensely in one spot, his back and hands seeking respite but not finding it, just freezing for a few moments in a rigid position like a Shakespearean actor before a monologue.

In the morning, on his way back from synagogue, Grandpa Yosef would pick up a roll. He would sit Moshe on the low fence next to the red mailbox and put the roll in his hand. He would wrap Moshe's fingers around it and squeeze lightly until Moshe's hand stirred. Then he would put down a plastic water canteen and a little hat with a picture of an anchor. When everything was ready, Brandy would take up her position and the shift would begin. Moshe, from early morning until sundown, alone on the fence. The birds, the lawns, the paved path, the old almond tree—their groans, their rustles, their bows. Moshe was at one with them.

As the long days sailed across his face, Moshe did not withdraw in the face of crises, fearless of danger. Around him, in the neighborhood, nature took its toll, disasters befell the shores of the gardens and the palely whitewashed houses. But Captain Moshe remained silent and erect, his face watchful. He stood on deck when life beat down Regina from the second floor and Adella Greuner from next-door. By all appearances, he concerned himself only with his bread roll. Took bites out of it, chewed, massaged its body with rhythmic, sleepy prods. Only the sun frightened him, and he moved his cap and tilted it according to some internal mechanism, defensive and respectful of the one who was always above. And sometimes, making a Captain's decision, Moshe would get up and set off on a voyage. He was blessed with two strong and sturdy legs, which he exploited for long journeys. From his still position on the low fence he would suddenly erupt into purposeful walking, as if called to duty. But the journeys' endings—at a garage in the industrial zone, a butcher in the next *Kirya*, in the middle of an intersection—put to question the existence of any organized plan. Before Brandy came along, Grandpa Yosef was the one who took him back to the fence, where he rubbed his feet and back. Once Brandy entered Moshe's life, she handled everything.

But Moshe's outward journeys were rare. He usually remained on the fence, internally a Marco Polo. In wonderful China he discovered silk, drooling a thread of saliva for us, hinting, hinting as hard as he could, if only we could concentrate and understand. He discovered gunpowder. His eyes black, pain traveling from his extremities to every part of his body. Rapid, bustling commerce across all borders, over all waterways and land. Undeterred by the Mongolian wilderness, the Yellow Sea of China, or the overflowing Yang-Tse River, Moshe closed his eyes for a moment while blocks of pain changed hands. Goods in return for goods. A bustling city, and Marco Polo stares inside, wide-eyed.

Sometimes children kidnapped him from the fence and led him afar in merry processions. He would be returned hours later. They were always careful to put him back where they had found him, on the fence next to the red mailbox. And they carefully removed any hint of the last few hours—something stuck to his shirt or hanging from his neck or glistening in his hair. But when Brandy arrived, all trade in Moshe ceased. The children didn't dare. Captain Moshe was left master of his own time. He sat on the fence when he wanted to and set off on voyages when he wanted to. Got up suddenly with no hesitation and started walking on his strong feet. Quickly, quickly. A lot to get done. Other plans null and void. Only an army of ants could steer him off his chosen path. Moshe, in his enigmatic way, was in awe of ants. Something about their motion, the unspoken command that drove these little creatures one after the other, imposed the same law of procession on him. With heavy, hypnotic steps, he veered from his original path to join the convoy. Sometimes the line circled around a yard, or traveled far away to the fields beyond the neighborhood, in front of the row of eucalyptus trees that hid the train from the residents (but not its whistle—oh, the whistle). Moshe marched, his soul gradually changing, filling with antness. He was accompanied by Brandy, who trotted along at a safe distance from the black line, the blind procession that gathered up anything in its way. Sometimes she would hurry over to Moshe to make sure all was well, lick a few of his new bruises, sneeze, and run back to follow alongside the procession. By that time, in the center of the line, Moshe had already become an ant. A giant, anonymous creature in a long row, and his roll was a crumb for the queen. Only when they reached the nest, at the point where the ants disappeared one by one into a little hole, did Moshe encounter the inadequacy of his human form. He stood bewildered on the edge of the nest while harried ants angrily passed him by. The body of a human, the soul of an ant. One could imagine that deep animal desperation would erupt from his sealed core in a chilling wail, a howl of anguish. But no. After a few moments, Moshe would set down the roll—a delight for the astonished ants—and, having done his part, go home. Brandy led the way.

Every other Tuesday afternoon, Grandpa Yosef would put on a nice shirt, dress Moshe up elegantly, and together they would go to see a movie, preferably something by Walt Disney. Sometimes Moshe protested, presenting Grandpa Yosef with an impenetrable line of thought until the expedition was cancelled. Then Grandpa Yosef, disappointed, would go and study a page of Gemara and Moshe would go out to the fence to sit in his rightful place.

We usually found him there. When we came to visit Grandpa Yosef, Moshe would be sitting motionless, sparrows perched on his roll, holding it with their tiny feet and pecking. They were not afraid of the holder of the roll, apparently attributing a lesser consciousness to him than to the scarecrow in the yard across the way. The scarecrow belonged to Adella Greuner and for a long time we believed that this was the creature to whom she shouted through the window, "Kalman, *vi geystu? Vi geystu?*" The phrase was once clumsily translated for us as, "Kalman, where did you go?"—a fairly common shout among the bereaved neighbors. But Grandpa Lolek obligingly provided us with the more accurate translation of, "Kalman, where are you going?" This rendition testified to an ongoing dramatic state, a fixed presence in Adella's world, an event unable to become past tense, simply stuck. We thought we would have to set up a rescue team to get Adella Greuner out of her unfortunate situation, but Grandpa Lolek beat us to it. He started going up to her apartment for tea between two and four every Thursday, and ever since then the shouting stopped. Kalman, apparently, had gone.

We also practiced rescuing Moshe. Using methods that had proven successful in the books we borrowed from Mrs. Gottmartz's library, we furtively tried to cure him. We hoped to be able one day to present Grandpa Yosef with his new son: a cheerfully chattering, multilingual, musically talented Chief Mechanical Officer in the Navy.

"Here, this is your son, Moshe," Effi practiced the great moment when our Pinocchio, the wondrous wooden child, would be presented to Grandpa Gepetto-Yosef. In the meantime, we read him books and whispered secrets in his ear. We drew him cards with letters and tried to hypnotize him and find hidden reflexes in his body. But we had gravely underestimated the distance between Moshe and the light.

One day, for some unknown reason, Grandpa Yosef decided to build us an igloo. Excited by something he had recently read, he hurriedly set about his construction project. In the yard, he spread out a layer of white plastic sheeting on a truss of cardboard. He worked hard, laboring with the helplessness of a man not designed to perform handicrafts. But finally he declared: an igloo. We squeezed into the igloo with Moshe and were left to enjoy ourselves. We sat there, slightly cramped, and Grandpa Yosef abandoned us. Our condition was one of being in an igloo. It was a state of consciousness.

The state continued.

We did not know what came next. What does one do in an igloo?

We tried to think back to the seals from our *Tarbut* encyclopedia, and Neeluk the brave Eskimo boy. We sat across from Moshe with our limbs cramped, dripping with sweat, sweltering in the heat, playing at igloo. Suddenly Moshe began neighing in a strange, animal voice. Then he switched to soft bleating. After that, following a brief pause, he yelled at the top of his lungs. Traversing great chasms of damaged consciousness, the yell cut across like a wilderness train. Someone pulled the stop bell. Someone shouted to pull down the crank wheels. Moshe yelled with all his might and tried to get up, flailing his arms in all directions. Frightened, we rolled away from him. For a moment we got caught up in his reality, growing as distant as he was. We were lost inside the white sheets of plastic.

Grandpa Yosef came to the rescue. We were saved, but from that day on we understood how great the distance was. Moshe was farther than the expanses of wilderness illustrated in our Brawer

Atlas, beyond the Kazak plains, beyond Novaya Zemlya, beyond Franz Josef Land. Moshe could not be reached. Grandpa Yosef had been trying all of Moshe's life, and had not succeeded. Professionals had tried. We had tried. Good people had tried. The Moshe Pole was beyond reach.

Once we saw Grandpa Yosef helping Moshe get dressed in his room. He caressed Moshe's hair for a brief moment, and said, "My child, how shall I reach your inner sanctum?" in a desperate voice we did not know.

How strange, then, that the one and only person who not only could reach the darkness of Moshe's inner sanctum, but could come and go there as he wished, was Grandpa Lolek. As soon as his car appeared in the neighborhood, Moshe would change. The slow-witted figure became an energetic creature with volition, to the great satisfaction of Grandpa Lolek, as Moshe's primary desire was to wash the Vauxhall. Washing the car was his great love, one of his few privileges, and he kept a bucket and rag under his bed for the occasion. Moshe was so quick to sense Grandpa Lolek's presence that the scene would sometimes blur and it would be hard to tell which came first—Moshe running sprightly with the bucket, or Grandpa Lolek driving up in the Vauxhall, struggling to park. With rebellion bubbling in his body, Moshe also tended to add a certain majesty to his persona as he fished a wet rag out of the bucket and waved it, dripping with soap, to demonstrate his serious intentions. Perhaps he wished to banish potential competitors, guys who might emerge from nearby yards, buckets in hand, and Grandpa Lolek's car was willing to indulge them too. He would swing his bucket and run to the car like a crazed puppy. Then he would jump around the Vauxhall uncontrollably, interfering with Grandpa Lolek's parking maneuvers. He would begin scrubbing the windows with a sponge while Grandpa Lolek, a cigarette between his fingers, exhaled angrily into the windshield as he struggled to subdue the car into a parking space. Moshe would open the door to greet the newcomer and try to empty the ashtray, and would be left almost with the door in his hand when the car spluttered backwards.

The more profound layers of this relationship were evident

in the serenity of Moshe's movements when he was with Grandpa Lolek. Only Brandy reached deeper levels of influence. But Grandpa Lolek came first.

When we enthused over Brandy's accomplishments, Grandpa Lolek would repeatedly remind us, "I was the first."

It was true, but we betrayed him unflinchingly, increasing our excitement over Brandy. Grandpa Lolek did not give in. Hero of the battle at Monte Cassino, the man for whom Joyce-the-American-dancer had danced with two umbrellas on the rainy dock at Portsmouth kept up his fight.

"With me he really talks," he stressed.

"With her too, sometimes," we replied, defending Brandy.

"With me he explains what hurts!" he boasted.

"With Brandy nothing hurts!" we struck back.

Grandpa Lolek and Brandy were in a race to reach the Moshe Pole. It was a dead heat. The opponents had a lot in common—stubbornness, depth of thought, a shirking of kitchen duties. But there were differences, and most of them favored Brandy. In the race to the Moshe Pole, Grandpa Lolek felt like Sir Robert Scott left behind in the snow while everyone admired the winner, Roald Amundsen—licking Moshe as he stomped his paws and rubbed up against him. But we had to concede that it was only with Grandpa Lolek that Moshe spoke in charmingly complete, if somewhat clumsy, sentences and desires. As if the painful disarray inside Moshe managed to find its shattered hands and feet, and from the newly assembled fractures even table manners flowered.

Grandpa Lolek's approach to Moshe lacked the restraint we all embodied. The hesitation and the caution which, even when barely perceptible in the kindliest of people, was still real enough to shut Moshe behind a screen. Grandpa Lolek crossed the wilderness of Moshe alone, hugging him with ease, asking as he would ask anyone, "How are you doing?"

A blushing reply, struggling somewhat through his lips, crossed Moshe's dark throat: "Better today."

This was not his own phrase, but a plagiarized version of his mother Feiga's routine response. She always started with, "Better today," carefully maintaining the literary structure of the idyll, which first provides the reader with reassuring content, only to surprise him with imminent tragedy. "Better today" was directed at the past and hinted heavily at yesterday's sorrows. "Better today" also addressed the future. The persistence in this reply forced us to estimate a consistent improvement in Feiga's condition from day to day, going forth to some imaginary day in the future when she would reach Venus-like perfection, approaching the likes of Diana, goddess of hunters, whereupon she would kiss Rhea, Mother of the Gods. And then on to great Zeus.

Moshe's human voice filled anyone who witnessed it with admiration for Grandpa Lolek. They stared at him with glistening eyes. Grandpa Lolek sanctimoniously brushed off the respect, mumbling modestly. He hoped to plant the impression that if Moshe had been in his care from a young age, today he would have been, at the very least, a goalkeeper for the Israeli soccer team.

"Don't forget that Moshe is the only one who never asks him for pocket money," Effi noted, attempting to explain the wonderful relationship between the two.

Vested with this responsibility, Grandpa Lolek altered his manners and behaved carefully around Grandpa Yosef, even abandoning his tea bag *Selektion* ritual out of consideration. When pushed, he would go so far as to buy candy for Moshe, or preferably something they could share, like a poppy-seed cake. After recovering from the novelty of it all, Grandpa Lolek began to ponder out loud if perhaps there was a profit to be made from this relationship, some sort of respectable circus act. Of course, he unfettered his tongue only at a safe distance from Grandpa Yosef or from anyone who might inform on him to Grandpa Yosef—namely, us.

Until he dared propose his commercial ideas out in the open, the relationship between Grandpa Lolek and Moshe was exploited purely for medical purposes. Moshe suffered greatly from his adenopathy, and the doctors informed Grandpa Yosef that the disease had damaged his internal organs. His body was bound up in pain. Even if it was only slightly visible on the outside, his suffering was great. They prescribed pills to dull the pain, but they could not give

44

Moshe sedatives every time his face contorted with pain. The spasms might be simply the outcome of some internal rustle in the nervous system, or they might be due to intense pain. Grandpa Lolek would be called in to interpret. He would sit at Moshe's side and slowly decipher the complex language of his brow. "It hurts? Everything okay?" Based on the diagnosis, the pills were either administered or saved for the next onslaught. He drove without a grumble from his house in Haifa's Achuza neighborhood all the way to Kiryat Haim, sometimes at three o'clock in the morning, to ask Moshe, "It hurts? Everything okay?"

Grandpa Yosef used him sparingly. Fearfully.

But despite the language barrier, despite the four legs and the tail, the deepest reach of all was made by Brandy. Sometimes all that was needed was the presence of her clinging canine body to banish the pain and spasms. Not the pills, not Grandpa Lolek, but the maternal bodily warmth, the courage contained in those jaws.

Brandy.

One day when Grandpa Yosef walked home from synagogue, he had been joined by an unsightly little dog, panting and stubbornly trotting in the steps of her newfound master. Grandpa Yosef and Brandy walked on together, moderately aware of one another, he contemplating a Talmudic conundrum, she the hibiscus beds. After concluding their respective digressions, they returned breathlessly to the narrow path. Grandpa Yosef clucked his tongue. Finally, they arrived home, where Moshe was sitting by the fence. Grandpa Yosef wiped away a strand of saliva hanging from Moshe's mouth. Brandy joined in. She licked Moshe's face lovingly with her gentle puppy tongue. Grandpa Yosef did not object, amazed at her lack of aversion, at the simple way her paws rested on Moshe's knees and, moreover, at the ease with which Moshe's hand reached out to her, surprising, gentle, not recoiling, running five fingers over her furry head. Adoption was declared.

Brandy had been reared with no clear plan for her future. Her body had prepared itself for an ownerless life amidst the trash, a slow implementation of her original blueprints. The newfound bounty of food and rest necessitated constant repairs and improvements. Faulty supervision over this accelerated and architecturally unsound project impelled her tail to grow twice as long as her trunk and then, when it stopped, to give her legs exaggerated prominence over her tiny body. Her ears, never flattering, sailed like leaves in the wind. Her hips, destined to broaden due to the tendencies toward harlotry she was secretly harboring, first accumulated some meager flesh, small in comparison to her bulky chest, and then leapt forward like a canon muzzle, even gaining a pair of fleshy cheeks that protruded from her bottom like an extra face. No architect, no contractor, no accountant would have authorized these plans. But Brandy managed herself, willfully ignoring supervision and criticism, growing limbs that fought for precedence over one another, unregulated, working on requests from relatives, winks from patrons, kickbacks from thugs. This entire corrupt mess, a scandal that occurred against the public good and without any accountability (where were all the sausages, the chicken, the cheese, the *kishke*, the *gorgele*, the wings, the vitamins, and Feiga's pills—the latter were our own initiative—being invested?) eventually worked out for the best. Quicker than one could have guessed, a new persona emerged from the orphaned puppy. Brandy became a large, comfortable dog with only one thought in her mind: Moshe. Even for mating purposes, she refused to stray far from him, and the male dogs accepted her rules without argument. Many dogs sought the favors of the bitch owned by Grandpa Yosef the *Tzaddik*, whose reputation traveled far and wide. They came to her from the northern neighborhoods of Kiryat Bialik and the industrial zones near Kiryat Ata. Brandy, a modest soul, deprived no seeker of her body. Miraculously, this vast celebration of semen produced no puppies, most of the time. Brandy had trouble conceiving. Sometimes, a few months after being in heat, a passing dog would give her a questioning look, as if to ask, how much? But still, these creditors did not despair. Again and again, when the season arrived, they returned to her.

Brandy's relationship with Feiga was civil. Faced with Feiga's complaints—the dirt, the barking, the fleas, the ticks—she was considerate to a fault, making herself available for bathing whenever asked, and doing her business far away. Her barks served only Moshe's welfare. Our treatment of her was more fitting. Anyone who came to visit Grandpa Yosef remembered to bring something for Brandy; a little token of appreciation, usually made of salami. Although she was well fed by Grandpa Yosef, she never insulted the pilgrims, sticking her snout into anything they offered and even tasting a morsel. Once in a while, Feiga interfered with Brandy's feeding, furious at the waste. Weren't bones good enough? Grandpa Yosef, in trembling silence, repeatedly transgressed Feiga's laws, filling Brandy's bowl with the finest fare. He stroked her head, her ears, her shoulders. Whispered lovingly to her as her snout inhaled the aroma of chicken and the scent of pink sausages. With her tail, she would signal, "Your love has been duly noted."

1985 was a year of great consequence for Brandy. Due to some business in a distant neighborhood, Grandpa Yosef found himself doing the grocery shopping in a modern supermarket, where he discovered the dog kibble named Bonzo. That same day, his newly powerful shoulders hauled a forty-pound bag of Bonzo home, from which a few pellets were poured into Brandy's bowl as an introductory portion. Brandy sniffed and grimaced in surprise. She must have let something slip because Grandpa Yosef grew angry:

"What? No good? What now? *Nu*, enough. Every day, day in day out, twenty years, and never a word of thanks. I break my back and there's no regard, not one word. *Nu*, enough. How many years? How long can this go on? Just one kind word. Let me hear something. But *nu, nu*, we mustn't think badly…"

Grandpa Yosef pulled himself together and his anger was all but gone. He quickly restored his calm and put the world back in order. Brandy's bowl resumed carrying its normal contents: chicken necks and fatty bones. Only a few pellets of Bonzo, at Grandpa Yosef's insistence, were added to the menu to commemorate their fight. He asked us expressly not to bring her food—there was no need to spoil her. Only if there were leftovers, that was all right. The family ignored his request and brought Brandy the finest. Leftovers were for other animals.

In our homes, food was not thrown out. This was another basic axiom, almost as vital as the Law of Compression: Food is Not Thrown Out.

Why?

Because.

Why because?

Because Food is Not Thrown Out.

The true reasons:

Because people died for a single potato.

Because people turned their parents in for a morsel of cabbage.

Because people were so starved that they ate wooden planks in their huts in Buchenwald.

Because people stole soup. Because they had their heads whipped and they kept on eating. Because their bodies had already died from the beatings, and yet their mouths kept on chewing.

But we were not told these reasons, not given explanations. The third rule was that we had to be Old Enough to hear things. Becoming Old Enough was a purpose, a mission. Every year they told us stories about the war. Every year, the appropriate dose of horror. In order to climb up the rungs of horror we had to wait, restrained, until we were Old Enough. In the meantime, don't ask why. Food is Not Thrown Out.

My mother had a rigid set of rules. Hard bones were collected for the dog downstairs. Leftover tender meat and expired cheese for the stray cats in the yard. Dried bread that couldn't be toasted—add a little water and put it out for the birds. The fundamental law, the underlying notion governing her rules, was that any food could satisfy someone's hunger. Never throw out anything that contains protein, fat, or carbohydrates. Someone needs it. It can't simply be tossed into the trash to rot or rust. It must be given to someone, and not just given—arranged and presented so it becomes edible. Crack the eggs and remove the shells. Take the lids off the containers of cheese. Pour the milk into a bowl. Even orphaned leftovers (a moldy pickle, puff pastry forgotten in the freezer) were gathered into a little pile. Someone would eat them. Hunger leads to compromise.

In this kingdom of the living, surviving on my mother's generosity, there was only one exception: ants. In this Garden of Eden, ants had replaced the snake, persecuted to the point of total eradication. Terms of negotiation never existed between my mother and the ants.

Mom, why do you hate ants?

A question I never asked.

Why not?

Because you didn't ask. Because there were questions without answers, and questions you didn't ask.

At home, we led ordinary lives. Mom was two years old when the war started and Dad was nine, both young enough to recover from the Holocaust and eventually start a normal family. We children were not the "second generation" of the Holocaust—we were the second *and-a-half* generation. That slight shift, just half a rung on the generational ladder, gave us a simpler, healthier life, with parents who smiled, who found it easy to love, to hug, to talk with us. But beneath the surface was an enchanted tapestry of musts and mustnots. Questions you didn't ask Mom, questions you didn't ask Dad. And questions you did ask, but which had no answers. Hints picked up in a hesitant breath, answers that seemed disoriented—at first they were simple, benevolent, but then rather than thrust themselves into the light, they squirmed around in circles, lost in the darkness.

Where were you, Mom, in the war? Were you in the ghetto, like Dad? How did you walk barefoot in the snow for a whole winter?

Mom, why do you hate ants?

Don't ask.

We knew there was something in common, a shared basis that could provide all the answers, and it was called "the Shoah," although they usually referred to it simply as "the War." The Shoah could explain things, expose the truth—the real truth, not the answers passed off to us as the truth. It was a deep and hidden Shoah, unrelated to the one declared each year with a siren. That was the Shoah that made everyone angry at Effi year after year because she couldn't help bursting out in peals of laughter during the moment of silence.

The Shoah was a dual entity: there was the one declaimed at school ceremonies with torches and handmade black placards and the six million, and there was its twin, the familial one, the one that had not enlisted six million into its ranks but contained instead a vivid cast of characters—not only Grandpa Yosef and Mom and Dad, but also the banal personas on the margins of life. There was Aunt Frieda, whose life was no life at all, and Aunt Zusa, who had nothing but trouble. Aunt Riesel, whom God did not take because he knew what a mouthful he'd get when he did. And Uncle Lunkish, who had an unusual name but nothing else unusual—we couldn't find out anything about him: when we asked, we were shushed. There was Uncle Antek, the Auschwitzian prophet who could predict what happened there, and Aunt Ecka, who didn't seem to fit into any of our categories (was she animal, vegetable, or mineral?) as she sat clammy and wrinkled at the edge of every family affair. Always by her side was Mrs. Kopel, who had no children—she wanted them, but "her womb had dried up." And there was Uncle Menashe, the bachelor, who owned a little butcher shop in Netanya. When he showed up at weddings, unannounced, Aunt Frieda would faint because his hands always smelled of poultry, even after he had showered and put on aftershave. It made no difference to Aunt Frieda who was being slaughtered—she counted any death as a strike against her. In order for them to be able to sit together, because otherwise it would be embarrassing (and Uncle Menashe was actually a very nice man), he had to learn how to come up close to her instead of disappearing into a far corner, because with Aunt Frieda death was unaffected by distance—quite the opposite: you had to come right up to her, cautiously, taking apologetic and slightly peculiar steps that Uncle Menashe had invented and which could generally only be seen in nature films that showed male birds courting a female.

Our immediate surroundings were occupied by Mom and Dad and Effi's mom and dad. They were younger characters, who would hand down their stories to us every year when we were Old Enough.

Except for my Mom, who kept quiet.

What did we know of my Mom's past?

In a village among Christians, a five-year-old Jewish girl fearfully recites Hail Marys, a prayer differentiating life from death. Later, with her mother and father, in the woods with the partisans. And years later, when we were Old Enough: an ambush in the forest, shots fired, everyone escapes, leaving her behind. Her mother, alone, comes back for her. More shots. Mom wakes up hours later in the arms of her dead mother, hidden beneath her body. Her mother is covered with blood. And ants.

How could she not hate ants?

And what else happened to you, Mom?

You mustn't know.

By the time she passed away, only a few tiny episodes of her story had come to light. A detail here, a detail there, in between the gaps. But Mom's story was like Braille—it was the gaps that produced the content.

After Mom died, we went to Poland with Dad. I asked him, "Dad, is there anything about Mom that you know and we don't?"

No.

Mom and Dad were surrounded by uncles and aunts, grandfathers and grandmothers, people related to us by the Law of Compression. They all had their own stories, which we tried to understand, but mainly they spoke about each other. Although our families were small, they still tended to disconnect, to distance themselves. Calls were made on Rosh Hashanah and Passover. "We must get together," they would say, then dig themselves in—stations broadcasting not distress signals, but boxes of bonbons.

We were seldom bought candy, since there would be plenty of bonbons every holiday. We never ate the bonbons because they could be given as gifts. And so each holiday, bonbons were hurled from one family to the next. Happy holidays. And between the holidays, the boxes were stored on the top shelf next to Uncle Tulek's African figurine, which simply could not be displayed because of its huge black penis. Poor Uncle Tulek had lost his mind in the African heat. And you couldn't throw the figurine away because there might come a day when he would visit and want to see it.

We wanted to know what had happened to them *there*.

Why wouldn't they say?

Why did they keep their distance, not spend time together?

We knew their war had begun in 1939. Way back at the beginning of time, in 1939, the Big Bang had occurred, and the meaning of its visible crumbs would become apparent only if we could comprehend the instant of that explosion.

*

The residue left by the Big bang was evident in Grandpa Yosef's neighborhood. The crumbs, the people closed off behind blinds. The ill people, the strange ones. Gershon Klima, labeled a madman with the endorsement of district psychiatrists, but to us the greatest of friends. And Crazy Hirsch, undiagnosed, who lived in a scary hut in the woods and who must have possessed parts of the truth. And Rachela Kempler. And Eva Lanczer. And Adella Greuner. And Asher Schwimmer.

We got to know the neighborhood residents on summer vacations spent with Grandpa Yosef. Almost every summer, for half the vacation—after the unavoidable fate of going to camp, where there was horse-riding and pottery and swimming and soccer and team games—we came to the neighborhood, thirsty for the truth, to meet the people and their miracles. It was a marginal neighborhood, mostly paths and yards, with only one real street, Katznelson Street, and the rows of houses that branched off the main street made do with the proximity of its name. Grandpa Yosef, for example, lived at 8-B Katznelson, even though his house was some distance from the real Katznelson, the main one, which was a paved road. Katznelson Street ran down the length of the neighborhood, affixing its name even to the distant houses, but the name was shrouded in mystery. Which Katznelson?

The main hypothesis was Berl Katznelson, the leader of the Zionist labor movement, just like the streets in every other town in Israel. But some of the neighbors supported their own Katznelson, the poet and author, whose first name was Yitzhak. They remembered him from Lodz before the war, and from the days in the Warsaw ghetto. And Mr. Orgenstern recalled yet another Katznelson, a furniture merchant in Jezupol. It seemed as though the residents had enough problems—why did they care which Katznelson this was? But there was unrest in their hearts. They had to know—was it Berl or Yitzhak? They very much hoped it was Yitzhak. At least in their neighborhood.

He had perished in Auschwitz, poor man, after managing to escape to France. From there they took him, from Paris to Auschwitz.

Year after year, the doubt would suddenly be hurled into the most innocent conversations: Berl or Yitzhak? So one day I went to find out. I was fourteen, and wanted to put an end to doubt in the world. I went to the Municipality of Haifa, which had jurisdiction over Kiryat Haim, and found a clerk to interrogate. "Which Katznelson is the street named after? The famous Katznelson, or their Katznelson?" I demanded. The clerk made his enquiries with a grave expression and replied, "Berl Katznelson, of course." I told him that the neighborhood residents would prefer their own Katznelson, and would it be possible to change it? I explained that their Katznelson had been a great poet in Poland, and since he had perished in the Holocaust it made a lot of sense for his street to be in their neighborhood. The clerk nodded silently, then asked, "Kid, are you doing a school project or something?" To call me a kid that year was a very serious transgression. I left, hunching my shoulders in the leather jacket I wished I had.

Effi put an end to the problem.

She walked up to the sign, wrote "Yitzhak" in front of "Katznelson," and told everyone it was Yitzhak, not Berl. And ever since then everything has been fine. The residents are happy and the postmen don't get confused. Only Orgenstern, even though he's been dead for two years, still has a sour face. There really was a furniture merchant in Jezupol called Katznelson. You could order all sorts of bureaus from him and once a year, before Passover, he would bring all the orders in from town. He had two daughters, this Katznelson did, and the eldest one had married a *goy*.

It was a neighborhood of slow troubles. Every moment lingered long enough to have a bite taken right out of it. Even the sun was sober there. Every morning it carefully infiltrated the neighborhood and its rays climbed up the walls. As soon as they reached the windowsills, they encountered pillows, comforter covers and blankets waiting to be aired out. Heavy clothing hung on laundry lines. Waving excitedly, motivated partly by wind and partly by urgency, the damp clothes prodded the sun: Please start drying! That white shirt over there, for example, we'll be needing that tonight. And onwards the sun climbed. Blinds drawn. Why stop here? Why lash white-hot blinds with sparks of fire? Just get to work. Go up top, to the solar panels. Save these people some money. Theirs was a blue-collar sun, a day laborer, without benefits. They had no need for light flickering among the leaves, for emeralds of dew, mulberry rubies, shadows in the pitanga tree. What use was that? They simply needed it to dry, to warm, to flood with light. Before noon, a thorough job. Towards evening, indifferent brush-strokes among the shadows, another afternoon load of laundry spat out from the windows onto the lines, a few more tomatoes set out in Pyrex bowls: Please ripen these as quickly as you can.

If anyone thanked the sun, it was the garden plants. A stunning profusion spilling from one garden to the next, a large wave of lawns and bushes and flowers and fruit. Trees stood in every lot, their shadows falling on the lawns and bursting onto Katznelson, where they skipped over hedgerows of hibiscus and Turk's cap, oleander and wild roses. Crazed bees and flies flew around dizzily, not only in the springtime. Jostling one another, the bushes concealed an anonymous array of creepy crawly life. Ants crossed the paths, foppishly bearing colorful petals and pitanga berry carcasses. The treetops were abuzz with wind and birds, among the roots emerged toxic fungi, shoots and mole whiskers.

Even Mr. Bergner, who was highly educated, and only in Israel had become what he'd become, God help him, had a soft spot for the sun. When given a cup of tea, he would recount to whomever wished to hear that it was at Jagiellońska, the ancient university of Krakow, that Copernicus had first conceived the notion that the earth revolves around the sun. And since it had been back there in Galicia that human thought had first restored the sun to its rightful status at the center of the planets, and since many of the Galicians in the neighborhood remembered that in school they had dwelled at length on this affair, which illuminated Galicia with a scientific glow—somewhat surprising in a land of shopkeepers and small-time farmers—many of them turned to the sun with arrogance in their eyes. Just a little patronizing. Here you go, they seemed to be saying. Now it's your turn to repay the favor. They shot it secretive, Copernican sideways glances, as if they were partners in a galactic voyage.

And there was Asher Schwimmer, a man of the sun, who had been a Hebrew poet in Poland before the war and had taught beautiful Hebrew, and his poems had even been published in *HaSolel* newspaper. But after the war his Hebrew had simply disappeared and to this day he has no grasp of it, not even a word. This man who had once written, in intricately fluent Hebrew, lines like "Fleeces of raindrops unearth life from the inanimate," now has trouble understanding the bus driver. He no longer lives in the neighborhood, they say he's in Acre, or perhaps on a kibbutz with his brother. Sometimes he turns up and sits with the neighbors on hot *khamsin* days. Chatters in startled Polish, uses his hands a lot, doesn't laugh, sometimes in the middle of a cup of tea he gets a nosebleed.

The seasons bubbled in the neighborhood as if they were bottled up. The winter rain was cruel, cutting out paths for itself between the houses, appearing in windows like a frightened face. Summer entered the closed apartments, where it went mad, multiplied its heat, and danced and danced, sweat pouring down the blinds, the air turning practically white. Spring was lovely. The bauhinia flowers fell to the ground. The huge bombax tree blossomed. The bottlebrushes waved their spiky red wands. Tiny flowers rose up from the wild shrubs, frantic beetles flipped onto their backs. Spring was lovely, but people were unhappy. Gershon Klima, his own brother, tried to hospitalize himself almost once a week instead of every two months. Feiga would complain and suffer in her room. Mr. Bergner would do-what-he-would-do, only more so, and Mrs. Tsanz couldn't bear it any more.

There were not many possibilities in this neighborhood, only cracks of possibilities. Every day the same people walked to the same places with the same problems. Every day before sunrise, Rachela Kempler stood at the window of her house, 4 Katznelson, and stared into the expanses that ended at 3 Katznelson. Opposite her, with closed blinds and aching joints, crazy Itcha Dinitz, in love with himself, winked and blinked, some say giving his body to young men. This was no neighborhood for mortals. The great catastrophes had

already happened to them long ago, in the war. Now was the time
for the little catastrophes. Aging. Bad backs. Weak hearts. Brothers
from Ness Ziona dying suddenly. So young—what happened?

Tragedy was commonplace, a daily occurrence, like drinking.
They passed it by in much the same way that their looks skipped
over the uninteresting hibiscus shrubs in the yards. Those who had
not lost their entire families in the camps got no respect. Loss of a
spouse didn't even register. Loss of children was a little more touching,
but one child was usually not enough. Simple dramas were dwarfed
when compared to the lot of Rachela Kempler, who had lost her three
children and a baby she had carried in her womb for nine months
in Plaszow and had managed to deliver thanks to unspoken sins—a
silence fee. Her mantle of grief cloaked the entire neighborhood, casting a dampening shadow on such petty losses as that of one child, a
husband, brothers, parents. Nickels and dimes against the gleaming
piece of gold she had paid to the author of history, a glistening coin
that rose into the neighborhood's sky every day disguised as the sun
(not fooling anyone), a reminder of the cursed silence fee, a simple,
daily act in the reality of those days, because what else did a woman
have to sell, after all, and yet it would not let up, that reminder, perhaps because of the failure, perhaps because the baby she had paid
for was also lost.

The loss of Feiga's young rabbi was, for some reason, emo-
tionally captivating, acknowledged with profound grief despite the
relative shallowness of the case. No one felt sorry for Adella Greuner
because "she did it with Germans of her own free will." No one
apart from us, that is, even when we were older and understood
exactly what she had done with Germans. Her home, 7 Katznelson,
first floor, remained for us a pleasant sanctuary of aromatic smells.
Against the cooking odors that permeated the neighborhood—the
cholent, the *gefilte* fish, the chicken soup turning the sky a pale shade
of yellow—Adella Greuner's window insisted on infusing the air with
French perfume, floral bouquets, dried retama flowers, and the eau
de toilette that every proper woman should wear. Adella Greuner had
rows of neatly arranged colorful little parasols, white gloves and very
light purses. She stored lipstick, bottles of cosmetics and photographs

on immaculate shelves. Her closets held corsets and pantyhose and hairpins, all burning with the heat of her body. It wasn't only the scents tickling the air outside her house, but also the radio, which was always playing dancing music. Birds gathered to chat there, hopping along the branches of the dying bauhinia. And Adella herself, in the evening hours, behind closed curtains, sometimes leaned out the window and called out, "Kalman, *vi geystu? Vi geystu?*" and on rare occasions poked her head out the door, distraught. Adella Greuner took the quick route to the streets beyond Katznelson, to the bus stop, to freedom, wearing a handsome hat, a delicate dress, gloves and impeccable makeup. "She goes with men." "Wanton." Words said with ease. Who could be bothered to deal with other people? The Angel of Death would see to her. "He'll put gloves on his hands when he takes her," another venomous spark erupts. And more than that, no one could really be bothered.

It was a neighborhood of walking in pairs, in little groups. As if by chance the individuals met up to walk together to the bus stop, the greengrocer, Littman's corner store. Woe to anyone caught alone. Only Grandpa Yosef, protected by his God, and Gershon Klima, a radical loner, an Essene, did not fear solitary walking. And Genia Mintz. Crazy Hirsch didn't count.

There were those who did not fear the outside world. They worked, they functioned, everything was fine. Uncle Antek, 10-B Katznelson, served every day as an efficient clerk at the water commissioner's office, and only when evening came did he sit down in front of his huge radio and turn into a prophet. Even though Auschwitz was over and done with and the huts had become a museum, possibilities still stirred in the past. Uncle Antek roamed through the depths of what-was, writing his prophecies in a thick notebook, and every evening he went to sleep only to get up in the morning for work and make a living like an ordinary man. Not far from him, at 11-B Katznelson, lived Haim Mintzer, who managed a warehouse. In the war he had had an identical twin and no one could tell them apart. But the electric fence had known the difference; the length of fence over which Haim climbed was not connected to the current. He alone managed to jump over the fence and run to the woods. Today he walks with a limp and a hunched body, and the doctors can't figure out what's wrong. At 6-A Katznelson lived Genia Mintz, a survivor of the Ravensbrück Death March, who was a schoolteacher. A short, straight, single-mast sailboat with her black hair tied in a tight bun. She walked slowly. Alone. The neighborhood shook its head behind her back as if this solitary, peaceful walking was madder than any other behavior. Genia Mintz kept walking without fear and her demonic, tranquil isolation cast doubts about her true nature. Rumors flourished. People looked right and left, spoke cautiously. And when she died, collapsing at the tail-end of the Ravensbrück march, not everyone believed that Genia Mintz was really gone. They kept raising hypotheses, looking now not only to the sides but up above.

In contrast to Adella Greuner and the rumors, in contrast to Genia Mintz and the suspicions, in the window of 12 Katznelson there usually stood the angelic character of Eva Lanczer. She was young and beautiful and had come to the neighborhood with her mother, who died shortly thereafter and whose name they could barely remember. It was quickly discovered that Lanczer was searching for her fiancé. They sat her down by the radio to listen to the Bureau for Missing Relatives broadcast and went to great efforts, searching everywhere. Anyone able was enlisted for the benefit of Eva Lanczer, because she was young and beautiful and never smiled or wore makeup or met nice young boys—she had a fiancé. Grandpa Yosef spearheaded the campaign and made every effort to locate the fiancé.

The fiancé was named Meirke Geltzner, from Dynow, and the entire neighborhood searched for him. One day, they found him. In Dimona. They dressed up Eva Lanczer like a bride, persuaded her to put makeup on, and Yehoshua gave her a free haircut, modeled on the style of the Queen of Belgium. When everything was ready, one last thing was required: Eva Lanczer put on a smile and became a princess.

That evening, she came back home. It wasn't him. There were those who claimed that it was him, and others who simply said, Why not? According to the testimonies, this Meirke Geltzner wanted her to stay with him. But Eva Lanczer came home, turned off the Missing

Relatives program, gave back the clothes and removed her makeup. Only the smile remained.

The encounter with Meirke Geltzner from Dimona, who some say even came to the neighborhood once to try another proposal, happened before we were born. We had always known Eva Lanczer like a picture, standing in the window at 12 Katznelson with a frozen smile on her lily-white face. She stood in her window like Rachela Kempler, but without Rachela Kempler's strength. She dressed palely, in clothes that aged quickly, emphasizing how much she herself did not change. She lived a small life. No complaints, no sounds. Not even a murmur. She stood with pursed lips, arms hanging at the sides of her body, a white sentry. A man named Eliyahu brought her cotton threads and she made strange and colorful embroidery which he sold in stores. They used to find her sometimes in all sorts of places where she walked to without realizing she was walking, like Moshe but without Moshe's thwarted sense of purpose. She went out sailing, not walking. Drifting away. Floating like a fairy among the falling leaves, only to be discovered near the train station, in a kiosk, or at an intersection. Once, the doctors found that she had been taken advantage of. The virginal Eva Lanczer was no longer a virgin. Several times they talked to Grandpa Yosef, who acted as neighborhood consul for the insane. They explained the situation and sought his advice. But Eva Lanczer kept standing at the window, weakening, imperceptibly detaching, disappearing on little journeys with her white smile, her slender hands and her clean dress. It always ended with a voyage.

We always heard that Eva Lanczer was only doing "what she had to." That was it. Adella Greuner, they did not forgive. Eva Lanczer they did. Because they loved Eva Lanczer and she was only doing what she had to. Here lay the key to the delicate balance, the watershed line between hatred and compassion.

Her life trickled down into points of silence. You could not hear her living—eating, bathing, cleaning. A transparent silence lay on her house. Movement in the two little rooms winnowed down to the flickers of her mouth, bodily flutters barely detectible through the cracks. We did not bother Eva Lanczer. Her window image begged us to let her be, and we did.

With others, we were less kind. Not much further, at 10-A Katznelson, lived Linow Community. Her real name was Hinda Goldberg, but since it was said that she alone remained out of all the Jews in her town of Linow, Effi came up with her nickname, Linow Community. Right below her lived Sarkow Community, a similar case. They had lost husbands, parents, families. And every morning at precisely nine o clock, their two green front doors opened. Linow Community and Sarkow Community went down to buy vegetables at Sammy's. One tomato, one onion, a cucumber or a carrot. They peeked at the watermelons, prodded the apricots, bought another onion. They walked down the path, diminutive and unsteady. A green basket for Linow Community, a yellow one for Sarkow Community. They walked. Deadly afraid of Sammy the greengrocer. His voice. His huge belly. His chest-hair.

The mechanism kicked in every day at nine and there was no stopping it. Once every seven days: Shabbat. Malfunction. Linow Community and Sarkow Community walk down the path with baskets in hand. They get to the bars in front of the store and put their thin cold hands on the fence. Their knuckles turn white. Linow Community wears wine-red nail polish, reflected as dark brown in the store window. Who knows what is reflected on the vegetables beyond, lying in wooden crates, no reaching them through the fence. Sarkow Community gives in first and turns around. Linow Community follows. A dim recollection of yesterday, when Sammy put another cucumber in their baskets, another carrot, another onion. "All the best, Ma'am." They walk, swerving. Disappear until the next day at nine.

We used to follow the Communities. We suspected there were still a few remaining Jews from Linow and Sarkow and that they were hiding them; they had reason to. Linow Community had a kind face and we hoped to find her a little Linowik man one day. Sarkow Community, with a mole on her cheek, we did not like. We carefully checked every piece of mail she got to see if there wasn't someone from Sarkow corresponding with her. We read the addresses, in Polish letters that looked almost like English, and compared them with the stamps to make sure they matched. She wasn't the only one we checked up on. Whenever we heard talk about someone the others couldn't be bothered to deal with, we took the responsibility upon ourselves. We tailed the seven-thirty AM postman like crows behind a plough, removing everything he dropped in the boxes, just to check.

There were a few address-less people in the neighborhood. Crazy Hirsch, for example. A pasty old man, not much more than a yellowing beard with red lips that stood out against the pale whiteness of his face. Sometimes he roved the neighborhood in daylight, emerging from a distance and disappearing back into it. Roaming evil-faced on Katznelson, he reeked and jabbered, sometimes even sitting himself down on a bench. He had a long black coat like Orthodox men wore, and a book of Psalms in his hand. You never knew when he would start ripping out pages, tossing them into the bushes or up into the air or into houses through low windows. But you knew he would always find just the right minute to stop, stand in front of the neighbors or simply in front of thin air and scream, "Only saints were gassed?!" Rebuking. Spraying his question. His one and only question. Then he would disappear. We brushed his question off. Even when left without answers to our many questions, we never touched Crazy Hirsch's. First we needed the energy to gather answers to the straightforward questions. Crazy Hirsch could come later.

You could ask lots of questions in the neighborhood—it was populated by people with answers. But Grandpa Yosef forbade them from talking. "Don't get worked up about things that don't matter anymore," he said. He believed the Holocaust was not for children, and he imposed this opinion tyrannically.

We tried. We harassed old people. Interrogated them, told them what others had said, snitched and invented. It wasn't bad enough the fights they already had, the old accounts to settle, we had to add new reasons. "What do you mean by saying that—?" "I was in—?" We had no choice. We had to understand. Had to know. Effi had to understand why her mother cried at nights. Why Uncle Antek, who was a real relative of hers and also lived in the neighborhood, had numbers on his arm that never came off. We searched for hidden gaps.

Like Mr. Pepperman, whom we visited just to tell him that Grandpa Yosef had been to the Municipality for him and everything would be fine, but he offered us grape juice and told us he had had two children our age, and his daughter had eyes like Effi's. He told us, without being forced, how they took her in the *Aktion* at Kovno. Ruchaleh, ten years old. Then he said it was no story for children and that we shouldn't tell Grandpa Yosef he'd told us.

The fonts of knowledge were well-hidden. Sometimes we passed by blocked-up walls without sensing that behind the wall was a spring yearning to burst. Still, we developed subtle senses, able to know who was worth hanging around, and we learned to listen. The stories were not straightforward. The old people mixed up their time-lines. They jumped years ahead to the final moments before Libera-tion, then suddenly remembered the ghetto, their children, the camp commandant's dog, the Passover Seder before the war even started. Suddenly, a train journey, scared to death, no ticket. How could they have a ticket? It was only 1940, before the exterminations, before they closed them off in a ghetto, and Jews were no longer allowed to ride the trains. They talked about the Death Marches, a moment before Liberation, snow and summer got mixed up and they mentioned a man and the store he owned before the war, so they could tell about how he was shot in front of their eyes during the Death March two hours before Liberation. He didn't make it.

The stories were complicated, non-linear. But we were experts by then, knowing that time marched in a straight line only for those who slept at night. We listened quietly and later unraveled the stories and re-stitched them in the right order. We were not picky; it was hard to find people who would talk. The kaleidoscope of memories accumulated both successes and failures. Ella Pruchter, who wouldn't talk, went to Grandpa Yosef to complain—not only about that but also about what we did to her plants. Beady-eyed Uncle Antek, wear-ing a white undershirt, smiled when we asked what happened in Auschwitz. He spread his hands out. He couldn't help us. Auschwitz? Who could tell? He gave us toffee candies and went to snitch on us to Grandpa Yosef. And in contrast to them, at the last minute there was Zvi Alpert, who had already left the neighborhood with a new wife. He didn't mind talking. His father threw him out of the train on the way to Belzec. A Polish farmer took him in, a six-year-old boy with broken legs.

Sometimes there was no choice. We came to Grandpa Yosef embroiled in the tangle of a story, a congestion of details whose every partial component put fear in our hearts.

"Grandpa Yosef, we need to know about Kurt Franz from Treblinka for a school project."

But Holocaust Remembrance Day was still a long way away— we had barely scraped the mud off our boots from planting trees on Tu B'Shvat. Grandpa Yosef interrogated us. Where had we come up with that question? He didn't believe the school project story. His expression was stern. Who had told us about "Doll"? He tracked down the source of the leak and Mr. Levertov was caught. Grandpa Yosef picked him up by the scruff of his neck like a bunny and extracted an oath that he would never talk to us about the war again. Children shouldn't hear about Untersturmführer Kurt Franz, known as Doll.

But Kurt Franz had sunk in. Levertov's transgression had been brief and incidental, barely two sentences as he stood outside the grocery with a bag of milk in his hand. But Kurt Franz, Doll, had been sown within us. Slowly but surely he would sprout. Slowly but surely he would grow. We would yet suffer because of him. Doll joined the heap of fragments—Majdanek, Belzec, Birkenau—and the names that kept reappearing—Warsaw, Lodz, Vilnius—among the terrible screeches of glass—Herman Goering, Ilse Koch, Dr. Mengele. From the center of the kaleidoscope an inviting hand was outstretched by Untersturmführer Kurt Franz, Doll. He drew us in.

We never stopped trying to outsmart them. We counted the days until Holocaust Remembrance Day and then came to Grandpa Yosef, a pair of scoundrels. Effi spoke for us both.

"Grandpa Yosef, everyone in class has to have someone tell them about the Shoah, so we can write essays about it. Everyone else has already done theirs."

"Everyone?"

"Everyone."

"Even Yossi, Avraham Buskila's son?"

Grandpa Yosef knew the names of all the children in the classes and the names of their parents, because he had once glanced at the registers.

An awkward moment.

And then, without batting an eyelid: "The teacher said we could do it in pairs, and Yossi Buskila did it with fat Dorit whose dad was in the Shoah."

"But the two of you aren't even in the same class!" Grandpa Yosef pointed out, embarrassing us again.

We went for double or nothing.

"That's why we need two stories!"

And we won.

But Grandpa Yosef merely scratched off some stories from the outer peel for us, not even a hint of the burning core. Disappointment. He tried to interest us in the structure of the microscope, the life and times of Rashi, American Indians, and the 1920 riots in Palestine. But we demanded Shoah stories. The misshapen Shoah, the one on the other side of the fence, the one we were not yet Old Enough for. We weren't happy with what we were allowed and our senses picked up on what was beyond, the bigger Shoah, where the pale neighborhood characters turned into protagonists in a plot.

We were twelve years old when we began to rebel. Up to then we had settled for the random stories, the hidden fountains, what little our family consented to give—what they thought was appropriate for our age. At twelve, our sense of internal order began to make its own demands. We tossed out childhood materials to make way for consciousness. We wanted to know what our parents had been through, to know about the people who had been lost, the people that looked out at us from black-and-white photographs with handsome moustaches and serious eyes. We wanted Grandpa Yosef's story. What had he been through? Why had he gone through so many ghettos and camps? How was he saved? Everything we knew was punctured, perforated, full of pauses. Stories lacking continuity, with torn out pages, one episode after another after another, but between the events lay chasms. There was no integral whole, only a kind of Morse code, dot-dash-dot dash-dash-dot. Our rebellion declared: If we can't know about your Shoah, we'll find out about everybody else's.

We began to study, to acquire knowledge. We went to public libraries every day after school, just the two of us. Our day truly began after English and Grammar were over. We read, we studied. We made good use of our reading glasses. Auschwitz and Buchenwald, Treblinka and Majdanek flew across the pages of our books. Eternal, perpetual, in a solar system whose maps were becoming clearer. Now the questions burned in us from two directions. Not only, "Dad, what happened to you in the *Aktion* in Bochnia?" but also, "What did the Commandant at Magdeburg do to the prisoners with his dog?" Not just, "Why did Adella Greuner's husband complain to a Nazi general about the handsome ghetto commander?" but also, "What was the difference between the regular Bergen-Belsen camp and the exchange camp?" We cultivated questions at an age that did not yet enable us to completely understand them. We collected stars and comets, and later we would figure out the laws, the paths.

We wanted to bring what was written in the books to our family, to the neighborhood, to find out what we might read if they wrote books. We couldn't, we weren't yet Old Enough. Grandpa Yosef sealed off the shores better than the British had—illegal immigrants hardly dared approach. People knew how to close themselves off uninstructed, intuitively, a perk for anyone who had been through a life like theirs. We didn't have many chances, we were up against too many enemies, like the heroic Paladins in our *Tarbut* encyclopedia. But we declared an emergency mobilization. We mustered all our resources. Courage and schemes and flattery and lies and blackmail and planning. All orchestrated from the rear by a level-headed mechanism, relying on a childish confidence that our punishment would not be too severe. We collected what we could, picked everything that could be picked. We created a shape. Established a shuffled world of Shoah, a valid world in which the Holocaust was a geographical area, a district with a postal authority and a written history. Whatever we knew about the family, about the elderly neighborhood residents, found a place and was given citizenship and land. It was not organized research, it was begging. No—it was a hunt.

With slanted rifles and hunting caps, we marched through the forest on the lookout for prey. On the paths, in the branches, in the bare patches, we hunted. We hunted Mr. Orgenstern (1914–1991), Jezupol *Aktion*, and we hunted Mr. Cogen through the Vilnius woods, Majdanek, Sobibor. We hunted Littman, Buchenwald, and Mrs. Rudin. We hunted Genia Mintz (1920–1976), Krakow ghetto and Ravensbrück, and we hunted Olinowsky (1921–1980), Kovno. We walked up proudly to the fruits of our hunt and held out our hat for a penny.

"Mrs. Rudin, is it true you were in Stutthof? Tell us about Stutthof camp."

"Mr. Cogen, is it true that Ilse Koch used to mark up the Jews before the gas chambers, to make lampshades out of their skin?"

"Mr. Orgenstern, Dad says thanks for the pruning shears, and we wanted to ask, what happened at Magdeburg? In the book it says there was a dog that ate prisoners."

Once in a while, as we entered the thicket, we came across Crazy Hirsch, but we were loath to conquer that lying beast. We wanted none of Hirsch. We were after the nimble deer like Gershon Klima. We wanted our arrows to strike Adella Greuner, Mr. Bergman, Itcha Dinitz, one of the burrow-dwellers who might—if we could only penetrate their habitat—provide the magic key.

Disobeying the librarian, we furtively read Ka-Tzetnik's novel, *Piepel*, and we knew then what Itcha Dinitz was and what the kapos did with young boys. We read testimonies from the Vilnius ghetto. Now Mr. Cogen's mumblings began to make sense. Needy people from the testimonies had come to his father's pharmacy. The testimonies confirmed that the pharmacist Cogen had taken a hundred final pills with his wife and son. Mr. Cogen explained to us that he spat them all out when his father wasn't watching, went to sleep and woke up an orphan.

And once a year, there was a big surprise. Grandpa Yosef's font of knowledge opened up.

On the same day every year he would go to Tel Aviv. He wore a white shirt that was smarter than the usual ones, and insisted on taking the train. Despite three-days-closed-up-standing-upright-in-a-traincar-between-Ravensbrück-and-Sachsenhausen, despite the deaths on the way between Dora-Mittelbau and Buchenwald, between Buchenwald and Gross-Rosen, he rode the train. Against his better judgment, he took us with him. Once we arrived, he left us with a man by the name of Yehezkel, nicknamed Hezi, and disappeared for a few hours while we ran around the amusement park with its Ferris wheel and motorbike show and cotton candy. Meanwhile, Grandpa Yosef took part in the annual memorial service for the Jews of Bochnia. On the way home, with us still flushed from the haunted house and the rollercoaster and the bumper cars, he became a gushing fountain. Later there were regrets, but on the train, instead of telling us about magnetic fields or King Solomon, he spoke of *kiddush Hashem* and Buchenwald and the Warsaw ghetto uprising. He suddenly took an interest in what we were learning at school and what we knew (somewhat surprised). Unable to dam up his flow of stories, *his* Shoah erupted: the Lodz ghetto, children starving to death, the child he saw ripped to shreds by dogs, little bodies covered with lime so they wouldn't spread diseases.

Small stations pass by outside, faces on platforms, and the landscape sticks it tongue out at us. Large buildings with cranes above them, railway sleepers in heaps, trees as yellow as a lemon-ice ("Not now, we're listening"), and the stories somehow involve a real puppet show in a concentration camp and a lion trainer whom Grandpa Yosef knew and a merry-go-round on which Grandpa Weil rode in the middle of his escape from a death march, and there's snow in different colors and someone who ate twenty candied apples ("Not now, we're listening to Grandpa Yosef's Shoah"), and we wait for the story to come back to him—his story. The train charges on. Grandpa Yosef talks. Down below the pistons chug doubtfully, the *get your lemon-ice strawberry-ice here* man comes and goes, ticket collectors flow through the cars, passengers search for their tickets. Grandpa Yosef gushes. Outside, platform signs smear by—"Netanya North," "Hadera West"—many towns in all directions, all with train stations we must pass, and trains rush by in the opposite direction, their rows of windows as long as Katznelson, the air trapped between the two trains transparent, tremulous. Again the Lodz ghetto, again children starved to death. Again the boy devoured by dogs, again the bodies covered in lime.

By the time we get to Haifa it all falls apart. Grandpa Yosef dozes off. We go to the snack bar and use the coins he gave us. Kibbutz Ma'agan Michael has passed us by, Atlit floats behind the dusty window. Southern Haifa welcomes the train, finding a spot for it between the ocean and the neighborhood houses. The train whistles as it enters the station, waking Grandpa Yosef. A little confused, a little alarmed, he looks at our faces that are dotted with powdered sugar from cold donuts. The board says the train goes on to Kiryat Haim and Kiryat Motzkin, but Grandpa Yosef ignores these facts. As far as he is concerned there is no train to Kiryat Haim. As far as he is concerned we'd be better off without any trains. He waits for the train to stop so he can get off first, his body still a little slow, his face sleepy. On the platform, we flank him on either side, in charge of the bags, the packages, the bonbons from Tel Aviv. Our hands, sticky from juice, grasp his sleeves. Grandpa Yosef slowly restores himself, awakens, next to the eternally inaccurate clock, recovering just in time to explain why in our country we should have done without trains.

Grandpa Yosef was impassioned about this idea. Even though you had to take two buses to get from the Haifa train station to his house—a journey that twice defeated you—and even though he insisted on taking the train to Tel Aviv, he obstinately claimed that in our country we should have done away with trains. Trains could be used to transport anything you wanted, far away from people. Things should not be allowed to be transported far away from people. Everything should be on the main routes, on the roads, among cars, so that everyone knows what's going on. Year after year, Grandpa Yosef's explanation glimmered in the kaleidoscope of memories, recording itself as something-we-must-remember. Year after year, with slight variations, it asserted itself at the schedule board or on the way out as we passed by the kiosk without buying anything. Once Effi lost a ball while we were still on the train—we were the last ones in the car, hoping to find the ball before the train set off for Kiryat Haim. Even when we stood in crowded buses, dripping with uncomfortable sweat and holding too many packages and gooey boxes of bonbons, Grandpa Yosef insisted.

We would barely listen to him, still breathless from our Tel Aviv adventure at the amusement park and from the gushing well of Grandpa Yosef now sealed off, now regretting his words. But it was too late, the stories were already inside us, being marched down the road like hostages to a large camp, and new hostages were added every year. There was no choice, this was the only way to gather information. But the hoarded material still did not form a clear picture. The events, the people, the acts, were all fragments and crumbs, meaningless on their own, but an abstract picture emerged from their collective. Not a picture we could explain or describe, but a rich image whose details had no significance. Everything we learned, each additional story, formed a new sliver for the kaleidoscope, where the pictures spun around, erased themselves, and a new model was created.

We spent the nights after the trips to Tel Aviv at Grandpa Yosef's, lying wide-eyed in the dark, listening. Every so often we heard trains faraway. And in later years, when I was a soldier taking ordinary train rides, catching a nap on the way, suddenly there would be a click and the trains would change with the light whisper of a well-oiled machine. Something full of innocent passengers was taken away, lunch-boxes-scattered-newspapers-do-you-have-the-sportspage-and-children-running-around-yelling-and-even-an-impudent-spit-ball-flying-out-the-window-hitting-a-stunned-face. All this was replaced with narrow-high-windows-no-air-down-there-bodies-squirming-devilish-siren-who-knows-what-village-passing-by-long-stops-hours-and-days-without-moving-tiny-sobbing-stops.

Our trains would travel beyond the woods. We let them run over the tracks near our sleep, their chilling sounds setting music to our dreams. In our sleep we listened to the footsteps on the paths (someone walking), to the wanderers wandering (someone unable to find peace), to the quiet conversations, the calls into rooms, "Everything all right?" (someone worried about someone).

One person we could ask, even though he was officially insane, was Gershon Klima, his own brother. Three generations of psychiatrists had confirmed his madness and if anyone questioned him, Gershon Klima had the documents to prove it. He was one of the younger people in the neighborhood, born in fact in 1939, the year of the Big Bang. He came to Israel after the war with an older uncle and aunt and strayed through many places, living a virtually normal life, until he found the neighborhood. Gershon Klima was an expert plumber who worked for Kiryat Haim's department of sewage. He spoke Hebrew like ours and worked for a living. He gave out toffee candies, and there was always the hope that he would take us on a trip through the sewage system. We worshipped Gershon Klima. His privilege of going down into the sewer, trivial as it may have seemed to other people, was inestimable in our world, in which every dark opening was a gateway to our hearts. We were drawn to the secrecy inherent in hollow spaces. We liked caves, burrows, tunnels and hovels. Nor were we indifferent to always-closed-doors, basements or attics. But in our heaven, had we been asked to come up with one, we would have given first priority to the sewer.

We went to see Gershon Klima often. Not in his house—no one went there. But to the open manhole that marked his whereabouts. We would sit with our legs dangling into the hole—a test of courage—and direct our questions downwards.

"Gershon, can we come down?"

"Why not?"

"Gershon, when will you take us on a tour of the tunnels?"

Gershon Klima did not answer. Busy. He poked his head out only when he felt comfortable, like a turtle whose shell is all the sidewalks and yards and gardens around the manhole. He smiled at us. Asked how we were. Asked us to move a little so he could climb out, and told us what kind of problem he was fixing down there and why he was officially barred from letting anyone in. It later turned out that, officially, Gershon Klima himself was barred from going in because the neighborhood wasn't even his work area. But the Kiryat Haim sewage authorities turned a blind eye: Gershon Klima solved all their problems, and besides—you didn't mess with Gershon Klima.

Gershon Klima was a quiet, wise man. But he did peculiar

things and lived a peculiar life, so he had a bad reputation. No one in the neighborhood wanted to talk about Gershon Klima and no one wanted to talk with him, apart from Grandpa Yosef, who was above the normal rules. People thought Gershon Klima was scary just because he lived such an utterly different life. But Gershon Klima was a wonderful friend and a very useful one. Before Brandy, whenever someone had to find Captain Moshe, it was usually Gershon who came through. He had a sense.

His craziness came in an orderly fashion. Usually Gershon Klima beat the craziness to it, arranging his own hospitalization with one calm telephone call. Neatly following an internal debate that led to a clear-cut decision, he would leave his house after dawn and sit on the little bench beneath the huge Indian bombax tree. A little bag lay beside him. In the bag, Gershon Klima had packed a few clothes, some medications and a large, heavy pipe wrench. His skilled hands were exploited even at the mental institution in Tirat HaCarmel, where there was always a repair or two for him to do. Of all things, it would be the arrival of the four male nurses which enraged him. He would leap up like a demon at them, thrashing against their grip. The struggle was quickly decided. Gershon Klima calmed down. Mumbling, his arms slowly waved in the air. "Never mind, never mind…" he would reassure himself, the commotion with the nurses suddenly seeming needless and inappropriate. He would drape his arms over their shoulders, then smile and mutter, "It was…that was it," as if having explained something fundamental, something that had always darkened his sunlight. Now he could rest. But then he would squirm in their arms again, almost wrenching one arm free, his eyes glistening with the possibilities should he be able to free one arm. The nurses would overcome him and Gershon Klima was swallowed up inside the ambulance.

Once or twice we went out at night and were able to see Gershon Klima being institutionalized. When he caught our eyes, he stopped fighting his captors. He smiled at us like a rabbit slung over a hunter's shoulder. "Everything…it was…it's all right…" And he was taken away.

We wanted to know why he was known as 'his own brother.'

But no one would tell us. You could peek into his home from 17-B Katznelson, or boldly climb the huge bombax that rose from his modest yard halfway up the sky. He had an empty apartment. Utterly empty. No furniture, no tables, no boxes. Nothing. Walls and white-wash.

"I've always lived this way, this is how I like it," he explained. He didn't ask how we knew what the inside of his apartment looked like, just smiled sheepishly and promised to take us down the sewage tunnels one day.

"How far?" we wanted to know.

"Caesarea. Or Tiberias."

He debated pros and cons to which we were not privy, then secretly settled them in his mind. "I lived like this on the kibbutz too." A late-blooming thought to explain his empty apartment.

A few years after immigrating to Israel and bouncing around various places until the age of twenty-five, Gershon Klima had joined one of the most severe of the Shomer HaTzair movement's kibbutzim. There, his request to live in a room without objects was reviewed and they allowed him to live between bare walls in a drafty room. They were impressed. His name was even mentioned at one of the national conferences as a model of ascetic extremism. Gains were reaped. Gershon Klima was briefly upheld as a paragon but was soon forgotten, to the relief of the kibbutz representatives. Better to suffice with brief symbolism and not expose the embarrassing flaw in his character, his insistent tendency to collect expensive fabrics as bedding. In the center of his room, on the bare floor, he scattered lengths of utterly non-socialist fabrics: satin, velvet, brocade and silk. A princely bed was formed from these broad sheets of fabric with cascading folds which, if not for the sour odor of perspiration and hay that clung to it, might have engendered thoughts of a harem. When he was kicked off the kibbutz because of something that happened, he gathered up his fabrics and came to the neighborhood. Peering through his window from the bombax branches, one could just make out his luxurious bedding in the corner of the room. We once stole a few silk shirts from Grandpa Lolek and gave them to Gershon Klima for his pile. He was touched.

"It's a gift," he explained our deed to us. He promised to get a permit and take us on a tour of the sewage tunnels.

"How far?" we pressed.

"Caesarea." This time he was determined. "Too hot in Tiberias."

His voice heralded a prediction about to come true. Caesarea! We could not immediately digest all the fun of anticipating this walk. For weeks and months we sat daydreaming, breaking the walk down into smaller units. We imagined a dark passage, numerous dangers and enemies, a treasure trunk. Arguments broke out—would there be bats? Would they bite? How many candles should we take? Were flashlights allowed? Would we ever return to our worried families? A sewage-full Caesarea was about to cleave our souls before we could even see it. Every few days we had to unload a dose of excitement upon Gershon Klima:

"Will you really take us to Caesarea?"

"All the way to Caesarea, not just half-way?"

The promise was ratified and a bag of toffee candies placed in our hands, to fortify mind with matter.

Sometimes, usually at summer's end, Gershon Klima surprised the neighborhood residents by appearing in an IDF uniform, thanks to the reserve duty for which he continued to volunteer even at the age of fifty-three. As soon as Gershon Klima turned up at his army base somewhere in the south of Israel, his fellow unit members showered him with respect and praise. They walked him inside and danced around him. Senior officers came up to shake his hand, quickly asking, "Gershon, where are the mains?" Because, as it turned out, Gershon Klima was the only person who knew how to find the water mains that united the water and sewage systems of the entire base, and he had been jealously guarding the secret since 1963. The visible mains, the straightforward ones, which any hand could touch, were nothing but an empty vessel—a superfluous component that had been maliciously circumvented and left completely without function. The real mains were hidden somewhere, probably in the thick of the earth, lording over the supply of water to the base with demonic whims. Only Gershon Klima could work his magic on them to make them

73

keep working. A certain deviousness snuck into Gershon Klima when he put his IDF uniform on, a-completely-different-Gershon-Klima, and in order to keep the scandal to a minimum he was willing at any moment to turn up at the base and repair the mains, even if it meant leaving in mid-hospitalization. He had already been summoned by two base commanders to offices with brigade maps hanging on their walls, where, with grave expressions, they pressed, "Gershon, where are the mains?" The maintenance commanders, who were replaced every few years, hated him. One of them once spent thirteen thousand shekels on sophisticated equipment to locate the real mains. He reasoned, how difficult could it be? It was simply a matter of following the pipes. But the operation failed and the pipes lay still, never betraying Gershon Klima. As Grandpa Yosef served him a slice of watermelon, Gershon Klima recounted gleefully, "They almost struck oil with their thirteen grand, but they didn't find the mains." He chuckled, treating the thirteen thousand shekels as if he had donated them to an important cause.

Gershon Klima was unaware of the role his apartment played during his reserve duty days. In his absence, we reconstructed the terrorist takeover of the Savoy Hotel in Tel Aviv (we were both the late Colonel Uzi Yairi, the first of the forces to be killed), and we freed the Sabena airliner hostages at Ben-Gurion Airport (united against the terrorists but resentful of one another, since we were both the commanding officer of the Sayeret Matkal special forces unit, neither of us wanting to be a hostage). In '76 we would have freed the Entebbe hostages seven days before a government meeting authorized a similar operation, were it not for Gershon Klima's early return.

We needed Gershon Klima. His hands alone could uncover manholes to reveal the thrilling, multifaceted belly of the underworld. Ever since we had been given a *Tarbut* encyclopedia set, we had become acquainted with the properties of Planet Earth, and knew that it was made up of layer inside layer inside layer. We envisioned us humans as tiny people who stood on the outer layer, not knowing that down below it was burning—not even knowing that there *was* a below, that below was the source of everything that occasionally burst forth up here, volcanic eruptions and streams of lava, and steaming geysers and earthquakes, and a horrible smell of sulfur in ordinary-looking places. Our minds wrestled with the structure of the Earth's layers, the thin layer we lived on, only its outer skin viable. Underneath was the cloak layer, in moderate burning colors, and finally the core, storing iron in a fluid state. Effi claimed Gershon Klima had never gone down deeper than the Earth's layer. I believed the core of the Earth was within his reach, as evidenced by the fact that his clothes were covered with grey and brown stains, which must have come from the iron and manganese so plentiful in the Earth's core. In any event, Gershon Klima had the key to the heart of Planet Earth.

He also held another key: if he was born in 1939, the time of the Big Bang, well then he must have known what had happened, and he was obliged to tell us.

We never walked up to him and asked questions just like that. We were conscious of the magnitude of caution required, of the once-in-a-lifetime opportunity we would be given one day in the future to ask the true questions, and of our obligation to wait, to ambush, to sense the right moment. We circled Gershon Klima, giving each other meaningful looks before each question and conducting silent consultations to avoid asking the wrong question, the kind that might destroy our chance to one day be able to ask: What happened to you in the war? How were you saved as a baby? How far down into the earth have you reached? Why do the people who come to take you away to the hospital call you 'your own brother'? And above all, when will you finally take us on a tour inside Earth? We proceeded with caution. Edged around the nerve centers with a subtlety beyond our age, a concentration beyond our abilities.

"Gershon, how do you know when you need to go to the hospital? Do you feel it? Can anyone feel it when they need to?"

"Gershon, is Adella Greuner really a whore, or did she just do it once of her own free will?"

And the questions branched off:

"Gershon, what's it like to be a whore?" (Effi.)

"Gershon, what exactly *is* a whore?" (Me. Whispered into his ear at an opportune moment when Effi wasn't around.)

"Whore" wasn't an entry in the *Tarbut* encyclopedia, despite illustrations of Cleopatra and pictures of amazingly curvaceous Romans, and an exciting picture of the French revolutionary Charlotte Corday murdering Jean-Paul Marat in his bathtub. Her stretched out hand, as it brandished the knife, revealed the curves of her breast beneath her blouse.

We investigated the Holocaust. Twelve years old, we charged into the barren wilderness, the murderous expanses in which Gershon Klima stood as a lone tree, and only rarely at that. We did not know how terrible and hostile the expanses were—we could not have imagined. We watched Grandpa Lolek play rummy with Holocaust survivors, winning money out of their compensation payments, and assumed the expanses were not all that hostile. We could step into their depths.

The case of Eva Lanczer exposed their true nature.

It was springtime, during Passover vacation. We were sleeping over at Grandpa Yosef's on the night Eva Lanczer couldn't bear it anymore. We were in bed by then, playing a game of "ten strokes for ten strokes," when a massive scream pierced the darkness. The lights did not come on—one scream was not enough for that in this neighborhood—but a second scream, right on Katznelson, alerted Grandpa Yosef. We followed him.

Before they made us leave we had time to see, or so we imagined, Eva Lanczer on fire—almost on fire—in a dress turned orange by the light, her bare feet glistening on the lawn and her two arms, in sleeves of flames, clutching her shoulders as her painted fingernails dug into her flesh. Her lips were painted too and there was a smudge of lipstick on her cheek. Small white earrings hung from her lobes, their dangling more kinetic than anything that moved and bustled on the lawn—the people, the lights from the windows, and the shouting. Neighbors came out in their white night-shirts and hovered like moths by the lamp in crazed circles. Exclamations of *"Oy vey, oy vey"* punctuated their sentences. A confused Gershon Klima came down with his bag and sat on the bench. Grandpa Yosef tried to impose order and calm, almost succeeding, until an ambulance arrived and drove over the lawn and Eva Lanczer screamed again. We wouldn't leave. We didn't want to move and didn't want to be in the world while this was happening. With our reasonably good grades and our teachers' notes about good behavior and the Passover vacation, everything should have been fine in the world. But nothing was.

The orderlies stepped out of the ambulance, skipped over Gershon Klima, and Eva Lanczer's mouth took control of her and screamed and scratched and bit. The orderlies grabbed her with stubborn hands, grasping her bubbling flesh. It was hard to discern a face and a body within the whirlwind—only her usual fey flickering and her mouth that seemed to grow and expand. Her screams rang back from the woods, pleas emerged from the puddles. Eva Lanczer's flesh was taken into the ambulance and her blood boiled on the path and on the orderlies' white coats and in her fingernails. When the doors were slammed closed, one last scream escaped and the whole world clapped its hands for a moment—the mouths of its lakes cried out, its birds turned to owls and its bats took to the sky.

And then, silence. They took Eva Lanczer away. Forever.

We tried to sleep that night, shutting our eyes tightly. Beneath my closed eyelids I glimpsed shapes of darkness, hovering stains. Letters, instructions, laws. That night, I think, my hatred of Germany was quadrupled. I hated Germans, hated Germany, would never go there. Effi, in bed next to me, shut her eyes tight as well. She wet the bed too, a thin trickle that spread through the mattress and over the sheets all the way to me. In the morning, Grandpa Yosef would have trouble deciding who was to blame. We should have woken up identical, both hating Germany. One night, one conclusion. When morning came we brushed our teeth without protest and ate what Grandpa Yosef served us without complaint. A silence had befallen the whole neighborhood. It was a day no one felt like starting. But Effi, who was quiet like I was and looked like I did, as if she too had spent all night studying by the light of Eva Lanczer, awoke carefree and forgiving. I learned years later that she had not thought about Germany that night, nor about Germans. She had not seen stains of darkness in the form of Eva Lanczer, had not read letters and laws, instructing: Do not forgive the Germans.

In the morning we roamed the neighborhood aimlessly, almost

without touching the ground. Two little hovercrafts with reasonably good grades—what was it all for? We wandered this way and that, not knowing what to do about Eva Lanczer. We wanted the story to go on. We couldn't accept the first ending, could not conceive that it would be the final ending, with no sequels. We waited many days for Eva Lanczer to come back, watched her window often, trying to persuade it to produce her. We came at daytime, on Saturdays, and sometimes when it was dark. We wanted to surprise her apartment and find it with Eva Lanczer outside, half-smiling, pale.

On one of our night-time excursions we discovered that we were not alone outside the dark houses. In the middle of the path we found a hunched character dressed in black.

"It's the Angel of Death, come for Eva Lanczer's soul," Effi said.

And indeed, the burglar turned to Eva Lanczer's house, although it turned out he was after more material assets than Eva's soul. Opposite, Adella Greuner opened her blinds and like a large cuckoo clock in a huge white night-dress, yelled out, "Kalman, *vi geystu? Vi geystu?*" just as usual. The burglar fled, half-cat half-bird, rolled over the flowerbed at the foot of the scarecrow and broke into a mad dash. He took all of Katznelson—which I could do in fourteen seconds wearing shorts and cheating the start gun just a little—in less than six seconds. Just before the end of Katznelson, he turned off into a side alley and was gone.

Autumn came. The days grew shorter. More tea was sipped behind the blinds, more memories. The sky waited for the rain to finish off autumn. "The splendor of Carmel falls / Bows / To the ends of autumns whose first rains are severed," wrote Asher Schwimmer back in Poland. In November a thuggish guava tree awoke from its slumber and flooded the neighborhood with its scent. The elderly neighbors seemed pleased. Guavas smelled of health, they claimed. And no less important, the aroma aroused their senses, emboldening their belief that not everything had weakened in them. All they needed was for someone to make a proper effort and everything would work fine. They tended to take their glasses off during guava days, dared to leave their walking sticks at home, reconsidered medication dosages. The guava flowed and flowed in a great stream. Hearing aids were cautiously removed, jaws moved in unabashed appetite. Once in a while, in random conversations, they expressed opinions and demonstrated knowledge.

"Lots of vitamin c in guavas," they would say. To show that modernity had not passed them by. That they too were in the twentieth century.

We would come on rainy Saturdays to visit Grandpa Yosef, careful not to track mud into the house—he had enough trouble as it was. We sat with the family and the neighbors, watching the rain, talking. Winter, the mire and the rain, for some reason did not bring back memories from the camps. On the contrary, winter was good. Their heavy faces were flushed from the heaters. The couches bore their weight. They flew. Childhood memories hovered. They themselves, their childhoods in snow and mud—they did not need us there. In their pictures they were fair-eyed toddlers sledding down the snow with a screech and walking with Father, holding his big hand. Always with them it was prayer shawls and Shabbat, narrow alleyways and, in the distance, the forest. The forests had long names. Niepolomice, Naliboki, Zielona. Sometimes there were weekdays too—haberdasheries, markets and synagogues. Tall *goyim*. Tomorrow it will snow.

And we were outside.

Sometimes other life forms tried to infiltrate the neighborhood. Young couples grew excited by the cheap real estate, and suddenly there were baby clothes hanging from the laundry lines. Crying at night, a soft, continuous sound. For some reason the young people did not last long. They moved away, leaving only the regular crying, lights on all night, the smell of old fabric on the lines. And sometimes kids were sent to the neighborhood to do fundraising.

On one side the children wait, sometimes giggling at the funny names on the doorbells. On the other side, life comes to a standstill. Quiet! Someone's at the door! The children of Israel wait with their vouchers in denominations of five, ten and twenty. Beyond the door the Gestapo is knocking—someone has turned us in.

Black clouds of starlings also invaded in season, finding the neighborhood a wonderful place for their needs, chattering on the trees, increasing the value of every branch. Footballs suddenly appeared in the air, kicked over from a nearby practice field. A young boy soon emerges and looks around for the ball, somewhat surprised at this neighborhood, this quiet. Sometimes he spots a resident in a window. Impudently, the boy asks Uncle Antek if perhaps he's seen the ball, not knowing that sundown is approaching and in Auschwitz the prisoners are being counted. The inmates stand for roll-call, the shadows of their tortured bodies hidden in the earth, and when the roll-call drags on and on it seems as if only a small step separates the natural state from its opposite: the shadow straightening up while the body falls to the ground to rest.

We invade too. Our neighborhood vacation. Halfway through summer, before we arrive, a sudden blossoming in the yards. Gloomy trees light up with color. Pink, red and purple glimmer trivially in the yards. Then we show up, Effi and I. Tanned, unkempt, full of ideas. After a whole session at camp, bursting with our little disputes, bitter grudges erupting every hour. How could Effi have made us lose the indoor-soccer match? How could I have forgotten the right answer in the group quiz? Effi still resentful over the gray horse I got to ride on horse-riding day. Carried on its back, I felt afraid, with a foolish smile on my lips, hesitant but victorious. Effi got a skinny horse without a mane.

Effi was older than me. She was always a year ahead of me and always beat me at everything. A poem she wrote was published in *Ha'aretz Shelanu*; mine wasn't. She got work as a photographer for *Maariv LaNoar* magazine; I didn't even get a response to my application. She managed to get herself a cast on her arm at least once every two years; I never even had one. She had braces and she was sent to have her eyes tested. Every other summer when she got her cast, everyone wrote lines and poems and signed their names with colorful markers. Every year I plucked up the courage to rebel, to reverse the order of things and try to lead. Effi would rise to the challenge. For that reason we set up a summer camp, an arena in which everything would be decided. Moshe attended our camp, and very quickly he also became the janitor and the judge. When Moshe wasn't quick enough and the fights were too great, Effi would declare—to the woods! That was where I lost.

Above us the Carmel mountains towered, and behind them the woods of Minsk. We were partisans and we were American-Indians and we were ghetto-fighters, day in day out. Time was thrown into disarray. German trucks were attacked and taken down whenever a path met a road. The rivers flowed with opportunities to wade through the water and join the partisans. Uprisings broke out in the ghettos every day. We escaped to the woods and hid. We poked around all the houses of Katznelson, climbing through windows, invading closets. We opened sealed boxes and read impenetrable certificates in foreign Polish on paper that smelled like dead countries. We picked up the rules from the grownups' conversations: if you get caught, better to be caught by the Germans. Worse to be caught by the Poles. Worst of all—Ukrainians or Lithuanians. We were afraid of Mrs. Dopochek, who was Lithuanian. We tried to find evidence to ascertain who was Ukrainian. We carved oaths of silence-if-taken-hostage on all the trees except Gershon Klima's Indian bombax, which we regarded as slightly holy. And we celebrated our childhood, our wildness. Apart from Menachem, the only child in the neighborhood, we had no competitors there, and we sucked everything we could out of it. Every year, the same things. Momentous events tried, unsuccessfully, to distinguish the years from one another, but one year skipped into the next and they all turned into one huge, borderless year. A year in which everything happened, then, now, forever. A tremendous year, its details bursting forth, every memory picking out arbitrary details from many places; contradictions and amazements jostle, huddle, one thuggish version wins for a moment then disappears into the pile, kicking and screaming. The Great Year plays innocent: I am not one year, I am all of childhood. But we think only of the summers with Grandpa Yosef and the Great Year quickly stands at attention, buttons itself up into the measurements of a single year, barely standing, rocking on its heels.

Genia Mintz, the teacher, who kept a little parrot on her windowsill, comes to complain that we threw chewing gum and toffees into the bird-cage. (She dies on a Saturday; they wheel her out of the house and take her away in a black car.) In the middle of summer, she pets Effi's head and asks math questions, questions for tanned skin and sandals. "Tell us about Ravensbrück, Mrs. Mintz." Little Genia Mintz walks down Katznelson, alone.

Mr. Bergman is hospitalized for a whole year, allowing us to investigate the contents of his home. Grandpa Yosef goes over to return a book in Polish about Herod and we agree to just stand at the window. Mr. Bergman's plants need to be watered, he's been in "convalescence" near Jerusalem for two weeks, and Grandpa Yosef goes inside with us and a watering can.

During that Great Year we were American Indians and soldiers and illegal immigrants and astronauts. But mostly we were partisans, of the vengeful type. We sought out victims. Once, on the side of the road that ran between the two forests, we found an abandoned car whose driver had gone into the woods for a pit-stop. Bleary-eyed, we crawled into the car. We stole candy from the glove compartment, let the air out of one tire and spat on the seats.

The road at the edge of the first forest was, for me, the final frontier, never to be crossed. Something about the way it popped up after a long run among the trees was inexplicably frightening. Nature, nature, nature, then suddenly a break, a road—human presence. Effi used to mock me. Complacently crossing the road, she would disappear into the other forest, then come back and tell me how she'd gone "to the edge." I didn't know that just beyond "the edge," behind another forest, was the Kiryat Haim soccer stadium where I went on Saturdays with Dad and yelled cheers that reached the heights of the treetops in the woods.

One day, when we accidentally discovered that the woods were where Crazy Hirsch lived, our blood curdled. We were too afraid to go back for a whole year. We made enquiries. Learned the facts. Pictured the hut he had built himself, with its wooden fences and the light coming from a little window. The next year there was a suffocating journey to the edge of the woods. Trembling steps. A darkening world, the scent of panic. More and more steps, until our surrender. We could not find the hut. In subsequent journeys we went deeper, further. Finally we found the hut. We fled with beating hearts and wild breath and footprints—that was what we thought about: the footprints, which would lead Crazy Hirsch all the way to Grandpa Yosef's if he chose to follow us. We went back, our breath ragged, our courage compelled. We erased the footprints and made others, leading the soles of our shoes to Brachaleh's empty house, to Gershon Klima's house—no one would dare harm him. And the year after that we went back to the woods and took up our games again, steeped in the knowledge that Crazy Hirsch's hut was right there, a gentle pattering of absolute terror, a suffocating veil descending upon our recreational pleasure.

When Crazy Hirsch suddenly appeared in the middle of the neighborhood, we would freeze as we waited, lifeless, for him to find an appropriate place to scream his question:

"Only saints were gassed?"

Then he would leave and we would breathe again. Children again, as usual, but those skeletal seconds before he left, long as the bones of a whale, exposed us to the true nature of the neighborhood. The character of the people. The family. The real truth. Stripped of the houses, the gardens, the paths, the trees, the sun, we clearly saw the people among whom we were playing. The dim message that could not be deciphered with words or with entries from the encyclopedia, like "tropical forest," "first aid," "the Stone Age." For a moment we comprehended the real figure, the one morbidly pushed into a corner. The dwellers of these little houses, tied to one another in a wondrous braid. Elderly gods, sitting on the Olympus of a senior citizen neighborhood, spinning plots of flesh and blood, determining the fates of us mortals. They were free of weak spots. Afraid only of the mailman, oddly affected by his shiny cap. Dining on ambrosia out of faded crockery. Orbiting through zodiacal constellations. From the early sunrise of Mrs. Kempler in her window, through Grandpa Yosef's route to synagogue, to the sunset of Adella Greuner's face as she waited in the evening breeze behind angry drapes, rolling in the image of a burning comet, yelling, "Kalman, *vi geystu? Vi geystu?*" Anonymous shouts discharged from dreams, shooting stars ineligible for wish-making. Grandpa Lolek like furious Apollo in his Vauxhall chariot, untouched by the suffering, a mischievous Pan in the forest of the miserable. And Neptune, Gershon Klima, his own brother, ascending from the water, a miracle being torn from its axis. The marching fire, Uncle Mendel, judging every being. And young Narcissus, crazy Itcha Dinitz. Saintly and amiable, walking to the grocery to the beat of an African drum, discovering new lands every day. Nobel laureates behind closed doors, sealed off geniuses living on pills. Their illnesses were picturesque, sprouting out of nothing. They went to the Sick Fund, that barn of pills, to ask the Pharaonic clerks to fill their prescriptions from the huge dark bottles on the upper floors. (We never got anything from the interesting bottles. No matter what disease we managed to catch we were always given syrup taken down nonchalantly from the lower shelf. The pitchers of pills, the wonders of the high shelves, were only for the patched up old people in slippers and layers of robes. And for Feiga, sometimes, there was even a trip behind the cabinet for a secretive pharmacists' huddle, and a little bag that emerged from the darkness full of yellow pills that we once tasted and which Effi promptly threw up; I did not.)

These prematurely old people waiting mutely on benches at the Sick Fund, spinning their memories around and around, were aqueducts that carried life and memories. Afterwards, at home, they philosophized quietly in their rooms, men and women of ideas (some were modest, having only one idea). Dam-builders, forest-choppers, mountain-climbers, gold-miners, land-birthers. A multitude of gold and wine-like light in impenetrable eyes—only memories could light sparks in those eyes. Crinoline dresses danced tenderly to the sounds of the radio at Adella Greuner's. The margosa trees dripped with barren fruit that turned yellow as it fell. Only the yard of Gershon Klima, his own brother, was blessed with a massive Indian bombax. Feiga also had a tree by her window, a mad poinciana whose branches groaned in the wind. As if her real demons were not bad enough, in the rain she imagined devils hanging from the stems of the leaves.

*

The Holocaust extended its reach beyond the neighborhood. Traces of Shoah lurked in the most surprising places, like the little shops where

Dad went to order wallpaper or buy light bulbs. He often took me with him to Attorney Perl's hardware store on Yonah HaNavi Street. Apart from buying plaster or little boxes of screws, it was a place where you could talk, ask questions and watch Attorney Perl at work. People used to stand with their elbows on the counter and gaze at the wall behind Attorney Perl, which was a patchwork of small metal drawers, each containing its own peculiar occupants: nails, screws, nuts, bolts, hooks, latches, washers, rubber bands. Attorney Perl would be up on the ladder in his blue smock, scaling the length and height of the wall like Spiderman, filling the customers' orders. Words cannot adequately convey the splendor of his motion. The slowness. The precision. His serene voice enquiring from above, "I've only got half-inch ones. Will they do?" Clinging to the wall as he moved up and down, right and left, Attorney Perl would descend for a brief moment to hand over the goods and take the customer's money. Then up the ladder again to retrieve something from another metal drawer. Measure out the contents. Wrap the correct amount in a small paper bag. Climb down. Deliver the goods.

Attorney Perl was born in 1900. Before the war he was a practicing attorney. In his town of Stanislaw, near Lvov, he was known even among the *goyim* as an expert in business, commerce, and property law. His voice echoed beautifully through the courtroom, as if the dimensions of the space had been designed precisely for his vocal chords. Had he not been Jewish, he might have been appointed a judge in Lvov. At the beginning of the war he lived in the Bochnia ghetto, in the same house as Dad's family, 7 Leonarda Street. Then he was sent to Auschwitz, and later to work in Dora-Mittelbau. This camp, with its tender, womanly name, is hardly mentioned in Holocaust stories because very few of its inhabitants survived. Attorney Perl would have been lost too, if he hadn't found his way to one of the Dora-Mittelbau satellite camps, where he operated Obersturmführer Jürgen Licht's puppet theater. After the war, he came to Israel. His days in the camps had not only left the attorney barely more than skin and bones, but had also rendered him skeptical of the validity of the law. So he opened a little hardware store. But even after all those years, even to people who knew nothing of his aborted career as a lawyer in the courtrooms of Lvov, when he called out from up top, "Coated or uncoated, the nuts?" he still exuded a stifling sense of eminence. People answered cautiously. Put their hands to their chins. Pondered.

Sometimes he would take Dad and me into the little chamber behind the wall of drawers. He would tell his assistant, "Yakov, mind the store for a while" (his assistants were always called Yakov), and take us to the back room. There, to my surprise, was a mirror image of the store. On the reverse side of the wall was another wall of drawers, containing the store inventory. The space below the counter looked just like its front-end counterpart. But the width of the chamber was different, and I soon noticed other dissimilarities, including a black-and-white photograph of a woman, a tea kettle, two fountain pens, and a book in Latin.

Sometimes Attorney Perl would point to the picture of the woman and ask Dad if he remembered her, forgetting that he had asked the same question many times. Dad would answer politely, "No, I don't remember her," and Attorney Perl, astonished, would wonder how this was possible. After all, they had lived together in the same house in the Bochnia ghetto until she was taken away. During those brief moments, Attorney Perl found the world to be a strange place. His fingers caressed the kettle as he contemplated how it could have happened. In Stanislaw, before they were married, half the town had courted her. Everyone knew her. And here, now—no one. Not even the people from the ghetto. Gradually, he would regain his composure. We would wait patiently as he went about making us tea in his calm manner. He talked with Dad, and a little with me. I liked to listen to the majesty in his voice, especially when he argued. He could quote from books in all sorts of languages and knew every minute detail of Polish history, as if it had been tailor-made for him. The only match for him was a wizard like Grandpa Yosef. Occasionally, one of Dad's responses to his questions would leave Attorney Perl hesitant, momentarily disarmed, but he would soon perk up and produce a witty retort, replete with dates and quotations. Still, there was respect in his eyes when he looked at Dad (*Nu*, and this is the boy who was so mischievous in the ghetto!).

I sat between them, coveting the appreciative looks. The kaleidoscope of memories came by like a large fish, swallowing up the flakes: *Attorney Perl argues with Dad. Dad wins. Attorney Perl slurps his tea and says nothing.* Colorful flakes. Soon they would be gone and I would no longer remember them. But the scenes still echo, chipped and crushed, inside the kaleidoscope.

Sometimes the arguments led to the topic of Attorney Perl's great plan—his despoiled, lost plan. He wondered out loud, now did they understand how far-reaching his predictions had been? At the end of the war, when Jews were thinking only of themselves, of food and of family members who may or may not have survived, Attorney Perl was busy scurrying back and forth among offices and embassies. His feverish momentum thwarted any notion of throwing him out onto the street. He was surrounded by desperate people trying to slip into offices and present their documents with trembling hands, petitioning bureaucrats on their own behalf or for a family member. Negotiations were attempted in reception rooms between a certain Yakov Zweig, tailor, and the government of the United States of America. People retreated in despair, sighed and went to try their luck elsewhere. They took no notice of retired Attorney Perl—his skin covered with eczema and his body little more than a skeleton—as he proclaimed his sacred mission at every embassy and bureau: Clemency must be granted to all the Nazi leaders. Under no circumstances should they be hanged.

This was the essence of Attorney Perl's position and the impetus for his bureaucratic endeavors. Fifty years from now, he explained, we will regret not having kept them alive, not having bothered to collect their versions. Not the rushed testimonies obtained from shattered officers during two weeks of interrogation. Not the court rendering, but rather a version for the history books. So that we might comprehend what exactly they were thinking, which orders were spoken, who said what. We must not be satisfied with the statements they give in court before they are hanged, their mouths contorted in contempt or terror. We must leave them to patiently document every tiny detail. Because if we hang the wretches, we shall never know both sides of the truth. We will keep digging our heels into our own versions.

Historians born after the war will try to understand the other side based on the inconsequential utterances of junior officers. We will all stand in front of the mirror that reflects us, our side, and we will deny the other side, the dark one. Regrets will be of no use. It is the heart's duty—humanity's duty, to keep these criminals alive, and it will be far more useful for us than any revenge could ever be. Many years after it had failed, after the Nuremberg hangings had disastrously killed all those who could testify, Attorney Perl never tired of his plan. What exactly were they thinking? What orders were they given?

Dad was practical. "*Nu*, but where would we have kept them? In the end they would have escaped, and then where would we be?"

But Attorney Perl had thought of everything. "Where? In the camps, of course. The barracks and fences were still standing. We could have housed the criminals there. Under guard. Why not? Every day we would have made them walk five miles to the testimony stand. In the freezing cold, yes. And we would have made them wear our clothes and eat our food, and walk in those 'fine' shoes, and they would have received medical treatment right there in their precious *revier*. And we would have whipped them. Yes! Whipped! Even unto death! Death to anyone who is careless with his testimony!"

He falls silent. His back hunches over, he shuts his eyes. A small vein throbs in his forehead.

We drink another cup of tea in silence. Birds of memory flutter overhead. Finally, my moment comes: Attorney Perl lets me choose whatever I want from the drawers of bolts, rubber bands and screws.

I don't know where Effi was during those hours when I settled down on the little chair at Attorney Perl's. Did her father also have a wise old friend who knew the names of all the Nazi criminals, the dates of their court cases, their sentences, and the extent to which those sentences were enforced? Did she sit in a little back room where the dense air was sweetened with tea, hearing about appeals, sentence mitigations, re-trials? Did she also hear a list of names—a long, long list naming criminals who had evaded trial and were living somewhere comfortably, hiding behind borrowed identities, ordinary members of communities—*forgiven*? Attorney Perl was mine, all mine, and when he was invited to family affairs, I didn't tell Effi quite how distinguished he was. It didn't matter. Her side also had anonymous guests who would show up unknown, ever-changing, recurring, replaceable, eternal. We maintained a certain distance from one another, fearing our similarities might one day make us virtually interchangeable. Attorney Perl, with his sublime hatred and his neat lists of Nazis carved out like steps, was mine alone.

When I was about nine, Attorney Perl gave my brother Ronnie the *Tarbut* encyclopedia set for his bar mitzvah. In my world this was an incredible gift, more precious than anything I could conceive of. A great deal of the affection which *they* did not know how to express in the usual ways was embodied in this gift. The Holocaust was concealed within the pages of the *Tarbut* encyclopedia, overshadowed by other entries. "The Massacres of 1648–49" and "The Pogrom Horrors" were more impressive, more direct. But even more powerful than the pogroms was the colorful, illustrated world waiting to be deciphered. The entries were arranged according to an unfathomable order, each entry following a set outline. First, an introductory narrative composed by the author, recreating the private meditations of Alexander the Great, behind-the-scenes secrets from the French Revolution, an encounter with a gorilla. After the introduction, printed in a different typeface and composed in formal language, came the encyclopedic data, a refreshing assortment of information, explications and subplots. Each page was embellished with an illustration, whatever the entry. That was where we learned how dinosaurs fought and what the Vilna Gaon looked like, how the Battles of Hannibal were won and how Thomas Edison gazed at the first electric bulb as it shone on his desk. The *Tarbut* encyclopedia paved roads, expanded the world, colored it and outlined its rules. It also clipped the wings of the Holocaust's voracity and defined its boundaries, demanding equal measures of attention for both *tarbut*—culture—and Shoah.

Grandpa Yosef wrinkled his nose when he saw Attorney Perl giving Ronnie the entire encyclopedia set, because he was the tree of knowledge in our family and encyclopedias were supposed to be his domain. When Grandpa Yosef himself bought me a very fancy book, *Sayings of Wisdom*, he suffered yet another setback, because that was exactly what Sammy the greengrocer had given me. When it turned out that Uncle Menashe had bought me yet another *Sayings of Wisdom*, an inquiry was conducted and all the *Sayings of Wisdom* givers issued a joint statement: It was on sale at Goldberg's on Shapira Street. An appendix to the statement clarified that the book was still expensive even after the discount.

We forgave them quite easily:

Grandpa Yosef, because of the money, of which he had none. Whenever he had a penny, he would find someone who didn't and give it to them.

Uncle Menashe, because he lived far away and there was an unwritten, dimly comprehended rule that defined a correlation between mileage and gift-size. Various distances and degrees of familial relationship were plugged into this formula, resulting in the appropriate expenditure for a gift.

Sammy, because when his son, Tzachi, had his bar-mitzvah, Dad had given him a very fancy *Interpretations of the Torah and Prophets* that was on sale at Goldberg's on Shapira Street.

Besides, Dad could never be angry at Sammy, because of all the people with whom he bought lottery tickets (they faced God in pairs, hoping He would hand out a measure of good fortune in proportion to their joint rights), Sammy was the only one who didn't cheat Dad when they won, or rely on his indulgence in financial matters. Hillel, the barber from Herzl Street, cheated him. And a guy from the army reserves cheated him. But Sammy would always run to find Dad and announce the winnings.

Sammy had a little fruit and vegetable store at the edge of Grandpa Yosef's neighborhood. He wore a gold chain around his neck and had a thundering voice, and his potbelly always stuck out of the bottom of a shirt that proclaimed, in English, "Harvard University." With his mustache and bald head, Sammy looked like a hardened thug, but he had small, green eyes that took on the color of tea in the sun. Inside the store, his eyes had a strained tone of green, sometimes Ganges-green, reminding everyone that Sammy was half-Indian. He kept two different kinds of tabs for his customers in the neighborhood: one for those who had to pay, and another for those who didn't have to pay because they had suffered enough in the Holocaust. Sammy spoke of the Holocaust like normal greengrocers talked about soccer. The Holocaust, for him, was a physical entity, a body with character traits. A transparent globe which you could hold in your hands and gaze into to see figures and snowflakes and all sorts of colorful things. "The Shoah…" he used to say, and coming from his lips the word sounded different. Finally, here was the perspective of a man with both feet on the outside, with true compassion and unexaggerated kindness. "They suffered over there, the poor souls," he explained, and nothing was hiding behind his words. "Suffered" did not conceal two-days-under-a-mountain-of-bodies-with-his-mother-and-father-dead-on-top-of-him-until-he-got-out-and-ran-to-the-forest. "Poor souls" was not their-children-died-in-the-ghetto-and-after-the-war-they-tried-to-have-children-and-could-not-something-in-her-body-or-her-mind-the-doctors-gave-up.

Sammy employed three assistants, and they were told to be nice to the customers. When he said "customers," it was clear that he did not mean the ones in sunglasses who stopped their cars outside for a minute to run in and get something for Shabbat, but rather the ones like Gershon Klima, for example, who would sometimes stand among the crates of produce without any idea of what he wanted. They had to let him stand there like a waxwork, with his own rhythm of confusion, no urgency, until a healthy thought about plumbing drew him out of the confusion and instantly cured him, and as if on the wings of Superman's cloak he would take hold of his six-inch pipe and emerge a regular customer, grumbling, "How much are the tomatoes today?"

Sammy worshipped Grandpa Yosef, and personally delivered his groceries for free. In the middle of the workday he would sit down with Grandpa Yosef and discuss the affairs of the day, the political situation. They explored various possibilities, like a truce between Sammy and Littman from the corner store. (Sammy's fight with Littman, who owned the corner store next-door to the vegetable store, had been going on for thirty years, ever since the business with the pickles. Sammy had attempted to market pickles made by his sister-in-law, thereby diverging from his legitimate domain of fresh vegetables.)

Littman was also a saint. Prices, with Littman, were a flexible matter. Bills were totaled in pencil on a little roll of paper, quick computations in Yiddish, impossible to follow. The neighborhood residents came, looked at a product, and whatever was reflected in their pupils—their past in the camps, the sum of their compensation payments, their pensions—formed an image that was turned into a price. They ran tabs that sometimes lasted a lifetime. Debts were dropped, erased. At Littman's, they could come and chat, and he would always ask how they were doing; this was as important as the shopping. His corner store was a valley of sorts, where shepherds came to rest with their herds in a place virtually untouched by the winds. Even Crazy Hirsch found refuge at Littman's, where he would idle with his elbow leaning on a barrel of pickles. Sometimes Linow Community and Sarkow Community came too. Littman encouraged them, reminding them that he had seen the greengrocer in the Turkish market buying spoiled pickles and then putting them in hot water to make them look fresh.

In the conflict between Littman and Sammy, the neighborhood's heart leaned towards Littman, who, after all, had a number on his arm from Auschwitz, and had also been in Buchenwald. But I preferred Sammy because he looked normal, like Dad, and a couple of times he took me to play soccer on the beach with his team, "Maccabi Sammy Vegetables and Son." Sometimes, when the store was empty, Sammy would ask me to toss him a mandarin orange, and he would cheerfully head-butt it back to its place. Sometimes he missed. Then we would look sheepishly at the mandarin as it rolled across the floor.

"You shouldn't throw away food," I said.

"You shouldn't say 'yuck' about food," Sammy retorted.

"People died for a bit of cabbage," I escalated.

"Bread is sacred," Sammy giggled.

We shouted out all the battle-cries, only after making absolutely sure we were alone.

A little of Sammy's hegemony was disrupted in favor of Littman during one of our trips to Tel Aviv with Grandpa Yosef, when we were delivered into the caring hands of Hezi for our day at the amusement park. We found Hezi in a garrulous mood. Until that day, we had believed that Hezi was created only once a year to welcome us in Tel Aviv and take us to the amusement park, then disappear into thin air until the next year. But there he was, not only talking and taking on the form of flesh and blood, but very quickly also revealing a solid connection to our life: he announced that he was the son of Littman from the corner store, didn't we know? He told us off-handedly about Buchenwald and the mad hunger. The people who ate corpses. Ate clothes. Ate wood from the hut walls. Their teeth crumbled as they gnawed on the wood but they could not stop. Only those who gained the protection of criminals or Russian POWs, the kings of the camps, could survive.

Hezi was an utterly unexpected fountain of information, and an incautious one. He was apparently reprimanded by Grandpa Yosef because the next year he was completely silent, as if the Hezi who had snuck into the previous year's amusement park day had been an impostor. We failed to see how he could be Littman's son, and how he could suddenly have talked. The year after that, Hezi was abolished altogether.

Hezi was abolished, but not the impressions of Buchenwald. We had finally found a magic key to the Shoah: hunger was something we too could experience. Hunger. That, we could do ourselves.

But it was hard to stop eating just like that. Mom's radar eyes would have picked up on it immediately, and things were no different in Effi's household. We waited for our chance, knowing that we had to taste Buchenwald. The opportunity did not come quickly, but it came. We were sent to the kibbutz.

The original plan was to spend summer with Grandpa Yosef as usual, but a severe deterioration in Feiga's health necessitated a change of plans. We oscillated between the threat of a session at camp (after already having announced that we were through with camp—thirteen years old, enough is enough), lounging around at my place, lounging around at Effi's place, or going to the kibbutz. We wanted to stay with Grandpa Yosef, even prayed for Feiga's health, but this time her decline was so severe that all the pale bones at the foundation of her illnesses were exposed, revealing a ruined network of body-soul connections. The die was cast: kibbutz.

The kibbutz was where Grandpa Hainek's eldest sons lived. Ze'ev had already been killed. It was the year in which Dov was to be killed, in November, but that summer he still welcomed us warmly. His task was to host us for a month, and he did just that, with the help of Eitan, Grandpa Hainek's third son, who was well-suited to the mission. He had just finished his army service and he liked to talk once in a while, which, by family standards, made him garrulous.

Most of the time we were left to our own devices, and we made the most of it: this was what we had been waiting for. Buchenwald. The rules of the game were simple: no eating. Then we replaced the absolute rule with less severe derivatives: eating was allowed, but only scraps from the kibbutz trash-cans, fruit peel, waste, bones. We were willing to be disgusted, to get ill. We toughened our spirits. It was not a game played for immediate victory, but in the service of the senses, to acquire skill, depth, and the possibility of touching the truth. Then we added another rule: we could eat whatever we stole.

It was not an easy time between Effi and me. She was fourteen, I was at bar mitzvah age ("Comfort, comfort my people," began the *haftorah* I was learning to recite), and all sorts of things were erupting in my body. Strange discoveries emerged constantly, everything seemed peculiar, in constant flux. Effi had begun to hide things from me and was often busy. She had recruited a staff of girlfriends. When I wanted to go to the library, she would say she was busy, and eventually she confessed: "I'm kind of sick of the Shoah." I felt betrayed. With great anger, I would go alone to read in the library, more diligent than ever, now representing the righteous, the neglected, the abandoned. I traded horrible thoughts and self-pity for studious reading. What I found out, I kept to myself, a little treasure for the treasureless.

On the kibbutz, the rift was somewhat healed. We knew it was Buchenwald time. Effi put her new interests (which, to my horror, had begun to take on the corporeal form of Yaron from the ninth grade) on hold. We played Buchenwald. We fasted and did not drink. We licked water from leaking taps, slipped behind the dining hall, stole old hunks of cheese and ate with trembling hands. We even sucked on straw, like Littman had done when he had escaped. We shared a sour, blackened banana peel in a tender moment of mutual destiny. Then, one day, there was an event of a different kind.

At the burning hour of midday we went to the distant fields near the entrance to the cowshed and the dairy. The heat was relentless. Our breath was lethargic from the Buchenwald hunger and the oppressive heat, colorful circles of sunlight hovered in front of our eyes. No one dared go outside in the heat wave. Only a few stunned pigeons wandered on the lawns and in the shade of the oleander shrubs, and the cows mooed plaintively in the distance. We walked slowly. I felt as if my legs were acting of their own accord. A strange sensation. Hunger had weakened my thoughts. For four days it had been nothing but sour banana peels, straw, cheese from a discarded container, and some apple rinds Effi had got hold of—the most nutritious thing I had consumed.

Effi dragged me into the oleander shade. She did not speak. She was breathing heavily and I saw a strange look in her eyes, beneath fluttering eyelids. Without warning, she lay down on her back on the slightly putrid bed of leaves, and slowly took off her blouse, crushing the leaves as she squirmed. Her nipples were presented to me with the hem of her blouse still draped over her forearms. Curiously, I surveyed the revelation, the fair mounds which bore her nipples on their peaks, and my heart did not demand a thing. Effi ordered me to come closer, laid down the law. She let me touch her with my tongue, but only on her belly-button, her earlobes, and the tip of her nose. She warned me against deviating from this crucifix of flesh. I knelt, examining my options, looking for interest in them. Effi breathed heavily. Nerve endings bustled just beneath the surface of her skin, invisible channels of sweetness perceptible only in her rosy blush. I kissed her earlobes undesiringly, cautiously touched the edge of her nose, then licked her navel. I sat up straight.

Effi sighed with her eyes closed. "Again."

I was scared. "Again?"

Effi felt for my hand. She dragged it over her skin, letting me find the tracks on my own. "Use your tongue too," she ordered.

I chose the safest looking path, the four points that had already proven themselves. I flitted over her navel, her ears, her nose. I sniffed. Effi exuded a new scent of budding perspiration. I gained courage and touched a nipple. I put my lips to it and tried to drink. I placed my hand on her abdomen and attempted to draw out a single drop, the way we had once both sucked on the udders of Lassie, the barn dog. She had not put up much resistance as we removed her puppies and tasted her udders, only a look that said, "Kids, it's not pasteurized," and slight amazement, perhaps also resentment at the temporary suspension of her puppies. (We didn't drink much. It was a little bitter and unpleasantly warm. Unlike Romulus and Remus, we preferred grape juice.) I could not find a drop in Effi's nipples. And she too, fairly soon, grew bored. But a new idea glistened.

At my cousin Zevik's wedding, Grandpa Hainek's son Eitan had been kind enough to explain to me about the schlong. He pulled me aside at one of the tables and went into great detail regarding whom he had given his schlong to, whom he was planning to give his schlong to, and how one gives one's schlong. Later, in the restroom, he pulled down his pants and showed me this mysterious creature, the schlong, which had-been and was-being and would-be given according to a carefully implemented plan. I discovered with Columbus-like excitement that I too had a fragile schlong in my pants, and that its thus-far monotonous functions (sometimes, to my chagrin, at night in bed) were merely a spiritual weakening whose time was up. Now I looked at Effi and was guided by an unspoken sensation—her fluttering eyelids, her trembling lips, her expectant look. I put my worlds together and enquired, "Do you want to get my schlong?"

The days were days of Buchenwald, and I was dizzy from barely eating, and Effi's slap sent me reeling into deep darkness. I could not believe how much Jewish strength still remained in the hand of this girl who had been testing her limits by starving herself for a week. Years later, she told me I was the only one who had been in the throes of Buchenwald starvation. She was secretly gobbling down double meals, fattening herself up in the dining room and at Dov's. "I thought about it," she generously explained, "about whether both of us really needed to do it, to understand." And she had a complaint too. "Do you have any idea how many apples I had to eat, to make you those scraps?"

I woke up alone. Effi had left and gone to Dov's room, where she sat comfortably eating jam and loquats, preparing me some apple rinds as she munched her way through a bag of toffee candies. The sun stole in between the oleanders, striking my face. I opened my mouth wide, feeling singed. Voices came from afar, people walking. My eyes could not see, shadows were distorted, glimpses of color danced around. I vomited, still lying on my back, almost choking. I could not open my eyes. How would I get up? I lay helpless, wanting to drink just one drop. I tried to move again, in vain. Nausea. I wanted to pass out, not to suffer the dizziness, the thirst. At the last minute, before giving in, I made one more effort. I rolled onto my side and sat up on my knees. Things were dripping inside my head. Circles running in my eyes. I vomited again. I got up very slowly and opened my eyes. I walked, lightly touching the branches, anchoring myself in the spinning world. I followed the shrubs all the way to where the path began and made my way to Dov's room. Got to survive.

I ate three dinners that evening, and for the next two days I kept drinking from every tap I came across, just in case. But at the moment when I touched the door to Dov's room, on the border between an Israeli kibbutz and Cell Block 55 in Buchenwald, I touched a speck of Shoah. Only a hint, just for a moment, but I will never again be as close. The Buchenwaldian moment was over as soon as I washed my face, but a glowing spot remained inside of me. And there remained Effi's look when I turned up at the door, my face and shirt stained with vomit and blood, my eyes vacant, unresponsive, as I walked to the sink with a strange quaver. A speck also remained deep inside her. I had been to Buchenwald, she had not. A solid stain of failure that no future victories could melt away. An Archimedean point that marked new directions in our relationship.

To console herself, she stood on the peaks of Monte Cassino with Grandpa Lolek the hero. When we went back to school, she brought him in to tell his story to her class. Despite his broken Hebrew and the hollow ring of his tales, when he faced an audience of thirteen-year-olds, Grandpa Lolek might as well have been a recruiter for the Israel Defense Forces: six armor officers, five paratroopers, two pilots and one Mossad agent were ready to sign up. At

the end of the class, Effi stood beside him on that glorious moun-
taintop with her eyes lowered modestly, basking in admiration. He
wouldn't come to my class. Even one free appearance was beyond his
emotional strength. For Effi, he agreed. She was always his favorite.
He had plans to marry her off for a good price one day. "What a
beauty! My woman! Men will be around her like flies!" The object of
these compliments, barely fourteen years old, was less excited. Men
were always like flies. Sometimes the compliments were dual. He
would gather us both in his arms and gush, "You are *mamelach*, like
my children." He shoved the word *like* to the front, its prominence
thwarting any ideas of offspring-hood we might have.

Later that summer the anarchy continued. Due to a coordination mishap, we were sent to spend two whole days with Grandpa
Lolek. There was no telling what he was promised, and he usually
collected his debts promptly and firmly. In any event, he managed
the first day nobly, took us to the Carmel Center and with a flourish of generosity bought us each two swimsuits. He even took us
out, like grownups, to a café, where he let us order chocolate cake
and hot cocoa while he smoked his cigarettes and sipped a cup of
tea. The cakes and cocoa were our reward for listening to him once
again recount the story of Joyce the American dancer, the one who
came with a troupe from Kentucky to entertain the soldiers, but
one of the generals took a liking to her and she was ordered to stay
behind when the troupe left and entertain him alone. Once he was
sufficiently entertained, he wanted to send her to entertain another
general, but our Queen Esther responded with a stinging slap on
his cheek. Lonely and tearful, she walked the streets until she met
her savior, Grandpa Lolek, a soldier in Anders' Army waiting to be
deployed to the front. On the rainy dock, she danced for him with
two umbrellas in her hands, etc., etc., etc.

We tried to ask him about the war.

"Grandpa Lolek, why won't Grandpa Yosef tell us about what
happened to him in Buchenwald?"

"Grandpa Lolek, what do you know about Adella Greuner?"

"Grandpa Lolek, what happened to my mom in the village
when she hid with Christians?"

But we gave up in despair. Grandpa Lolek knew only one war, his, and it sounded very similar to the wars we had here. The Six Day War, for example. His description of the battle at Monte Cassino, May '44, week after week after week, melted away the delight of chocolate cake and cocoa. Grandpa Lolek tried to impress us with descriptions of the final hilltop battle. "Seven days, we skip on foot, from rock to rock."

"It was probably cheapest to travel by foot," Effi whispered, her face a study of chocolate.

But I noticed the unusual words Grandpa Lolek used—'skip', 'from rock to rock'—and it occurred to me that he might have read about Monte Cassino in books, impressed at his own feats.

Grandpa Lolek grew animated as he continued to broaden our education. "Monte Cassino, what do you know? Germans were positioned there, not to move. You move, you lose all of Italy, all the war. Fighting there, the Germans. Everybody against them, no good. No passing. They bomb from the sky, day and night. From the land we try to get up. Germans slaughter everyone. Through the rocks, not possible. Uphill. Difficult. Anywhere a soldier walks, a German is hiding, and bang-bang. They tried everything, the generals. No more soldiers of theirs left, and the Australians tried and the New Zealanders tried. Fighting, fighting, and no doing. All day, all night, they bring bodies down. No getting by the Germans. Strong, those Germans. Animals. They decided: Send the Poles in. Anders' soldiers. Why not? Soldiers for free. In May, we start to conquer. Fifteen of May, the beginning of the end. Last battle, they said. Well, ask your father. That was the day when his mother, Rachela, went in Auschwitz. Exactly that same day. Fifteen of May. Ask him, ask him. And me on the hilltop, Monte Cassino, fighting the Nazis. There were casualties, you should know. For two weeks now, we, the Poles, on the mountain. The Germans were men, lions. Us Poles, we had more hate. Up we went, and took the Germans, one at a time, with bayonets. Until no more. We slaughtered the last German. Anders' Army on the mountain. Me, the Jew, on the mountain. Your father's mother, Rachela, a righteous woman, Auschwitz. Your father and his father in train car, to a new concentration camp, they have luck, not

Auschwitz. Strong. Your father is good boy, his father sick already. But me, a Jew, on Monte Cassino, up top, and no one has bad word for me. Germans, only with bullet in the head, and if all Jews were like that, no Hitler. There would not have been…"

He calmly ordered another cup of tea, leaving us wide-eyed, with many new questions racing through our minds. For me, my mother's birthday, May 15th, now connected with the new date, the day of Grandma Rachel's death in Auschwitz. I would have to ask Dad about it. But I soon forgot. The loyal mechanism worked every time: whatever we weren't allowed to ask, we forgot to ask. Dad would continue to hide the date, celebrate Mom's birthday with her and quietly think about his mother. Mom mustn't know, not to ruin her celebration. Only after Mom died, did he tell us how all those years…

The cup of tea came. Grandpa Lolek stirred in three teaspoons of sugar (courtesy of the café) and jolted the teabag around in the boiling water to get everything out. After fishing out the bag, forgoing his usual *Selektion* process, he put it with its predecessors in the saucer and sighed. "Such a pity you cannot smoke what's left of tea." He stared at us with his crystal blue eyes and sighed again, from the depths of his chest.

Fake.

If not for our keen senses, he might have been able to trick us. But something about the sentence rang false, something in the sigh he had amateurishly copied from Grandpa Yosef. Since when did Grandpa Lolek sigh? As we left, we were not surprised to see him stealthily collecting the used tea bags in a little plastic bag, intending to produce another eight cups out of every bag, and then on to his great mattress plan.

We had fun at his house. We learned new shades of miserliness, ones that were not evident to us during regular encounters. In his kitchen window boxes we found herbs he had planted following the guidance of a television program, with plenty of sun and a little water. In his lamps he used only monastic low-wattage bulbs, which produced a brownish-golden light. In the kitchen, he required every match to last for three uses. When he tried to make us soft-boiled eggs, the first match completely failed and Grandpa Lolek looked at us accusingly. Before bed-time we took showers. We wanted baths with water up to our chins, but Grandpa Lolek recommended showers. "After beach, it washes better the sand." We reminded him that we hadn't been to the beach, but our protests were drowned out in a stream of water. He kept us apart ("No romances should be here") and sent Effi in first. To pass the time until it was my turn, and since I was going to wash soon anyway, I helped him polish shoes, wash the dishes in the sink, throw out the trash.

After my shower, Effi and I shared our astonishment at the soap. We discovered that not only did he dilute the liquid soap by the sink down to nothing, but that the bar of soap for use in the shower had also been subjected to his artistry. In a painstaking process, he had hoarded and united the tail-ends of countless bars of soap, and with the skillfulness of a goldsmith had fused them into one multicolored lump, a bumpy hedgehog ready for use. This hedgehog, when it reached the end of its days, was also reduced to a soap tail-end and used, in turn, in a further welding. Through this process of reduction and fusing, Grandpa Lolek created a new entity, a bar of soap in which every particle had its own age and its own parent-soap. This alchemical creature, "a wise man's soap" that resulted from the filtering down of hundreds of initial bars, astounded us with its multitude of colors. At home, our soap had only one color, usually a faded shade of brown.

And we discovered more rules. When he had a headache, he left his house to have a cup of tea with a neighbor. Then he would suddenly murmur, "Happen to have a pill for my headache?" That way, he also gained a glass of water to swallow the pill with. He was distressed by the red light on the hot water heater, which lit up every time it was turned on. Grandpa Lolek wanted hot water, not light. They explained to him that the light was in fact intended to conserve power, to remind him to turn the boiler off. Grandpa Lolek could not comprehend this. How could anyone leave the boiler on? Who would do that? He blamed the boiler for the waste, as if the hot water was designed to pamper the heating elements.

We came to believe that Grandpa Lolek existed on a level of miserliness that few could achieve. We could not have known that he was still only half-way up the peaks he was yet to scale. But even then, we sensed how to wind him up. "Starting next month, it will cost money to call an ambulance," we told him. Or, "They said on the news there's going to be a tax on bus fare." (He rode the bus to preserve the Vauxhall.)

By the second day of our visit, Grandpa Lolek was shirking his duties. He handed a thimble-full of cleaning fluid to the maid who came in the morning, instructed her to wash everything twice, then hid the container. He took us for a measly trip to the Carmel Center, where he walked around with us impatiently. Too many hours had already been robbed from his life. When lunchtime arrived, he did not hesitate to set off to his regular restaurant. He left us at home without much remorse. The maid had left us a pot of mashed potatoes to heat up with beans, two rolls wrapped in plastic, and compote for dessert. In disgust, we ate nothing but the rolls, saving time for the main event: a thorough rummage through Grandpa Lolek's house of wonders. We cautiously opened closets, bureaus, draws, cabinets. We found account ledgers and binders and lots of pictures of smiling people, including some of ourselves at Nathan's bar mitzvah. We found a crystal swan with a broken neck—more precisely, we found only the hook of its neck and head, with no body. We found two envelopes stuffed with stamps, all in the same color, red. When I stood on a chair and Effi risked her life by climbing up on my shoulders, we discovered a treasure. From that height, Effi saw something in the rug on the floor. The rug was nicely spread beneath the table, with its edges under the armchairs and couch, but from up above she saw an indentation down the length of the rug. A bunker! We quickly uprooted the table, the couch, the armchairs and the rug, revealing a trapdoor that led to a cellar. And there it was. Our dreams had come true.

Grandpa Lolek's house stood on a small hill, a position which created interesting geometrical possibilities. It had been built by a founding member of the underground Haganah movement in the thirties, and he had exploited every single possibility. When the Haganah man was killed, the house was left to its tenant, Grandpa Lolek, who managed to defend it against claims by the legal heirs.

After a generation of fighting, the heirs were exhausted, but to this day, every few years, a feeble legal bleating comes from the direction of Ness Ziona.

Now we stood over the opening of a hidden cellar, a weary cloud of dust rising up from below. We looked inside. All we could see was a dark staircase winding its way down. We were drawn to this Pharaonic tomb, and despite our familiarity with the curse (*Death shall come on swift wings to him who disturbs the peace of the king*), we had to go down. Guided by some force of maturity, we descended, older than our years, and crossed an invisible line between childhood and what comes after.

We advanced slowly. Effi went first. We stood blinded on the cellar floor, inhaling a stench of dead lizards and bricks touched only by dampness. Dust, dust, wormy and horrible. The moment was too sacred for words. We tried to accustom our eyes to the darkness. No light deigned to enter. Above us, through the cellar opening that faced the living room, daylight loomed, but in the heart of dustiness darkness reigned. We could vaguely see that the cellar continued far on into the darkness. We walked slowly, hoping for the best, until we touched a damp wall. There were two windows of a sort there, which gave way to the yard above, but no light shone in through them. Mosquito screens had been hung long ago and they were thick with spider webs, allowing only a slim line of light to barely penetrate and drag its shadow behind with a limp. Effi decreed that someone had to go up for matches.

It was me, of course. Out I went, passing through the rooms like a short apparition, pausing in astonishment opposite the hall-way mirror to scan the mass of cobwebs on my body. I found two flashlights in the kitchen cabinet (the battery was kept separately, of course, in the refrigerator) and I also took candles, matches and a lighter. I looked around at the house. The furniture and rugs were coated with dust. Punishment hovered over our heads. I went back to the cellar, concealing the dusty horrors from Effi. We turned the flashlights on and dark objects sparkled and crackled in surprise from every corner. Light! Light!

Together we scanned a cellar crowded with items, furniture

parts, pictures, and an inexplicable blonde wig that took our breath away. We went a little further inside. The dust glimmered in the beams of our flashlights, exposing cobwebs of withered geometry. Effi led us further inside. At the edge of the cellar was a hidden open-ing, concealed behind two kerosene heaters that stood like eternal guards—reeking sphinxes.

"This is probably going to lead to some secret army headquar-ters," Effi decided, in a voice grown weary of secret tunnels. But when we opened the cover we found only a recess, and inside, oddly, two more kerosene heaters. The heaters were guarding heaters. The dust kept billowing out. We cast our flashlight's glow on a small metal box and opened it, revealing envelopes and pages written in crowded Polish characters. We trembled. These were not our first stolen docu-ments. In the houses in Grandpa Yosef's neighborhood we got our paws on any available box. But this time we knew—these were secrets. This was a clue to something.

We made our way out and collapsed on the dusty rug, our faces colored with war-paint of soot and dust. We looked at the distant ceiling and did not talk. We saw the room around us envel-oped in a frock of dust, but that was not what we were thinking of. In our hands shone the box that contained letters, possibilities. We each pondered separately but our breaths were intertwined, our souls melded. There would be no more Effi-without-a-little-Amir, no more Amir-without-a-little-Effi.

Later, we spent three hours cleaning the house meticulously to eradicate all traces of dust. We unrolled the rug, and restored the overturned furniture. And we stole the box.

The letters were in Polish, in Grandpa Lolek's handwriting, except for one page. The page at the bottom of the box was written in a different ink in an unidentified, square handwriting, and it had no illustrations of blood-red hearts. We needed someone to translate them for us. We had an entire family of Polish speakers at our disposal but we could not give them the papers just like that and say, Please, translate these letters we stole from Grandpa Lolek's secret cellar. We hatched a plan to translate the sentences word by word, separately, each word from a different source. We copied the words onto separate pieces of paper (we knew the English alphabet, so the Polish characters did not pose much of a problem). Next to each word we wrote down the name of the person we intended to ask. We were careful not to give any one person a sequence of words or too many words from one letter. We set off on every mission with one word and, in a roundabout way, deciphered its meaning. Each deciphered word was written on a new page. Using this mosaic approach, we slaved with a dedication usually associated with pyramid builders, and slowly created the Hebrew translation of the letters.

There were a few hitches. For example, the stubbornly puzzling sentence, "Life is a roll." Cross-referencing, enquiries, parsing and assembling, led to the decipherment: "Life is a *partnership*." Instead of *spółka*, partnership, we had copied down *bułka*, roll.

Some people were dismissed after being found unsuitable—suspicious, questioning. But we did discover a few great talents. Uncle Pessl, for example, whom everyone in the family had always considered—to put it mildly—an idiot, asked no questions, made no enquiries, and was utterly unsuspecting as he sat gobbling down a dish of chicken and providing us with translations of entire sentences.

And then there was Uncle Menashe from Netanya. We came to him and asked about the word *brzoza*. But Uncle Menashe looked us in the eye and said calmly, "You've found a letter in Polish and you're trying to figure it out. Why work so hard? Bring me the letter, I'll translate it."

We held a brief and silent consultation with our eyes. And two days later, with the box on our knees, instead of going to school we were on our way to his butcher shop in Netanya. We sat in Menashe's shop for a few hours, surrounded by freezers full of meat and slaughtered chickens hanging on the walls like *sukkah* decorations. He read out loud and translated, no wise-cracks.

What we had found were Grandpa Lolek's letters to his dancer, Joyce. (He must have written them in Polish and had someone translate them into English for him, keeping the Polish copies himself). The content of the letters was not rewarding—silly love lines, promises, pleas, plans for a life together. For a while we were partners to this mythological episode in Grandpa Lolek's life. With him, we were left for the Viennese pianist. We sent her pleas. We hoped. We knew in the bottom of our hearts that now, after the war was over, the future belonged to the pianists of the world. But still we tried, even writing poetically, "…you know, battles on the plains are still sadder," but we did not win back her heart. We lost Joyce. We also lost interest in the letters. We asked Uncle Menashe to skim them, thinking perhaps he might come up with something of interest after all. Then we showed him the last page, written in a different ink, the one without hearts. This page piqued Uncle Menashe's interest.

"This, you must not talk about!" he ordered. "And put the box back straight away, so no one will know you took it."

"What is it?" we demanded.

It was a letter from Moishe Finkelstein, a Jew from Bielsko-Biala, dated September 1st, 1939. That was the day the war broke out—the occupation of Poland, the Big Bang. We had found a dark moon orbiting the glowing planet of Grandpa Lolek.

Uncle Menashe made light of the matter: all that had happened was that Grandpa Lolek had received a lot of gold from Finkelstein, which he was supposed to deliver after the war to Finkelstein's son in America. Half was to go to the son, half to stay with Grandpa Lolek. "And if I know Lolek," he added, "gold, he didn't see, Finkelstein's son. Oh well, not to worry. It's only money. Believe me, Jews over there did worse things than that."

"Worse?"

"*Nu*, it's not for children."

We were not Old Enough. But we were reminded of Crazy Hirsch's yell. Until that day we had not devoted sufficient attention to his recurrent question, "Only saints were gassed?"

We were not Old Enough.

Before childhood could end, we had to fit it all in:
 Find out what happened to Finkelstein's gold.
 Understand the important things.
 Discover all sorts of things.
 Invent something important.

Find a profession for Effi, something that would combine her desire to always be tanned with her hatred of hard cheese.

Descend, finally, into Gershon Klima's sewer.

Stand facing Hirsch. Without fear.

And for that we had to remain kids. We had to investigate. The tea bags, the mattress, the hidden gold, it all joined into one enigmatic picture of a land begging to be explored. Finkelstein's moon hovered above us, dimming, shining, dimming, shining, trembling in its orbit. In order to understand the Kepler Laws of this astronomy, we would have to go back into the cellar.

Having no alternative, we landed—two small space-ships with reasonable grades—on Grandpa Lolek's planet. A search party. Into the cellar. We forced ourselves. Sensing the uncompromising smell of hidden gold within the odor of a-punishment-we-could-not-even-imagine, we positioned ourselves on Planet Lolek. We replaced our deadly fear with a dry sense of purpose. We sorted items, catalogued. Over and over we went down to the cellar, creating opportunities out of thin air, plots hatched behind Grandpa Lolek's back. One slip and we'd all be exposed. Once in a while, we delved deeper. The forest of dust revealed itself to us, vaults, treasures and all. We found camera parts arranged in towers, the smaller ones on top. Hundreds of neatly rolled mosquito nets. Metal objects that gave light in return for light. Aluminum strips robbed from windows, blinds, closet hinges. A washing machine engine leaning on its side like a sunken ship in the sandy floor. A fan with all its blades broken, like the prop for a bad joke. We found an accordioned roll of barbed wire that we tried, unsuccessfully, to unroll, and had to grow accustomed to it jumping up suddenly every so often, like Archimedes submerged in his bathtub, shouting, "Eureka! Eureka!" but without revealing a thing. Rapidly adapting, we learned to use the barbed wire to rake the cobwebs, forming dusty clumps. We exposed more and more. Empty bottles that always glistened, like a chorus hungry for the light of a flashlight. Empty packing crates. Matted bundles of rubber bands, sticky and crushed. And finally, a mouse on its back with its feet sticking straight up. Its eyes turned golden in the flashlight beam.

The mouse opened the door to desperation. Finkelstein's moon was disappointed in us; we had not found wonders or secrets. Not even a note. Only worthless material treasures coated in dust. We hoped for a miracle, hoped to stumble upon a box containing Grandpa Lolek's confessions, explaining what he had done with the gold, or an incensed communication from Finkelstein's son demanding to know where the gold was. We looked for envelopes with American stamps, papers written in foreign languages, Polish letters.

In between one descent and the next, we continued to orbit within the gravity of Planet Lolek. We tried to approach the core issue—the gold—with words. Out of the blue, we would ask him about the price of gold. Where did they sell gold? How did you get gold? We talked to him about El Dorado, the mythical land of gold. We talked about golden retrievers and asked him to buy us a golden hamster. We showed him the picture in the *Tarbut* encyclopedia of the Indian chief whose wife and son fled his cruelty and drowned themselves in a river, and every year he threw gifts of gold into the river to plead for their return. To our surprise, Grandpa Lolek showed no interest in where the river was, how one got there, or how much gold exactly this Indian had thrown in there. He only wanted to know if the gifts had helped, if the wife and son came back.

Again and again we went down to the cellar. And once, as expected, it happened. Just as we were starting to roll up the rug, Grandpa Lolek, who-was-only-supposed-to-be-back-in-an-hour, caught us. In his hand was a glistening new camera and on his face a furious suspicion. "What goes on here?"

I was the first to respond, before Effi. "Grandpa Lolek, my pen got lost under the rug."

That was practical-Amir, a distant relative of regular-Amir. He was hardly ever seen. Sometimes, at weddings, he would choose the furthest slice of cake from the one Aunt Ecka had touched.

Effi did not cooperate. She should have said, "Yes, the pen," but instead she stood facing Grandpa Lolek with her hands on her hips and demanded, "We want to know, what did you do with Finkelstein's gold?"

Eyes met eyes. One look said: more locks, more bolts, fewer guests. Two looks said: have mercy, Sir, take pity on these small children.

Flashes, looks, thoughts, prayers. A breeze passed through us as we stood sturdy as cypress trees.

Finally, "Finkelstein got the gold." Simply put.

Meaning, no punishment (for now). Meaning, Grandpa Lolek was unaware of his entitlement to punish children when there was no other way out. When asked a question, he answered it.

"Got more than was he deserved," he added.

"He deserved half," Effi said, representing the parties in absentia.

"Half?!" Grandpa Lolek came closer, furious.

Effi continued cautiously, "According to the letter…"

Grandpa Lolek sat down slowly on the couch. A mistake. We immediately flanked him on either side.

"Tell us about Finkelstein. How much gold was there? How did you give him half? Was it hard? What happened to Finkelstein?"

Grandpa Lolek put his new camera in his lap and drummed on it with two fingers. Perhaps he was waiting for us to ask about it and forget about unnecessary questions. But he had no choice and so he spoke. He told us the entire story, omitting no detail, as if what we had found in the letter was needless, as if he had always been willing to tell us everything, but hadn't thought anyone cared to know. He talked at length and also stole in a little bit of Joyce, her umbrellas, the dock, the rain, the damp rose in her hair.

"What do you understood about half? After war, no getting money out of Poland. No doing. Not allowed. And where I buried the gold, to send to America, to the son over there, a lot of money I gave people, so gold will arrive to America good. My head was having shiny with sweat, not with money, until there came for me a telegram that okay, that says to me thank you from Finkelstein the son, that his wife she says thank you also. Half mine, what was left, not so big this half, after the people took for them."

"And what did you do with your half?"

We hoped to hear that he had kept the gold without touching it. We hoped he would open a secret door and reveal a room full of cobwebs with a stack of pale bars of gold on the floor.

"What I used, when was needed," Grandpa Lolek said disappointingly.

But we were relieved. "So you weren't a bad Jew?"

"Bad Jew?"

"Who did bad things in the war...?"

"Who do you think you are, Haim Nachman Bialik?! There is no bad Jew, good Jew. There is alive and there is dead. That's it."

Grandpa Lolek's philosophy. A dogma handed down from on high. Dead Germans, bodies of Anders' soldiers. All our lives, Grandpa Lolek showered us with sayings coined on that mountain:

"What you take, you have not give back."

"Hold in your teeth, and not yet is yours."

"If hit, hit back. No hit, very good. That means, you hit."

We disagreed. "No bad Jew, good Jew" was too simple. We had stored up enough thoughts of Adella Greuner, Mr. Bergman, Itcha Dinitz. For too long we had become acquainted with Finkelstein, with Crazy Hirsch's words. Something strong, an evil Jew, had to exist—the opposite of Grandpa Yosef. The war could not have sufficed with bad Germans. We rejected Grandpa Lolek's philosophy but felt that he himself was becoming purer, not a bad Jew or a good Jew, but rather, our grandfather. We breathed a sigh of relief that flung open floodgates, an eternal, lucid horizon, over which anything could gallop, anything could fly. Spotless light flowed easily. Two little spaceships with reasonable grades could finally let go and Finkelstein's moon lifted off like a balloon and disappeared. We felt like going out with Grandpa Lolek so he could buy us popsicles, or so we could buy them, whichever—as long as we could sit and lick them and no one would be to blame.

Only a single letter in Polish stayed on its course through space. What had the textile merchant Finkelstein written to his son in America? For many years in the dark, Polish characters concocted a frightening truth. The letter opened with the hackneyed lines, "When you read these words, son, your mother and I will not be among the living..." Then more words, Finkelstein the textile merchant's explanations of what was about to happen in the world, why he did what he did, and what the son should do.

Today, now that I am Old Enough, I know. Finkelstein realized, days before the war broke out, what the Holocaust would be. His thoughts were lucid, with none of the enveloping mist of illusion. Crystal clear. Even before the Nazis imagined how far they would go, before Adolf Eichmann hatched his ingenious plans, before Hitler conceived the only solution to the world's troubles, the textile merchant from Bielsko-Biala knew—*knew*, not guessed—the future in great detail. He sold his business. He instructed his only son to stay in America despite the hardships. He had all his gold fillings removed and forced his wife to do the same. Even before Auschwitz was built, before the incinerators, before the Sonderkommando and the "Kanada" commando that collected belongings from the dead, he had deprived himself of the immediate reasons to send him to his death. He melted down the gold from their teeth, from his wife's jewelry, from the sale of his shop. Then he waited for an opportunity, for a man to whom he could give the money, someone he could trust who wouldn't ask questions and would survive the imminent war. On the street in town he met a hardened corporal from the Polish army, a Jew by the name of Feuer, son of the headmaster of the Hebrew Gymnasium in Kielce. Finkelstein the merchant looked the Jewish corporal up and down and knew he had found his man. They settled on the terms. Shook hands. Corporal Lolek Feuer went back to his unit. The next morning, the war broke out, inflicting six years of suffering upon the world. Finkelstein the textile merchant and his wife perished. At a certain point during those years they joined the six million Jews, perhaps in a ghetto, perhaps in a concentration camp, perhaps in a death camp. They may not have been killed as Jews but simply, without ideology, like the ten million other citizens who died in the war. One moment they were human beings, parents of a son in America, and the next—dead.

One Jew, before the war, knew everything. And even in 1942, with the extermination at its height, Jews would disbelieve living witnesses and refuse to accept the impossible. A man by the name of

Rosenthal would manage to send a postcard to the Bochnia ghetto from Belzec, reporting explicitly what befell those who went to Belzec and exposing the true purpose of the transports to "resettle the Jews in the East." People would doubt him. Suspicions would flicker, fear too. But they would refuse to believe. A letter from the Rabbi of Grabow would be smuggled into the Lodz ghetto, explaining precisely what the Chelmno camp on the Ner River was. People would not believe. At the height of the war, the *Aktionen*, babies' heads smashed against walls, still they would not believe that there could be such a thing as death camps, such a thing as gas chambers, such a thing as industrial use of hair, skin and fat. War, people perpetrating horrors on other people, yes. But gas chambers? Incinerators? Not possible.

Zagazowani.

That was what Rosenthal would write from Belzec to the residents of the Bochnia ghetto. The first word that would explain that people were being put to death with gas. (Dad tried to explain the Polish grammar to me, the way the noun *gas* is inflected as a verb that kills people. *Zagazowani.*) A word that would be a gateway to the coming years. Secretly, the congregation leaders in the ghetto would pass the postcard from hand to hand. My father, a curious child, playing down among the chair legs, would listen. Above him there would be doubts, suspicions—why would the Germans let someone send a postcard out?

Only one Jew, in 1939, the textile merchant Finkelstein, knew everything, and he wrote a letter to his son. Not a historical or scholarly record, but a practical abstract of thoughts. The textile merchant had no spare time to sit and write at length. What good would writing do? Leave the writing for the intellectuals. All he needed was to explain to his son what would happen, what to watch out for, how much gold to demand from the soldier and where to invest it.

Once I became Old Enough and was allowed to know more, I asked Dad about 1939. That year, just before it all began, when only Finkelstein knew, is more frightening than anything Dad could tell me about "afterwards." Because 1939 is similar to the years I live in. In 1939, level-headed Jews had moderate opinions. They had worries that could be dismissed by reason. Sensible people made assumptions, felt apprehensive, found solutions. The Jewish newspapers were full of keen, thorough editorials. Everything was so reasonable, so progressive, so modern. In the cemeteries, deceased Jews were led to their eternal rest. Kaddish prayers were whispered. A little before September 1939 they still recited, *Let He who makes peace in the heavens grant peace to all of us and to all Israel*, and the congregants responded, *Amen*. The year 1939 is the year I could be living in. Every year could be 1939. Everything around me is so democratic, so reasonable. A world of public statements, petitions, strong protests. Everything could be reversed in the blink of an eye. Sometimes I know that if a totalitarian regime were to be established here, decimating minorities, only time and a few moral convulsions would delay a Jewish incarnation of the Reich. Here too, it could rise. There would be opponents, yes, even in the mainstream. But they too would disappear. Not straight away, but all of them. I recognize around me the types who would construct the new regime. They are all here already: the king of the black market, the collaborator, the informer with eyes torn wide in terror. The chief of police, the loyal soldiers, the implementers of orders. They are here, they are living and multiplying. They are decent citizens concealed by comfortable circumstances. Never (one assumes) will their dark natures be exposed. Throughout their lives, perhaps only a moment or two will touch the core of their souls. Commonplace life produces moderate versions of these people, the outcome of routine and of the flourishing State of Israel. The king of the black market will be no more than a crooked insurance agent. The collaborators will be tailors, policemen, physicians. The chief of police will be an unlikable man, perhaps the manager of a supermarket, that's all. If the day comes and reality is overturned, Grandpa Yosef will be an intellectual opposing the regime. His skull will be cracked in the public square, crowds will cheer. Or in secret, three thugs will knock on his door in the middle of the night. The car will drive away. Neighbors will murmur sorrowfully. Someone will make a derisive comment about him and a few will nod in agreement. The regime will provide them with material and they will recite it. They will forget.

Yes, it is here, but it will not come to fruition. There is too much good sun, blue skies. But what is important is that it is here, that it threatens my Yariv, that it will want to take my father away again to Plaszow camp, but I won't let it. That I do not know how I will not let it. I pick Yariv up from kindergarten. We walk down the street and pass by the collaborators, the volunteers, the informants, the black market merchants. People with simple faces. At any moment it is possible. The wind will change, the makeup will scatter, and Yariv and I will stand facing them. It would take even less than a change in the way the wind blows. They could be exposed just like that, simply because they want to be. And my skull too will be smashed on some night-time street in some immaterialized reality in some world which I am mocked for even positing the existence of. Anat too. Why, for God's sake, don't they see it?

I raise my Yariv to be strong, to know how to suffer, to survive. Anat takes the seeds out of tomatoes before he eats them. I get annoyed. She does, too. "Yariv belongs to both of us. You can raise your half in Buchenwald, but I'm sending mine to Mira's Daycare!"

Anything he has not been fully prepared for deters him, afraid, confused. I want him to peel his hard-boiled egg. He refuses. The shell is hot, it scares him. Anat takes it and peels it for him. My father was in the camps. He knows what can happen. But Yariv's babyish fears don't bother him. He plays with him, sees how afraid he is of the ball, how he starts crying. He runs to reassure him.

I cannot understand them. *Zagazowani.*

How good it was then, two little spaceships resting beside Grandpa Lolek, our voyage over, and Grandpa Lolek between us with a camera in his lap. I did not know everything I know today: that you don't need a Holocaust to have bad Jews. That people like Grandpa Lolek, even if they do steal gold, are not the bad ones. We only knew that that was it, we could breathe easy, Grandpa Lolek was not a bad Jew. The camera on his lap started to glimmer, capturing half and more of our attention, pushing aside letters and dust and bad Jews. We started to take an interest. The price-tag was intriguing; it was a very expensive camera. We looked at Grandpa Lolek full of hope.

He who was absolved of all guilt erased his anger. "Here, Nikon make this, is very expensive, I brought for Effi as present."

We passed the enchanted object between us, a gift for Effi, not for me. His preference for Effi was immortalized.

Grandpa Lolek hadn't meant it. He did prefer Effi, but hadn't intended to insult one of his "like grandchildren" on the couch in his home, after a dark moon had melted away. There was no reason for tears, even though they almost burst from my eyes. (It was at that moment that I made up my mind: I would go to the Municipality on my own and find out who Katznelson Street was named after.) In any case, the bestowal of the Nikon upon Effi was unplanned, and it was not the product of generosity. An hour earlier the camera had still sat in a display window at Carmel Center, scanning with a shuttered eye the passersby who did not buy it because it was too expensive, who only lingered briefly, eye to eye, to exercise their longing, to covet, to finally glance askance at a cheaper model displayed two shelves below. The look in their eyes changed—this was something they could afford—and they gazed at the plain model with the loathing of compromise, as if to say, "We're doing you a favor." Eyes yearned, calculated, went into the store to buy the simpler models. Two gentleman stood opposite the camera, ignoring the display window, busy doing business. The one wondered quietly whether the other was capable of meeting his financial obligations—he'd been warned against doing business with him. The other, dressed in finery, a hero of Monte Cassino with blue metallic eyes, sensed the man's doubts and feared the transaction would fall through. He had to make a quick impression. His look fell on the camera in the display window. He scanned the price. Panic. Contemplation. Vacillation. Decision. The hero of Monte Cassino walked into the store and came out with the Nikon in hand, explaining to his interlocutor, "This I bought for Effi, so it will make her happy. She is like my granddaughter, Effi." This time the *like* was intended to clarify that he gave his *like* relatives expensive gifts without a moment's hesitation. Imagine, then, what gifts he must give his real relatives. Imagine how financially secure he must be.

"Thanks, but what am I supposed to do with a camera?" Effi asked. And a minute later, "Oh well, stand up and pose, we'll give it a try." And we stood up.

At first she photographed everything she came across, then landscapes on Saturday hikes, and finally family affairs. This blatant invasion of Grandpa Lolek's domain came after he had been defeated by Brandy in the fight to reach the Moshe Pole, and after the family members had begun, one by one, to buy small, modest cars, doing away with hegemony of the Vauxhall once and for all. The battle was fought through two weddings and one *briss*. Finally, a moderate victory was achieved because:

Effi took nice pictures.

She didn't ask for payment.

Grandpa Lolek was in her pictures.

The latter was an advantage praised even by the loser. In almost all of Effi's pictures stood a tall, serious man, a hero of Monte Cassino, and his look at the lens took into account generations to come, who would ask, who is that? The masculine one, standing in his finest suit?

Effi did not like spontaneous photographs. She preferred the formal kind, arranging people like bowling pins. One click and they were dismissed. Then, "No, actually, stand that way again, it may not have come out well." Smiles were arranged in rows, lips frozen. At weddings, parties, everywhere. Rows, lines. Little trapeze shapes with the adults in the back row, gathering with-gentle-hands-on-shoulders the children in the front row. It was the beginning of the photography era. Effi with a camera around her neck, always arranging people. As soon as people saw her, they would arrange themselves in rows. Women would reach up to their hair, men—down to their flies. They smiled when they saw her; you never knew. Always flashes, always instructions. In winter she blended with the lightening. In summer—the heat, the flies. "Stand, I'll take a picture." "Smile now." They built her a fully equipped dark-room with chemicals that only two or three years earlier we would have tried to drink. Now she was careful, gave warnings, behaved responsibly, sealed the bottles, made labels with thick markers, separated containers.

Grandpa Lolek's passing on of the photography obsession and the natural effects of age began to come between us. Effi signed up for a photography course, and I for an amateur radio course (which was a little too amateur for my taste). She graduated to a photography course for gifted children. I responded by winning an essay competition on Jerusalem. The distancing continued, became more sophisticated, swept along deposits of grudges and hostility. Substances long ago fixed into the river banks were swept along, renewing forgotten arguments. At the apex of the route—the apogee—Effi's photographs were accepted by *Maariv Lanoar* magazine. My turn. I was appointed head of a ship in my seafaring course (salt water when falling overboard at the port, filthy water when falling in at the mouth of the Kishon River). That wasn't enough. In a desperate step I defected from *Tarbut* encyclopedia and switched to the *Hebrew Encyclopedia*. I began at "*a cappella*" and started reading.

Then we started to divide our assets. Effi demanded the four-part poster of Yehoram Gaon, which we had both labored to compile. I demanded that she apologize for her comments about Mike Brandt.

No.

Me neither then.

The poster stayed with me, a hostage for an apology never given.

It had started two years previously, when news came that Mike Brandt had committed suicide in Paris. I was overcome with grief. He was from Haifa, one of ours, and had become a famous singer in France and in the world. Then suddenly they said he had jumped out of a window, and despite all his success in Paris it was decided that he would be buried here in Haifa, in the same cemetery where Aunt Zusa owned a plot. Effi said, "So what?" and showed no understanding. I was used to national grief, when everyone was sad for a lot of people, but this time I felt a new sadness, only for Mike Brandt, the way I felt when I read in the encyclopedia about Katznelson the poet, the Katznelson for whom we had named the neighborhood street. It said that he had managed to escape the Warsaw ghetto and get to Paris, and there he sat, a brand snatched from the burning fire, lamenting his perished wife and children. He wrote poems, expressed hope—if only he had died with them. And it was this prayer that was heard, of all the prayers uttered in all those years all over the world. A train came especially to take him from Paris to Auschwitz, to the gas chambers. A whole train for one weeping Jew, while war was raging and trains were an expensive commodity.

I thought about Katznelson when they brought Mike Brandt back here. It was a sorrow that Effi could not comprehend. We fought, with hatred. We found more and more things to divvy up. We halved joint collections and erased each other from important lists. We left no detail in our lives that did not bear the stamp, "Inspected. Proper procedures followed." We even divided the grandparents, all of whom had been tirelessly collected under the Law of Compression. Borders were demarcated. Partitions that had previously symbolized mere preferences were lined with barbed wire fences: No Entry. Grandpa Lolek and Grandpa Weil went to Effi. Grandpa Menashe to me. Grandma Eva was divvied up as an afterthought. Grandpa Yosef was undecided. It seemed that if there had to be a decision, Grandpa Yosef would prefer me, because of the scholarliness. But we found Grandpa Yosef high above territorial borders, even during this nationalistic frenzy of the separation of grandparents. Grandpa Yosef remained the only thing that would still connect us.

Agreed.

And what about Grandpa Shalom? After all, he was my real grandfather, only mine, my mother's father. The only actual grandfather. Ostensibly there was no question that Grandpa Shalom was mine. At my *briss* on the ninth of Av he had held me in his arms. He had looked at me, his second grandchild, and seen yet another root struck in the new land. He had watched me grow up, not knowing that inside of him someone had already rapped three times on the door, that in the dressing room his disease was already preparing for its performance. One final moment before it came out. A glance in the mirror. A long breath. And the curtain began to rise. Grandpa Shalom got Parkinson's disease and sunk into his trembling body. The Gestapo tortures, the room in which he awoke on the floor after being interrogated, bathed in his own blood, would be portrayed in a symbolic illness—his body was now his prison. Grandpa Shalom the strong man, championed by all, helper of the needy, a poor man in aid of the poor, would become Grandpa Shalom who smelled of medicine, his tortured body emitting vapors of rotten fruit. Barely walking, barely talking, only Grandma Chava could understand what the thin purple lips were saying. And the cold mouth that tried to kiss us, which we dreaded even before leaving home and on the way there. Grandpa Shalom, who loved through all obstacles, but whom we could not love. We simply could not.

Effi could. When we came to visit (preferably during Chanukah; on Passover Seder and Rosh Hashanah we had no choice), only she hugged and kissed him without hesitation. It was not courage or purity of soul—she simply had no problem doing it. Effi with a camera round her neck and complaints about everything. How could we not have seen how obvious it was that she would grow up to be a doctor? A merciful mother to the Sick Fund patients. She did not photograph Grandpa Shalom in rows of people, but always alone, looking straight at the camera.

How would we divide Grandpa Shalom? It seems we did not. We left a grey area, a demilitarized zone in the interest of both parties. After a while there was a truce of sorts. We emptied out our pockets into one joint pile of grandparents for us both. What did we need the silly division for? We reconstructed from memory what we had been before the fights. We gathered the strength needed for what was about to occur in just a few weeks, the affair of Levertov and the Formacil pills.

In Grandpa Yosef's neighborhood, medicine healed the body and uplifted the spirit. Prescriptions were status symbols, property, business cards, legal tender. Your medications were who you were. Everyone in the neighborhood knew their neighbors' prescriptions. A few who had unique prescriptions were modest in their pride, walking along their Mount Everests, shrugging their shoulders—they really didn't know what they'd done to be so fortunate. But it was a dynamic world. Prescriptions were renewed and terminated at doctors' whims, based on pharmaceutical trends. Everyone in the neighborhood knew the rules well and they knew they needed to stay vigilant. You had only to look away for a second and a prescription could be lost. And then no amount of pleading ("it was so good with the old pill," "the new one's no good") would help. Dishonest complaints during medical exams wouldn't help. Does it hurt here? Yes. Here? Yes. And here? Yes. Everything hurts? Yes, but with the pill from before it didn't hurt at all! Narrow-mindedness grew naturally, like weeds on the edge of a puddle. If you were taken off a pill but your neighbor was not, the insult was threefold—where was justice?

Feiga's prescriptions were a relatively constant anchor. Her diseases complicated one another and no physician dared touch this house of cards—one false move could bring it tumbling down. This stability was a thorn in the side of some of the neighbors. People were jealous. Sometimes we heard remarks. We stored them up as if sensing that one day we would make use of them.

It happened with Mr. Levertov.

It happened with the Formacil.

It happened during a ceasefire. And during the days when we had stopped wondering about the Shoah: There was a war, and the Germans wanted to murder all the Jews, and they managed to murder six million, and the ones who survived lost so much that even they did not emerge completely alive. That was it. That explained it. The questions had settled down to a lower level. We were able to connect the Shoah we found at home with the one we learned at school, the black placards, the recitations, the minute of silence. For a moment we believed everything was clear. And it was then, of all times, just when we didn't want to ask anything more and everything had become simple, that Untersturmführer Kurt Franz from Treblinka, known as "Doll," emerged like a sandbank for us to run aground on. Something made us think of him again. Levertov had once tried to tell us something about him but Grandpa Yosef had put an end to it. And now, despite what we'd thought we wanted, we simply had to know everything about him.

The idea percolated for a long time. Two river banks faced each other. On the one was Levertov, yearning for the Formacil they had taken away from him—Why did Feiga still have hers? On the other bank was Treblinka, where Levertov had been with Untersturmführer Kurt Franz, Doll. The two banks glistened, the water turned silver at night, churning and rising in daylight. One ferry ride with the Formacil in our possession, and Levertov would agree to tell us about Untersturmführer Kurt Franz, Doll, the Commandant of Treblinka, despite Grandpa Yosef's prohibition. Levertov was afraid. He had already turned us down twice. But he was the only one in the neighborhood who had been in Treblinka—one of the few who had been with Doll and survived. We had to know.

From the heart of the kaleidoscope, Kurt Franz, Doll, looked out at us. *I am the Shoah of Shoahs*, he seemed to be saying. I am what you will not understand even if you understand everything. I am the only one who, even twenty or thirty years from now, when you're grown up, when you're old, when you understand—you will not understand. I am Kurt Franz, Doll, and I had Levertov in Treblinka. He escaped during the little uprising here, but that's not important. My commander, Stangl, was dismissed and I remained, no longer Deputy Commandant but Commandant. Me, Untersturmführer Kurt Franz, Doll, Commandant of Treblinka. Finally. Levertov did not see me when I was Commandant, he had already escaped. But he can guess, he can tell you. He saw me when I was Deputy Commandant, subject to orders, restrictions, rules. He can guess who I became afterwards, alone, here in Treblinka. Ask Levertov.

We did.

Levertov was afraid. "He was a terrible man. It's not for kids. And anyway, your grandfather asked me not to talk to you about it and he's right. Why don't you tell me what you learned in math today?"

But Feiga had the Formacil on the other river bank. The two sides of Katznelson glimmered: Levertov at 7-A, Grandpa Yosef at 8-B. The Formacil here, Levertov there. What if we brought him some Formacil?

After many days we said it out loud. "And if we bring you Formacil?"

It was a sentence we had practiced saying, recited, encouraged each other. A sentence Levertov had hoped to draw out of us. A sentence both sides were expecting.

Now the waiting. We got down on our knees to offer our gift. Now Levertov had to say yes. Let him say yes. How long could we wait?

It was the height of summer. Scorching heat. Katznelson was

a river, a dreamy Nile. At midday we passed by its banks to check the other side. Was Levertov there? Would he call us? Say yes? No? We walked back and forth. We passed by Mr. and Mrs. Tsanz, Uncle Mendel. From the mud Gershon Klima appeared like a frog. On the fence was Moshe, sitting alone, a captain. By his side an empty space waited for a dog named Brandy to be born, to be adopted, to sit down and keep watch. Menachem, the neighborhood kid, called to us to play with him. He said we could build a tree house in the eucalyptus. He looked at Effi, his thick thighs a pale pink color. Girls were allowed too, he stressed. We got rid of him. On the banks of Katznelson we sat among the reeds of hibiscus, Turk's cap, and orange honeysuckle, waiting for a signal from the other bank.

Finally it came. "Yes. But I will decide what to tell you."

Our hearts trembled: Levertov said yes. The kaleidoscope overturned. But one spot still remained inside, calling us. We had to. We would give him Feiga's Formacil. We would steal it and give it to him. Within the kaleidoscope was one dot of fear named Kurt Franz, Doll. We could hear him calling: I will not leave you, children, I am the Shoah, I am the elucidation, I am the explanation that will not help you comprehend, but without me you have no chance of understanding your family. Your mother, Effi. Your mother, Amir. Grandpa Shalom. And Grandpa Yosef. Do you think he doesn't have a story of his own? You steal the Formacil from Feiga and give it to Levertov. If he tells you what he saw, you'll know who I was. Untersturmführer Kurt Franz, Doll, Commandant of Treblinka. In the library you read that I was a very cruel Nazi and that my nickname was Doll because I was handsome and my face was like a young boy's. Did they mention that I was tall? That I loved to be seen riding horses? But Levertov will tell you, he'll tell everything. Ask Levertov. Steal the Formacil.

Levertov gave us a precise description. We wrote down Hebrew characters, Latin characters, color, size and shape. We memorized F-O-R-M-A-C-I-L from one pill, a refugee from an old packet that Levertov found in his cabinet. We had to remove the Formacil without Grandpa Yosef noticing. He was used to whole packets of pills disappearing occasionally, because Feiga would sometimes secretly throw things out the window, acting on some logic known only to her. She would throw things out and then complain, where is the napkin? Where is the pill? Where is the soup spoon? When we were guests of Grandpa Yosef, we took over his chore of collecting the objects (until Brandy came into our lives and spent her morning walks gently picking up what she found with her teeth and bringing it to Grandpa Yosef). In order to barter with Levertov, we had to make the pills completely disappear, something that would explain why we could not find anything under the poinciana tree. We considered a few methods of deceit and finally adopted Effi's idea. To add to Grandpa Yosef's perplexity, we hid a slingshot among Feiga's things. He would find it and wonder in astonishment, could it be? And would vainly expand his search all the way to the edge of the hibiscus at 6-B Katznelson.

When we finally got hold of the Formacil, we went to see Levertov. He panicked. "No! Not here! All I need is for…" He rolled his eyes as he scanned the paths along Katznelson to see if anyone was giving us unwanted looks. He greedily snatched the Formacil and forbade us to come to his home. He gave us a meeting place, a real one like in the movies, in the neighborhood across the way, next to the drapery store, a bench, a tree, next to a payphone, where we could talk.

Effi snatched the Formacil back from Levertov. "You'll get it there," she announced, staring at him with Grandpa-Lolek-eyes.

And that was how we found him, waiting on the bench with restless eyes. We sat down full of questions and excitement, our souls practically bursting out of our shirts. Levertov demanded the Formacil. Effi handed it over. He gave it a long look to make sure everything was in order. He checked the expiration date and made sure the pack was sealed. He mumbled something nervously and shoved the bag into the pocket furthest from us. Then he breathed heavily. "I'll tell you, but I'm deciding what to tell and how far to go."

We nodded, prepared for anything. Our questions were clambering over one another to get out. But we remained silent, a spot in the kaleidoscope spreading large as an ink-stain.

"I was in Treblinka only two weeks before we escaped. They bought weapons from the Ukrainian guards and we killed the

Ukrainians. Fools! Then like heroes we hid in the woods. Until the war was over, in the woods. But first, before Treblinka, I was a Jew from Radom. Then I got married and moved to Siedlce. I have many stories to tell about how they slaughtered the people in the ghetto, how I escaped alone to the partisans, and how they tried to kill me too, the *goyim*, anti-semites. I hid in a village with good people but in the end they informed on me and they took me to a camp. Then Treblinka. I arrived in a train car. When they opened the doors I was almost dead. I don't want to talk about what went on next to me. It shouldn't be told. Outside was a little station with a clock and a schedule for other stations. Everything neat and orderly, even a small shop. So we'd think the suffering was over, that now was no time for problems. If we had known where we were, we wouldn't have done everything they told us so well. I was strong, not like today how you see me now, an old man without strength. I was well-built, with good muscles, and they chose me for the work group. Every-one who came with me, one-two to the gas, but me, they took me aside to work. God help us, what hard work. Right after the gas with what was left, we had to do what the SS told us. All sorts of things. Whatever they said. And anyone who couldn't, who didn't work well—gone. One-two."

"What about Doll? He killed children, right?"

"I didn't see everything. That man, *Lalka*, whom you call Doll, there were things he liked. There were things that made him angry. Children who slowed things down, yes. And naked women, it angered him if they didn't go in quickly. If in the middle of the gassing the engine broke with people stuck inside, and outside another load was waiting, then he would go wild. Then the whole Lager would be afraid. That he liked, to punish. To beat with fists and with a whip. But he had a huge dog. I remember he was beautiful, his name was Barry, and together with the dog, or sometimes just the dog, they punished prisoners. God help me for telling this, but the dog would finish people off. Eat them. Yes, I mean he ate them. And especially he was trained to bite there, *nu*, you know, in the pants, where the thingamajig is, to tear it. And it was better if the dog finished off the prisoner completely, otherwise he would suffer. And all this we had to see in front of our eyes at the roll-calls, everything there happened during roll-call so that everyone would see, and we thought how we would be next, always we thought about the dog, that it would be us if we made a mistake. One day a Jew went berserk by the gas and attacked an SS man. Commandant Stangl ordered Doll to have a roll-call and kill one out of ten. But he killed one out of ten and then kept killing, slowly but surely. Time, he had plenty. We stood there wetting our pants, really and truly, and he kept pulling people out, sometimes to kill, sometimes to whip them and leave them alive. When it would end we did not know. We were happy every time it wasn't us. That they took someone else out, for the dog, or for a bullet in the head, or just lashings, as usual. That was every evening, the lashings. All day he walked around, and for little things he would say how many lashings he would give that evening. He would have a roll-call, and everyone who was getting a punishment had to come, say he needed to be lashed, and say exactly how many lashings. No one lied, it wasn't worth it. And the men had to count the lashes themselves. Even if they were almost dying from the beatings, they had to count out loud. And if they lost count, they would start from scratch. Some did not get up from those lashings, better to get a bullet in the head..."

Levertov fell quiet. Thought quiet thoughts. We sat silently.

Suddenly he said, "That's it for today. Enough now."

We were amazed—so little? We wanted to rebel but something within us did not. Something inside completely agreed and told us to go, there would be time to hear it all. Effi got up first. I stood up too. Levertov stayed behind. We didn't look back until we'd rounded the corner, and then we ran down the main road back to Katznelson, to Grandpa Yosef's neighborhood.

The next day we wanted to hear more, but we discovered that Levertov was not in such a hurry. He had enough Formacil for a few days. He would tell us when to meet by the bench again. We were annoyed, but it was no use. It was during the school year and it was hard to get to Grandpa Yosef's just like that. Still, we tried twice, until Levertov found us, and we didn't even need to say anything. "In an hour," he told us, and we synchronized our watches.

We got to the bench half an hour early and Levertov was already there. Effi gave him six Formacil and kept the rest in her pocket. Levertov got angry.

"I need it all!" he shouted.

Effi kept her cool. "It goes by how much you tell!"

Levertov looked at her and at me, wondering what he could say to prevail. His look was hateful, but he simply said quietly, "Two more."

And Effi agreed.

He grabbed the pills from her and looked around, waiting for the street to empty out.

"Today I will tell you about how he was, Doll, from a work point of view I mean. He was the Deputy Commandant in Treblinka and he wanted to do well, so they would make him Commandant. He was always making plans to improve, to fit in more of the transports that arrived all the time, day and night. Long before I came he already had an idea that went very well for him. He realized that he wasn't getting as much done as he wanted, because elderly people and cripples did everything slowly. So he had an idea. Near the beginning of the route he closed off a piece of land as if there was a hospital there, put up a sign and a red cross. Anyone who was elderly or handicapped was sent there straight way. Inside there was nothing, just a pit, where they did away with people on the spot. Doll was pleased with his idea. With my own eyes I saw how he went up to an old man and asked him politely why he wasn't keeping up with the group. The old man answered something and Doll graciously pointed to the hospital. He even got a thank you from the old man, you see. That, he liked. One-two, no more old man. And he always made sure to receive the transports himself, for this pleasure. Where people were stripping down he interfered too, and did things. If he found that women were trying to keep their babies and children with them, he got angry because that was against his rules. He got rid of the children himself. And listen to this: Once I saw how his assistant, Hirtreiter, took hold of a baby by both feet and, hear this, he slammed the baby against the wall until it was over. And Doll got angry and yelled at Hirtreiter that that wasn't the way to do it, and he stopped everything, even though that was a waste of time, so that he could teach him. He grabbed a different baby by its feet and with one blow, that's it. Then he told Hirtreiter that was how it was done, with one blow, and he left. God help me, the things I saw. He had strange behaviors, this man. One minute he would go through the camp on his horse, tall you know, and clean. The face of an angel, he had, the Angel of Death, and on the horse he was distant from it all, thinking to himself, clean sort of. And another time he would sneak into the latrines where the Jews went to get a breather, and shoot people doing their business. He found that very funny. There was a man, Itzik Konchinski, whom he hit right as he was using the latrine, and he fell inside and Doll was very happy, as if he had succeeded at something he had wanted to do for a long time. Sometimes he did things where you couldn't tell what was going on in his mind. Once, so I heard, there was a Jew who came to Treblinka and he was injured when they took him out of the train car. He begged for water and Doll gave an order to bring him a bucket. And they said that the Jew tried to drink and then Doll attacked him and shoved his head in the bucket and kept hitting him with the butt of his rifle until it was over. They always told stories about him quietly, and I can't explain how frightened we were to think that it would be our turn soon. First the man to your left, then the man to your right, and all the time you had the feeling that that was it. I was there for only two weeks, thank God, until the uprising. Afterwards, this was only what I heard, because of our uprising they got rid of the Commandant of Treblinka and made Doll the Commandant, and that was his dream. That, thank God, I did not see. I was in the woods until the end of the war."

That was the end of the conversation, for eight Formacils. Effi tried to offer him more, to make him go on, but Levertov refused. He had decided to teach us a lesson. "Same time tomorrow. And bring me a whole packet, otherwise nothing," he threatened.

We left. We had to find a way to steal more medicine. We thought about substituting similar looking pills and searched our medicine cabinets at home, but we found only one little packet that looked almost the same. We exchanged it for the Formacil. We volunteered to help Grandpa Yosef prepare Feiga's pills and lukewarm tea and arranged everything nicely on a tray, not forgetting a saucer for the teacup.

Those were trying times. We would come up with all sorts of excuses to come to the neighborhood. After school, even on Saturdays. We met Levertov to hear more of his stories. We stole Formacil and gave Feiga replacement pills. Feiga did not complain but we detected something menacing lurking under the surface of her silence. We imagined Feiga turning blue or yellow. We imagined a multicolored Feiga. We imagined worms erupting out of her body and Feiga erupting out of the house like Godzilla, people scattering. Our imagination spun around the true fear, the one we could not imagine—what would we tell Grandpa Yosef if we were caught?

The neighborhood lived its life in ignorance; Katznelson flowed slowly while we secretly passed Formacil pills from one bank to the other. We felt empowered by the pills Levertov grabbed from us, his eyes glimmering with redness and guilt, and by the secret that went everywhere with us. We were filled with the power of the traitor and the smuggler. It showed in our eyes, in our gait, in the way we held our heads up high. Menachem, the only kid in the neighborhood, dragged around behind us. He was older than us, our undisputed leader, but he surrendered to a force he could not comprehend. He built us tree houses but we refused to enter them, and found all sorts of petty faults in everything he did. He brought Effi new pedals for her bike and gave me books he'd been given for his birthday.

We went to Gershon Klima and asked menacingly why he wouldn't take us to the sewer. We faced Grandpa Yosef, supported by the force of fear and betrayal, and instead of being ashamed of ourselves, we made demands:

"Why did they move you around in the Holocaust through so many places?"

"Why weren't you in Auschwitz?"

"Tell us about Hirsch, when did you meet him?"

"Why do you apologize so much when Mrs. Tsanz gets angry?"

Mrs. Tsanz came from Lodz, and for some reason Grandpa

Yosef was self-deprecating in front of Lodzniks. A constant tone of self-justification and apology, even when it wasn't us who had kicked the ball into Mrs. Tsanz's window.

Our latent power affected the neighborhood. Unlikely events occurred offhandedly. The Frequent gave way to the Rare. A red-capped parrot took up residence in the treetops and for two days squawked from up high, "I'm lost, come and get me!" Or "I ran away, I promised I would!" Then it disappeared. Over at Sammy the greengrocer, a crate of plums was found covered with strange little bite-marks. A great mystery, until they found a small bat and a hole in the wall that had operated in tandem. In the middle of the day, a eucalyptus tree crashed down from the woods into the garden at 12-c Katznelson. We took a book out of the library and from the pages fell a postcard sent from Cypress to a woman named Hedva. Someone had written her a love letter and signed it "Everyman." Even Adella Greuner sensed something. In the throes of the Era of Things That Should Not Happen, she came to visit Grandpa Yosef. In her hand was a letter from the Municipality. Her dress was light blue and clean. She asked Grandpa Yosef for advice.

"Please come in," he said.

Adella Greuner and Grandpa Yosef sat at his desk for a long while, but the world could not tolerate such behavior. Feiga fluttered in her bed. The fridge rattled in the kitchen, emitting a series of complaints. Planes overhead shocked the neighborhood with distant sonic booms, the windows shook and rattled, even the walls could barely stand up around the two of them. The Frequent knocked and asked to come back—enough already with the Rare. But Grandpa Yosef sat with Adella and explained what the City wanted, who she must see, what to say.

It was difficult. It was up to us. We had to hear as much as we could about Doll, to fill in the empty gaps, to get it done before everything blew up and we would have to explain ourselves, standing in a shower of shrapnel, facing Grandpa Yosef and hoping everything would scatter and there would be an end to it. We had to get through.

Levertov kept talking.

"He planned 'portions' for the gas chambers. He knew exactly how many went in with each portion, the children and everything. They kept the children for last and when it was already crowded they threw the children in between the heads and the ceiling, and finally the babies too. If he couldn't push them all in, he got angry. That was when you wanted to escape his look. Us, and the Ukrainians, and his SS."

Six Formacil.

"One day I'm walking through the camp. On duty, not just like that. You didn't walk through the camp just like that. There was a man from my hut, Yankel Klein, standing there petting the dog Barry. Petting him! And Yankel says to me, completely calm, that when Doll isn't around there is no sweeter dog than Barry. He was one of those big Saint Bernards that never really do anything, just drool a lot and have a stupid look on their face. And Yankel said I should pet him, he was a good dog. God help me, I didn't pet that dog. That, I would not do. But exactly one week later, just before the uprising when we escaped, I watched that dog finish off Yankel Klein. He bit Yankel until he stopped yelling, and Doll stood on the side, lashing him with a whip. That, I saw."

He got a whole packet of Formacil, even though we had agreed on only six pills. He looked thankful. The next day, a horse with a shiny chestnut-colored coat passed through the neighborhood, stopped briefly on Katznelson opposite Gershon Klima's house, stood up on his hind legs, his coat glimmering in the sun, neighed and ran away.

From Adella Greuner's garden, the scarecrow disappeared. The one we thought she was yelling at, "Kalman, *vi geystu*? Kalman, *vi geystu*?" Peculiar hypotheses were suggested. There was even an explicit accusation against Grandpa Lolek, who snorted disdainfully, "I am to be lucky if I can get ten shekels for the wool hat, and nothing at all for those clothes, which the rain eats, and his plank also worth nothing. Who would buy from me such plank?"

From which we surmised that he had given the scarecrow an economical appraisal but had rejected it. We tried to picture Grandpa Lolek in his suit, haggling over the price of a scarecrow with a rag merchant. We couldn't. Proof. We acquitted him beyond a doubt.

"Once he went up to an old man to offer him his 'hospital,' but suddenly he couldn't hold back and he started to strangle the old man. He didn't shoot him, nothing, just strangled him, like a madman. Suddenly he stopped, as if everything was fine, and after a moment not fine again; he strangled him and strangled him until that was it…"

Two Formacil, even though we had promised more. There was no more. Levertov was angry, but to no avail. And the next day it rained hard, out of season. (Asher Schwimmer, having learned from the pioneers' letters about the strangeness of the Israeli skies between the dry season and the transition season, wrote in Poland, "A land of trespassing clouds / Their constitution of wilderness.") The laundry had not yet recovered from the miracle of rain when Grandpa Lolek's Vauxhall suddenly showed up. He brought Grandpa Yosef a wonderful edition of the Babylonian Talmud, with all volumes intact. He'd found a good deal—seventy-five percent off on the whole thing—and he gave it to an excited Grandpa Yosef for free, why not?

"Doll, he fancied himself a boxer, and he trained in the camp. He would get hold of a prisoner and that was it. The prisoner had to hold his head straight so Doll could hit it, and Lord have mercy on anyone who couldn't hold his head up straight after a round of boxing. But it didn't matter anyway because after Doll was finished they didn't stand much of a chance. SS Miete, damn him and all the rest of them, who was in charge of the 'hospital' that Doll invented, he would always walk around wherever Doll had been because he knew he'd find clients for his hospital. A bullet in the back of their neck, straight into the pit and that was that. And anyone Doll left after the boxing, this Miete would come quickly to take him to the hospital, one-two. Once, so they said, this was before I came, back in '42, Doll heard that a real boxer from Krakow had come on a transport. He made a big deal, organized a fight with gloves and everything, on a Sunday, their day of rest. But Doll was well-prepared. Inside his glove he put a little pistol, just in case. As soon as the fight started, while they were still facing each other with their gloves, he couldn't resist. Through his glove he shot the young man from Krakow. On the spot, that's that."

Four more Formacil and some other pills we had gathered up to offer Levertov because we couldn't get any more Formacil.

One Saturday, we came to visit Grandpa Yosef with our parents. We were strong, fortified by our betrayal. We glanced at Feiga, everything seemed fine. When it was time for tea and the conversation began to slow down to make way for the silence, the dreams, we went outside to play. We walked slowly down Katznelson. In the midday heat only Moshe survived outside, rubbing his hands together, something passing across his face, a kind of smile, as if inside he had completed a quick transaction. The shade from Gershon Klima's bombax attracted us. We went to see if the trunk had grown any new thorns (someone, perhaps one of the night wanderers, liked to abuse the tree, cutting off its thorns every night). We found a few that had slipped by. We touched them carefully, pricking ourselves painlessly. Our eyes traveled upwards, to Gershon Klima's forbidden window. We didn't have to look at each other. The Formacil, the power, the boldness. We decided that today was the day Gershon Klima would take us to the sewer.

We started climbing without a second thought. We skipped easily among the branches all the way to the open window. From there a small jump, and we'd be in the bathroom. We poked our heads in. Before us, inside the bathtub, lay the scarecrow from Adella Greuner's garden. We wondered, frightened, what was it doing there? We pushed our questions aside to make way for more important matters, but our astonishment kept showering us with its sparks. We found Gershon Klima standing in his room (Not sitting? Always standing or lying?), and before we could formulate our request, he said, "I'll tell you whatever you want."

We wanted him to take us to the depths of the earth, to the core, but the power of the Formacil had gone too far and had mistakenly melted away an ancient emotional strength, a cloak of silence forged over many years. All of a sudden Gershon Klima agreed to tell his story, to explain why he was "his own brother." We had subdued him by way of error, or perhaps (so we contemplated), Gershon Klima had captured us in his lair and we were finally caught, so he could tell his story.

Effi struck a hard bargain. "Do you have any juice?" she enquired.

I was anxious that we were about to lose Gershon Klima. Here he was, willing to tell us his story and make us the first to land on that moon, when suddenly—juice. But still Effi guided the ritual, in control of all aspects.

"I have no juice. I have no refrigerator at home," said Gershon Klima, and the simple politeness of his response became, in the air of the room, something greater. Gates were opened, the room filled with the sense of his clear declaration: This is Gershon Klima and this is his empty home, and his life, and we would hear his story here in the heart of the being that created it. "His own brother" was about to be deciphered. His own brother. So simple.

When Gershon Klima was born, he had an identical twin brother. Only their mother could tell her two drops of bliss apart. In a bunker during the Görlitz *Aktion*, sixteen adults and two children spent two days underground. Gershon and Hezkel Klima, aged one-and-a-half, were given sleeping pills so they wouldn't cry and give everyone away. But the Germans didn't need cries. Someone informed. In return for his life or the lives of his family members, or in return for one of the things that functioned as currency during the *Aktionen*, someone gave up the bunker. One by one, the people came out. The first were shot even before the last emerged. A moment before the mother went out into the light to be shot, she threw her twins into an empty water barrel.

They lay there, still, for an unknown length of time. First drugged, then dazed by the darkness and the shock. When one of them began to cry, someone heard him and crawled into the hiding place. He found one living twin, crying, and one dead twin. No one knew which of the two had survived—Gershon or Hezkel? But not only the external name had been lost. The sleeping pills had also taken the inner name. A warm child had woken up beside his cold brother, everything was dark, no one around. For several long hours a one-year-old soul had stirred, lost in the dark, crying, in a slumber that came and went, lowering blinds and partitions. Years would pass and only prescription pills could raise those blinds even a crack.

He spent the entire war hiding in the woods and in the homes of kind *goyim*. When the war was over, relatives came to collect him and they raised him devotedly, giving him generously from what little they had. Their looks enquired—Gershon or Hezkel? Not once did they call him by name, so as not to make the decision. He silently bore the appellations, "good boy," "our beloved," aliases that evaded the need to use an explicit name. Years went by and no decision was made. When they arrived at the port of Haifa in Israel, the immigration officer leaned down to the boy and pinched his chin affectionately. For some reason, after hundreds of children, all wide-eyed and imploring, the officer was moved by this boy grasping his uncle's hand.

"What should we call you, boy?" he asked in crude rustic Polish.

Gershon Klima, frightened and suddenly obligated, found himself committing. "I'm Gershon."

End of story.

We listened to Gershon, who now was quite possibly Hezkel, and understood everything.

"Is it because of Hezkel that you go to the nuthouse?"

Gershon Klima smiled. Yes, all was understood. Hezkel wanted a life too. Sometimes he demanded everything, sometimes only a little—just a walk outside.

We were not happy. "His own brother" had been deciphered but we felt empty and worn out. Something we should have left with its owner had been given to us. We should not have taken it. We left Gershon Klima's home in the usual way, through the front door, remembering to observe how the world looked from inside the house, through its windows, from its doorway, from its porch. We walked very slowly, already thinking about our meeting with Levertov later that evening, and even before that, our task of stealing more Formacil from Feiga.

We were not prepared for the next surprise. Trapped in broad daylight in the middle of Katznelson, we ran into Hirsch. His feet were planted solidly in the middle of a row of hibiscus flowers, his coat raised in his right hand above his knees. He was peeing on the flowers. In his left hand he held a book of Psalms, lifting it as high as he could, far away from the urgent downward stream. We stood frozen opposite this statue of liberty—we were immigrants in America, standing dazed at the port with a suitcase at our feet and our brother's address in our pocket. We thought about Mr. Bergman, who had a brother in America. About Finkelstein the son, of whom we knew nothing except what had been addressed to him. We recalled Adella Greuner's brother, who once came to visit from America, rolling into the neighborhood in a taxi. After less than half an hour at Adella's, the whole neighborhood watched through their blinds as he slapped her on the cheek, got back into the waiting taxi and left. Astonishing. Everyone stood limply behind their blinds—imagine coming all the way from America to slap Adella Greuner and go back home! That evening, the sky had seemed higher over the neighborhood, although the swallows had come down at twilight as usual, following the insects that stuck to the lamps. By morning, the neighborhood had not yet wiped off its look of astonishment. People pondered the broadness of life, sensed a Mississippi River that had burst onto Katznelson for one single day and submerged it. All the way from America for one slap and back home!

Hirsch concluded his business and walked onto the paved portion of Katznelson. His right hand still lifted his coat, his left shook the Psalms up and down. Up and down, as if he were clutching a JNF donation box, listening to the letters jingle inside. We saw him turn to us and approach. We thought he would choose us, stand facing us and open his terrible mouth:

"Only saints were gassed?"

We stood. Eyes closed. We felt Hirsch's breath on our face. Then he was gone, leaving his leaden dramas at an insignificant point near the plumbago shrubs far behind us.

We went home and we were almost unsurprised to see Levertov coming out of Grandpa Yosef's apartment. He looked at us for a moment like a captured jackal, exposing his teeth in an evasive sort of smile. We didn't have to ask. We hurried to Feiga's room. The Formacil had already been swapped. Grandpa Yosef scurried after us, explaining, "Mr. Levertov came to see how Feiga was. It's so nice that there is someone willing to sit with her a little when I'm busy. And Levertov, he has enough problems of his own."

We left. Our hearts yearned for the woods but our feet took us only as far as the upper border demarcated by long yellow skeletons of leaves and little pieces of junk tossed, over the years, into the point that connected the place of human residence with the beginning of savagery. At the point where the neighborhood disconnects from the rest of the woods, we returned to Katznelson. That was the precise moment when childhood ended.

We walked quietly back and forth along Katznelson. We wanted to vandalize something at Levertov's, to go to Grandpa Yosef and blurt out a confession: Feiga has been poisoned, someone faked the Formacil! Or perhaps do a good deed and carry Linow Community's shopping for her or rake some leaves from the path next to Moshe.

We had wasted our power and we sensed it ebbing away, beaten down, weakening. So many things had been missed. We had not gone to Hirsch's hut to knock on his door and see what he did when he wasn't shouting on Katznelson. We had not gone down into the sewer to walk all the way to Caesarea. So much truth we could have acquired, enough to fill our pockets with. But we had wasted it, wasted it all. Childhood was over. We were thrown out and barred from taking anything with.

The following Saturday, when Mom suggested a visit to Grandpa Yosef, I asked instead to go hiking in the Jezreel Valley. (In class we had learned about Hankin, the Zionist who had redeemed lands in the valley). Effi, at home, used the flu.

We began to withdraw from the neighborhood, from Grandpa Yosef. We abandoned the Shoah. We were repelled by something. Levertov's betrayal was the seed of something greater, and it only grew larger and darker, with onion-like layers. We gave ourselves up to maturity.

We were fourteen when Levertov betrayed us. After that, we were seduced by a new world. With Tal Brody, we led Maccabi Tel Aviv to victory in the European Cup Championship. With Yizhar Cohen, we won the Eurovision Song Contest. The world glowed with

lights of victory and we lapped them up. It was the start of our years
of Imaginary Purposefulness. Growing up. Aspiring to things that
were bigger, less alive. We allowed ourselves to be painted with the
right colors, to assimilate, to blend in. The instructions were precise
and we followed them, no questions asked. And whatever we didn't
do, our bodies rushed to achieve on their own, treacherously, with
an apologetic grin but pleased with the changes.

We were dropped off on an unfamiliar platform. Adolescence.
Things happened.

Occurrences.

But only to us.

Around us, stagnation. The years passed by. In the family,
everything stayed as it was. Grandpa Yosef's neighborhood remained
unchanged. The people we knew added twenty years on to their ages,
years swallowed up like pills taken and forgotten. For them the years
were pushed into drawers, closets, lives with secret bottoms. Things
stopped changing. A spell brought it all to a standstill and let us run
ahead and grow up. Blindly, we ran.

There was Rachela Kempler, every day before dawn in her
window. Opposite her, with drawn blinds, was mad Itcha Dinitz.
Linow Community, Sarkow Community, swayed slightly more as
they walked with their baskets of vegetables. In season, the bombax
bloomed. The bauhinia. The poinciana. Katznelson, calm as always,
flowed in numbers and letters. A frozen world where nothing changed.
Not even Eva Lanczer. Twenty years have passed since they took her
away and she still lies in a hospital bed all in white. Eliyahu goes
to visit her. Wondrously, she still embroiders strange and beautiful
things for him to sell. All those years she spent resting, we devoted
to growing up. The people around us grew older, sicker, much the
same as always, determined to go on without aging, as if the secret
of longevity was unhappiness. Avoid happiness and you have as good
as avoided dampness, wetness, any danger to your health.

The family stuck to itself and clenched its teeth against change.
Nothing could happen. When someone died, everyone rushed to the
funeral and huddled around the muddy grave with wintry umbrellas, or sweltered in midday in a desert of white gravestones—just as

long as we huddled around the plot, piled up the dirt to stop a hole in the ship.

Grandpa Shalom died in 1980. Effi's camera captured Aunt Ecka for the final time. We had her face as a souvenir, next to a table spread with whipped cream and desserts. Uncle Tulek also died (finally, the African statuette could be removed from the living room). In the unknown distances at the edges of the family with-whom-we-never-met, people died. But the bonbons still arrived at the holidays. People died, but the bonbons could not be stopped, they were like a herd of buffalo galloping by on the holidays, kicking up dust. Every year a Passover Seder managed to somehow be arranged. We managed to meet at the dinner table. If we had photographed ourselves and sent the picture to a lab, the report would have come back and certified: this is a family.

The family friends did not abandon us either. Attorney Perl was still in his store. Now he had two assistants, both named Yakov, but only he went up the ladder. A ninety-year-old Spiderman in 1990. And it wasn't only Dad sitting with him in the backroom—I started to sit there too. The years brought Attorney Perl and myself together in an unexpected way. At the age of fifteen I tried my hand at a woodworking course held near his store. I wanted to drop the course almost immediately, but the teacher was a friend of Dad's from the army reserves and lots of warm regards were exchanged between them. I stuck it out for more than a year, fulfilling my messenger duties, and built a wooden *menorah*, a bookshelf, a wine rack, and a model airplane. My consolation was that I could go into Attorney Perl's store on my own, without Dad, as a grownup. Attorney Perl welcomed me into the little back room, the mirror room, where he made me tea, told me about his late spouse, about the Nuremberg Trials that had put an end to all hope, and about Eichmann, who was put to death just like that, without us knowing his thoughts.

I kept going to see him even after squirming my way out of the woodworking course, sometimes before seeing a movie in town, sometimes for no reason. During my army service, too. I was welcomed respectfully, pleasantly, with a cup of tea that suspended all commerce. He ordered his assistant, "Yakov, mind the store for a while," and took me to the back room, the mirror reflection of his store. Every visit opened with a short discussion of my military service. A meeting of the special staff. "How's it going at your Lager?" Attorney Perl would enquire. They have their own words. *Camp*, with them, is *Lager*. A *pass* is a *Certifikat*. Even here in Israel, after years of independence. But they do have Hebrew words. Even those who speak only broken Hebrew acquire essential words. *A draft*, for example. They must have stepped off the boat and enquired, "How do you say in Hebrew when the windows are not sealed properly? A draft?" And that was it. Absorption in Israel.

Attorney Perl did not allow the Holocaust to disappear. He regretted the Nazi criminals who had been hanged before we could understand their thoughts, and he regretted those who were not hanged at all and whom the world had found swift ways to forgive. His memory catalogued hundreds of names of war criminals, their deeds, their verdicts. His map of the world included every country that had taken in Nazis after the war, every country that had served as a means of transit, every country whose agents had assisted the criminals in their escapes. In the air of the little room among the shadows of tea, he made long lists, calmly, meticulously.

—Martin Sandberger. Sentenced to death during the Einsatzgruppen Case for having engaged in mass extermination of Jews in occupied territories. Set free as early as 1953.

—Dr. Carl Clauberg, "the sterilizing doctor." Conducted horrific experiments on Jewish and Gypsy women in order to improve methods for quick sterilization. His lethal experiments were carried out in a special hut at Auschwitz. Released in 1955 from a Russian prison and transferred to Germany. No legal proceedings were initiated against him there, and only under pressure from the Jewish communities did an investigation begin. Preparations for his trial were cut short due to his death.

—Dr. Wilhelm Beiglböck. Conducted human experiments designed to ascertain whether man could subsist on seawater, and concluded that he could not. Sentenced to fifteen years in prison in 1947 but set free in 1951.

—Dr. Karl Genzken, physician. A typhus 'researcher' who

killed hundreds of prisoners in his experiments at Buchenwald camp. Sentenced to life in prison, but his sentence was reduced to twenty years and he was released to live in freedom in 1954.

—Wilhelm Speidel. Convicted of participating in the extermination of Serbian Jews and in war crimes related to the expulsion of Greek Jews to extermination camps. Sentenced in 1948 to twenty years in prison but released in 1951.

He listed some familiar names too:

—Untersturmführer Kurt Franz, referred to by the prisoners as *Lalka*, meaning "Doll." Arrested only in 1959 and brought to trial. For almost fifteen years, he lived a normal life in his community. Despite the harsh testimonies, his punishment was only imprisonment. As an exceptional case, the court also addressed the culpability of Barry, the St. Bernard dog who took an active part in killing prisoners. The dog was adopted after the war by a German physician, Dr. Strobe, and harmed no one. He reached old age and was euthanised in 1947.

—Erich Lachmann. The original owner of Barry, and the man who instilled his murderous tendencies in him. Also charged with murdering inmates in the Sobibor camp, but acquitted of all charges.

—Heinrich Lohse, Reichskommissar of the Baltic areas. A brutal implementer of the Final Solution, who ordered that Jews in areas under his control be rationed no more than the minimal essentials to sustain life. Sentenced to ten years of penal servitude, but released after three years for medical reasons. Lived in freedom until his death thirteen years later.

—Wilhelm Koppe. A leading figure in the establishment of the Chelmno extermination camp, a ghetto "liquidator" in the Wartheland and a senior SS commander of occupied Poland. Lived under an assumed name after the war and was only captured in 1961. His trial was discontinued due to medical problems. Lived in freedom until 1975.

Endless lists.

Again and again, I am struck by one mounting impression: how quick the world was to forgive, to mitigate death sentences, to release life-term prisoners. Something larger than the Nazis' crimes was at work here. Something global. It was not only the Nazis whom Attorney Perl was condemning. His explanations encompassed all human beings—otherwise, the Nazis would not be understood. He spread before me the treasures of the Holocaust, rolling them out like a fabric merchant. Together we tore up everything I had learned at school; the Shoah recited in ceremonies, the placards displaying numbers of casualties. It was a competition of sorts, a hope to impress, to shock, to emphasize the magnitude of the catastrophe.

Attorney Perl led the conversations. I, in turn, modestly provided material from encyclopedias, from school, from the books on the shelves in Mrs. Gottmartz's public library. I also brought to our conversations what little I knew of my family history. Minute details in punctured containers. But Attorney Perl removed our families from his words, so as not to divert the line of logic. His own private Shoah grief rarely emerged, and was quickly covered over when it did. He was authoritative in his speech. Precise, impartial.

"In order to judge the Nazis' deeds," he explained, "we need something moral and axiomatic that includes the obligations of both the judged and the judges. Feelings must not be an active factor, but only an additional examination method."

And when the explanations got complicated, we always went back to the endless lists.

—Heinz Schubert. Sentenced to death at the Einsatzgruppen Case. Released in 1951.

—Erhard Milch, head of the Nazi regime's Central Planning Board. Charged with exploiting the slave labor economy throughout the Reich and overseeing morbid medical experiments conducted by physicians on camp inmates. Sentenced to life in prison in 1947 but his sentence was commuted to fifteen years and he was in fact released in 1954.

—Walter Kuntze, a general in the German army. Responsible for the murder of thousands of Serbian Jews with the SS. Sentenced to life in prison in 1948 but released in 1953 due to reasons described as "health considerations."

Outside Attorney Perl's store, life went on as usual. Yehoshua the barber had to make good on more and more promises to cut the hair of loyal customers at their homes until their dying days. He arrived punctually, not reneging even on the vaguest of vows, but boosting himself by mumbling around his customers' heads, "Believe me, I'm certain it was you in '64 over at Golchik the barber on HaNevi'im Street. Not anyone else. So help me God, I shouldn't have come to you."

In the neighborhood, the fight between Littman and Sammy raged on—proof that the world did not change. But it did change: Littman installed air conditioning in his corner store ("enough suffering," he said), paving the way for two frenetic months during which the entire neighborhood fattened up their walls with little air conditioners. A victory for progress.

Littman did not grow old. Neither did Grandpa Lolek. Why would he? He had already been eligible for discounted bus fares for a while now, and besides, there was not much to be gained by old age. His Vauxhall was not what it used to be; every time the engine was turned off, its cooling body trickled out grumbles and complaints. But Grandpa Lolek remained loyal. Thanks to Green the Mechanic, the Vauxhall could still make it to Gedera and back. When Anat was pregnant with Yariv, Grandpa Lolek bought her a car. One day he simply placed the keys to a Fiat Uno in the palm of her hand, as if to say, "I always buy cars for pregnant women." We tried to graciously refuse, and finally, perplexed, we consented. There were no words. Only the *Tarbut* encyclopedia could express the sentiment (Everyman, Plate Tectonics, Seventh Wonder).

Grandpa Yosef did not grow old either. His justification was the bike. His wrinkles deepened, his wisdom grew heavier. The university studies breathed new life into him, dragon wings that he politely dragged through the shrubs along Katznelson. His decision to continue his academic adventures even after obtaining his Masters' impressed us. The topic of his doctoral thesis, Jewish heroism in the Middle Ages, aroused a certain curiosity. By the time he reached the graduation ceremony in 1985, Effi was a medical student and I was an officer—two perfect icons of *naches* for Grandpa Yosef. Except in our case it was the grandfather who brought *naches* to his grandchildren. Each of us secretly vowed to fill our lives with rich content, to somehow aspire to be the equal of Grandpa Yosef, who struggled against a lack of time, a multitude of worries and old age. Many other family members seemed to be in a constant flux of hidden motion—a change perceptible only to those proficient in this morphology.

We would come to Grandpa Yosef whenever we could, to eat the ever-changing contents of the fruit bowl, to talk, to fortify ourselves. Around us strange years flew by. We sat with Grandpa Yosef. Things occurred outside. Grandpa Yosef came and went, brought cold fruit, juice. We saw the books on his desk change. Less of Rambam and Radak's scriptural commentaries, more *Traditional Anti-Semitism in Western Europe* and *The Jewish Leadership's Interpretation of the Crusades*. We went to make coffee in the kitchen and came back. Effi began her studies. Still taking pictures in bursts, but the periodic excess now concealed an impaired desire to photograph. I became an officer and completed a short term of service in the standing army. Grandpa Yosef reveled in the anti-aircraft weaponry I was put in charge of, slightly miffed that I wasn't allowed to try my hand against real aircraft. Effi's books, *Introduction to Surgery* and *Biology for Physicians*, were respectfully leafed through.

Grandpa Yosef did not have a porch-and-a-loquat-tree-to-sit-beneath. When we came, sometimes both of us, but usually only one, we made do with the big wooden table. There we sat, all grown up, comprehending the amazing power with which its location had been selected: the precise center of an equilateral triangle between Brandy's calls (Moshe's needs), Feiga's calls (Feiga's needs), and the window (public needs). Grandpa Yosef, the loyal emissary, left his post once in a while to head this way or that to answer a call. Sometimes he went far, if the summons required it. Moshe, Feiga, someone else, Moshe again, Feiga once more, someone else again. Grandpa Yosef on his orbits, never resting, never finished. And he always came back to us, looking straight ahead with severity, even threatening: No pity. God forbid, do not dare pity me.

Sometimes serendipity brought Effi and me together at Grandpa Yosef's. Like a pair of lemmings, we dropping everything—university, marriage—to answer the call of our species and come to Grandpa Yosef. We convened with him to debate the problems of life, offer advice, comments, slight derisions and sometimes encouragement. We never left Grandpa Yosef without playing a game of "Categories." It was good to lose, as we had done in our childhood. Grandpa Yosef showed no mercy when it came to Categories. He became a vengeful warrior. His arms thickened. His voice turned crude. In the interest of fairness, we made him come up with two terms instead of one to gain any points. Grandpa Yosef obeyed, but in return, we agreed that he could play his beloved double turns—once as Grandpa Yosef, once as Feiga. He placed two pieces of paper in front of him, one with his own name, and on the other he wrote tenderly, "Feiga."

Feiga was the winner. Always. Grandpa Yosef left himself the common terms and decorated Feiga's page with the best of exotica. An animal with "Z" was "zebra" for himself and "zebu" for Feiga. A vegetable with "T" was "tomato," destined to battle our own identical choices, leaving Feiga as the lead with "turnip." If the letter H was called out, Grandpa Yosef would blink, his Adam's apple bobbing, bits of thought dripping down his temples. He would write down "Honduras" or "Holland" for himself, and for Feiga, "Hungary." A very mediocre stroke of genius, connected to the as-of-yet-unexplained escape by Feiga and her family from Bochnia to Hungary one fine day before the *Aktionen* and the Holocaust horrors. The insult was not yet digested, Grandpa Yosef still did not dare take a first bite out of the affair: one moment the two of them were in the ghetto, engaged, and the next—Feiga was gone.

After the games he would make sure to pad into Feiga's room and announce, "You won!" Pleased with his achievement, he would pamper himself with a piece of pickled herring or some lox or a pickle spear. Happiness radiated from his stubble, from the wrinkles on his face. He happily sipped a cup of weak tea right in front of our eyes, restoring in himself the powers dissipated by victory.

Every time we visited, we asked about the doctorate. Grandpa Yosef was secretive. "Grandpa Yosef, let us read it," we would beg, but our attempts were met with raised eyebrows and waves of the hand. He would grumpily complain: there was progress, but not the progress he wanted. Something…something was missing. Something to give life…validity. He was waiting for an omen, a sign from above. As if engaged not in scientific research but in a kind of religious purification.

"Maybe if you wrote about Jewish cowardice in the Middle Ages you'd have more ideas," Effi says, annoying Grandpa Yosef. Jewish cowardice. Not funny at all.

Angrily, he responds, "I knew a man in the camps…Adler… *nu.*" And falls silent. As if he has touched a thought not yet fully molded. He suspends our fruit bowl rights by taking the bowl into the kitchen to preoccupy himself, to hide his anger, leaving us with a hankering for grapes. The hasty reference to "Adler" gives rise to a common thought: Grandpa Yosef had managed to successfully ford our childhood without telling us much about his Shoah. A series of Morse code was all we ever had, event-event-occurrence, that's it.

There are moments when Grandpa Yosef lobs a confession attempt in our direction. "The things I saw…the people I recall…in the Lord's name! Sometimes I sit here in my chair and think: I am alive. And I think about them, so many years have passed since they too hoped to live, to survive the camps. I sit here and tremble, children, I sit and tremble…"

As if he wants us to sit and listen as he talks, but there is no one to talk to. We look back at the years during which we chased down the questions of the Holocaust. Caged years that began with ordinary days, when we were ten, and ended with Levertov's betrayal and our banishment from childhood. We did not find answers to our questions, and it seems we stopped seeking them.

Grandpa Yosef's dissertation was to continue at a painfully slow rate, and in fact is still not complete today. But during the lucid days of 1985 we imagined it was just within his reach. Every meeting with him opened with the question, "How's it going?" and with the answer, "Still not…still not," with a grumbling sigh. If we had focused our attention correctly, the delay would have revealed to us the secret of the stagnation that had befallen the world around us. We should have taken the hint. The neighborhood had come to a standstill. Everything had frozen. The world does *not* change.

We would run into the neighborhood residents and find them

identical to the characters of our childhood, unchanged, not a comma or a wrinkle different. Continuing to survive. Magical people. Day after day, experts at survival. Forces of nature pushed them into the neighborhood (volcanoes disguised as historical dates; raging fires known as Auschwitz, Belzec, Bergen-Belsen; thunder storms on train tracks; the thick fog of transports; sub-zero temperatures—the locals' indifference) and now they sit in the depths of their compensation payments—the only support they have, a flow of coins from Germany. Only the Germans are left to atone, to compensate them every month for their suffering, for families lost and lives unblossomed. There are no professors among them, no big-time merchants, statesmen, legislators. Their lives have been diverted to this neighborhood, to this wasteland. Their lives are unlived. They came here as a torrent of refugees after the war, to the heat waves and the rationing, to a place with no trees and no snow. They were forced to live other people's lives, chosen from a pile like clothes in the camps without trying them on, no exchanges allowed—pause too long and the whip will crack. They took tattered lives, lives that fit no one, and lived them complacently. They married. Had children. Listened to the radio. There were holidays—Rosh Hashanah, Passover. But what could compare to the Passover Seder at home in Sosnowitz, where Father blessed the *matzo* with Elijah's trembling cup of wine on the table? Where were their lives? The continuity? Things begun during the first year of studies at the Polytechnikum or a renowned *yeshiva*? In a successful business inherited from Father, full of ideas to double and triple the profits? Where were those lives?

They sit. They sigh. Sometimes a thought creeps in, a certain sacred relief: We are not to blame. Our lives have been nothing, but it is not our fault. The Shoah. The war. We were saved, and more than that we could not do. We were absolved from a life that demands successes, accomplishments, proof. Not like our children, who grew up here and were given everything—and what do they have? Nothing. We are here, surviving.

We looked at them with wonderment, amazed and alarmed— they did not change. The years passed us by like a cat's scratches. We could feel each one of them. Those later years were not as easy as our childhood had been. Life surged around us and we clung to our seats trying not to drift away. We were abandoned, weak, in need of Grandpa Yosef. We came to him: Go on, Grandpa Yosef, pull us along, you are the strongest sleigh dog. We sat with him to catch our breath. To rest. To check in—was the world changing? Not changing? And us? What about us?

The neighborhood does not change. Every evening, Uncle Antek turns on the huge radio and the inmates are counted in Auschwitz. Gershon Klima is down in the sewer. The occasional hospitalization, slightly less frequent. Twice a month is just too much at his age. Adella Greuner is still despised behind curtains. Haim Mintzer limps along Katznelson.

Sometimes outside, for a moment, the yell comes:

"Only saints were gassed?"

The world does not change, just grows old and more complicated. A scruffy beard and cracked lips. Doesn't it ever get sick? Doesn't it ever need help?

And Moshe? What will happen with Moshe? There he sits on the low fence.

Everything remains as it was.

Without even noticing it, we grew Old Enough. Dad started to talk with me. Cautiously laconic, only the bare facts. He told many stories—at-age-twelve-condemned-up-against-a-wall-in-the-ghetto-a-German-SS-officer-puts-a-bullet-in-raises-his-rifle-suddenly-a-messenger-comes-with-an-order-to-stop-shooting-the-German-lowers-his-rifle-what-did-you-think-about-Dad-a-moment-before-the-shooting?-I-don't-know-I-just-thought-let-it-not-hurt. Then-in-the-camp-during-*Selektion*-they-sent-him-to-die-put-his-name-down-on-the-list-of-condemmed-then-they-couldn't-find-him-on-the-list-he-didn't-wait-around-just-ran-to-the-ranks-of-those-chosen-to-stay-alive-and of all these stories, the most moving was a particular moment after the war. Dad tried to finish his primary school education. In the entrance exam he was required to submit an essay in Polish. The school headmaster asked him to write on "My Life Story." And so Dad wrote his life story. When he came to get his grade, the headmaster asked him, "All this, everything you wrote in your essay…Did this really happen to you?"

Dad said, "Yes."

The headmaster said, "Poor boy." And caressed his head.

A simple gesture—an educator pats the head of a boy whose life has been difficult. But Dad was not a boy. He was already sixteen. The hand was caressing the head of the boy from the essay, who had already lived, who was no longer, whom no one had caressed when he was selected for death in Plaszow camp, on whom no one took pity when he was ill, when it was clearly just a matter of time before they put a bullet in him. The boy who stole food to keep his parents alive. Who was unable to keep them alive. Whose friends—all his friends from school, from the playground, from the screaming and shouting during recess—were dead. Gone. The hand caressed a subterranean boy, a non-boy. The caress was too late.

That caress had to traverse many light years and cross many firmaments to land, to settle, to show a natural motion, an educator-patting-the-head-of-a-boy-whose-life-had-been-so-difficult. Six years earlier, German educators had joined the ranks of the SS and the Gestapo. Polish educators had cooperated willingly, even when the victims were little children. Six years earlier, Dad had come to school for the first day of the third grade, and the homeroom teacher, Professor Wronewitz, had called the five Yids up to the front of the classroom to inform them that from that day onward they were no longer students at the school. He was following the orders of the Germans, who had recently occupied Poland. Just following orders. But the Germans had not ordered him to refer to the children he had been educating since the first grade as *Kikes*. The Germans had not ordered him to sweetly add, "Goodbye but not farewell." Dad still remembers his smile.

A country beginning with P? The Philippines, Peru, Portugal, Pakistan. We silently agreed never to choose "Poland." Revenge.

And Attorney Perl in the back room:

"Let us closely examine words from a command issued by Walter Von Reichenau, Commander of the Army Group South, as a spiritual guideline for the operating forces of the liquidation: 'The soldier must fully understand the necessity of meting out severe yet fair retribution to the Jewish sub-humans.' These words were intended to strengthen the spirits of soldiers engaged in the liquidation, and they represent an extremely prevalent frame of mind, which informed the way Jews were treated even by those who had nothing to do with the SS, such as anti-semites among the Polish civilian population, the collaborators."

Circuitously, Attorney Perl found his way to Grandpa Yosef. A respectful friendship grew. The presence of the elderly man enriched our games of Categories. Attorney Perl observed the game, respecting its rules, amazed at the treasures of knowledge to which he was not privy.

A city beginning with M? Minatitlan. (The points go to Feiga.)

A country beginning with T? Tuvalu, the capital of which is, of course, Fongafale.

But in the back room of Attorney Perl's store, the directions of amazement and knowledge were reversed:

—Emil Johann Puhl. Actively engaged in handling gold teeth collected in the death camps and storing them in the Reichsbank coffers. Sentenced to only five years in prison.

—Franz Rademacher. One of the greatest 'desk-bound' murderers, in his capacity as head of the German Foreign Office's "Jewish Desk." Escaped after the war to Syria, returned to Germany in 1966 and died before legal proceedings against him were concluded.

—Hauptsturmführer Hans Krüger. One of the most efficient and energetic murderers in the SS. Served as commander of a small border station in the Stanislawow district of Eastern Galicia. Although he commanded a tiny force of about twenty-five men, he managed to organize and implement the executions of some 70,000 Jews, possibly more. After the war he was not arrested at all, and was even bold enough to assimilate into public life and run for local parliament. Only in 1959 was he placed under investigation, and in 1968 sentenced to life in prison. He was released in 1986 and died two years later.

—Erich Koch, a founding member of the Nazi party. Reichskommissar of the Ukraine. Sentenced to death in 1959 for his actions, but his sentence was not implemented due to poor health. He lived on in prison until 1986.

—Alfried Krupp. Chairman of the Krupp family industrial conglomerate, which employed close to one hundred thousand forced laborers under conditions of slavery and terror. Sentenced in 1947 to twelve years in prison, but released in 1951. In 1953 he was restored to his previous position as head of Krupp industries.

—Richard Korherr, statistician. Author of the "Korherr Report," a publication containing updated data on the number of killings and the number of Jews still populating each area throughout Europe. His work was used by Adolf Eichmann to enable the planning stages of the extermination. After the war he was investigated but never brought to trial.

Endless lists of bad Germans swarm through my memory like frenzied flies.

I asked Attorney Perl an ancient question. "Mr. Perl, were there bad Jews?"

Attorney Perl prepared for his reply. Rapped his knuckles on the empty kettle. Twirled a finger behind his ear as if pulling an imaginary side-lock. "Bad Jews...you have to understand that the Germans...they had methods. Jews...they wanted to live."

He fell silent. A preparatory silence.

"First we must understand how far it is possible to go with the law. Where is the line from which we draw conclusions about who was good and who was bad? Up to a certain point, a person's morality struggles and he must choose between options. After that, there is no control, you cannot judge or accuse. A person commits an act—turns in his mother, his father, his brother. And it is not his thoughts that issue the command, and not his faith that interferes. It is not the person who acts, but the molecules of his body. The molecules wish to exist, they tell the Germans, 'There is the door, behind the oven, the bunker.' They desire only to live, to stay together in some human form. Families turned in, friends turned in. It was not the person who betrayed, but the molecules, the corporeal level, and that cannot be judged. There was in our ghetto, in Bochnia, a family by the name of Zomer. One day the Germans caught them—an informant had told them that the Zomers, father and son, knew where other people were hiding in bunkers. I believe they were bakers and they secretly delivered bread to hiding places, so they knew everything. They were told to inform, otherwise they would be shot immediately. The son, a young man roughly your age, wanted to live and so he started to talk. The father ordered him, 'Shut up and start undressing,' because the Germans would not shoot people in their clothes, that would be a waste. The son obeyed. They took their clothes off. They were shot. They did not give up the bunker. And the son? Like you. He wanted to live. So where are good Jews and bad Jews? Where?"

He told me about good Germans, bad Germans. Good Poles, bad Poles. Good Jews, bad Jews. He told me about Landau, a Jewish collaborator whom the Gestapo used to drive proudly through the streets of the Bochnia ghetto. And Count Simon, who was a fool, not a bad person, a persistent collaborator. These were not the worst, he cautioned. And he told me about the Jewish Kapo Yehezkel Ingster, and the Jewish Kapo Yakov Honigman. I was Old Enough.

Effi was also Old Enough. "Mom, why do you cry?"

Some things were told. Some were not. Even though we were Old Enough, questions still remained.

Why don't they spend time together?

Why is Mrs. Kopel infertile?

Why is Uncle Menashe from Netanya still a bachelor?

What about Mr. Bergman?

Suddenly, like a redemptive wave of nausea, we remembered: What did Grandpa Lolek do with Finkelstein's gold?

The wave of nausea went off to ask Grandpa Lolek. We were Old Enough.

"I give it to people without food after war, I give so they make graves for families, make new graves that the *goyim* destroyed. Also my family I made graves. Everything I gave, I thought after war there will be world without money, that is what I thought."

Grandpa Lolek's ideological era.

"On that, I was much mistaken," he admitted.

"You gave it all? All of it?"

"All of it."

To believe, not to believe, to believe, not to believe, to believe, not to believe—an entire field of marigolds was picked, petals plucked off. Believe, not believe, believe, not believe.

A hurt look from blue eyes interfered.

We believed.

The years passed by, Moshe celebrated his fortieth birthday, still sailing away as he sat on the low fence. There were no more attempts to find him a framework. He had found his framework. Maturation had given his face a stamp of contemplation, a gravity which brought to mind an internal change, perhaps a thought about to burst through, finally erupt, a thought that had been stymied all his life by a mind too bureaucratic, too clerk-like, and now the dull era would be over and the sweeping thought would burst forth to make amends, to express with simplicity everything that had not been understood his whole life, had been hidden in a distorting mirror. Brandy at his feet, an old dog now, tired of lovers, knowing her duty, loving the essence of her existence. A heavy slumber had spread over her limbs. Over the years some of Grandpa Yosef's qualities had poured into her. The altruism, mainly. When Moshe was resting in his room, if there was no urgent canine season, she could be seen hurrying to the pedestrian crossing nearby. She excelled at helping the elderly and children, granting confidence to those who lacked it. Every visit to Grandpa Yosef's began with a thorough indulgence of Brandy. We scratched the soft spots behind her ears and the hard box of her forehead. Looked straight into her eyes, trying to find the nobility that lay behind that canine face. Whiskers straight as a wand. Open mouth. Dots of foam always on her tongue. Not a face to break hearts. But still, Brandy.

Over the years we could sense how even Brandy went through changes. Death, in particular, was reflected through her—it tried her on like a suit of clothes. When someone came close to her she perked her head up, wagged her tail and yawned, as dogs do. But if you concentrated you could pick up certain notes. Death was apparent in her. Something not yet issued, a license held up by a clerk dazed from the heat, subject to continuous delays and the capriciousness of a bureaucrat. She strode down the paths with exemplary steps, careful not to skip too far into the next world—bad enough the trees she sometimes forgot to circle and the walls she crossed distractedly. Fifteen years old in 1991, Brandy was a demonic and yet tranquil dog. A sober island of wisdom, only the scruffy face preventing her from taking on a saintly halo.

Sometimes, on Katznelson, we would run into Menachem the neighborhood kid. We would stop and smile. "How's it going?" And in his eyes was wonder and astonishment. You left me here, he seemed to be accusing. You went off and I'm still here. I went to military school, got a job in Haifa, and I can barely make ends meet, and when we were kids we went to the woods together and climbed trees, even Gershon Klima's bombax, and you left me here. We say goodbye, somewhat awkwardly. I head to Grandpa Yosef, Menachem makes his way to the parents who gave birth to him many years ago, in the neighborhood, with wonderment, with embarrassment, as if they were being accused—where did this child come from? After all, we barely have the strength to live, so how did you find enough joy to give birth?

I too am amazed. When we were kids—I am certain of this—he was called Nimrod. I remember everything, and he was called Nimrod. When we were kids, Nimrod. There were no other kids in the neighborhood, so it was easy to remember. Grandpa Yosef remembers Menachem, everyone remembers Menachem, and yet I am certain: Nimrod. After the birth, for a short while, the parents had been filled with a placental life force, they grew impudent and named their son Nimrod after the biblical hunting hero. But now suddenly it was Menachem. According to him it had always been Menachem. To his mother he was Nahche, with teary eyes, after her brother, Nahche Osterman, may God avenge his blood. Fourteen years old, sent to Belzec. The eyes are the same, but her Nahche is heavier set.

If Grandpa Yosef wrote down 'Leibeleh' for a boy's name with L, we did not point out that for us 'Leibeleh' was not considered a boy's name. We trusted him. Our game of Categories was played in a spirit of generosity, which came easily. Sometimes, though, disputes arose. Effi, a charming ignoramus, fanatical over every point, once insisted that marshmallow was a vegetable. A radical player, she spread her hands out to the heavens for proof that might spring from the evening night. "Isn't marshmallow a vegetable?" Then she demanded points for Sodom. Sodom, she claimed, was a city!

Tasked with finding a country beginning with "B," Effi got points for Britain, I for Bahrain, Grandpa Yosef for Bermuda, Feiga for Barbados. Grandpa Yosef commented, "Interesting, we all chose islands…"

Effi was astonished. "Britain is an island?" She looked around at us. Was she being mocked? "But Germany isn't, right?" Just checking.

I consulted Grandpa Yosef's eyes. Geographically, the answer was clear. But Effi's question had raised a thought-provoking cultural image that could not be dismissed at hand. Could Germany be an island?

Grandpa Lolek interrupted our thoughts, manifested in his role as geographer. "What island?! Germany is connects nicely with Poland, and is connects nicely with Austria, where I have been when my Joyce got mixed up with the player on the piano in a café."

He was sitting with us because his neighborhood game of rummy had been cancelled. And as long as he had dragged the Vauxhall all the way here (and now it needed to rest), why not sit with some company, smoke a cigarette, drink some tea? He could also dangle a tea bag in front of Grandpa Yosef and do his *Selektion*, deciding to let the bag live but regretful that it would live on at Grandpa Yosef's. But not to worry, dinnertime was nearing, which might offer some prospects. He could browse Grandpa Yosef's papers and circle some notices. Then we'd see. He often turned up at our meetings, where he existed alongside us without wasting his time on our games and conversations. We would find him sitting quietly, diluting his cigarettes with tea, thinking. He never allowed his thoughts to be revealed, only their shadow exposed, disguised as tea vapors or wisps of smoke.

A more frequent guest than him, steady and respectful, was Gershon Klima. His tiger-like nostrils, unscathed by the sewage, always detected our arrival. Then he would hurry to Grandpa Yosef's and sit down to watch us play Categories. He never dared play, confounded by the supra-terranean concepts. He sat stiffly on his chair without even reaching for the fruit in the center of the table, which was meant for him, too. We respected his presence and looked forward to the letter S coming around so we could demonstrate our fondness. We silently conspired to all write 'sewage' under 'inanimate' (except for Feiga, who put down 'skippet' and took all the points again). Gershon Klima thanked us with a nod of the head, but seemed to disagree with those who did not know that sewage was in fact 'animate' and sometimes even 'vegetable,' and perhaps also 'personality' or even 'boy/girl'—two of them, begging to be taken down into the mystery smelling of mildew and zucchini.

Gershon-please-take-us-on-a-tour-of-the-sewer had been a failure, when childhood was said and done. During our games of Categories we began to comprehend Gershon Klima's strategy of promises. He employed a miraculous mechanism of rejection, one thousand and one nights, and in each promise the next rejection was ingrained. We looked for guile in the eyes of our childhood friend, but all we found was a desire to keep himself a little piece of the world, one freedom, a place that could act as a sort of balance to the empty, unfurnished house that contained only a bed made of satin, silk, brocade and velvet. This was Gershon Klima: three generations of psychiatrists had certified him as insane, hospitalized him when he asked, diluted his gentle personality with pills and taken slight advantage of his strong hands to do a few repairs here and there on the hospital pipes. We sat across from him, grown up. 'His own brother' deciphered, cracked. We had imagined this deciphering for many long years of toffee candies, believing that the moment of discovery would shatter planets in our face, alloy saliva and breath in our throats. But no. Gershon Klima talked, we listened, and nothing. Was this the moment of maturation? Compassion exceeding curiosity? Even before the betrayal of Levertov, which had dispossessed us, banishing innocence into exile?

We kept growing up. We changed. Sent forth versions of ourselves to live, to try things outside. Every version that succeeded we wore as an overcoat, layer upon layer. But inside, a wholesome core still enquired once in a while:

Why don't they spend time together?

Why is Mrs. Kopel infertile? (The long years sent forth the tail-end of an answer. Dr. Mengele.)

Why is Uncle Menashe from Netanya still a bachelor?

What about Mr. Bergman?

Versions of us asked questions. We did not abandon the Shoah but we bundled it up into one single day like everyone else did. Holocaust Remembrance Day. Like a pile of leaves neatly raked. We stood for the moments of silence. Watched the national ceremony. Communed. But daily life overcame us. The passing years. Only one connection remained to the lands of Shoah, one single flimsy ladder in the form of Attorney Perl. In his store there were debates over the culpability of the German nation, of the Nazis, of the SS. Everything I quickly convicted, Attorney Perl delayed, sentencing to caution and investigation. He walked his conclusions in a cold row of facts, enslaved by data and evidence.

"Every factor must be considered independently, and every pair of factors together, in terms of their influence on one another, and every group of factors, and so forth, in a neat order, with a settling of the conclusions at every stage, integrating them with what has already been concluded and what we aspire to.

"Let us read as testimony the words of Hans Karl Moeser, given during his trial in August in the year nineteen-hundred and forty-seven. Listen: 'The same way, with the same pleasure as you shoot deer, I shoot a human being. When I came to the SS and had to shoot the first three people, my food didn't taste good for three days, but today it is a pleasure. It is a joy for me.'"

Attorney Perl constructs ineradicable sentences within me. The bottom of my soul is paved with words. "With the same pleasure as you shoot deer, I shoot a human being."

And always, always, it ended with the recitation of lists.

—Erich von dem Bach-Zelewski, Obergruppenführer. A general in the Einsatzgruppen. Sentenced to only ten years in prison, released after five years. In 1961 he was sentenced again to a period of four more years.

—Erich Fuchs. A mechanical expert who installed gas chambers in the Eastern death camps. Arrested only in 1963. Sentenced to four years in prison and revocation of citizenship.

—Dr. Karl Blaurock, chemist. An expert on asphyxiating gases, a consultant for the gas chamber program. Not found to this day.

—Hermann Michel. SS member, nicknamed "the Preacher of Sobibor." Not found to this day.

—Adolf (Karl) Müller. One of the more brutal of the Sobibor staff members, whose name came up repeatedly in survivor testimonies. Not found to this day.

"What do you mean, 'not found to this day'?" I asked. How do people disappear in such a precise nation? It was unacceptable. Unpaid sins. Names and more names. The list was merciless. Its length, its breadth. One after the other in an orderly march. The hatred was fanned. The helplessness. How could so many have got away? Who forgave them? Who let them live, and bear children?

The hours I spent with Attorney Perl passed through underground burrows. These were hours unaware of the questions that arose: Does the world change? Does it not change? Outside the store, in the silence that prevailed when my footsteps returned to the world, the underground hours reunited with real time. Maturation. Grown up life. Continuity. Within the store there was still the reign of logic and precision, the Holocaust up for study. Inside his little back room we spun a world and attempted to comprehend it. I suggested it might have been a different world back then, with different rules, incomprehensible to us.

Attorney Perl dismissed my claims. "People were as they are today. Everything worked according to the regular rules, it was not a different world. It was our world, familiar and examined. My Laura came to Belzec on a train whose travel time was precisely the distance of the route divided by its average speed of travel. The gas in the chambers behaved according to the laws of gas formulated by the chemist Avogadro. The engine output determined the speed at which the gas diffused through the given volume of the chambers. And from there, physiology. The duration of time until death was determined by certain parameters: the ratio of gas to air, lung supply, the rate of metabolism in the body. Even Laura's final seconds, inside, can be described. Everything she went through during her final breaths. Doctors and experts have helped me to understand. And I talked with a survivor from the Sonderkommando who was somehow saved from death. His job was to clean the excrement and blood from the gas chambers. He described, at my request, everything he saw inside the chambers themselves. So you see, I know everything. I can go on with her until the last moment. And my Laura was so concerned with cleanliness and aesthetics. Even in the ghetto, despite the difficulties, she was so good about maintaining hygiene. Never let the crowdedness and the hunger sabotage her upbringing. And to die like that. Damn them…"

He breathed heavily.

"Damn them…"

A vein throbbed in his forehead.

"Damn them. Damn them."

Outside his store, time passed by. The hours piled up, massed at the door like uncleared snow. When I went out the spell was lifted, the crawling time in Attorney Perl's store disappeared in the flow of reality. A bus home. Falafel on HaChalutz Street. Car horns and stoplights. Only inside me the accumulating hours still lingered, constructing the only thing they were meant to construct: hatred for everything that went unpunished and still lives in our world, gazing fondly at its grandchildren. All the "not found to this day" who water their little suburban gardens, pay their taxes, wait for the weekend when their oldest son will come to visit with little Hans.

But the burrowing hours at Attorney Perl's did not dam time completely. I met Anat in 1986. I got married in 1987. Alongside my life, Effi grew up. She had loves. She studied. In the army, they sent her to take photographs too. After the army she chose medical school, seemingly for all the right reasons: they told her it was hard to get in but then it was easy, you just needed a good memory. She wouldn't have to stop taking photographs. But inside her, a hidden well of natural healing talent was crawling, waiting to spring. After seven years of school, she forgot about the camera.

1989. She earned her M.D. An impressive ceremony. She stood in the heart of a proud family while one man, a hero of Monte Cassino, clicked the button on a black Leica as if finally shutting a stubborn lid. Then two years at Ichilov Hospital in Tel Aviv. A shabby job, her hands longing for patients but touching only sterile bottles. Later, a partial transition to Carmel Hospital in Haifa. In the meantime, a position at the General Sick Fund in one of the Haifa suburbs, until a full-time position opened up at Carmel Hospital. But the temporary job won her over. Like a scientific researcher who does not find his place in human society, but in the heart of Africa, with a tribe he discovers (and perhaps names after himself—a simple matter of finessing the reports), he suddenly finds tranquility and love. The simplicity of the people wins him over, their love is the emotion he never found at home.

The Sick Fund patients loved her, and affection breeds affection. Sometimes I went to visit, surprised to see Effi's tribe at the entrance to her room, huddled in their troubles, talking about the doctor inside with a few complaints and a lot of love. They came bundled up in heavy clothing or flaccid robes, to gain her listening ear for their suffering, to present documents and test results. Among them were the shamefaced, the secretive. Apologizing for their illnesses, they kept their suffering folded up in little plastic bags. Their eyes were watery, frozen on a particular point on the floor (no doubt a puddle of memory had gathered there). Others were more demanding, masters of their illnesses. Standing in line, they regaled their fellow patients with the wondrous thicket of their aches and pains, and when their turn came they could barely bring themselves to leave the crowd—they had not yet given their opinion on the latest blood test. Determined, on the arc of a storm, they would sit down with Effi, charged with strength and courage, their illness practically escaping. Their debates were lengthy, involving pills, prescriptions, tests, forms—a hybrid treasure clutched in the palm of their hand, which they waved victoriously at the waiting congregation as they left.

The patients came to her one after the other, with more than simple illnesses to be treated. They did not always remember the true nature of their needs. Sometimes, like a watch forgotten at home, they left their complaints behind and came only with memories. They brought a mixture of backaches and service in the Russian military and new desires and the constraints of reality. Effi sat the mixtures down in a chair and talked to their memories. She had the depth to sense, to treat what needed to be treated. They acquiesced to her genuine compassion, to her concern for their welfare. Her fingers touched them and the touch said, "this body is important, someone cares that health should prevail here, too." She asked questions, remembered minute grievances, the fingerprint of each of her patients.

There was one disadvantage to the relationship between Effi and her patients: Effi was the first to get any round of flu. She could easily have served as a public alarm system, like canaries in a coalmine. She always fell to bed and turned red, then pale, her breathing labored. Then her patients would come up against a note that said, "Out sick," and would be referred to someone else, Dr. Reut or Dr. Mitelbien or Dr. Sachs, who were never sick. Whenever a flu outbreak began, the patients ran quickly to storm the clinic, hoping to beat Effi to it. But no. Already sick. Dr. Sachs instead. Her absences were no great crises. Most of her patients had flexible illnesses that happily accommodated delays. Only a small minority, a demanding handful, packed up their grudges in little boxes and came as soon as Effi was well to demand compensation. More pills, perhaps. Another test. Maybe the medication they were taken off that the doctor wouldn't give them, now she had to! Effi did not give in. The hagglers left her office, roaring their complaints and sometimes cursing Effi. Horrible words were uttered. Neither hisses nor utterances of "you should be ashamed of yourself" from the crowd could calm them. And Effi forgave, always. The curses were never mentioned at the next meeting. How did she forgive?

The old people from Grandpa Yosef's neighborhood could not come to see Effi. Sadly, the neighborhood had its own separate branch of the clinic. Only just over a mile away as the crow flies, but the distance of infinite Sick Fund bureaucracy. So they had to make do with *naches*, proud of Effi, whom they had known as a child, now with the most precious of gemstones in her hands: a prescription pad. Only one person in the neighborhood, Levertov of all people, somehow slipped through the fences of bureaucracy and got himself registered as a patient of Effi's. He came and sat down in her office. The world *does not change*. Effi prescribed Formacil, knowing he needed it. Levertov said "thank you" and sometimes wanted to tell her about Treblinka. He wished her well. "May you marry soon." He thanked her again and left.

I got married. Effi did not. From the beginning she took the path of multiple lovers, trying out men of all kinds. Almost every time we met she talked of someone new, predicting eternity for the new love, but completely aware that there was no eternity and that there was still a long list of men ahead. She was like a competitive eating candidate, preparing to eat a hundred and four crabs, two more than the current record (set by a Korean student). The rules were clear: every crab must weigh at least one pound after cooking. One ten-minute rest every hour, on the hour. Three hours at most. Water is allowed, with lemon. No alcohol. Someone set the rules and Effi obeyed. A long, observant attempt, whose chapters were conveyed to me in dry, embarrassed reports.

To transfer our relationship from childhood to adulthood, we sawed the connection between us in half so it could squeeze through. We assumed we could put it back together again on the other side. And indeed, here and there the halves came together. We remained wondrous, suspicious. The halves were in our hands, everything was intact, but the relationship did not connect. Something had gone wrong.

Time passed. Thunder slammed against the ground. The sounds of a drumbeat. My Yariv was born, fanning flames of *naches* in the family. An echo came from Netanya: Aunt Frieda's Rina gave birth to her first son. Then Miri, then Ronnie. Roots erupted into the air. Grandchildren, great-grandchildren. You could take pictures, put them in your wallet, pull them out when necessary and proudly present roots. Fertility came easily. Not sadly, not sorrowfully. Children and more children. How many more would you like?

The family was stirred up with births and deaths. We could no longer take the stagnation. Something was about to change. We had to choose a moment of flux, a worldwide event that would give us momentum and cancel out the years-without-occurrences.

We chose the Gulf War.

In August 1990 the Iraqi army invaded Kuwait, shocking the world and surprising both experts and laymen. The cracks continued to emerge until 1991, alliances formed, tempers raged. In January the war broke out, but by then we were completely different than we had been in August 1990.

*

We were the first to understand Iraq's intentions, to absorb their significance through the short moments of history.

In a game of Categories, the letter "K" was declared. Panic! We knew there were not enough countries beginning with K to go around! Years after we had disallowed Kurdistan because Iraq had stubbornly prevented the independence of the Kurdish region, forcing us to rely on the same old Kenya, Korea and Kuwait over and over again, often resulting in a draw, suddenly "Kuwait" was gone too. The plot of the dictator from Baghdad, a malicious step impenetrable by all strategic experts, was revealed as clear as crystal on our Categories score sheets. Alongside his plot, the events also exposed an ancient scheme of Grandpa Yosef's. As if he had been waiting for the Iraqi tyrant to make his move so that he could comfortably complete a maneuver of his own, he stunned us by writing down "Kiribati" on Feiga's sheet. It was a tiny republic in the Pacific Ocean. Disputes arose, the old Brawer atlas was summoned, and evidence presented itself on page sixty-five. How had it gotten away all these years? Grandpa Yosef hurried to Feiga's room to report to the island princess how polished her game was this evening, how sweet her victory.

After a few months the war itself broke out. Rockets fell. Perhaps Saddam Hussein was after more than annihilating the letter K. But even before the rockets, the main events had already occurred in the family. An era of traveling had begun. Effi decided to take advantage of a school vacation to go to Japan. In her room she piled up guidebooks, descriptions, recommendations. She was too lazy to read them, demanding instead that I give a brief, efficient summary—after all, I had read all the encyclopedias. I started my attempt, but after a moment she cut me off in astonishment. "Wait a minute, Japan is an island?" Fearful, perhaps she wouldn't go after all. "An island? Tokyo is in the ocean?"

We took a trip with Dad to trace our roots in Poland, to see it all. Ronnie came back and then squeezed in a trip to the US. Effi finally set off for Japan. A frenetic pace took hold of the family. Something had decided to iron out the creases and reorganize things. We were all troubled. Business. Pleasure. Roots. Constant travel. Ostensibly independent trips—what did Japan have to do with Poland? But from above, something larger was waiting to rip out everything and dismantle it. Even the backdrops would be torn apart, destroyed (just in case we thought we might come back one day, everything was demolished).

First, Feiga died. Just like that. The impossible occurred without a second thought. One morning a trembling phone call came from Grandpa Yosef. Then a momentary dizziness. With him. At the graveside. With neighbors. At home at the *shiva*. We allowed him to mourn. Even Moshe improvised a quiet *shiva*. People went into Feiga's room to believe. Her death, which had occurred opposite the surprised branches of the poinciana, was not yet apparent. The blankets did not look as if they had given up their place. There was still an odor of medication in the air. On the windowsill, the same delicately peeling old paint. The same thin branch staring inside. The impression of death was delayed.

Effi was in Japan. I had to locate her. She cried a lot. I had not realized how attached she was to Feiga. She was incomprehensible. She wanted to come home right away, but something went wrong, constraints beyond her control. When the *shiva* was over, I received postcards she had slipped one by one into a Japanese mailbox. She wrote how much she loved Grandpa Yosef, how everything was different now, how impossible it was. How could she have missed the funeral? I tried to locate her so I could cheer her up with the existence of Grandpa Yosef and replace him with Feiga, but in the meantime she had traveled home, just in time for Moshe's death.

Moshe died.

It happened suddenly, not even as a result of one of his diseases.

Heart failure. Another infliction he had been cursed with and which had hidden among his disasters, taking a backseat to the dramatic lead roles of retardation, brain damage, autism, adenopathy. A modest ghostly infliction, an unassuming stagehand to the great dramaturgy of Moshe's life, turning up all at once to lower the curtain.

We could not ignore the proximity of the events. Moshe's death followed Feiga's as if a lifeline that had been obscured in the shadow of Grandpa Yosef's grace had suddenly erupted, proving its vital existence only in its absence. Moshe had survived, ostensibly, with the support of Grandpa Lolek and Brandy and ourselves. But Feiga's death had pierced the gentle artery of his will to live.

A slow, merciful wave enveloped the house. Mourners gathered from the edges of the neighborhood, from the city, taking routes usually traversed by Grandpa Yosef in the opposite direction. Even those who had not come to the house for Feiga's death uprooted themselves and came this time. Adella Greuner, fragrant and despondent. Itcha Dinitz, unsure if it was the right thing to do. Mr. Bergman, restrained and heavy, sat and spoke in Polish about the sun rays.

We never noticed the disappearance of Brandy. On the day Moshe died she wailed like a wolf, and at some point during the *shiva* Grandpa Yosef asked if we had fed her.

Feiga was gone. Moshe was gone. Brandy was gone. *The world does change.*

During that *shiva* Grandpa Yosef conducted himself silently, with internal precision. He sat small and covered in his corner, addressing us only seldomly, to clarify confusing customs. "Now we need a *minyan* for the evening prayer." "Tomorrow is Shabbat, no *shiva* tomorrow." A lone sailor, leading himself on without us, we could not even pick up an oar to help him. At the end of the *shiva* he rose, his skin yellowing, his eyes bloodshot, and with a decisiveness that could have only emerged from focused contemplation, he announced that he intended to sail to the Caribbean islands.

The family was taken aback. The Caribbean? Haiti, Guadeloupe, Tobago, Martinique?

The Caribbean.

Why?

That question was not asked. And there was no answer.

We waited for the peculiar idea to pass, along with the sorrow and the layers of shock. This unwise plan would surely fade away as a mere fragment of thought that had offered him some consolation. It was an incomprehensible notion and would soon be gone. But the days went on and Grandpa Yosef went about his business, keeping secrets, making preparations.

The Caribbean?

Events proceeded at a surprising pace, and at the end of 1990 Grandpa Yosef took off in the estimated direction of Bermuda. He was a tourist with maps and a suitcase.

1991: Grandpa Yosef's Travels

T hey eat lots of coconut and pork here," his first postcard announced. He sounded disappointed, as if he had expected to find an observant congregation on the Caribbean islands. But his second postcard focused on the "amazing dark-skinned ladies," whose supple gait made a great impression on the wise scholar. On the front of the postcard, to our regret, were only a modestly-topped palm tree and a stretch of blue ocean. A disgruntled Grandpa Lolek suggested sending a quick telegram demanding to see the glistening dark buttocks with our very own eyes. We ignored him and continued to peruse the postcard, on which Grandpa Yosef detailed his impressions of a cave he had toured and his pending voyage to an abandoned island (a pirate stronghold from the good old days), but Grandpa Lolek would not let go. Finally, he confessed: his dancer, Joyce, was black. We were amazed. We quickly had to repaint a reel of memories in Joyce's new color and add the necessary features, somewhat awkwardly, to each imaginary scene. Even the color of the umbrellas with which she had danced for Grandpa Lolek on the rainy dock at Portsmouth had to be revised.

"Did you leave out any other details?" we asked firmly. We

meant to straighten out the memories once and for all. These recollections were the fruit of so many stories, and suddenly, in the midst
of a postcard from Grandpa Yosef—the first to lose his mind—now
this grandpa was going mad too. We waited.

"She had a little yellow parasol. She carried it rain or shine."

We were a little thrown off by the combination of rainy England and yellow parasols. How did the dance fit in? And what was the
difference between an umbrella and a parasol? Like weary painters, we
were forced to refinish our imaginations with the right colors. Joyce
the dancer grew darker and more beautiful. The trivial objects that
surrounded her also took on the appropriate characteristics (we threw
in scarves, high-heels, purses). The exhausting engagement in color
and details almost caused us to overlook the true hero of the evening,
the supposedly unruly Grandpa Yosef. We still did not understand his
fascination with the Caribbean, nor how these islands of palm trees
had found themselves caught up in a life of prayer shawls, chopped
liver and pickled herring with onion. At the edge of his postcard we
identified a grease stain that demanded rigorous investigation. Was
it possible that Grandpa Yosef was secretly committing transgressions
over there? Ultimately, the source of the stain was officially determined
to be okra, or possibly coconut. Case closed.

In his third postcard he claimed to have discovered fruits
whose existence he had not previously imagined. For the first time
in his life he was eating without knowing the names of the foods.
He also expressed his astonishment at the color of the ocean, the
peoples' eyes, the way night-time appeared. He wrote that as far as
the purpose of his travels was concerned, he was not getting much
closer, but the bottom line was that he did not find himself sensing
any regret. We remained puzzled by all the mysteriousness—what
was he up to there?

It was a good thing the Gulf War broke out, replete with Scud
missiles, plastic sheeting, and gas masks. Grandpa Yosef's postcards
tumbled into our post boxes as if from a faraway world, filled with
coconuts and treasure chests and his increasingly worried enquiries
as to what was happening over here. On a series of grease-stained
postcards, he attempted to commiserate with our missile anxiet-

ies. Even years later, when the synagogue congregation reminisced about the Gulf War days, Grandpa Yosef would whisper apologetically, "And there I was in the Caribbean..." He was never sure how to utter this truth, especially in front of guests who had come to spend the Shabbat with relatives. They looked at him in astonishment—the Caribbean?

And indeed, he tried to come home early due to the Gulf War, so he could worry with us. He informed us of his intentions and was rebuked—he should stay there and complete his trip. We told him to stay where he was and agreed to follow his instructions regarding what to do with his needy neighbors during these stressful days, for as long as he was gone. The instructions were precise, like those for tending to plants. The postcards specified what to watch for with Mr. Bergman and what to do if Mr. Pepperman turned up again with old papers from the Municipality. The names of Mr. Cogen, Ella Pruchter and Itcha Dinitz reached us like the coconuts in the *Tarbut* encyclopedia, traveling the seas in their tough shells, finding islands to wash up on and take seed. Each postcard was signed by the palm tree himself, Grandpa Yosef, always adding a tail-end of questioning—Perhaps he should come home early after all? He did not imagine the extent to which his early return would have gotten us into trouble. Because in his empty apartment, in the meantime, a tenant had been installed. A tourist.

A short while after Grandpa Yosef's departure for the Caribbean, I received a phone call from Professor Shiloni, his academic advisor. He informed me that Dr. Hans Oderman, a research colleague from Frankfurt University, was arriving on the next El Al flight to make his way to the University of Haifa, where he would spend time on a research grant.

And the problem?

"Well, we agreed that he would be a guest in my home, but all of a sudden my in-laws from New York have turned up. They heard about Saddam Hussein's threats and came to show solidarity, the nuts, instead of inviting me to their place. And now this young man, Dr. Oderman, tells us he's decided not to cancel. He too believes that now is the time to support the people of Israel. So I thought that if Yosef's apartment was empty, perhaps, just until I find something better, we could put him there. Only temporarily, until we come up with something. Just until the first missile lands here, and then all the friends of Israel will be gone in a flash."

"He's German?"

Embarrassment in Professor Shiloni's voice. "Yes.... Is that a problem?"

"No, no, of course not."

The elderly residents in Grandpa Yosef's neighborhood were trying on gas masks, and I would be housing a German in 8-B Katznelson.

I didn't have to pick him up at the airport. Someone else brought Dr. Hans Oderman of Frankfurt to the faculty lounge at the University of Haifa, where we were introduced. Six-foot-three-sapphire-blue-eyes-golden-locks shook my hand.

"Nice to meet you."

A limp handshake.

I politely carried his luggage and led him to my car. A simple drive. No conversation. We drove down the Carmel hillside through Neveh Sha'anan and round the bends that hug the mountain. I looked at him as he sat erect and glanced at the cascading landscape. He stared at the lights, the intersections, the industrial zone in the valley below us. Our eyes met briefly. His were islands of steel. I looked at his hands resting firmly in his lap over the safety belt. Six-foot-three-inches of neatly divided parts. We passed by traffic lights, junctions, and the colorful commercial area. Heavy industry sprawled on both sides. Fences, chimneys, guard towers. The objects stood out against the landscape, distant deviations that looked as if they were running toward the road, waving, urgently introducing themselves. I drove among barbed wire and guard huts with a Nazi poster child sitting beside me.

The industrial stench provoked a look of discomfort on Hans Oderman's face. He wondered where he was being taken to. Breaking out of his polite silence, he tried a few lines. But the conversation did not progress much. Hans Oderman sensed the reservation in my voice and wondered whether everything was all right. He began to apologize even before I could reply. He was afraid something had been imposed upon me and asked again if everything was all right. He could always find a hotel room, he said.

"Everything is all right."

But then I took advantage of an uneventful stop light near Volkan Intersection:

"I just want you to know that, personally, I have a bit of a problem with Germans. That my parents' families were obliterated in the Holocaust. That I won't buy German appliances. That I fought with my wife because she bought a German washing machine. That I won't drive a Volkswagen because I haven't forgotten that in the war they employed Jews as slave laborers at vw factories. That all the cars you see on our roads, including lots of vws, are to my mind a desecration of the honor of those who died in slavery. That even so, I have nothing against you personally."

Silence. The light turned to green. We were saved.

As we approached Kiryat Haim, trees and residential buildings began to appear around the intersections. I said, "It will be a bit of a schlep for you to get to campus every day."

Hans Oderman nodded.

We turned onto the road leading to Grandpa Yosef's neighborhood. We passed by parks full of mothers and children, and I said, "If you need something, anything, just call us."

He nodded. He looked at a group of golden-haired children trying to take over a see-saw from a stubborn little girl, and possibly remembered his home. In Frankfurt.

I told him that if he called because he needed something and there was no one home, he could always call my parents or leave a message.

He nodded.

We reached the edge of the neighborhood, marked with a cypress tree at the beginning of Katznelson Street. I stopped there. When we got out of the car I had an idea. I took the suitcases out of the car and walked away, to make it clear that this time he was carrying them all by himself. I hoped the three suitcases would make him look slightly hunched, just a little ridiculous. So he wouldn't appear before the elderly neighbors in his full glory. Why shouldn't *they* carry things for once? I saw no curtains pulled back but I knew they were watching. Eyes at every window. They were experts at it.

Hans Oderman carried his suitcases with a straight back. He walked slowly, erect, elegant. Too elegant, to my mind. He walked down Katznelson just ahead of me, without slowing down, without even glancing at me to enquire which house to go to. I looked at his steps as he strolled down Katznelson as if it were his own street, and from beyond the windows, from behind the blinds—they saw.

They saw Hauptsturmführer Amon Goeth, commandant of Plaszow camp.

They saw Gruppenführer Jürgen Stroop, liquidator of the Warsaw ghetto.

They saw Hauptsturmführer Fritz Suhren, commandant of Ravensbrück camp.

They saw Hauptsturmführer Josef Kramer, commandant of Bergen-Belsen camp.

They saw Obersturmbannführer Rudolf Höss, commandant of Auschwitz.

They saw Hauptsturmführer Hans Bothmann, commandant of the Chelmno death camp, liquidator of the Lodz ghetto.

Marching in front of me. Come to stay. Soon he would put his suitcases down in Grandpa Yosef's home, place his ironed clothes on the shelves in the closet, hang his suits. Make himself a first cup of tea. Him. Here.

But when we reached Grandpa Yosef's apartment we found Effi standing in the doorway, eating a carrot. It turned out she had been settled in at Grandpa Yosef's for two days now, and was painting the apartment. She looked at Hans.

"Oy, the Nazi creature!" she said. She wore a long tank-top and nothing else.

"Effi, what are you doing here?"

"Look at you! You've really brought a Nazi," she continued, examining Hans, offering him a carrot and pulling him into the apartment as if introductions had been made and all that was left was to divvy up Grandpa Yosef's apartment.

"Effi, what are you doing here?" I chased after her, stepping over the plastic tarps she had spread throughout the apartment. "Effi, what are you doing here?"

She turned to me and promised, "Adolf and I will get along just fine."

And that's when I began to feel bad—he had suffered enough cruelty.

"His name is Hans," I said to Effi, but you could tell he had picked up on the 'Adolf.' With one awkward wave of the hand he played out the entire requisite sequence—expressed shock, indicated that he understood the humor and knew that it was imposed by his persona, voiced his objection nonetheless, then downplayed it—he would give in if he had to.

"He can stay here," Effi said generously, "we'll be two doctors in one apartment."

It seemed to me that she already had her eye on him. Him, Dr. Hans Oderman, six-foot-three-sapphire-blue-eyes-golden-locks. She led him to Feiga's room and opened the windows to banish death, if there was any still remaining. She helped him lay his clothes out on the empty shelves (in the midst of the *shiva* Feiga's clothes had been donated to an old age home; Grandpa Yosef's charity campaigns never rested for a moment). As her hands took control of Hans's property, with her face buried in the closet, she explained that her apartment lease was almost up, it was close to her work here, and the apartment needed to be fixed up a little before Grandpa Yosef got back.

A short while later we sat drinking tea at Grandpa Yosef's wooden table. We talked. We asked Dr. Hans Oderman about his plans, his intentions, his family, the city of Frankfurt. We generously bypassed questions about things that should not be discussed, but tried to extract an admission of guilt—a happy childhood, grandmas and grandpas, the whole thing. Hans Oderman pleaded not guilty: he never knew his grandparents on either side. Things were not that easy for him either. His father had been orphaned as a child.

And what did he think about Israel?

We demanded love. Not just for us but for the elderly people who lived here, who would see him as he left the apartment every day, walked through the yard and down Katznelson. We could not imagine how easy it would be for Hans to integrate into the life of the neighborhood. Within a few days we would find that he had already been enlisted to perform the requisite tasks, helping the old people choose a room to seal off, measuring sheets of plastic as they buttressed themselves inside in preparation for another battle. (They grit their teeth, their elderly fingers caught up in masking tape, their faces wearing determined expressions—they would survive.)

During the first days of his stay we plodded around behind him responsibly, checking up—Effi in her capacity as roommate, and myself as liaison with Professor Shiloni. I felt obliged to report to him should anything occur, some fatal mistake or a case for the authorities to handle. We did not need to report his lingering visits at Sammy's vegetable shop. Nor the cups of tea at Mrs. Rudin's. We gradually eased up our supervision. We came to check up, to see how the neighborhood was getting along with Dr. Hans Oderman, and found him nicely assimilated. Sipping tea with Mrs. Rudin. Eating Mrs. Tsanz's *kugel*. Chatting with Sammy about the crisis in German soccer, complaining about the price of tomatoes. He was doing well. He even had an encounter with Hirsch. Later, he asked for explanations. What was he yelling? Why did he yell? And finally we had an opportunity to explain this neighborhood, these people, the hidden significance of what occurred here.

We carefully monitored his opinions and actions. On his free days, we learned, he liked to go to Jerusalem, to Lake Kinneret, or to the Galilee. He also went to Masada, the Yad Vashem Holocaust museum, and the Ghetto Fighters' Kibbutz. Our courteous offers were met with dismissal: Hans Oderman preferred to take the bus, so he could meet people. He came back from his travels full of impressions. He connected easily with people and learned to understand the different pieces of Israeli existence. He sat with us trying to fill in the gaps in his knowledge. Were Jews of Bulgarian origin considered Sephardic? What was the difference between a cooperative moshav and a regular moshav? Where exactly had the Cochin Jews come from?

He also found the beach, and he took slow walks there with

his lustrous Atlas-like body, regally scanning the seashell-clutching women who stared at him and engaged him in conversation. He made no effort to avoid the streets of Haifa, especially the Carmel, amazed at the mottled mass of Eastern, Western, Southern and Northern notes. Women and young girls strolled up and down the streets of the Carmel—a miracle ignoring its own importance, coming and going from the houses, the stores, the cafés.

It sometimes seemed that an impenetrable contemplation flickered in his mind, something that might have taken on the shape of a thought—You mean these were the kinds of people they wanted to annihilate in the gas chambers? But the thought did not ripen. It remained in its crude form, hovering, bothering every other thought like a troublesome grain.

People asked us what he was doing at the university.

"Hans is completing a historical study on the subject of orphanhood," I replied.

Meaning?

"Meaning, how they treated orphans in different cultures and through the prism of history."

("Very useful," Effi pointed out.)

They wanted to know if he himself was an orphan.

I answered, "No."

Anat said, "He looks a bit like an orphan." (Finding even in Dr. Hans Oderman, six-foot-three-sapphire-blue-eyes-golden-locks, the orphan in need of help. Anat.)

We slowly came to understand his personality. Hans Oderman from Germany was an expert at awkwardness. Like a mouse trained to find cheese, praised every time he makes it through a maze, so was Hans, finding in every situation the way to be embarrassed, to hesitate, to grope his way out with cautious words. Six-foot-three-sapphire-blue-eyes-golden-locks was only a camouflage.

Towards the end of January the war came true. Missiles started falling. Worried, we scurried around on Hans's behalf, trying to get him a gas mask. He didn't want one. It wasn't necessary, he believed. And in general, he had a tough time with masks and found it difficult to breathe with them because of respiratory problems. In between the air-raid sirens he cared for the sealed rooms, replacing plastic tarps and fixing strips of tape that had fallen away here and there.

Effi's liked to look me over and say, "You see, there are good Germans."

I never said there weren't. There were back then too. Dad told me about German soldiers who cried when they saw a pile of dead children in the Bochnia ghetto. Who said there weren't any good Germans? But within the current admixture of euphemisms—New Germany, the New Germans, Democratic Germany—hides the thing that allowed the criminals to keep on living, the thing that granted sweeping clemencies, gave them back their status, let them raise sweet grandchildren—Hans and Peter and Jorgen, who sometimes came to plant trees here in the Land of Israel. I despise those unwilling to confess to their crimes, the banks that traded in gold teeth, the factories that killed prisoners through slave labor, anyone who allowed these institutions to continue being part of the nation, to function under the patronage of national denial. I despise the hands raised in the Bundestag on May 8th 1960—only fifteen years after the war had ended—and voted to allow the expiration of the statute of limitation for minor crimes such as manslaughter, wrongful injury resulting in death, and denial of freedom resulting in death. I despise those hands, a democratic majority. But who ever said there weren't any good Germans?

We invited Hans over to our place on weekends. As we sat around waiting for air-raid sirens, we grew more friendly. We slowly roamed through different conversation topics. First, orphanhood. What exactly was he researching? Then, the war. Germany. The Holocaust.

Hans Oderman took part in the conversations reluctantly. His scripted role was that of the culprit, and he took it upon himself without protest. We set him free in the swampy reeds of our intentions, a jet-black wolf for us to target and hit. But Hans Oderman sat frozen like a frightened duck. His function was to stand before us, accused. But we could not draw the lines that would differentiate us from him.

"What did your father do during the war?"

"My father? He was only born during the war."

"And his father?"

"He was a soldier, killed on the Russian front near Leningrad."

"And your mother's family?"

"They were soldiers. One was a pilot. And there were two dissidents, one was imprisoned in Dachau for five years."

But there was an uncle who belonged to the SS, he remembered, sheathing himself with the blanket of culpability after all.

Even without words (after all, many of the worst Nazis found these sorts of biographical responses for themselves), there was in him a sort of innocence. Guilt did not stick to him. A hidden line of defense came together from his looks, his embarrassment, his explanations. He was exonerated by the words we sensed hiding within his thoughts. He did not say everything, and what he left out was not damning—on the contrary, it might even have connected us to him. A riddle.

We introduced Hans to the family so he could wriggle under the light of their looks for a while. If he survived that, we would know he was innocent.

The family was enchanted by Hans's politeness. Grandpa Lolek interrogated him and observed, "I killed a lot like him."

The days went by and the Gulf War began to die out. Everyone was used to Dr. Hans Oderman, no longer excited by the appearance of this man who seemed to have been drawn from a Nazi leader's dream. And then suddenly, in the midst of the routine days, without warning, Grandpa Yosef was back. He had been struck by a mysterious virus, courtesy of the Caribbean humidity, which had graced his pale yellow cheeks with a healthy flush and quickened his breath. He returned with a newly ardent and life-loving temperament and seemed agitated by the slow pace of routine events. He did not object to Hans Oderman's presence in the empty apartment, which was now full of dead people with whom Grandpa Yosef had a thing or two to sort out privately. He warmly hosted him in his home. In fact, he deepened the intensity of the German doctor's residence, cooking him

179

food and washing his clothes, willfully and affectionately melting away Hans Oderman's intentions to move a little closer to campus—there wasn't even a bus route in this sleepy neighborhood.

In a sort of destruction of the sanctity of grief, in this house without Feiga and without Moshe, Grandpa Yosef and Hans organized a cooperative life for themselves. They cooked, cleaned and studied. They seemed thankful for each other's company. Grandpa Yosef enjoyed the refreshing proximity of scholarliness. After the heat of the Caribbean days, he happily breathed in the cool air of science. Hans was charmed by his host, easily won over by Grandpa Yosef's personality. He was especially happy to speak fluent German in the Holy Land. And he made the mistake of asking where Grandpa Yosef had acquired such fine German.

"I was in your land," Grandpa Yosef clarified. As if he had spent time in Germany to inspect some furniture.

They sat often at Grandpa Yosef's wooden table, talking about the problem Hans was working on at the university. Grandpa Yosef understood little, and was sorry that no miracle occurred, such as a brilliant idea that would come to him in a flash after one hearing. The Caribbean force still pulsed in him, and slow business irritated him.

Every evening, Hans Oderman came home from his studies and Grandpa Yosef from his do-gooding. They unloaded their daily baggage, two hunters laying their loot on the table. They talked, debated, argued. Our visits were not rejected, but were received somewhat indifferently. As if for our sake Grandpa Yosef was keeping up a demeanor appropriate for a man in mourning. We would come and find them walking around Katznelson together, in the parks, even the woods. They talked. Like two intellectual giants projecting their charms upon each other. They would stop for a moment to exchange an opinion and glance at one another. Two magicians, mutually awed, but each suspicious of the other's tricks, wondering what was the secret of the other's magic.

When Hans Oderman went back to Germany, the vivid impression he had made continued to accompany us in conversations, in thoughts, in meetings, until it became doubtful whether his physical presence could have added anything more. We felt as if he were with us. Phone calls also fostered the relationship. After one such conversation, we thought he had said his research was not done and that he would have to come back soon. We nibbled out of the air a feeling that such a promise had been made, and we nurtured it. (Effi tried to tempt him: "Come, come back. We have lots of wars here. Every decade or so there's a good orphan season.") We perceived Hans Oderman's appearance in our lives as having a greater function than what had been revealed thus far, and could not accept that his return to Germany had put an end to it all. With uncommon generosity, we agreed to wait for months, even years, until the true role of Hans Oderman would be revealed. Only Grandpa Yosef turned out to be a realist. He viewed the separation straightforwardly: Hans had left. But a sadness befell him. He cut down on his bike rides and even considered a moped or a car. With an increased sense of charity he fell on the patients he had neglected for weeks in favor of the Caribbean, and still we did not understand—what had he found in the islands?

But we did not ask. The Caribbean adventure was over. That was it, and it was best forgotten. Why would we go searching for something that would supposedly explain a connection between the mourning in Kiryat Haim and the coconut trees of Tobago? We offered him a trip to Jerusalem, he hadn't been to the holy city for years. We even suggested, somewhat anxiously, the reckless city of Eilat. Maybe there, in the Caribbean sphere, he would shake off the burning in his blood. But Grandpa Yosef rejected our offers and quickly accustomed himself to a life with new troubles. There were many needy people and no time to rest. He forged relationships with elderly people outside the neighborhood, and reconnected with an old love, the community of Belz Chassidim, where he found some good to do. He volunteered in the northern neighborhoods, where new immigrants began to look forward to his frequent visits. He was quick to commit to any affair, rushing to lend a shoulder.

It was clear that new powers had taken control of Grandpa Yosef. This was evidenced by the fact that one day, while he was being driven by a colleague to visit a mutual acquaintance who was sick, a policeman popped up and accused the driver of disobeying a stop sign. Grandpa Yosef was overtaken by a rebellious spirit.

Disobeying?

Failure to come to a complete stop with all four wheels behind the line?

The wheels, after all, are all on one axis. If one stops, they all stop. And Grandpa Yosef was prepared to testify that the front wheel had stopped. And if *it* had stopped, it stood to reason that its siblings had too.

The policemen, at first, was extremely patient, responding calmly to his elderly interlocutor. But Grandpa Yosef entered into Talmudic debates and arguments, later telling us how he struck down the policeman's claims one after the other until victory. The policeman grew angry and began to make threats. Grandpa Yosef fumed as well. Things were fast approaching the most dreaded outcome. Grandpa Yosef was not hauled off to jail, but he came close. He gave the policeman quite an argument, and earned a ticket to show for it.

He dug through his pockets and pulled out the official confirmation for us, then looked at the report covered in Hebrew letters. "*Nu*, at least it's one of our own policemen." And he breathed a breath of calmness, inhaling the flavor of a Hebrew ticket, in Hebrew characters, from "one of our own" policemen. Even the argument seemed to take on a renewed form in his thoughts—softer, entirely conducted in the language of Eliezer Ben-Yehuda, inventor of the modern Hebrew language.

We hoped the pale light and the tart aromas of cooking from the neighborhood windows would quiet his blood. But in the Turkish market Grandpa Yosef found curry powder, and from Sammy of the vegetables he demanded mango, fresh coconut and ginger. He replaced his tea with strong coffee. Then he began researching names—Arabica, Robusta, Segafredo, Jamaican Blue Mountain.

At times it seemed as if the new, temporary persona would soon settle down and put forth roots. Grandpa Yosef scurried around even when he had no reason to. He could not find tranquility in his armchair, and changed outfits a few times a day. At some point, a great secret almost escaped him: since his return, the Gemara had struck him as too slow, too lingering. How long could one debate a *seah* of carobs? And so instead of studying Gemara pages, he sometimes took off to the beach—the actual beach. Red sunsets. Beautiful young women, excuse-me-sir-what-time-is-it? And an oceanfront café where you could buy cocoa and fruit juices. The Caribbeanism within him radiated to the outside, pulling out his personality like a rabbit from a hat. But we gradually sensed that a great weight had sat itself down in Grandpa Yosef's garden, clarifying: things will be tough. There was no Feiga, no Moshe, no one to make an effort for.

Grandpa Lolek continued to visit. When the Vauxhall showed up the yard looked briefly as it had in days past. Hope glistened; perhaps Moshe's quick figure would emerge from the distance to wash off the nettlesome dust. Grandpa Lolek sat down for a cup of tea, his face respectable, and inspected the new reality. He missed Moshe and, more than Moshe, he missed the wondrous miracle that could flourish thanks to him. (There was something disrespectful about the way he missed him, like a magician who had lost his rabbit.) We were amazed to learn that it was he who had bought a triple burial plot for Grandpa Yosef and his two loves. He had gritted his teeth and financed the erection of two marble tombstones. For now, Grandpa Yosef had saved him a third. No need. Grandpa Lolek had no qualms about taking pride in this act of charitableness, recounting in great detail how he had acquired the triple plot against all odds, outdoing competitors. As if he had completed a winning row of three in a game of tic-tac-toe.

"They said, take two, this here and this another separate, they said is expensive here, no possible three because of wall. They said here is good plot, no possible three, one in middle is already taken. Not possible to cancel. Very expensive. Here in middle is already taken, there is others who want three together. That's it. Must give up. Then suddenly, yes! On the side, in shade. A good plot! They already jumped on it, to take it. From between teeth I took it away, bam! There is nothing which that money cannot do."

And yet it was with him, of all people, one fine day, that the incident occurred.

We were drinking tea (strong "Eva" coffee for Grandpa Yosef), and as on every day, Grandpa Lolek waved his tea bag, hanging it from the edge of a cake-fork by its string. *Selektion.* When he held the bag up close to Grandpa Yosef's face, teasing him in his customary way, Grandpa Yosef suddenly snatched the bag away. He held it in his hand and contemplated whether to throw it in Grandpa Lolek's face or do something else. But in the end he just crushed it in his fist. Dark brown rivets of tea trickled from his hand to the table as Grandpa Yosef squeezed and squeezed.

All his life Grandpa Yosef had held back, exercising restraint for the sake of the little miracle that was Moshe. We could actually sense the word, RESTRAINT, appearing on his face, and further inside. But now it all fell apart. There was no Moshe. No Feiga. No one to make an effort for. With the tea bag in his hand, Grandpa Yosef hurried to the kitchen, where he traded his anger for some trivial business and then returned to us slightly calmer.

Grandpa Lolek, in a rare outburst of sensitivity to what was occurring, quickly found a reason to leave.

Grandpa Yosef was left alone, not only on that day. There began a period of isolationism. He had finally found the strength to declare himself a mourner with rights. He fenced himself off and avoided the family. He made us feel punished, unworthy. We tried. We came up to the foot of the cliff of righteousness, and there we broke down, wretched, spilling over with shortcomings.

Grandpa Yosef taught us a chapter in remorse. He did not have to use many looks or words, he trusted that we would sense the nuanced emotions, the hidden meanings of his gestures of withdrawal. But with Grandpa Lolek it was simple and determined. As if to pay him back for many seconds, many hours, for the six million whom Grandpa Lolek had continuously humiliated without anyone doing anything about it. Instead of the whole six million, *they* usually focused their grief on one or two people, becoming their voice.

Grandpa Lolek's response was surprising. It would seem that he could have avoided Grandpa Yosef's presence—what was bringing them together? But instead he repeatedly asked for Grandpa Yosef's forgiveness, insistently, innocently, without complaint. He admitted that he had behaved badly. And he was prepared to apologize, to atone. We could see that he cared. Delegations were sent. Grandpa Yosef welcomed the guests with his usual humbleness, taking his doughy cakes out of the oven, serving herring and home-made pickles. But despite the normal hospitality, in the matter of Grandpa Lolek he would not budge. His face hardening, his temples sprouted veins as he announced that he was unwilling to make up. "May he go to hell and go in peace," he blessed the banished relative.

We kept trying. Our self-declared role as mediators allowed us to feel objective, outside the fan of Grandpa Yosef's anger. We were merely the organizers of a transaction, not a party to the affair. A number of times the reconciliation was about to come to fruition. The two were already positioned on either side of the bridge, the exchange ceremony about to begin, when suddenly Grandpa Yosef would brush off the agreement—he would never forgive, never! We tried to persuade him. Tried to demand explanations. Grandpa Yosef extricated himself from us. Trembling. He wagged his finger, mumbled, grumbled, rubbed one fist against the other. His temples lit up in rage. Words tried to escape. Commotions. Little crackles in the pipe works. Sweat glistening on his forehead.

We were amazed. This was not the Grandpa Yosef we knew. This was not the Grandpa Yosef he himself knew from looking in the mirror. And so we summoned time to come and heal. We invited the months to pass by, to place cold compresses on his face. We sensed that Grandpa Yosef did not wish to alienate the Caribbean-ism in which he was slowly coming to know himself, his condition, his widowerhood. He fumbled alongside a dark wall, finding only a grieving father and no one to make the effort for. No one at all. He was preparing for a great battle, a desert front: life ahead without Feiga, without Moshe. With a burning silence he shed colorful layers, rainbow-colored feathers, war paint. He shrunk down to the right size, a life of austerity around the darkness of routine and family events. Only towards Grandpa Lolek did his resentment maintain its tropical nature, devouring our attempts to alleviate, to lighten, to conciliate.

Grandpa Lolek stopped relying on us and tried a few of his own reconciliation methods. He failed. He tried again, and failed again. Then he made up his mind that he had no choice. As an emergency ploy, like a pilot abandoning his plane, he produced his final attempt:

a cancerous tumor in his head. He may have six months left to live. In the meantime, tests were to be run.

After Grandpa Lolek lost consciousness on the steps outside his house and was rushed to the hospital, the harsh prognosis was pronounced: the growth was cancerous, his chances slim. Later, a more moderate possibility emerged. There might even be full recovery. We sat there, Grandpa Yosef and I, on a little bench in Rambam Hospital, waiting for a doctor, for solid information. Anxiety took hold of Grandpa Yosef's face, somehow looking more natural than the Caribbean vigor.

Effi arrived, alarmed. "What happened? He lost consciousness? On the front steps?'

She pushed open closed doors and talked with doctors. Grandpa Lolek suddenly became the most urgent case there, although he himself was by then lying calmly on a clean bed, his blue eyes shut, tranquility in his bones. After an hour Effi calmed down too. She sat down tiredly on the bench with us and became a worried relative once again. No more being a doctor.

Grandpa Yosef was curious, still clinging to her in her role as a doctor. "What does it mean that he passed out like that?"

"Lots of things. It could be lots of things."

"But to pass out? All of a sudden, in the middle of the day?"

"That was so he wouldn't have to make the call to the hospital, so someone else would pay for the call, that's why," Effi said, completely restored.

"My Feiga never passed out. It was hard for her, but she always kept her eyes open." Already making comparisons between the new patient and his patient. (Feiga won. Her refreshing morbidity was inimitable.)

We organized shifts when Grandpa Lolek woke up and wanted to know what the fuss was about, when he could leave, and whether the Sick Fund would cover his expenses. The doctors told him he had suffered "a kind of stroke." There seemed to be something pressing on his brain, a tumor—no, not cancerous, it could be lots of things. They reassured him that the Sick Fund would likely cover all the treatments. For now they would leave him under observation. They needed to do some X-rays. And a CT. They left me with him while the family went to get some sleep and organize things.

We waited for the CT. Grandpa Lolek, from one moment to the next, grew stronger. He demanded food, cigarettes. He tried to get out of bed, embarrassed—how could a hero of Anders' Army be lying on a stretcher bed in a hospital? By the time they were ready for the CT, he had worn me out with his plethora of demands, opinions, schemes (three escape attempts in four hours, one grab for a meal in the closed kitchen). Grandpa Lolek flew into a rage when they would not let me in the CT room. I whispered to the nurse, "I'll just go in with him and come straight out." We went in. Grandpa Lolek was very alert, waving a stick he had gotten hold of the devil knows where. He held it close to him, giving the impression that the stick was an old friend and no one could possibly take away this old man's support. He also used the stick to rap on the side of the CT machine and wink at me inexplicably, a wink I suspected was related to the tumor in his brain. He rapped impatiently on the machine, again and again, as the nurses grew angry. Finally I saw it. A little label on the side of the machine read, "Donated by the Society for the War on Cancer." Grandpa Lolek was clarifying that for this machine, he had not given a penny. I went out and sat on the bench while inside the CT machine scanned Grandpa Lolek for free.

After half an hour a commotion broke out in the room. The closed space into which Grandpa Lolek had been slid like a cake in an oven had a negative affect on the old warrior. He lost consciousness. The doctors, alarmed, rushed him to the treatment room. For long hours, it turned out, Grandpa Lolek fought for his life. A kind of sudden collapse. Not something the CT was supposed to cause, it was a completely routine test. But still, tubes were inserted into his nose and body while the doctors tried to save him. In the morning his condition was stable but he lay in bed unconscious. The family came. Even Atalia and Grandpa Hainek. They were amazed to hear about the overnight crisis. Why hadn't I called anyone? How could there be such a sudden deterioration?

Everyone thought of Uncle Pessl. Uncle Pessl had been a robust man whose eighty-five years were apparent only in his Austro-

Hungarian opinions. We had always admired him, despite his dim-wittedness, because he was a partisan and had strangled five Nazis to death with his bare hands, and even when anti-Semitic peasants had turned him in he had gone on to survive the camps and even the death march from Gross-Rosen. Since then, he always walked upright, elegantly. Always with few words and a bow tie. Last Sukkot he was walking through the shopping center and fell down. People quickly helped him up; he only had a slight bruise on his knee. But since then, Uncle Pessl had not recovered. Now he was in a nursing home and wanted to die.

One after the other we went into Grandpa Lolek's room and examined the silent figure lying quietly in bed. We were filled with thoughts and worries. Anat came and sent me home. In the evening we changed shifts. When my shift began, I was amazed to find Grandpa Yosef sitting at the bedside of excommunicated Grandpa Lolek as if there was no more natural a feature than him in the hospital landscape.

We sat on either side of the bed in a small room of which Grandpa Lolek was the sole inhabitant. To the west was a pleasant window, where Grandpa Yosef stood and attempted the afternoon *mincha* prayer. His short figure covered half the window. A Caribbean sun set over the ocean, winking with its final strength, trying to stir up Grandpa Yosef's new personality. Its efforts were in vain. He was here, a praying Jew, come to care for a needy patient, to do good, to give support in times of trouble.

When he finished praying we talked about this and that. Our eyes avoided Grandpa Lolek's figure, as it was still unclear whether the ban had been lifted, the excommunication called off. We talked about Yariv, about Anat, about the weather. We shared our astonishment at winter's failure to arrive. It was almost November, the days were getting cool, the nights still cooler, but it had yet to rain. Everyone knew the rain would come, but for now there was a drought. Between our sentences lay Grandpa Lolek. My presence seemed natural. And Grandpa Yosef also blended into the landscape of unsurprising elements—the curtain, the water pitcher, the little sink. Between us, slightly more out of place, lay Grandpa Lolek.

His eyes were closed, but his right one was open a slit, just to make sure the world remembered that he always said, "People have to die of something." He would not close his eyes until the world admitted that he did, indeed, say that. He had lived with that one opinion and would die with it. In fact, we should bury him with that victorious belief, like a Pharaoh entombed with his jewels so they can serve him on his eternal journey. We could leave his suits outside the grave, as well as his decorations, his certificates, the promissory notes and the papers for the land near Gedera—a good piece of land, one day its value will increase—but his opinions would be placed beside his body.

Grandpa Yosef broke down first and acknowledged Grandpa Lolek's presence. He pointed to the silent man and tried to rationalize him. "*Nu*, after all, one cannot forget. Jews in the war went like lambs to the slaughter, exterminated in the gas chambers, and this man here fought heroically. I heard stories about him from people who were there. A true lionheart. And me, with all my wanderings, all the pain and suffering, perhaps it would have been better if I had been like him."

Fresh envy in Grandpa Yosef's eyes. His look roamed worriedly over the still body, which somehow did not appear helpless. Grandpa Lolek was silent on his bed, stiff and still, like a Viking set adrift by his friends for one last voyage. The glory still enveloped him. It was hard to pity a body so taut—it seemed at any moment this Viking might sit up and smoke a cigarette. But for now he was afloat on the current, summing up his life with satisfaction, eyes shut. If not for the tiny slit in his right eye, which turned to a tremor like a wink, his image would have been perfect. The slight wink tarnished the glory. Grandpa Lolek was alive and planned to return.

Grandpa Yosef prepared for his defense. "Believe me, in the camps and the ghettos I also saw heroism." His voice strengthened. "Individuals sacrificed themselves. Lone soldiers, without uniforms or orders. At the moment of truth they flung themselves into death. And who will tell their stories?"

His question lingers in the air.

Who will tell their stories?

Grandpa Yosef stands up. He thinks he saw some "Swiss coffee" in the vending machine at the end of the hallway. That was what the label said. He has no idea what it means. Would I like a cup too? No.

Grandpa Yosef goes off to examine the mystery of the vending machine label. By my side Grandpa Lolek lies tall and still, ready for inspection.

Who will tell their stories?

Grandpa Yosef managed to traverse our entire childhood without giving away too much. His attempts at concealment were successful. On the train, on the trips to Tel Aviv, the spring poured forth once a year. No more. Strategically, Grandpa Yosef had won. And now he cautions—who will tell their stories? As if now of all times, from within his victory, he is considering the possibility of taking a loss. Perhaps he wishes to offer himself up: He will tell, I will listen. We will sit on either side of Grandpa Lolek and whatever manages to cross over his bed will be mine. But I have my own reservations. It has been fifty years. Whatever has been told, has been told. I once pursued these stories. I poisoned Feiga with fake pills for them, and knelt before any old man willing to talk. Now we have grown up. We are the second-and-a-half generation to the Shoah, living our lives, and we have no need to adhere to the past anymore. Life flows vigorously enough. I still visit Attorney Perl and talk with him. With him the Shoah lives on, a climbing plant that never ceases to sprout new branches. But the conversations with him are the *malkosh*—the last rain of the season. The final rains of a great winter that has come and gone.

When we went to Poland with Dad to see his stories made real (the imaginary pictures solidified, we could even take photographs), we discovered that we did not need the Holocaust stories as much as we wanted the stories of his childhood—the happy one, the forgotten one, in Bochnia before the war. Dad showed us places, houses, abandoned gaps of time. He gestured with his hands—this happened here, that happened there.

The house he was born in.

The soccer field across the street.

The rooftop where he chased pigeons and almost fell off.

The chestnut trees whose fruit he used to gather with his friend Penek Lamensdorf (1930–1942), intending—based on a personal scientific hypothesis—to manufacture sophisticated glue.

There was a certain discord between our childhood stories and the reality we found. Things turned out to be the opposite of what they had seemed. Our memories stood gravely in attendance, prepared to defend the childhood stories in this complicated suit—after all, this conspiratorial reality was scandalous. But as we walked behind Dad through the ghetto, reality went through the stories with a fine-tooth comb, dismantling everything. Dad left nothing whole.

"Here, look," he pointed to a little path between pretty houses, trees and greenery. There, in front of our eyes, was the-lane-Dad-zig-zagged-through.

Since we were little kids, every year, Dad had told us about the day he and a friend had tried to hide their stamp collection. The Germans called out to them to stop. They ran away down the alley. Dad's father had instructed him to always run in zigzags when shots were being fired. (I think of Yariv. What will I teach him?) His friend ran in a straight line and was killed. It was a simple story for Dad. We became Old Enough for this story fairly early. Perhaps from his point of view it was a trivial tale—only one child was killed. But it was imprinted in our memories, and its visual traits gave us many versions of Dad running, dodging the bullets, the zigzag overcoming everything. We did not hesitate to dramatize the different versions in dusty lanes on dry, colorless, pitiful gravel. When we were older we learned to add shades of color we came to know in the alleys of Gaza, in Khan-Younis.

We gazed in wonder. Here, in front of us, was the zigzag lane. It was raining, everything was glimmering, giving off a fresh smell. And the ghetto. The ghetto where people had to line up on the sidewalks to die. A violent and pale ghetto, surrounded by walls, crowded, morbid. But we walked down narrow streets and stood in front of the house at 7 Leonarda Street, the mythological house from the stories. We looked at a little yard where a swing hung from a tree, and there were bushes, and flowers. At this moment it became clear that of everything in this journey to Poland, we would remain with only one accurate link between the childhood stories and the Polish reality: The famous window from which a cat willingly leapt sixty years ago after Dad gave it a bottle of ammonia to sniff. A thousand forms of this window had been imagined since Dad told the story, a thousand cats leaping, a thousand versions of its hesitant return home a few days later.

Dad pointed to the window. The thousand windows of our imagination murmured satisfactorily, pleased with the father who begat them.

In the meantime a small door had opened at 7 Leonarda. Mr. Petrovich, the resident, came out to see us. He was the son of the man who had owned the house at the time when its owners were thrown out so that Jews could be housed in it. The father, an educated Polish Christian, was sent to Auschwitz, one of the first from Bochnia. The son was friendly. He recalled how his father used to send him to the confiscated house to see how it was getting along. He even found an old document listing the Jewish tenants during the ghetto period. Someone had written everything down in neat handwriting, every single detail, seemingly assigning the utmost importance to the lives of these people, most of whom would soon be murdered in the gas chambers at Belzec.

Dad read the list and filled up with new memories. The Marsend family. Father, mother, little Etinka.

Who was little Etinka? Why didn't you ever tell us about her? Where is Attorney Perl on the list? Didn't he live with you at 7 Leonarda?

Dad struggled to explain, to bring order. The Perls were taken in the first *Aktion*. This was a list from the time between the first and second *Aktionen*. The Marsends came after the first *Aktion*. They were taken in the third *Aktion*.

And who is little Etinka?

Before I can finish the thought, Grandpa Yosef comes back carrying two cups of "Swiss coffee." One for me. Didn't I ask for one? He thought I did. Really? Won't I drink it? It's a pity to waste it.

Grandpa Lolek's eye gives its quick wink. The scent of wasted money disturbs his rest.

I take the coffee and sip unwillingly. It has no sugar—a double punishment.

Grandpa Yosef makes himself comfortable, surrendering to the flavor of the coffee. He looks up at me and says, "When it comes down to it, the ghetto was not completely bad." As if finishing up a story, or starting one, or interfering in Dad's. Unclear.

He sips from his cup. One hand rests on the edge of Grandpa Lolek's bed.

"Up until they closed us off in the ghetto, the lives of Jewish people were not too bad. Everyone suffered, *goyim* and Jews. The beginnings of the ghetto did not foreshadow what was about to happen to the Jewry of Bochnia, to all Jewry. The ghetto commandant, Müller, was not an evil villain. Perhaps if he had been as abusive as some other SS officers, we might have been more on our guard, might have dared to find any way possible to escape. Even the Gestapo chief, an older German by the name of Schomburg, did not help us divine the true circumstances faced by Bochnia Jewry. He did not treat us harshly, and in return for bribes he was willing to issue authorizations, certificates, whatever was needed. We were closed off in the ghetto, waiting for the gloom to lift, not imagining what lay ahead. It was crowded, there was little food, there were worries. But Bochnia was known throughout the region as a good place to live. Jews flocked there to become a part of the imprisoned community. The Germans did not stop them. They sat in their offices and rubbed their hands together gleefully. This was their plan, after all. First, to gather the Jews from the small villages and farms into the towns. Then, to concentrate the town Jews in the district centers, and finally, to lead them all into the large cities. A diligent and thorough cleansing plan. They implemented it with force, with decrees, with train cars. And at the same time, Jews flowed in of their own free will. Bochnia was filled with them. And what can I say? Until the first *Aktion*, life was bustling. Within the crowdedness and the density, people grew closer—some through love, some through strife, some through communal study, some through screaming to high heavens. It was hard, but life burst through. There was a little field on the outskirts of the ghetto in a deforested piece of land, where I would meet Feiga every day. We would sit and talk of important matters like spring, the prophets, silly Marushka. But the ghetto children also liked the field, those rascals, your father too, and when we wanted to be alone we had to go up to an isolated wooden hut on a hilltop on Leonarda Street. In the middle of the little ghetto was this magnificent hilltop. Around it were crowded houses and noisy masses, but on the hilltop—not a thing. Our own Noah's Ark. You could sense the gathering, more and more Jews streaming into the ghetto from the villages of the Bochnia district. Tiny ghettos were shut down and their Jews were sent to us. Slowly and diligently the Germans labored to convene all the rural Jews in our ghetto. The crowdedness became worse and worse, you wouldn't believe how the skirmishes and the screaming outweighed the love and friendship. How people became less happy with the imposed communality, and the Jewish heart with its righteousness and patience could no longer suffice. Something had to break—even Noah's Ark had room only for couples.

"But I had Feiga, and what else did I need in the world?

"One day, all of a sudden, no Feiga. Thunder on a bright day. Her family disappeared, and the rumor was that they had secretly escaped. They were heading to Hungary, which was often the destination at that time for those who had the means or the connections."

"Your rabbi did that too, the Admor of Belz," I charge. "But his disciples stayed behind for the *Aktionen*."

"*Nu, nu*," Grandpa Yosef protests.

Grandpa Lolek's winking eye stirs a little; it seems his opinion of the religious in general has been voiced.

"What will be the end of this?" Grandpa Yosef sighs, straightening the blanket on Grandpa Lolek, short, elderly fingers expertly tucking the blanket beneath his body.

I begin to be frightened that he might stop talking. I suddenly realize that Grandpa Yosef is sitting here about to tell me his story. The entire story. Childhood bustles within me excitedly, gratefully. I must not disturb him, he must not stop talking. Grandpa Yosef comes through.

"I could not understand how Feiga had left without saying a word," he says, returning to the point at which he left off. And he quickly rejects my unvoiced question. "No, I was not hurt. At first perhaps, there was a grain of anger, but even before the grain sprouted, my heart was flooded with joy: my love was in a safe place, a great worry had been lifted.

"But after a few days the rumors began. They said her family had been betrayed by its guides, they had been captured. They said some were dead, some taken away. Feiga had been taken north, for some reason. The Germans were lacking a beautiful Jewish woman in northern Poland, so instead of killing Feiga they fished her out of the south and handed her over to the north, to balance out their world. *Nu.*"

"How did the rumors start?"

"They just did. In the ghetto, rumors had the healthiest of legs. All day long they hurried around from here to there, never tiring. They ran around and built up strength, not like us humans. *Nu.* And there were people who still traveled around in all sorts of ways among the ghettoes, bearing news and rumors. They knew what was going on. Everyone knew. The only thing they didn't know was that only thirty days away, death was waiting for us all. Feiga disappeared in July, and in August they suddenly declared a roll-call. They ordered us to line up in the military camp courtyard adjacent to the ghetto.

"It was the *Aktion*, which meant a transport of Jews to the death camps. We knew nothing of the liquidation. We were told of a campaign for resettlement in the East, where they would turn Jewish people into productive citizens. We were even ordered to pack bags for the journey. The deceit worked beautifully. We gathered obediently in the empty camp, where they would separate people intended for the transport from those permitted to stay. Anyone who had a permit to stay in the ghetto felt safe, and the others, without knowing a thing, sensed death. People hid out, dug themselves into attics, hollows, anywhere they could. The Germans went from door to door, aided by Polish policemen and local assistants. Whoever was caught was shot on the spot. Women, elderly people, children. The whole ghetto filled with the sounds of screaming and shooting. Bodies rolled down the streets.

The *Aktion* continued for three days. To the credit of this *Aktion* one could say that it was easy compared to the two *Aktionen* that would come later in ghetto Bochnia, until the liquidation. I myself saw no more than the first *Aktion*. I was destined for a transport.

"I stood there indifferently, facing death in the gas chambers but pondering the East, to which we had been promised we were being taken. The rumors about Feiga had spoken of a northern camp, but how could the rumor-mongers know where she had been taken? Why not to the East? Had the Germans who had captured her bothered to show them their orders? People gossip, they want to be considered knowledgeable, and so they embellish. I stood in the large courtyard, around me much grief and chaos, commotions erupting once in a while when people were separated from their families or holders of legal permits were suddenly placed in the transport group, their protests to no avail. In my family too there were many tears and much confusion. My mother fainted and I ran to ask for some water for her, but nothing. Two Jewish policemen returned me by force to the row, humiliated me. Nearby a commotion broke out and someone was shot. I was overtaken by a sense of apathy. I thought about Feiga. Will we meet in the East? Might we have a marriage ceremony there? Set up a home for ourselves?

"Suddenly, my name was called out. I was told to go with a small group being sent to the labor camp at Rakowice airfield. I was simply pulled out of the transport waiting to die in the gas chambers of Belzec, and sent off to live a good long life. Why me? Who was the angel who had put my name on that list? I do not know. Perhaps it was Yanek, your father's uncle, who was in the Judenrat and had very helpful connections. They were not much help for him, though. In that very same transport he himself was sent away with his family. To the gas chambers. And the same for my mother and father and sister and two brothers. Also my uncles, friends. Everyone. Only me, to Rakowice..."

Grandpa Yosef stops talking. Rakowice pads through the room. An unfamiliar name, its letters tread firmly. Ra-ko-wi-ce.

Grandpa Yosef's thoughts wander. I assume he is thinking of

his family, their last moments together. But he is dwelling on the wonder of his being sent to Rakowice.

"Strange. Craftsmen were sent to Rakowice. A small group of skilled laborers. And me. Why me? Rakowice was not just another camp. Airplanes! An airfield! Engineers worked there."

He sounds almost boastful. He is short of breath. For a moment he scans his surroundings—me, Grandpa Lolek, the bed, the room. As if only at this moment has it become apparent to him that he has begun to tell his story. He needs to devote his attention to the place, to observe before he opens his mouth, as all good orators do. Here, in a wondrous way, is a coming together of opportunity and the need he has harbored for a long time. In this silence, which only Grandpa Lolek can disturb, we will spread out the story. There is plenty of time, every detail is important. Outside, night has fallen. Silence in the ward, silence in the room. Grandpa Yosef sets the time for his story: evening.

"We arrived in Rakowice in the evening hours. They rushed us into a group of huts. They started yelling. Beating us. What they wanted from our shattered souls, we could not tell. And in the distance was the airfield with the runway lit up. We squinted at the lights, fearful. Everything was too overwhelming, happening too quickly. We wanted just a moment of reprieve.

"Our gazes were drawn to beyond the fence. There, near the ugly barracks that formed the staff housing, was a fancy black car. In the chill of the night, against the backdrop of the runway lights, the body of the car shone like marble. So shiny and black, standing still and demanding our attention. But we were not permitted to look at the car for long. We were soon thrown from the gate area onwards, into the camp. Then there were beatings, searches, shouts. They acted as though they did not understand why we had come, and the whole business of our arrival was an unnecessary nuisance. From their point of view, we could have left. But I say this only jokingly. Leaving, even attempting to leave for just a second, was a death sentence. They hit and yelled just indiscriminately, for no reason. Shouts and lashings that made your mind dizzy with fear. We could not contemplate anything, not even the town we had left, or our families. All we could do was bow our heads and obey orders, ignore what was going on.

"But still, I must admit, once in a while my thoughts strayed to that black car. For some reason I sensed that I would be brought together with that fabulous machine in a few hours. There were beatings, punishments, crazed thoughts, and yet the car took hold of my mind. What was such a car doing in this ugly camp, among the crude trucks and a few simple vehicles parked in the mud? Was a high-ranking official about to take off from the airfield? Was the car waiting to pick up an official about to land here? The soldiers and personnel moving around in the distant airfield seemed unconcerned with the car. Why here, then? All that was happening here was our absorption into this pathetic, wearisome camp, implemented by low-ranking cruel beasts. Yes, this was what I would contemplate as the blows were being delivered, punishments and yelling around me. Still, I was drawn by the idea that the car was there for us. As if the absorption in Rakowice was an exemplary act, an operation to which senior officials were invited to watch and be impressed.

"As I contemplated these nonsensical thoughts, a sergeant suddenly grabbed hold of me, a Scharführer in uniform, and asked me to my face, 'Speak German, kike?'

"I replied, 'Yes,' with terror in my soul. My father, may God avenge his blood, Reb Mordechai Halevi Ingberg, had always admired the Germans. He learned their language and read their books. In the First World War he even served in one of the Austrian army's regiments. He taught me the language too, and I was fluent. But why did they need my German?

"I was not given much time to think. I was pulled away from the group to an isolated courtyard near a black wall. Did they shoot German-speaking Jews immediately? And for that they had dragged me all the way from Bochnia?

"I was left alone for a moment or two, and then came two prisoners, Jews, servants of the camp. They silently instructed me to strip, so they could wash and disinfect me. I obeyed, saying nothing, but my heart wished to know—what would be my fate?

"At first the two men did not speak much. They left me to my

thoughts, which were few: *Shema Yisrael*, Feiga, Mother. Why disinfect me if I was condemned? Would I dirty their bullets? Or did this
mean that I was not going to die? It seemed unreasonable, after all,
to wash and disinfect someone about to die. Then again, the Germans had already shown us quite clearly in the ghetto that they had
their own logic, a very cunning kind, which became apparent only
in retrospect—usually too late.

"The Jews gradually began to loosen their tongues. They whispered to me that they didn't know much, but a Nazi general was
waiting with the camp commandant. He had demanded to be given
a German speaking inmate. They had heard him ask for 'a short Jew,'
and they had no idea why. The car, over there, had I seen it? It was
his. More than that they did not know.

"I was terrified. What did he need a 'short Jew' for? What was
he going to do with me? My throat closed up, images darting between
the walls of my imagination. What would the Nazi do with me?

"The Jews finished washing my body. I was freezing, naked
in the night air. They rubbed me dry, then sprayed me with a foul-
smelling disinfectant. Then they rubbed me again with a different rag,
doing their work carefully like loyal servants. All that was left was to
dress me. Not in a prisoner's uniform, but in civilian clothes. They
were instructed to dress me well, neatly and cleanly. As if I were a
bride being lead to her *chuppah*. And my heart sank—what misdeeds
would they inflict upon me? Why did they need someone short?

"First they put an awful pale pink shirt on me, as if I were a man
of leisure in Krakow, one of those debauched people I had heard so
much about, and had even seen in Brzesko once. And they gave me
shoes that were almost the right size, a small consolation, and plain
brown trousers. Then an overcoat to cover the pink shirt.

"I asked my fellow Jews where they were from, what their names
were. But they were silent. Their eyes showed fear. They were forbidden to talk. A single word could result in lashings. But one of them,
who must have been naturally garrulous, was eager to convey something, and he began to whisper. The general was very senior. He had
earned commendations on the Eastern front. He was high-ranking.
'And they say he has a lover,' he whispered secretively. A little SS

sweetheart somewhere in the north, and he was traveling to her. She had fled him, the lover, and he was pursuing her. A whole affair.

"'A lover?' I asked. The man said he had overheard the German policemen gossiping. More than that he did not know.

"More than that I did not need. Horrific images sprung up in my mind. My heart trembled. What would they do with me? Would he present me to his SS woman? A lover's gift? And why did he need 'a short Jew'? I had known great fear in the ghetto, but now I could no longer abide it. From the *Kadosh Baruch Hu*, from Him I asked for strength. Perhaps I will kill myself here and now, in the name of the Lord, I thought, before they do to me what they wish to do. But then I thought of Feiga. And like a white feather descending from a dark sky, I suddenly found determination in a new thought: I was going to Feiga. To rescue her. This whole journey, the plan of this Nazi general, damn him, was nothing but a trick being played upon me by the *Kadosh Baruch Hu*. He was making the villain lead me to Feiga. And so it was. I had asked my Lord many times: Take me, lead me to Feiga. And how had I thought my Lord would answer my prayers? Would he provide me with a private jet? An automobile? No. Instead, he had given me a Nazi general in pursuit of a fleeing lover. For some reason the bastard had concocted a need for a Jew, and he had to be short, and had to speak German fluently. Of the whole shipment he had chosen me. And now I was going to rescue Feiga!

"The newfound joy in my heart must have transferred a spark to my eyes and face, because the two Jews looked at me in amazement. My fortitude had sent a shudder through them.

"'Are you not afraid, Reb?' the talkative one wanted to know.

"'With God's help, *chazak chazak venitchazek*, be strong, be strong, and we shall be strengthened,' I whispered, and they stood up straight in the darkness upon hearing the holy prayer. My strength imbued their limbs with power too. And that force that I showered upon these two poor Jews, servants of the Nazi camp, strengthened me even more. I had become a leader of sorts, a small-time leader, who saw the trouble of his people and gave them strength. Like Moses our Teacher, who smote the Egyptian, I whispered words of encouragement to them, now completely separate from the torture, the nightmare, the terrible fate of Jewish souls from all corners of the Nazi land. And me—I was going to Feiga. I could barely contain my impatience. Let the Nazi come, that evil Haman, and lead me like Mordechai on his horse.

"I was eager and excited, but they left me alone for two days in a frozen room with no windows, with only a waste-water container to keep me company. My heart was burning, my body freezing. The cement dug into my bones. The cold tortured me, but worse was the loneliness, the uncertainty, the harsh anticipation. I wanted a journey! Right then and there! Every twelve hours a door opened and a 'black,' which was what we called the Ukrainian guards, placed a dish of rotting food out for me. Two days later, in the evening, I was sent out to the yard again. They undressed me. Washed me in freezing cold water. Dried and disinfected me again. Gave me back my clothes, including the pink shirt. They added a hat. Even gloves. Yes, yes. Yosef Ingberg in kid gloves!

"After all these arrangements, one of the 'blacks' led me to the huts and then my eye caught sight of the black marble car, washed and shining, waiting. Oh horror and fear, an SS general was already sitting in the driver's seat, his black uniform stifling my courage—perhaps I was wrong about Feiga. But a moment later I found encouragement. How could I be wrong about the Lord's salvation?

"I was put in the passenger's seat next to the general, a large upright Amalek, and when I shot him a trembling look the Ukrainian guard hit me. Kikes mustn't look! The SS general had been still, but now he moved his hand slightly, as if brushing something off, and the guard who had struck me pulled away. I realized he had been ordered to leave me alone. There I was between two Amalekites, and one cancelled out the wickedness of the other. I was certain of the Lord's salvation, but in such proximity to a Nazi's body, the soul takes fright. His cap especially, shiny black on his head, put fear in me.

"The general reached out and turned the engine on. Policemen, Gestapo and Ukrainian guards bustled outside. And camp staff. They all came to see the general off on his journey. They did not realize it was my journey. My journey to Feiga. And off we went. An SS general holding the wheel, and me, Yosef Ingberg of Bochnia, beside him. Really and truly on the seat beside him. The seat was soft, made of fine leather. My fingers found pleasure touching it, feeling it. God forgive me for saying so, but it was as fine as the *paroches* that covers the holy ark. Through the windshield in front of me I could see everything clearly. Beneath the windshield, on his side, was the instrument panel with its dials and gauges. And the wheel—a butting ram, driving the engine that roared in its innards."

Grandpa Yosef blushes slightly at his own excitement. After all, this is a car he is describing. The air is charged with a sense of confession.

"*Nu*, you see, back then I had never driven in a car before. It just hadn't happened. And here was this wonderful carriage, all in black, and the whole world hurriedly making way for us. Trees, houses, even the clouds. Every time we passed a security point or a group of soldiers, they saluted us in fearful reverence. I had no idea where we were going. My heart was frozen. Was I bound for her? Terror struck me from my knees to my chest, but one sliver of thought did not abandon me: Have no fear, we are going to Feiga. But elsewhere was gloom and darkness. What would they do to me?

"We drove without stopping until midday. He was untiring, the general. His face was frozen, fixed on the wheel, and on he sailed. At noon we went into a military camp for lunch. I was left in the car and a guard was posted to watch me. I realized that I had eaten nothing for twenty-four hours. I did not yet know what days of hunger were ahead of me in my miserable future. But when we got back on the road, after some way, Amalek reached into his coat pocket and took out a wrapped parcel of food. Meat and salami and beets and cabbage. I gobbled it all down without saying a blessing, without a thought. The food was like pebbles in my throat, but I overcame that.

"So we kept driving in silence. In the evening he stopped again and had another meal. Again he secretly put aside a portion of food for me. Even poured me a hot drink. Such a merciful caretaker! And it was all done in silence, without so much as a glance in my direction. As if I were nothing but an object. Still I did not know, what did he want? What would he do with me? My mouth gobbled, my heart quavered. My knees trembled, my gut rejoiced. In between meals this

Pharaoh needed no rest. He kept driving the whole night through. I, in great terror, fell asleep. I woke up with an empty stomach. My body ached from the endless sitting. And he, the devil, acted as if he had not been robbed of any sleep. Around us, although it was summer, the pine trees were sparse and it was very cold, mud piled up alongside the roads. Forests came into view to the east. To the west as well. I wondered about Feiga. Was my little bird near or far?"

Grandpa Yosef comes to a stop with screeching brakes. "Do you know what *Feiga* means? *Feigaleh*? It's a bird. A female bird. A little female bird."

He continues his story.

"This Amalek did not let go of the wheel until the roads led to another camp. I felt them immediately; the fences, the huts, the terror. My general was tensely welcomed by an SS man, the camp commandant, who gave him their *heil* salute. It seemed my general had taken him by surprise. They both disappeared into a building, where they sat down to eat and talk. They spent six hours there while I was trapped in the car, watching the camp routine through the windows. The daylight was dark through the heavy glass and the scenes were dim. No sounds penetrated the car. Beyond the fences were inmates, exhausted and skeletal. No one came close. They did not dare. I sat watching, not knowing at all that I was in the height of the days that would come to be called the Shoah, believing that my suffering was due to loneliness, with Feiga somewhere out there, unrevealed. I believed my family was in the East, perhaps in the Ukraine, working hard, if they had not met with some disaster on their difficult journey. I myself was at the mercy of a Nazi general and I did not know what would be done with me. There was terror in my heart but there was a certain sweetness too—I was going to Feiga, I was destined for a great adventure. A black car was driving me through places I had only dreamed of as a boy, when I used to sit at the edge of Bochnia looking at the faraway landscape, my heart hollow with vague longings, weeping with love—Feiga, Feiga.

"A faint smell wafted into the car. My senses immediately conjured up a thought—potatoes! But that smell belied something else, and to the left of the car I could see a billow of smoke. A hut obscured my view of the source of the smoke. I stretched my neck out, my body leaning as far sideways as possible, but I could not see around the hut. The smoke billowed upwards from the earth as if someone were stoking that fire well, and the smell became more and more pronounced as the smoke thickened. For a moment I contemplated moving to the general's seat, where I would be able to see, but the mere thought was enough to cover my heart with ice. I must not! I remained in my seat, turned away from the billow of smoke, and a moment later I thanked my lucky stars because the general came out, surrounded by officers. They looked excited, as if they had been vigorously commended, their fear of criticism gone. They saluted him and walked him to our car with ingratiating looks. They did not move from the road until the car drove through the gates.

"We drove north. All the car's movements, the official stops at SS camps, all were directed northward. An iron plan was in his heart, to reach his escaped lover, and he did not sleep, and did not cease, and only for the sake of good order, damn them, did he visit his officers on the way.

"By that time I had already found a name for him, for the Nazi general. From the first I felt the need to give him a name. A nickname. If I were to die at his hands, he might as well have a name. I had already named the woman he was traveling to, Little Lover. And him, I had already silently called him Amalek, murderer, cruel soldier, Pharaoh, Haman, murderer. And possibly because of Haman, I suddenly determined to name him after Ahasuerus, the King of Persia who was incited by Haman to kill all the Jews. Perhaps this was not emblematic of his character, not an appropriate name for such an evil man, but it was what my heart decided.

"Evening came. We visited our fourth camp in a single day. My heart was dimly terrified, sensing we were getting closer to the end of our voyage. Ahasuerus would deliver me to the Little Lover. Sacrifice me on her altar. May God have mercy. But when we left the camp gates, Ahasuerus's face had changed. I dared not look at him directly, knowing it was better not to, but out of the corner of my eye I could see a glimpse of his face. It was gray and drawn and deadened. As if he had learned of a great disaster that had befallen his family. His hands, seemingly uninformed of the bad news, grasped the wheel strongly as they drove the car. These people seemed to have no connection between their hearts and their hands. But then finally the broken heart reached the hands, and Ahasuerus slowed down and drove his car onto the shoulder of the road, where he stopped beside a small puddle of mud. He did not explain the stop to me, as if I were nothing to him. He sat clutching the wheel, his back straight. He sat that way for a long time. Ahasuerus was silenced. The whole world was still. Ahasuerus's breath counted time—the seconds, the minutes. In and out it went, heavy and slow. Ahasuerus was tormented.

"I stared straight ahead, careful not to look at him, God forbid. Suddenly, there was a sound. The door opened and Ahasuerus got out. He walked alongside the car. He dug into the hollows of his eyes with his thumb and finger to rub the tiredness and trouble away from them, as I used to do when I was studying. Then he put his hand over his eyes as if he were crying. Suddenly he moved his hand to reveal his eyes and there was nothing to separate him from me. He looked at me, the Angel of Death.

"Ahasuerus got back into the car. The end is near, I thought, and suddenly it seemed that a bundle of pictures I had stored away in my memory was erupting. The Nazis shoot Metzger the baker in the hiding place he made for himself behind the oven, and while being led to Rakowice, I pass his body, bullet-ridden and white as ice. The body of young Yehezkel, my classmate, on his back, his eyes facing me. Mrs. Otkova yelling, running through the courtyard, no one knows what she wants. And Rabbi Halberstam, what of Rabbi Halberstam? With his wife, both shot against the wall.

"Nothing in my heart was apparent to Ahasuerus. He wanted to get back on the road, to keep going north. But the car would not cooperate. He could not start it. He got out, checked the engine, got back in. In and out again, he hurried around, regal and slow, but his concern was apparent. Around us night was falling, the woods, wild beasts. *Nu*, may God protect. For some reason, I was confident that he would manage. In my mind I could not envision a Nazi general failing, damn them. We believed in them so, those sons of death. But the car did not fear him. It remained silent and still, as if this marble angel was insulted at having been made to stop on a muddy road.

"Ahasuerus got back into the car. Silence prevailed. The cold began to seep in. Night was falling. Not a soul was on the road. Forests on both sides. Trees. A few birds fluttered through the treetops, screeching, groaning, demanding to know why the Creator had brought them to this remote land. And suddenly I sensed sleep fossilizing on the general's face. But then something moved in the stoniness of his strong chin and he left me in the car again, going out to explore the wilderness. His boots creaked in the freezing cold. Birds screeched and an echo passed from one end of the world to the other. We were alone. Around us an endless forest. No salvation.

"I looked through the window of the car. Ahasuerus's fingers rested on his eyes. His figure was hunched over for a moment. Tired and irritated and helpless. Lightening struck in my heart: He will kill me here with his gun. I tried to diminish my presence, shrinking into my pink shirt like a miserable reptile—perhaps he would take pity. Indeed. An evil Gestapo man, a general, and from him I expected mercy. Still fresh in my mind were pictures of shattered babies, Rabbi Halberstam shot with his wife. And there I was, expecting compassion. Still, my body was taut, hoping for mercy, mercy.

"Ahasuerus returned and sat down beside me in his place. I dared to steal a quick look. His face was still hard and his sorrow evident. What was going on in his soul? Had he heard bad news of his escaped lover? Had he seen her? Was she not impressed by his efforts, had she simply told him that everything they had told each other previously was revoked?

"Silence.

"Suddenly a small, sharp sound. Forgetting my vigilance, I looked straight at him. Ahasuerus was cracking a nut. With the fingers of one hand, with Herculean strength, he broke the shell and removed the debris. Carefully, unrushed, he took out the fragments. The nuts cracked like skulls between his hands. I looked away from him, frightened. I remembered that he had forgotten to give me part of his dinner. He had been lost in thought when we left the last camp and forgot about me. But it was not hunger that rose in me—rather, it was fear. The smell of the nuts terrified me. Ahasuerus pressed on. Breathing slowly. Cracking nuts. Every nut got its turn.

"Thoughts rushed through my mind. Metzger the baker came back again, as if his body wanted to tell me something. Lying, shot dead, in front of the bakery where every Friday we used to feast our eyes on the window display, the soft *challahs* and the raisin bread. In our home, Mother baked the bread, the *challahs* too, but to this day I can smell the aromas from Metzger's. Feiga used to go there to buy bread for her family and Metzger would give her a little crown of *challah* for good luck. I thought about Mother. The last time I had seen her she had fainted in the military lot. Who knew where she was. My heart filled with self-pity. My loneliness enveloped me. I took consolation in the distant memory of a walk I had taken with Feiga before the war. Against that backdrop I saw a scene from the last camp Ahasuerus had taken me to: a prisoner stands looking at me with wild eyes. His whole face is black. A skeleton of a man. He stands and stares as if it's worth looking at the car despite the risks. He tilts his head for a moment, hearing a sound. Then he leaves. I, for some reason, wonder what his name is. As if there is any importance to the name of this suffering man behind the fences, who looked at me for two minutes and in a few days will be among the dead. And still I ask myself, Yanek? Hetzkel? Shmuel? Perhaps Yosef, like myself? Suffering and tortured and about to die, and his name is my name?

"Ahasuerus moved briefly beside me. He had collected his nuts and hid them somewhere. He sat erect but his weariness was now obvious. He had not shut his eyes for two days, maybe more. For his lover's sake he overcame tiredness, hardened himself, but the car's breakdown had collapsed everything. Now his eyes demanded sleep. Ahasuerus struggled, there was no salvation. I was tired too, but fear would not allow me to close my eyes. First the villain had to sleep, then we'd see.

"Ahasuerus gave in first. He prepared himself for sleep, wrapping his body in his officer's coat and digging his hands in his pockets. He turned to look at me for a moment, as if remembering that this human package sitting beside him still existed. He seemed to be considering something. Suddenly he turned to me. Truly turned his head to me and spoke:

"'I've always hated Jews, but not like this.'

"When he said 'but not like this,' his hand made a gesture in the air as if to envelop the entire world, the *Aktionen* and the torture and the blood of Rabbi Halberstam on the street in the ghetto. He turned his side to me, mumbled something and fell asleep.

"Those were his first words to me and, in my innocence, I thought that from then on we would talk. But I was mistaken. He never addressed me again as long as we were together, except one more time to say one sentence. But that day is still far off. Perhaps you'd like some more of the Swiss coffee? Tasty, isn't it?"

I decline. Grandpa Yosef patters down to the end of the hallway. It's night time here in the hospital ward. Absolute night. Ahasuerus is asleep with his hands folded beneath his black coat, and Grandpa Yosef has positioned himself as a guard. The night is dark and there are sounds of menacing creatures. Trees sway in the wind. Grandpa Yosef's eyes will not shut. He sits and stretches, and thoughts pass through him unfettered.

Grandpa Yosef comes back from the vending machine, looking bitter. The machine is broken. Someone poked their fingers into the mechanism and stuck something in there and now nobody can get any coffee.

Grandpa Lolek sighs as something inside him stirs—perhaps the stroke, trying to heal—and his body emits a kind of whimper. Grandpa Yosef sits silently, his flow of talk ceased, wondering if there might be an awakening, a feeble word uttered. We watch Grandpa Lolek, lurking for a disturbance in his deep rest. Only the strange wink moves slowly. The eye opens to a narrow slit, then closes, as if satisfied by one open instant. His still body convinces us that there will be no more motion. Grandpa Yosef hurries on, reminded by the soft sigh that his time to tell the tale is not unlimited. If Grandpa Lolek wakes up, if he recovers, it will put an end to the time allotted for listening, for telling, for continuing his journey.

"The general slept the whole night through. His sleep was not peaceful. His head moved, sighs and whimpers erupted from his chest.

I wondered if he was plagued by scenes of babies smashed, children with heads cracked open on the walls of houses. Or perhaps his Little Lover, the SS woman, who had fled him. And myself—if I closed my eyes, would I be in the arms of Feiga? Or would I too reach the walls of the ghetto, our elderly neighbors, like Bergman, shot in the back of their heads? My eyes would not shut. Forbidden. My eyelids kept drooping, but then I would see Kowalska Street, covered with people lying dead as I walk among them. And the eyes would shoot open. No sleep. By my side Ahasuerus moved his head restlessly. Two people suffering; around them, wilderness.

"Just before dawn, the birds began to chirp and a car approached. I looked at Ahasuerus. He did not wake up. He lay restfully, curled up in a dream, perhaps having found peace in the arms of his Little Lover. He had no idea that a car was about to pass us, that he would sleep away an opportunity. I asked myself if I should let the car pass and leave us there, the two of us, hungry and cold, perhaps unto death. That would be my revenge for Metzger the baker, for Yehezkel, for Rabbi Halberstam.

"The car was audible now, its sounds clear. My hand reached out and one finger impudently tapped his neck. Ahasuerus woke without even giving me a glance. He got out and stopped the car. The soldiers in the car were eager to help. They rescued us. A short soldier reached under the engine hood and did something in there that fixed the problem. In the meantime, they danced around the general, star-struck, offering him their food. They saluted him and asked if they could do anything. Confused, they saluted again. They shot glances at me but did not dare ask what the general was doing with a Jew in a pink shirt. But their looks were curious. Ahasuerus dismissed them and I thought we would set off on our voyage again, determined. The breakdown had cost us precious time. My body was slowly thawing, its heat eager to get to work, to find Feiga's camp. But Ahasuerus was in no hurry. The moment the car was fixed, he began to plan the day ahead. From his coat pocket he gave me a hunk of bread. He had put it aside from what they had given him. Then, to my surprise, he went off to do his business.

"Even crouching behind a shrub, he still looked regal. Straight as an eagle. I allowed him some privacy, turning my face. But the odor of his bowel movement spread through the fresh air. The smell was unpleasant but I persisted in inhaling it, sensing his health—for months, begging your pardon, everything with me had been sick and watery. After a while he reemerged and walked toward me in his neat uniform. He rubbed his hands on the leaves of a bush and was spotlessly clean. He proceeded, not to his side of the vehicle, but straight to me, motioning with his head at the bush. I grew frightened. Was I to die there? But my fear was unfounded as I soon understood. There was a long way ahead of us, most likely, and I too, begging your pardon, had to relieve myself. My heart wished to lead me to a different bush, far from the one he had used. But my legs positioned me behind the very same bush. *Nu.* I pulled my pants down and looked aside. There were two of them, laying like babes in a cradle on the leafy grass, solid and identically sized. I hoped I would not emit the soft stream again, not the usual output, not in front of those two. But my bowels quickly erupted in a dirty, unpleasant flow. Flies had already appeared. I could barely stand up and tuck my pink shirt into my pants. Disgusted and miserable, I sat down beside him in the car. I recalled the sentence he had said to me and, for some reason in that moment my heart believed that the journey had somehow brought us closer, that perhaps we would talk. But the general's concern was only for his car. He drove the marble angel back onto the road to his lover, to my Feiga.

"At midday we visited a camp. Again I sat imprisoned in the car while Ahasuerus met with the camp personnel. This time I saw women. Female prisoners and policewomen. Was the journey to Feiga over? Suddenly there was a knock on the window. A prisoner, an actual prisoner, was knocking urgently. His face looked like the skeleton I had seen the day before. That one had just stood and looked at me, a nameless figure with crazed eyes, but this one was more daring. I opened the window a crack and asked hurriedly, 'Feiga, née Blau, is she here?'

"'Bread?' the prisoner asked. 'Anything?'

"His skeletal face was crazed with fear. My reaction was too slow for him and he skipped away and disappeared among the huts without waiting for my answer. A moment later two SS men passed by and stared lengthily at the car. In my heart I knew that Feiga was not there. When I reached her camp I would know, I would not need conversations.

"I waited for Ahasuerus and did not trouble my mind with thoughts of the prisoner, that skeletal face of his, the likes of which I had never seen in the ghetto. I did not bother with thoughts of the type of life that engenders such terror. My heart was directed elsewhere, to an uncomfortable flutter, a dense sort of desperation. As if my heart was a true prophet, when Ahasuerus came out his steps seemed weak, his expression strange. I looked at him and suddenly all was clear: the voyage was over, no more. Ahasuerus had given up on his journey. Why the confidence? Why the certainty? It was his face. I could tell without a doubt that he was no longer determined, that he had lost his purpose. He got into the car without even glancing at me, and started to drive. The previous night had broken something in him, something greater than mere time lost. I could see this with certainty. Though in fact he appeared more at ease, as if something in him had found calmness, or had been lost, disappeared. But my heart was not available to study the inner workings of a Nazi general. It was Feiga that I was thinking of. Was my voyage still going ahead as planned? Ahasuerus, after all, knew nothing of the journey's purpose. Only the Little Lover was in his head, and now, no Little Lover, and no more need for the 'short Jew' he had wanted to bring her as a gift. What would he do with me?

"The roadsides began to be dotted with villages. The villages grew denser and denser. We were driving through the outskirts of a town. German army guard posts, roadblocks, inspections, examinations. Everyone let Ahasuerus go on his way, retreating with a salute. We sailed deeper in. I slowly began to read names on the road-signs, and realized we had reached the city of Lodz. Why Lodz, I did not know. Had Feiga been taken there? Why was Ahasuerus bringing me to Lodz? What was he scheming? Was he planning to get rid of me now that I was unnecessary? And why not simply put a bullet through my head right there?

"From the fear, not only my heart shrunk. Begging your pardon, my bladder did too. To this day I remember the endless, painful pressure. My life was on the line, but it was my bladder that preoccupied me. If only Ahasuerus would stop for a moment, I could jump out and urinate. He might think I was escaping. He might shoot me. But my thoughts could not tolerate the caution that might delay urination. Still suffering, my bladder so full that it was almost erupting, we reached the gates of a low wall, and beyond it, I knew immediately, was a ghetto. Far larger than the Bochnia ghetto, unfamiliar and crowded, but there was no mistaking it. A ghetto is immediately recognizable. An entire town of hungry, ill Jews. The Lodz ghetto.

"To this day I wonder why Ahasuerus brought me to the Lodz ghetto. Was it so I would be killed in the *Aktion* that was planned for the next few days? He must have known about it (perhaps even ordered it). Or maybe it was just the opposite—it was life that he ordered for me. He knew what everyone knows today, that after the next *Aktion* this ghetto would be allowed to survive, the last of the ghettos. So his was an act of grace. Or maybe it was neither. Here was simply a place where he could leave me among the hundreds of thousands of people crowded into the ghetto, who walked its streets daily, characters coming and going with the wind. Here no questions would be asked. But why would a Gestapo general need to be so cautious? In the Bochnia ghetto they shot hundreds like me, lined up against the walls, so why would a general inconvenience himself for one miserable Jew? He could have shot me, no questions asked, on the side of the road.

"Back then, much like today, I was full of questions. But Ahasuerus was indifferent. We were destined to meet again several days later, and as I have said, Ahasuerus would address me one more time. But on that day he left me by the entrance to a building. He gave me some sort of *Certifikat* and a little bag which contained, I discovered, Polish and German currency. Dispensing with niceties, he left me and disappeared. As if the neglected regions of the world had never been traversed together by these two: a Nazi general and a short Jew. At that moment I still did not know how much future we were yet to have together.

"I soon realized that I had been left outside the German police headquarters. I was promptly led to the office of the Jewish police by two German officers who treated me with inexplicable respect. The Jewish clerks I was delivered to also treated me with caution, even deference. They interviewed me, asked questions. They explained to me about the difficulties, the rationing. They promised to help with housing, although the situation was practically hopeless, and in any case it was warm on these summer nights and the street was a good option for now. Better the street than the houses, where typhus and boils were raging. The streets were cleaner. They dared to ask, in hushed voices, if I had any particular desires, if I required assistance in my mission, any requests?

"No, they said, they hadn't heard of Feiga, née Blau, but they would find out. Two-hundred thousand Jews in the ghetto, but not to worry, everything was in the records. Order, there was. Law, there was. The clerks would do their jobs and Feiga would be located. Did I wish to make any further inquiries of another kind? Any orders, for example?

"I was naïve. I did not realise that to them, a man dropped off in the middle of the Lodz ghetto in the black car of a Gestapo general, dressed in fine clothes and a pink shirt, had to be an agent. They were in awe of my unabashed scheming; I had not slipped into the ghetto dressed in plain clothes, but had arrived demonstratively in a black car that had stopped right outside the police headquarters. And they must have pondered the pink shirt. What kind of an agent dressed like that? In my innocence, I did not divine the thoughts surrounding me. I did not yet conceive of the size of the Lodz ghetto, the two hundred thousand Jews crowded into it, the hundred Jews who died there routinely every day, in hunger and in sickness, in suicide and over-crowdedness. I did not imagine the thieves, the agents, the informers, the policemen, the underground activists, a great tapestry of people in conflict with one another, fighting over a hunk of bread, over a sliver of authority. An entire city full of passions and torments. In this city there were people who jumped out of windows, and there were those who were selflessly charitable. There was a woman in this city, a simple daughter of Israel, who was accused of having eaten from the flesh of her own son's body. And there were martyrs who died for *kiddush hashem.* A city that even had strikes and labor riots, instructions from foremen, and weddings and prayers and distinguished gentlemen. And into this cauldron, the vast Lodz ghetto, tenfold larger than our ghetto in Bochnia, I descended in a pink shirt.

"The clerks asked if I had any further desires. Amazingly, I expressed my urgent desire—begging your pardon—for a place to relieve myself. My bladder could take no more. And thus began my time in the Lodz ghetto.

"The first days were terrible. All the ghetto streets were so clean as to be practically spotless. Countless people made it their business to clean them, countless others supervised their work. With untiring efforts, they scrubbed the streets to stop the spread of disease as much as was possible. But on top of this bed of cleanliness teemed terror and fear. Everything was crowded and morbid. People were hungry. The money on my person was of practically no use. I was afraid to take out a coin. I was among Jewish brethren, but there was hunger in their eyes, and thieving looks. And my own fear was dwarfed by everyone else's fear of me. The rumor had already spread: the high priest of agents had come to the ghetto.

"At first I walked alone. Without a friend, without a living soul. Around me the streets bustled with the furor of life, thousands of people going about their business. Troubles and pleas and lobbying and attempts to deceive bitter fate. There was no going outside the ghetto. Closed off. But inside people flowed, together or alone, including a few strange creatures like myself. Who could imagine the travels that had led a driven leaf like myself from our little Bochnia to 32 Dolna Street in the Lodz ghetto? One way or another, all these scattered leaves seemed to gather together in their wanderings, and I quickly found myself some company. Not wise men. Good people, also lonely. We wandered the streets like ragamuffins, and it was good. We spoke of our loved ones, our homes. Each man extolled the place he had come from, his family, his loves. There were lies, and foolishness, and it was all in good spirits, to warm the heart. I alone did not have to lie: I described Feiga just as she was, unembellished.

"I found consolation in this gang. By all appearances, they were lonesome unworthies. But the closer our ties grew, the more confessions we made, and each man shone through with the miracles of his life. You would look at one of us, a lifeless man dressed in rags, the dregs of the dregs, and an unparalleled story of life would emerge, a unique, wonderful soul that could not be imagined.

"We walked and we talked. All like me, driven leaves. Brought from distant places, each with his own story, longing to tell it thoroughly, to amaze, to share, to sigh a little together. It seemed, at times, that life was not yet that bad. We were hungry, but a sweet sorrow lingered in the air. The two trees on Balut Street, where our 'parliament' met, were like an orchard to us. We did not imagine that on September fifth, 1942, the terrible Lodz ghetto *Aktion* would begin—the one infamously known as *Sperre*. Afterwards, the ghetto was untouched until 1944, the last of the ghettos allowed to live out its life. Outside the ghetto, Jews everywhere were taken to concentration and extermination camps, murdered and tortured, while the Lodz ghetto was left in peace. But the ghetto paid a price for this respite in the form of the *Sperre*.

"I have already said that I was naïve. I did not imagine that even as I was wandering around among the unknowns, I was not anonymous at all. Many in the ghetto took an interest in me, for various reasons. People often turned up in the ghetto like I had, sent by the Germans as agents. And just as suddenly, they disappeared. No one could keep track of all the movements and transports. But I had come straight from a general's car to the police headquarters, and such a thing had never been witnessed before. People privately commented that this was no way to plant an agent—so publicly, wearing a pink shirt like some sort of peacock. And rumor soon spread that I had no shortage of money. There were many thieves in the ghetto, as well as real murderers. But apparently they were afraid of me. I am ashamed to say that I had gained a reputation as a high-ranking secret agent of the Germans who should not be messed with. All my efforts to refute the rumors were to no avail, and within a few days I began to comprehend that in fact I might be better off protected by them.

"I would walk through the masses, sad and hungry. All sorts of people attached themselves to me, mostly intrigued by my alleged role as chief agent, and undoubtedly also drawn by the rumors of my money. Fearful characters stole up to me, pressed my arm and offered me a piece of wax, or cabbage, or a lock. They tried to complete the transactions quickly, retreating in haste when I hesitated. In the morning I would hear that a supply of boots had been stolen from the warehouse, and in the evening a Jew would come up to offer me a pair for cheap. Others behaved like royalty. *Malchus*. Turning to me, they beckoned secretively, hinting at a proposal, expecting that we would gradually reveal our business to one another. The one would expose his money. The other would name a price for a fake authorization, for getting a letter to any address in Poland, for a special favor at the ghetto organization offices. They were surprised I did not want these services, which were offered only to the distinguished—to those who could pay gold for small favors.

"Not only merchants hassled me. Some came to me with complaints about this or that official, expecting the grievance to make its way to the powers that be. Some came with bubbling anger, regaling me with stories of wrongdoing. Demanding compensation, threatening, saying, 'The day is not far…The day is not far.' And some did not speak. They followed me around with hawk-eyes for a day or two. My money put them on my heels, the title of agent melted their hearts. For one or two days they did not dare approach, but did not give up. And every such attempt increased my resolution: I would cloak myself in the rumor and the thieves would stay away. Better that way. I had no idea of the danger lurking beneath the surface.

"There was in our gang a narrow-eyed Jew from Koźminek. His wife had died of typhus in the ghetto and he had lost his children to pneumonia. He hung around with us, not entirely belonging, sometimes talking of his wife, sometimes of his children, but his main concern was potatoes. His mind was completely obsessed with the topic, and he would stand among us discussing a shipment of potatoes he had seen being unloaded on Limanowa Street, which would probably go to the sycophants of the Authority. He discussed potatoes distributed in the public kitchens, which were damaged from faulty storage over winter. This was his entire preoccupation: potatoes that were, that would be, that he intended to get hold of. Potatoes. And between them, like drops of rain, a word or two about his children. Antek, three years old, had died in the hospital. His Rozka had not even seen the inside of a hospital. For two days she lay coughing at home, and suddenly one night she got a high fever. He wrapped her in a blanket and took her in the middle of the night, hoping they would treat her. They told him the hospital was over-flowing with typhus and boils patients. She should have hot drinks and she would get better. He offered all his food stamps and a small treasure of hoarded potatoes as bribery. But the sacrifice did not help. She died in his arms, six-year-old Rozka. He would have given his entire stock of potatoes, but they did not want it. Why would they? Bursting with fatty foods, hiding huge storehouses from the masses, full of potatoes, only for them. And here the potatoes erupted again. The unfair allocations. The shipment rotting in a warehouse because a few clerks in the office were lazy. A certain type of potato that was a curse, causing the stomach to bloat, God save us, we had to watch out. And so on and so forth.

"One day, when there was great hunger, this Jew from Koźminek decided to attach himself to me. He stood close to my body and for a moment I thought that was it—a knife and I would be done for. He had a thieving look in his eyes, which led me to believe that it would be him, of all the men in our gang, who would overcome the force of the rumors and rob me for my potatoes. But the Jew from Koźminek, it turned out, was seeking my wellbeing. Standing close to me, his words crazed, frightened, he was actually trying to warn me:

"'In our circle...*hmm*...they think about you, *nu*...Where did you come from? And some believe we should...*nu*, in the neck...there are youths here...'

"He was trying to tell me that my life was in danger, and at the hands of whom?! The rumors protected me from regular thieves, but the underground, the people who acted in the name of ideology, considered me a target. Oh dear! Why did Ahasuerus bring these troubles on me? He could have left me at some distance from the town, where I would have ended up wherever I ended up. What did he care? I knew my condition was grave. I did not know how grave it was yet to become.

"In the meantime, something of note occurred. The chairman

of the Lodz ghetto Judenrat, Rumkowski, the "Elder of the Jews," who lorded over the small kingdom of two hundred thousand ghetto subjects, summoned me to see him. He wanted to talk. The most important of the ghetto Jews, the 'president,' as we were required to call him, invited a lonesome Jew of the Wesoła Street wanderers to his room.

"He talked to me for a long time, trying to figure me out. If I were an agent, how did he not know? There were agents about whom the Gestapo notified Rumkowski, and others, if the Gestapo hid them from him, Rumkowski the fox uncovered on his own. And me? Who was I? He stared at me. An elderly man with a strong face. He asked where I had come from, what I did. He chatted about himself and the troubles of his kingdom. And all this time his eyes were watching me, wondering who I was. A cunning and wise man, this Rumkowski was. Some say he was bad for the Jews, some say he did great things for them, finding himself between a rock and a hard place. Who can judge? He met his end in Auschwitz too, may God avenge his blood. With me he was relaxed. He asked if my life in the ghetto was adequate, if I was finding nourishment, if I was treated well by his subordinates. He asked how he could help. I gave him a detailed description of Feiga, which he wrote down, and he said his people could make enquires in nearby ghettos.

"All this time I wondered—should I confess? Open my heart to this grandfatherly Jew and tell him that I was no agent and no nothing? Should I restore myself to the people of Israel, or cloak myself in secrecy and preserve the confusion? After all, it was only my secret that protected me from the robbers, like a coat of armor. Perhaps I could give him my money to keep? German and Polish bills were forbidden in the ghetto and were of no use in any case. But I did not reveal it to him. Not a thing. I went back to the street, and he, in his office, was left wondering who I was.

"I kept roaming here and there through the streets. A lonesome Jew, longing for life. Thieves in pursuit, murderers lurking for the money hidden deep in my coat pocket. I could not spend a penny of Ahasuerus's treasure. And whom did I fear? The underground youths. I did not want to die like an agent, a traitor. Better to be killed by a robber, better tuberculosis, typhus. Every young man who came in my direction looked like an assassin to me. I tried to find ways to contact the underground—perhaps I would knock on their door and settle the misunderstanding. Take the entire treasure out of my coat pocket and say, Here, all my money can go to your cause. But what door could I knock on? How could I, the chief of agents, find out on the streets where the underground met? *Nu*, what an affair!

"One day there was a chance of sorts. On Dolna Street, I happened to meet a man by the name of Yanek Leib, a Jew of short stature who used to be in our gang of misfits and then disappeared. A peculiar sort of Jew. His eyes were extremely large, made even more pronounced by a pair of bushy eyebrows. From the first I had sensed something odd about him, as if despite spending time with us, he did not wish for human company, only needed it so he would not stray too far. He was silent when he was with us, his head bowed, and he never made any efforts to introduce himself. If he was forced to talk, he would immediately grow anxious, emitting sort of 'humpf humpf' noises between his words, waving his hands, wishing to finish his piece in any way possible. He behaved as if a secret were burdening him and he was afraid it would escape—he could not find anyone to share his secret with. Then he found me.

"When I met him he was in a fever, walking towards me as energetically as a defense attorney hurrying to defend the town dignitaries in court. When I enquired as to his destination, he at first tried to conceal his excitement, as if our meetings were a daily occurrence—why would today be anything special? But within a moment or two his appearance changed. He wanted to tell me something right away. I have already told you that, sadly, ordinary Jews, regular people, kept their distance from me, while certain characters stuck to me. And Yanek Leib, he was the greatest of characters. He sat me on an odd-looking staircase that was not connected to any building, serving only the backsides of two conversationalists. He began to talk. Then he stopped. He inhaled, as if trying out his words. He whispered, 'humpf humpf,' preparing his vocal chords. Finally he looked at me.

"'I am a simple Galician, as you know. Yanek Leib, from the

township of Okhanow. From a young age I aspired to reach great distances, humpf, and great distances I have reached…'

"He briefly scanned my face. Was his story making an impression? Then he hurried on, likely short of time.

"'I was a merchant's apprentice and an aid to a *tzaddik*, and also, forgive me, I was a thief. Humpf. I tumbled from land to land, I crossed Silesia, and I crossed the land of Czechia. A merchant and a tramp and a juggler. Yes. Hungry all the time. And the police in pursuit…humpf. Locked me up in winter, let me go in summer. Until I crossed the Alps, yes, the great mountains! Humpf. And in the land of Italy, where it was warm, I found the world famous Enrico circus. Having no choice, for my stomach, I became an acrobat, performing magnificent feats for the audience. But then I twisted my foot, to this day it is crooked and makes me short, shorter than the day I was born. For seven days and seven nights I lay in pain, bedridden, and Mrs. Gazella, the wife of Enrico, cared for me like a mother, humpf, and on the seventh night something went wrong with the lion tamer, his head was bitten off. He put it into the mouth of a lion but never took it out. Humpf. They gave me a choice: they needed a lion-tamer, and acrobatic jumps I could do no longer. I could either tame lions or go back to the dumps, humpf. Of course, I preferred the dumps. There, I would have my head intact, humpf. But the circus master, Enrico himself, hovered over me for seven days and seven nights, entreating and persuading. After all that time I didn't know if I was coming or going, and then he added a final temptation, humpf. He would teach me a magic whisper to subdue the lions. I said no, of course. What good would the magic whisper be when I was in the lion's gut? But Enrico put his lips to my ear and whispered the magic whisper, which had been passed down through many generations in his family, and which included one Hebrew word. Yes, one word in *lashon hakodesh*, the Holy Tongue. For some reason, humpf, far from my people, from Okhanow, one word was more enchanting than the wholeness of my head. Yes, a Hebrew word. I did not even speak Hebrew, except for a few prayers. And so I became the lion tamer in the famous Enrico circus, traveling through the towns of all the world! I had seven lions and seven lionesses, all at my command. No thanks to my stature, which was not tall, humpf, but due to the whisper. After I whispered the charm, looking into their eyes, I fearlessly put my head between their jaws and sometimes placed my neck beneath their paws. Humpf. Humpf.'"

Grandpa Yosef looks serious. "I was beginning to believe that his 'humpf' was the magic whisper, but it turned out not to be. And the whole story turned out to be a long introduction to one more secret.

"Yanek Leib purses his lips and his eyes sparkle. 'Here in Lodz,' he says, 'I discovered that the lion whisper also works against the Nazis, damn them! Yes, humpf, it calms them like little lambs, it calms them. Indeed, only yesterday one such man stood opposite me and I faced him coolly. I began to whisper the magic words and looked deep into his eyes, damn him. He opened his eyes wide—how dare this Jew stand right across from him? Humpf. He was already thinking of his whip, perhaps his pistol. But after a moment his heart became as tender as a lamb. An innocent kid stood before me with no thoughts in his head. Had I wished to, I could have taken his handkerchief from his pocket, blown my nose and put it back. But no! The authorities must not be provoked. You should not be too smart for your own good. A lion is a lion, and a Nazi is a Nazi, damn them, humpf. So I simply walked away and left him to his perplexity. In a moment or two he would awake and have no idea where he was, what he had done, or indeed the name of the cursed mother who had borne him. Humpf!'

"Yanek's face was flushed and excited, he was agitated. His 'humpfs' became more frequent, sticking in his throat.

"'I have already offered myself to the underground. I could play my trick on the authorities, transfer information. Humpf. But they are disbelieving, humpf, they almost threw me out. Humpf, they demand a demonstration, humpf. They'll get one, humpf, tomorrow. In front of the congregation's eyes, I, Yanek Leib, will subdue a *goy*, humpf.'

"He subsided for a moment. His breath grew quiet. But suddenly his face filled with fear. 'I will not reveal the words, I will not!' he screamed, and started digging through his coat pockets, and bleating and mumbling.

"It had never occurred to me to steal his whisper—this whisper was his only asset, worth a multitude of food stamps and more. And in any case it was the underground I was thinking of. Was he connected to the underground? Perhaps he could help me with my affair. There was a sword hanging over my neck, after all. I laid out my plea before him. Yanek Leib arched his eyebrows and gravely considered the request. He could not promise anything. But I was already excited and I urged him, 'Please, for me.' Yanek Leib stood up as if in a hurry again. I chased after him, one block, two, urging him, my heart pounding, 'The underground, the underground, please help.'

"Finally he consented. He knotted his eyebrows together, sighed, and agreed to present my case before the underground the next day. But from that day onwards, until the end of time, I never saw Yanek again. What happened to him, I do not know. I wanted to ask, but people kept their distance. As far as they were concerned, the chief agent had conversed with a man, and the next day the man was gone. And a few days later came the *Sperre*.

"Have you heard the word? *Sperre*? That was what they called the Lodz ghetto *Aktion*. What can I say about the *Aktion*? Every horror you can imagine occurred. A baby taken from its mother's arms, speared on the gun's bayonet, and put back in her arms with wild laughter—she wanted her baby back, didn't she? People were thrown out of windows...children too. Lying broken-boned on the sidewalks, no one coming to their aid. Your heart could not contain all that the Nazis inflicted, in the streets, in houses, lines of people going to Chelmno, the death camp. To this day, sometimes, still, my eyelids close in the middle of the day, my head droops, and from that cursed place those scenes pour forth in front of my eyes.

"First the announcement went through the ghetto: the Gestapo authorities had given an order to evacuate some of the residents. 'Evacuate' was the term they used. At first it was the sick and the weary, then the elderly. Then—the children. The ghetto community leaders had to hand over a list of twenty-thousand people. And to where would they be evacuated? God help them, now we know it was to Chelmno. Back then? We knew and we did not know; we understood and we did not understand. And what can I say...the entire ghetto was panic-stricken, and an uprising was organized. In our hearts we knew where the evacuees would be taken, and it shook people up. The demand passed by word of mouth: Do not give anyone up. Let the *goyim* come and take them themselves. Even the Rambam decreed it is forbidden to give a person up for death, even if it is to the advantage of the entire congregation. Forbidden.

"President Rumkowski gave a speech. He entreated us to hand the people over, otherwise it would get worse. Committees began to meet and divide people up. There were lists. People looked out for their loved ones, pushed people off the lists, wrote others in. Anyone with power, anyone capable of accessing the lists. And there was wailing all the time. I myself was not on the lists of those going to death. No one dared write down the name of the chief agent, for fear their own name might replace it at the last minute, reversing their fortunes.

"On September fifth a curfew was declared. The *Aktion* had begun. Eight days and eight nights of terror. I have said already that in our hearts we knew where they were going. And testimonies had crept into the ghetto. The Rabbi of Grabow sent a letter, a voice of truth to his brethren in the ghetto. True, there were also denials, letters signed by people in the deportations, even rabbis, asking how we were and reporting how fortunate they had been. A moment or two before the gas chambers they were forced to write comforting letters, planting doubt against the cautioning testimonies. But in our hearts we knew the truth. We believed there was annihilation. Everyone thought about their relatives and stopped imagining their lives in the East, trying instead to come to terms with their deaths. I too, from the little window in the room I called home, peeked out at the goings-on in the streets and my memory called up the *Aktion* in Bochnia, the military courtyard, Mother, Father, my sister, my brother. I thought about the large group from which I had been removed to be sent to Rakowice. In the streets below mothers begged, children were dragged kicking into carts, and I recalled four-year-old Irenka standing next to me in line, waiting quietly. A little angel with golden hair. I remembered how she used to sing for us in the ghetto when they organized concerts. Her mother, Bronia, who was a musician at the Krakow Conservatory, would write songs, and Irenka would stand with a violin, playing and singing."

Grandpa Yosef begins to sing a Polish song:

Bo ja jadę dzisiaj do Palestyny
Po radośniejszego życia los
Tam przy cichem gaju pomarańczowym
Będę snuć życia radosnego nić

Grandpa Lolek's eyelid flutters a little. How far are the Polish words reaching?

I ask for a translation.

Grandpa Yosef thinks for a while. It will be hard in Hebrew, he thinks; the words embrace one another less. His lips test the words, gain confidence. Then he hums Irenka's song in Hebrew:

Today I travel to Palestine
To the fate of a more joyful life
There in a tranquil orange grove
I will spin the thread of life's joy

"It sounds better in Polish," Grandpa Yosef emphasizes. "And the song was so beautiful when Irenka sang it. She sang many songs, but unfortunately only this one remains in my memory. They took Irenka, with Bronia, and with her father Leon, to Belzec. *Nu*, four years old, with such angel eyes and golden hair. *Nu*, that was how Irenka went. For many years Leon waited to be blessed with that daughter. In the First World War he fought in the Austrian army. He was taken hostage and held for a long time. When he came home he worked with his father as a barber, he had to make a living, but he never gave up his dream of studying music, and every spare moment he played his violin in the barbershop. 'Chasing away the customers,' his father used to grumble. That was your father's grandfather, Sigmund Shlomo. At a late age, Leon was able to see his dream come true, and at the Conservatory he met the woman of his dreams, Bronia, whom everyone called Ronia. They fell in love and got married. How beautiful the world seemed when Irenka was born, such an angel. All their dreams were coming true, and then Belzec. But our Irenka was just one little angel, and there in the *Sperre*, through my window, we saw dozens of angels crowded onto a wagon and taken away. People followed the wagon, screaming. Shots were fired. People lay in their coats on the street, blood spurting, as the wagon went off into the distance. Screaming, wailing.

"*Nu*, imagine all this, and when the *Sperre* was over, I found out that word on the street was that it had been my mission. I, the chief agent, had brought about the *Sperre*. So went the rumor. *Nu*, me. Nothing could have been further from the truth. But the rumor persisted. People talked. I could not go around to everyone and convince them. Rumors had the strength to walk, while we no longer did. And who would talk with me? To this day, I hate to think of it. I was taken forever from the Lodz ghetto a few months later, and perhaps there are still survivors who remember Reb Yosef Ingberg as an agent of the Germans, their error never corrected. Who knows? Perhaps in the gas chambers at Chelmno, in the minutes during which they convulsed before death, not only the faces of their loved ones passed before their eyes, but also those they hated, and they whispered horrible curses unto death. Was there a Jew who whispered my name? Did I rise up in front of the eyes of so-and-so, in my pink shirt, as his lips entreated?"

Grandpa Yosef stands up and faces the window. In the west, over the ocean, the light from the east is reflected. The day has begun. Grandpa Yosef cracks his knuckles, moves this way and that. Time for prayers, a cup of coffee perhaps. He must go and see when the doctor is coming, we can't just leave Lolek this way. The door opens. A nurse comes in and announces that a doctor will be coming soon. Grandpa Yosef nods, calmly bobbing his head, as if having measured the time between his wish and its realization, he is pleased with the speed. The nurse leans over Grandpa Lolek's bed to check on him, straightens his head on the pillow, smoothes his sheets. Grandpa Yosef watches her movements—perhaps he can learn something new. Then he disappears from the room. Praying, no doubt. But he comes back with a cup of "Swiss coffee" (someone fixed the machine) and the physician follows him in with Effi at his side.

We are asked to leave the room. Effi stays—she is a doctor. Grandpa Yosef stays—he is not moving. I go out and call Anat. Yariv picks up the phone. He tries to figure out where I am and when I'll be back, reducing the complicated topic to his true interest: Will I bring him a present? We agree on a ball. Red. The kind that squeaks when you press it. I think about Irenka. The thread of life's happiness. I want to hold my son. What, I wonder, do you tell a boy in a train car on the way to Belzec? What do you explain to him when the doors open, orders are barked, and everyone must get off? The kid would be screaming, wouldn't he? But he mustn't scream. And if he is quiet, if he asks questions, what do you answer? Anat takes the phone and listens to the night's events, also wanting to take part in the shifts. She's giving a benefit evening for foster children, but she can find the time, perhaps not tonight, but tomorrow. She will look after Grandpa Lolek too, it's her prerogative. Strange, I think. Anat is half Iraqi, on her father's side, and in her huge family there are at least two celebrations almost every week. How is it that there are hardly any troubles? There should be a proportional relationship, shouldn't there? Her family is large. But with them we go to weddings, *brisses*, bar mitzvahs. With us—visiting the sick, funerals. How is that? Once we went to the funeral of Uncle Shmuel, her mother's brother. That was the Polish side. Strange indeed. I can hear Yariv in the background, wanting to be part of the conversation. He grabs the phone again and clarifies: The ball must squeak. A strict engineer, my child, formulating his desires in precise detail.

The doctor comes out. Not much news. They have to run tests and keep him under observation. His current condition may continue for some time, the bodily systems need to recover. We look at Grandpa Lolek. The change in him cannot be ignored. His face has taken on a tenderness, a strange glow. As if his soul has found an unfamiliar tranquility that he has no intention of giving up so quickly. Perhaps what is so striking is his silence. Finally, the ever-present handicap of his defective, limbless Hebrew has disappeared within the silence of his body, removed from Grandpa Lolek's face like a mask that has held him back all these years, a barrier between him and us. We look at him as we stand there, and it's like looking into a small pool of water. We perceive with clarity, finally seeing him as he was seen one day in the fifties by an anonymous photographer who needed to produce a suitable picture—perhaps for a poster, perhaps for a new Israeli stamp—and had found Grandpa Lolek a good model for his needs. He had tried to photograph him as a Zionist leader observing his vision, his gaze turned slightly upwards and forward, somewhat diagonal. But in the wonderful picture in his album, Grandpa Lolek wears an expression reserved for golfers, a second after the swing, his eyes searching for the ball in flight. Now we understand the photographer. On Grandpa Lolek's tranquil face lies the quiet radiance befitting leaders of nations.

Effi goes over to the window and draws the curtains. Grandpa Lolek's face fills with a dark sleepiness. "Go home, I'll sit here for a while," she says.

I agree. She comments to Grandpa Yosef, "You can take a break too. I'll be fine here."

Grandpa Yosef refuses. "No, no," he replies, somewhat hurt, "maybe later." Alex had said he would come, and Atalia too. She would come alone. Hainek had to go back to Beersheba for some urgent business.

We sit there and try to imagine Grandpa Hainek having urgent business.

*

Grandpa Lolek was in no hurry. The critical condition of the first few hours had been exchanged for the comforts of a sleepy empire where the king held court in bed. The doctors concluded that a benign tumor had developed in his head, which could be removed with one or two operations as soon as his body gained some strength. This diagnosis gave rise to a general sigh of relief, but the object of the diagnosis remained indifferent to the turn of events. Resting on his bed, he was quiet and free of worries. Only his fluttering wink reminded us of the life currently trapped inside a stroke.

Word of Grandpa Lolek's hospitalization spread through the

family by the usual means—phone calls and the fluctuation of the stars—and they came, teeming with urgency, soaked in sweat, three-busses-from-Netanya, local trains, aging cars, all come to peruse Grandpa Lolek and let out a murmur. A massive force collected them piecemeal from the troubles of life. The secret wings of the family that were scattered around the country, their connections normally hidden and disguised, were suddenly exposed and there they all were, summoned by the urgent alarm call of true trouble. The white room groaned, chairs were dragged in from the hallway, from the waiting room, and surreptitiously from the room next-door. The iv stand was wheeled against the wall. The empty bed next to Grandpa Lolek's became populated with visitors who settled themselves down close to one another, four or five in a row like heavy parrots.

And there were guests too. Unlike the family, they were notable for the temporary sense of their visits—they came for just a short while, didn't want to tire anyone out. What distinguished them from the family was also the absence of calculating looks at the other inhabitants of the room. Neighbors came. Friends came. Old creditors came. As they looked at Grandpa Lolek, they saw the silent debts within him, pondered their money and sighed. The elderly court clerk came, the one who delayed cases in return for stories of Anders' Army. He looked at his sleeping hero and sighed. There were visitors whose business with Grandpa Lolek was not apparent even by the end of their visits. They sighed and left. Green the Mechanic came. Why hadn't he been told anything, he asked angrily. He had begun to grow suspicious when the Vauxhall hadn't shown up, so he had made enquires and here he was. He stood with his hands spread wide and announced to the room: the Vauxhall, he would handle.

From the moment Grandpa Lolek began to command all horizontal attention as he lay in bed, Grandpa Yosef took the vertical attention, dashing this way and that, welcoming visitors and doctors, handling all the necessities. A great deal of motion circulated through Grandpa Lolek's room, and in the center of it all was Grandpa Yosef. He hardly left the hospital, devoting himself completely to care-giving. His shirts were clean but a faint odor wafted up from them, and from his body too. His eyes were bloodshot, his cheeks damp with glistening perspiration. He chopped up the endless time into shifts and handed them out to anyone who asked. Uncle Lunkish turned up with two umbrellas—so what if it wasn't raining—and got one shift, just one. Aunt Frieda came from Netanya, declaring, "*Nu*, you know I never got along with Lolek, but family is family," and demanded a shift. Uncle Menashe left the butcher shop and demanded a shift. Uncle Mendel came, inspected the *mezuzah* with his fingernail and sat down. Another shift.

Even at the end of the distribution, plenty of shifts were left over. Most of them were taken by us, Grandpa Lolek's *like*-grandchildren. We were recruited in different permutations, usually linking up with Grandpa Yosef, the lead caregiver. The *real* family—Grandpa Hainek—was represented by Atalia. She demanded and received one shift every day. In the hospital Grandpa Hainek wandered restlessly. Haifa. The north of the country. It might snow. And he rushed back to his southern city of Beersheba before his Polish destiny could awaken and strike, taking Atalia away from him. Every day he brought Atalia at the beginning of her shift, drove back to Beersheba in a taxi with the windows rolled up, and showed up again when her shift was over. He was consistent in the way he gave the obligatory ten minutes which Atalia forced him to allot to his oldest brother. He sat there polished, heavy, boots sticking out, sternly scanning the place.

In light of the grueling job he had taken upon himself (twice-a-day-Beersheba-Haifa-and-back) for Atalia's sake, and to ward off his fears, we hoped to discover something new in Grandpa Hainek. We looked at him and tried to comprehend. It was a good season for a little compassion. We thought about the beginning of the war. We tried to envision an eleven-year-old boy taken to a village he had never seen before, his father telling him this would be his new family, that he could not see his mother and father for a while. *You mustn't ever say you are a Jew.* He had to memorize prayers. *Here, this is your father, only him. Here, this is your mother, you cannot say she is not. Here are your brothers.* An eleven-year-old boy, left alone despite his tears. The farmer takes him to the barn and silently shows him how to work. From that boy our thoughts returned to the man sitting here in heavy boots, and we tried to envelope him with understanding, with tenderness. The thoughts lasted a second or two but then fell apart with a clatter and we had to think again about the eleven-year-old boy—if we wanted to.

The obligatory ten minutes passed and Grandpa Hainek escaped to his taxi. He spent a few minutes looking for passengers to take to Beersheba, but either way he was soon headed south, before the flakes could begin to whiten Haifa and clog everything up with mud and snow.

In the world, meanwhile, it was a dry winter. No rain. Freezing at night time, sometimes warm during the days. People said, "It's already November and no sign of winter." They gazed at the sky with astonishment, even some pride, practically hinting at a secret partnership in this decision of nature to flood the days with what had not ended in summer—light, heat, and strange winds. A violent and sterile winter, trying with all its might, but forgetting the main point. It glanced at the deeds of the previous winter and reproduced the freezing winds, doing its best, but there was no rain. Every night leaves fluttered through the darkness. The sea opposite Grandpa Lolek's room was full of great waves. Grandpa Yosef liked to stand at the window. At night you could hear the waves, and the wind sweeping paper from notice boards along the street.

In between visits, shifts, doctor's examinations and nuisances, Grandpa Yosef's journey continues. I try to time my shifts so I can continue on the voyage with him. My shifts are punctuated with essentially normal life. I come and go while the voyage waits. But gravity pulls the chapters together and the times between shifts are forgotten, dismissed from memory, leaving a continuity, an energetic and impatient journey.

Every time I come, Grandpa Yosef is in the midst of some burning matter, rushing past me, does-he-look-like-someone-who-has-time-to-sit-and-talk-about-what-happened-fifty-years-ago? Yet he is eager to talk of the voyage raging inside him, and very soon he sits me down, rids himself of all sorts of nuisances, including the ones I bother him with, and tells me offhandedly about Grandpa Lolek's status. He looks at me sternly: What do I mean by coming here and demanding miraculous improvements in the health of someone lying in bed like a sphinx? What could be new? Then he reaches out with impatient fingers to the bag I've brought, pulls out the clothes Anat prepared for him, the neatly cut sandwiches with little stickers noting the content of each one and whether they should be refrigerated. He nods, mumbles, "Thank you very much," and can't resist biting into the first sandwich, supplementing it with some coffee from a thermos. He sips and munches.

It seems to me that we both try to time our shifts so that we are together. But in fact Grandpa Yosef does most of the shifts, sharing days and nights with Effi too. One morning, between shifts, she asks me, "How many *Aktionen* were there in Bochnia anyway?" Atalia, at the end of a shift, asks me something about the ghettos. And I slowly begin to comprehend that the voyage is taking place during their shifts too. Or perhaps there is a completely different voyage going on there. The same places, the same events, and yet a different voyage. Grandpa Yosef does not divulge—he divides and conquers.

I come to take over from Dad on one of my shifts and find him and Grandpa Yosef laughing. They were recalling a day in Dad's childhood in Bochnia, when his mother sent him with his sister to the *dayan-posek*, the arbitrator, to check if the chicken for Shabbat was kosher even though she had found a tiny imperfection in it. Dad and his sister spoke only Polish, the *dayan* only Yiddish. With great effort they memorized their mother's question, learning the words by heart: *di mame hot geheysn fregn a shayle oyb dos hindl iz treyf oder kosher.* But on their way to the store, the syllables scattered in disarray. The two walked on worriedly, rapidly losing their arsenal of words as they neared the *dayan*. By the time they arrived, only a few confused letters and one simple phrase remained, a few sounds at the end of the sentence.

Dad and Grandpa Yosef laugh as they reminisce, and I realize there is no happenstance here: Grandpa Yosef is in the same era with everyone, the era of the voyage. I am not enough for him. During Dad's shifts the voyage slips through. It is planted in Atalia's shifts too. In Effi's shifts a twin voyage sneaks in. Grandpa Yosef is producing enough baby voyages to conquer the expanses of the family.

*

"Life went on after the *Sperre*. Those who had gone, were gone. Those who remained were overcome by hunger, thirst, and a will to live. It is hard to believe how quickly people went back to discussing the affairs of the day—potatoes, soup, the prospect of a cabbage shipment. Gradually the streets healed from the *Sperre* and, wondrously, new Jews flowed into the ghetto. As if the Germans had forgotten that they had evacuated Jews because of over-crowdedness, they continued to bring in more and more. Although I had not been taken away, I myself became a ghost after the *Sperre*. No one came close to me; they wouldn't dare. But I needed friends. My town of Bochnia was far beyond the mountains and the darkness, and the Jews here did not want me. Feiga was gone. I was not going to find her. It seemed the hunger and loss had weakened me so much that I no longer had the strength to get up and continue searching for my little bird. My legs longed to take me to Feiga, to awaken my heart. But my heart, what could it do? I could not just pick up my hat and go. All I could do was tire out my legs. There was not a day when I did not roam the ghetto in circles. I needed people, needed to talk, to socialize. I wanted to pray, to share a prayer with other Jews. I wanted to join a prayer *minyan*, to contribute my voice. But after the *Sperre* all religious life was forbidden, holy studies punishable by death. Even marriage ceremonies, when permitted, were conducted by Rumkowski. He was given sort of captain's duties. People gathered secretly to study and went on praying in underground groups. Me, they fled like the devil, exercising extreme caution.

"About a week after the end of the *Sperre*, Yom Kippur came, on September twenty-first. The ghetto was preoccupied with work, food and sickness. I walked far, as far as my legs could carry me, as if that were my way to somehow mark the torments of the holy day. And behold, from one of the houses emerged a distinguished Jew. He looked at me with penetrating eyes and asked, 'Would you like to pray on this holiest of days?' And wonder of wonders, he took me into an alcove in the house, where a secret prayer group was squeezed into the cellar. Jews wrapped in prayer shawls looked up at me and nodded their welcomes. I was handed my own *tallis*. A moment later, I, Yosef Ingberg of Bochnia, was praying in a *minyan*.

Guess who this miraculous man was, who dared to come out to me, to look into my eyes, to see that I was merely a Jew seeking prayers, not an agent or a chief agent?"

Grandpa Yosef wants me to guess. I give up. "Well, who was it?"

"It was Mr. Hirsch. Yes, Mr. Hirsch, the man who sometimes wanders through the neighborhood." He looks at me, detecting trains of amazement running over my face.

"Hirsch?"

"Yes, Mr. Hirsch. Now you have to make an effort and replace the person you know with his image from the ghetto days, when he was still an honorable rabbi, one of the senior beadles of the Admor of Tipow. Soon after I arrived in the ghetto I had noticed him on the streets; he stood out because of his great height, which did not result from the length of his body but from his gait—upright, arrogant even. He walked proudly through the ghetto, fraternizing only with similarly Orthodox men. They lived as a collective, a cohesive group from Tipow, obeying the rulership of their rabbi, the Admor, daring even to defy Rumkowski and his gang. In every matter they held Rumkowski accountable. They negotiated with him fearlessly over food rations and work quotas and housing. Everything. The Admor of Tipow gave the word, and his disciples went to battle.

"After the prayers, where I had been the tenth man to complete their *minyan*, Hirsch did not dismiss me. For some reason he attached me—not to his group, God forbid, but to himself, solely to himself. I found myself strolling the streets with him, just the two of us. We spoke a little, but mostly we were silent. Most of the words were spoken by Hirsch. He thought out loud, gave me his homiletics, and the things I heard from him I never imagined I would hear. Until the war I had been a man of Torah, I had studied diligently, but what I had learned was unlike anything I heard from Hirsch. He spoke pearls of wisdom and his persona was lofty and exalted, splendor in his appearance and splendor in his heart. To him, only to him, I poured out the entire truth, that I was not an agent nor anything of the kind. Only with him was I bold enough to let down my guard. I also gave him Ahasuerus's money. I told him to take it and give it to charity. But Hirsch only shook his head and laughed bitterly. 'Why would we want your money?' he asked mockingly, as if I had offered something forbidden.

"Sometimes he would erupt in fits of anger, accusing the whole world, accusing assimilated Jews, modernism, even myself. Sometimes there were long silences and I walked beside him quietly, waiting for his foul mood to pass. But usually he was in good spirits, and his Torah was as sweet as honey. During the hours I spent with him, life seemed to grow larger. It was so easy to believe that there was a world beyond the ghetto walls, and it was as if my soul had already been set free, comforted. I felt myself a man of freedom, walking wherever I pleased.

"We met almost every day. Each morning I hurried from my home on Dolna Street to meet him, and if he did not arrive, the whole day went badly. But when he did, we soon began to walk around the ghetto in conversation. He gradually began to unfetter his tongue. He asked me, 'Wherefore the destruction?' Standing at a crossroads, he grasped my shoulders and repeated the question: 'Wherefore the destruction?' It was a custom of his, to ask questions, when he was the one who had the answers. He came up with a question and repeated it over and over again, but it was not from me that he sought an answer—rather, from himself. Again and again, 'Wherefore the destruction?' And his reply: 'Due to the diminution of life.' What did this mean?

"Rabbi Hirsch explained. 'Even before the war, long before we could have imagined this state of affairs, I used to look around at life in our rabbi's court. Everything was so simple, the usual worries. In the *cheders* the little boys studied, and in the yeshivas the young men, and rabbis expounded upon the Torah, and Admors guided the simple people, and our minds did not engage in the greater questions of life. These wise men wished to delve deeper into rabbinic writings, to amend and revalue the laws, to interpret the sages' opinions. And the questions grew smaller and smaller, down to the scale of a feather, a bone, an egg. Oh, how small the questions grew. I gave notes to the rabbi on trivial matters—an onion fallen on an impure stovetop, or a crumb hidden among the straw. Tiny questions—shadows of questions. Where was the richness of life, the mystery?!

"'And when the questions grow small, so too does the soul and the faith. Our eyes suffice with small sins, and our hearts follow our eyes. Exploitation does not gnaw at one's conscience, lies do not sour one's breath. And life is pleasant, and worshipping *Hashem* is done offhand. Jews needed their lives to grow large again, after having diminished so. This is why everything now descends upon us. Because we stopped asking questions. Effortless existence weakened our questions. And here, now, everyone is asking questions…'

"Rabbi Hirsch's look turned cruel for a moment, vengeful. I had yet to learn of his tragedy, the tears he wept inside while he spoke so finely. Nothing I had learned had prepared me for such opinions. It was a desecration that was, somehow, not desecrating. As I lay in bed at night, I turned his words over and over in my mind. Life that had diminished…and what had befallen us because of it. I revisited scenes from the *Sperre*, the children, Rabbi Halberstam from Bochnia on the street, just like that, lying on the street, and for a moment I thought of Feiga, the comfort in her arms, and back came pictures from the *Sperre*, and up floated Hirsch's words.

"The diminution of life.

"In the morning my feet were drawn to Hirsch, and I spent entire days with him, with his relentless, unforgiving theories, and his words, which were unbefitting, and the likes of which I had never before heard. They were so sharp, and they compelled my heart to listen, to examine, to self-examine—was my own life so small? Were my questions small?

"I noticed that as the days passed, the fire of hatred grew stronger in him. His claims were harsh, bitter. 'How can we remonstrate?' he asked. 'After all, we ourselves are commanded in the holy Bible to destroy a people, Amalek. What is the difference between a command from our Lord, *Ribono shel olam*, and a command from their mustached god? What is the difference between annihilating Amalek and annihilating the Jews? We are commanded in the holy Torah, *Thou shalt blot out the remembrance of Amalek from under heaven;*

thou shalt not forget. Why, therefore, should we complain that the *goyim* too have been given their own Torah, in which they are commanded to kill us?'

"'And the children?' I asked. The children. Scenes of the *Sperre* flickered through my mind, and scenes of Bochnia, and beautiful Irenka, but Hirsch stood and faced me and his voice thundered, 'It is said in our Torah, *Now go and smite Amalek and spare them not...but slay both man and woman, infant and suckling...*do you understand, sir? *Infant and suckling*!!'

"He spoke the holy language, and it was so beautiful to hear it in the tortured ghetto, but his words were intolerable and I did not know how to respond, and at night the words mingled and Feiga appeared in a dream, and the infants of Amalek, and in the morning I ran to him to hear more.

"And so it went every day. I did not know the tragedy Hirsch bore in his heart, and I did not know that already then his soul was dismantled, that he was then the persona you know today, but under the authority of the Rabbi of Tipow, his Admor, all his parts were held together as one. To the outside he was still an elegant rabbi, the beadle of the Admor, and on the inside he was falling apart, betrayed, seeking revenge. Today, all that I did not know at the time is known and can be told. Today I know that during the *Sperre*, the Tipow group was required to hand over some of its members. The Admor of Tipow pronounced the names—these shall live, those shall die. And right in the midst of the *Sperre* days, he discovered that a relative of his wife's had recently arrived in the ghetto but had not yet joined the cohesive community, and all of his children were listed for deportation. The Admor ordered that the names be changed. Two of Hirsch's six children were put on the list. The searchers burst into Hirsch's house and pulled out all six of his children, although he had been promised that only two would be taken. By the time Hirsch learned of this awful affair and rushed to save his children, they had already been given to the Germans, from whose claws even the Admor of Tipow could not rescue them.

"And so his six children were lost, and his wife was lost—she jumped onto the wagon that took her children away. After the *Sperre*,

Hirsch was left on his own, and the Rabbi commanded him, 'Jew, take strength in the test that our Father in Heaven is giving you.' The Admor's authority was enough to strengthen the outer shell. But inside, Hirsch's soul was weeping, it did not want to live, and it was ashamed of its cowardice—his wife had thrown herself to death, and he? But Hirsch had no choice. Life had to go on. Even in the ghetto, the Admor's court carried on, and no words of mourning could be voiced because everyone had lost loved ones. Thoughts of revenge and heresy were forbidden. Then Rabbi Hirsch found me, Reb Yosef Ingberg of Bochnia, a Jew from the outside, and to me he released his thoughts—the question of destruction, the question of justice. Thanks to me, that which was confined within him could survive, and I served as a vessel for his anguish.

"I had no idea whatsoever of what was going on in Hirsch's soul, and was utterly unaware of my role, that by talking to me, a stranger, he was draining his embitterment just a little. I only knew that I heard wonders of wonders from him, terrible things. He would put his face close to mine and quote to me from the sages: 'Even if an Amalekite converts, we are commanded to smite him.' He would wag his finger in my face and ask, 'Where are these laws from?' And continue walking as if having spoken calmly, as if his words had not beaten my Jewish heart like a mallet, and I stayed behind him in the heart of the bustling ghetto. And the next day, the same thing.

"One morning something happened. It became known in the ghetto that the Admor of Tipow had escaped. To where, or how he did it, was not clear. But that morning his disciples awoke orphaned. Imagine to yourself what a betrayal that was, without warning, without a hint. The Admor had simply fled with his family. The disciples were not given much time to mourn. Rumkowski's people immediately saw their chance to nullify agreements, break up power, send the poor men off to work groups and deportation lists. They took the Admor's cronies out of the best places in the hospitals, out of the comfortable factories. All at once their privileges were revoked and given to those who found favor with the Judenrat. But worst of all was Hirsch. The Admor of Tipow had disappeared, and Hirsch's dismantled soul, which had been held together by the power of his authority, shattered into smithereens. Why go into detail? In short, *nu*, he completely lost his mind. From the moment the Admor abandoned them, not only did Hirsch's mind weaken, and not only did the Tipowik group's power fall apart, but all its secrets blossomed and spread through the ghetto, including the story of Hirsch. Only then did I learn of the fire that had been eating away at his heart. I was regretful—perhaps I could have offered him some consolation.

"One week later, Hirsch was taken away. I thought he was killed, but as you know, he was not lost in the camps; he is here with us in Eretz Yisrael. And it was the Admor of Tipow, may the memory of this *tzaddik* be a blessing, who did not survive. He was caught and taken with all his loved ones, may God avenge their blood, to Treblinka. He was captured near the town of Shedlitz, and instead of Chelmno, where the Lodz ghetto inhabitants were sent, he went to the gas chambers in Treblinka."

(Treblinka. Untersturmführer Kurt Franz, Doll.)

Grandpa Yosef seems to read my mind. "Yes, that was where that 'Doll' was, *Lalka*, but what difference does it make, one way or the other. Hirsch went, as did many others. And I too, just as I was getting used to life in the Lodz ghetto, I was grouped with some Jews sent to slave labor in a camp near Poznan. Someone dared put my name on the list and kick the chief agent out of the ghetto. And I, Yosef Ingberg, not an agent and not a chief, found myself leaving the Lodz ghetto forever. I cannot recall the name of the camp. How could I? As soon as we arrived, battered from our ride in a truck, after they whipped me and pulled out two teeth, and after two men were shot in front of my eyes (Why? No way to know), my gaze fell briefly on the camp personnel standing in the distance, and I saw the figure of Ahasuerus.

"There he stood, next to the camp commandant, and he seemed to be tutoring him, teaching the inexperienced commandant. I stared. I must have stood out from the distance—a Jew looking straight at death. Suddenly his eyes met mine. I saw him give the commandant an instruction and then all the personnel came up to us. Terror fell upon our group. All around me people sensed the shadow of death approaching. Only rarely did the senior officers interfere with the

Jews' lives. They left that job for junior officers, sergeants, the Ukrainians and the volunteers, damn them.

"I whispered to the Jews, 'Do not worry, he is a decent man.' They looked at me as if I had lost my mind. They could not have imagined the storm raging in my heart as a thought that was all but forgotten began to reappear: Feiga. We must set off on the road again. Here, the *Kadosh Baruch Hu* was renewing my voyage! I had no doubt of Ahasuerus's intentions. He might not have remembered me at all, but simply been astonished at this Jew staring at him. And yet he might have recognized me, only to wonder how I had not been killed in the *Sperre* as planned. Still, I was certain he would not kill me.

"Ahasuerus came closer. He stopped some six steps away from us. The personnel stood behind him. In front of him the Ukrainians and the sergeants, they too were frozen. They had ceased kicking us, cowed by the presence of authority. What did the general want? They did not know of my Feiga. Perhaps they did not conceive of his Little Lover either. We stood there, everyone around us completely unaware of the true significance of the situation, only Ahasuerus and myself in the center as he stared at me with steely eyes. A brief moment of human expression flitted over his face, a wrinkle that perhaps came from the heart, and an instant later there was nothing but frozen wilderness. He turned back and disappeared into the distance, and with him, like the wings of a crow, went the personnel. Silence lingered in the air for a moment, then all erupted. The whips began again. The shouts picked up. We were pushed, whipped. We were rushed into flimsy wooden huts without windows. We knew neither the name of the camp, nor what they would do with us.

"A whole day and night passed. We were not sent to work. Twice we were brought some disgusting soup, and once we were allowed to use the latrine. Then, from the edge of the window, I saw the car. It had a new hood ornament, a statue of an eagle with its talons digging into the flesh of the car, its bird-legs lifting up behind. And as my heart had foreseen, we were quickly forced out of the hut for a roll-call. The reason for the roll-call was me. A sergeant took hold of me and removed me from the group. They washed me again. And again the bridegroom's clothes. They put me in a closed room.

"Ahasuerus had tormented himself for a whole day and night. All those months, while I was in the Lodz ghetto, he had managed with great effort to banish the Little Lover from his heart, to devote himself to his duties, damn him, and now here I was. He agonized for a whole day and night but was unable to put out the fire kindled by the sight of me, and early the next morning we set off again. This time it was winter. Cold. Ahasuerus's face was strained. Who knew what obligations he had abandoned hastily, and what his punishment would be, how determined he was to be swallowed up in the black abyss of this unrequited love? For four months, more than a third of a year, we had not seen each other. I wondered, should I report anything? He had deposited me in the ghetto and the deposit had been returned. I should say something, should I not? But reality quickly reminded me who I was, and who he was. The months of hunger in the ghetto had mistreated my body and he, the king of evil, now had a higher rank, and it seemed he had also grown taller. He did not talk to me, my existence did not bother him at all. I was an object, like a comb found at the bottom of the sheets, bringing up forgotten emotions. We were driving to his Little Lover, or so he believed. Storing up energy for a decisive conversation with her. Perhaps he would beg. The devil would kneel before the she-devil and weep. He did not know who Feiga was, for whom he was urging his heart, straining his eyes, squeezing out the power from his car. I permitted myself a pause for thought. Leaning back in my seat, I asked myself like a merchant, should I give him back his money? I had spent almost none of it. But that nonsensical thought soon disappeared.

"What more can I say? For two days we drove. The routine of the journey was much like the previous one, but there were no break-downs, no chance for a word to be uttered. Two people driving. Thus far we had accumulated only one spoken sentence, uttered by Ahasuerus before he closed his eyes to sleep. The landscape changed. Flat lakes, black trees. The sky drizzled constantly. We crossed huge rivers and one massive Tigris, which in retrospect I believe was the Wisla, that same Wisla that crossed through Krakow, on to Warsaw, and all the way to Danzig on the North Sea. I was afraid—was Feiga here? In this terrible cold? Here, in such a barren landscape? The car drove on and on as if Ahasuerus could not interfere with its maneuvers. She knew her way, the car. Bilaam's donkey.

"We stopped at a camp. It was entirely black. Black trees and black fences, and all the huts were black, dipped in freezing cold and puddles. The gates opened for us, the camp guards practically danced around in fear. We made a strong impression on them. The camp personnel hurried to welcome Ahasuerus, and I, knowing my role, stayed in the car. I was left in a large square beside the command house. My eyes were glued to the hunched, black images walking to and fro. Jews rotting away from cold and torture, while I sat in a royal car and fine clothing, looking for lovers. I dared not get out and ask the Jews about Feiga. I reprimanded myself—after all, that was what I had come for—but caution held me back. Slowly my silhouette became apparent to the inmates, and Jewish faces began to stare at me. From afar I saw them, but sensed them coming closer. I did not dare get out, and they dared not approach. There was terror in the air, I could sense it. Their caution taught me caution. Ukrainian guards in black uniforms, similar to the SS uniform, walked around the camp arrogantly. They passed by the car, pretending not to notice me. Darkness fell. Calls were heard in the distance. Many footsteps. My body had been freezing for two hours in the car. Inside, Ahasuerus was still meeting with the officers. They were probably presenting their fine achievements to him, boasting of impressive killing quotas, damn them. And then a Jew tapped on the car window. I could tell immediately that it was a Jew. I was horrified by his skeletal face, his body wrapped in rags, but I knew it was a Jew. Afraid, I opened the window a crack.

"'Give me!'

"His Yiddish was crude. His eyes darted around. Black knobs on his face, bruises and cuts. His flesh was covered with wounds. I reached into my clothes. I had no food and was hungry myself, but I still had Ahasuerus's money. I asked about Feiga.

"'No woman here. Give!'

"And then, disaster. From the darkness a figure emerged. A Ukrainian guard. Before I knew what was happening, the whip had landed. The Jew fell. Right beneath my window, he disappeared from my eyes. The Ukrainian went up to him and raised his whip. He thrashed and then turned the whip around and beat the Jew's body with the handle. Another figure came out of the command house. The noise had disturbed the convening gentlemen. The Ukrainian took one step back as an SS officer approached. He looked at me first and my blood curdled. I thought about Yanek's lion whisper from the ghetto. The officer looked away from me—I was nothing to him. In the dark he aimed his pistol downwards. The pistol was hidden from me, but not the flash of lightening followed by a bang. All beneath my window, a step away from me, on the other side of the door, and I could not see a thing. The SS officer straightened up and examined his handiwork. He turned to the headquarters, where Balshazar's feast was going on. The Ukrainian went up to finish the job. He dragged the body away, which was then revealed to me. My heart sunk.

"In the dark, in the silence, I stayed shut in the car. I barely noticed Ahasuerus coming out, throwing himself onto the seat next to me, starting the engine, far from my world. He drove the car, cold, quiet, and I thought of Feiga. For a moment I felt angry at her. What was this journey for? The torture. Jews were dying, for God's sake, and she was holding back. Where was she? Why did she not make an effort, as I was doing, to traverse the distance? A gloom took hold of me, not only anger. I remembered that in the distant days before the war, too, I had sensed a speck of something amiss. My time with her was enjoyable, and she had agreed to marry me, but the balance, how shall I put it...for her I would have run through half of Bochnia, but she? No telling. She had a rich world inside of her, she was quiet, noble. She had many suitors. And yet she had chosen me. That was her way, her world was shut off under lock and bolt, no emotions escaped, no closeness."

Grandpa Yosef tries to explain Feiga. Ahasuerus can wait. The journey can wait. The Shoah can wait. Now, Feiga.

"You know, long before I was bold enough to speak to her, my entire life was devoted to Feiga. In Bochnia, before she even knew of my existence, I would keep track of her daily routine. She walked down Zandetzka Street every day to visit her friend Gittel. And there, on Zandetzka, lived Jozi, a classmate of mine. Not a smart fellow, not a likeable man, in fact. But every day at three forty-five I would turn up at his house and try to tempt him with stamps to trade. That was his only hobby, and for Feiga's sake I began to collect stamps too. There was no better place in the whole street than Jozi's window, where I would sit and wait for her while Jozi crumpled the stamps I had brought, displeased. He would haggle and try to bring my prices down, negotiating back and forth with me, without knowing that it was time that I was buying. Only time. It was not easy to find stamps for Mr. Jozi. Your father used to get hold of some for me, I did not ask how. And I stole from Uncle Marek's collection. I did business with the Polish mailman, helping him out with our maid, Marushka, with whom he was head over heels in love. It was hard to believe how such a great love was possible for that Marushka of ours. Spoiled and sickly, all she ever did was complain.

"At exactly four o'clock, Feiga would appear from down the street. She walked alone, with a straight back. In her heart she did not address the world, but the whole world turned to her. It was impossible not to join the breeze in the trees, the birds in the branches, the fallen leaves scattering at her feet. I practically flew out the window like one of the birds. If only I could be allowed to roll at her feet. But I did not fly, I was no bird. I leaned out of the window towards her like a deer yearning for rivers of water, and she, innocent and pure, walked along. She was modest and knowing, fully aware of the man swinging between life and death at Jozi's window.

"Behind me, Jozi annoyingly complained that the stamps were too ordinary. His complaints increased from day to day, and the time came when he declared that he was sick of stamps. Stamps were for kids.

"And in what would the honorable Jozi take an interest now, if not in stamps?

"Jozi giggled. His eyes sparkled like two balls of grease. '*Nu*, you know...' He rubbed his palms together and the blood pulsed through his face as he pursed his lips. Then he confided the worst. Of all the women in the world, it was Feiga's name that he uttered. He told me how every day at seven in the evening she hurried down the street outside his window on her way home, and that the little lass looked straight at his window.

"Alarms rang through my head. It turned out I was missing an entire show of Feiga at seven in the evening. I would have to stay longer at Jozi's, missing one prayer service. *Hashem* would forgive me. And Feiga was apparently interested in Jozi. If that was true, what good were prayers?

"Imagine, before I knew how many obstacles there were and how difficult it would be. *Nu,* her family, and mine too, they thought we should wait. And imagine the joy in my heart, imagine how I thanked the Lord, when finally everything fell into place. Feiga agreed to marry me. 'I will love you,' she said. What happiness my Feiga gave me. And after the war, as you know, we were married. Almost fifty years of marriage I had with her, and every day was good. And then her strength failed her and my Feiga passed away. I would have liked twenty more years of marriage. I did not have my fill, my thirst was not quenched."

Grandpa Yosef walks to the end of the hallway. Coffee. Ahasuerus's car drives on north through low fields and creeks. Little villages. A flat landscape.

Grandpa Yosef has left a few words behind:

"For one moment there, while the Jew's body was being dragged away and I waited in the car for Ahasuerus, I felt some anger at Feiga, as if the prolonging of this journey was her fault, and the sacrifice of the Jews was unacceptable."

While he is gone at the coffee machine, the story continues without him. Grandpa Yosef and Ahasuerus pass through Mielejewo camp. Ahasuerus gets out to surprise the personnel with an inspection. His appearance is harsh, but his steps slacken, this whole adventure is a loss. If only he could turn back the wheel of time. He cannot. The obligations. The damned Jews. At home he has a wife and child, but without his beloved, life is intolerable. The officers salute, the car is welcomed with respect and amazement. The general's presence is unwanted—in this damned place there is no good time for an inspection. Fortunately, he only goes through the list of staff, enquiring, where is this one? Where is that one? Transferred where? And where was this woman transferred to? Ravensbrück? The answer satisfies him. He gets up and leaves without even finishing his meal. Did they pass the inspection? Would he give a good report? Ahasuerus leaves. The gates shut. And the journey continues. Pruchnik camp, Nadbrzeże camp. Tiny satellites of Stutthof camp on the shores of the Baltic Sea. The journey has only just begun, it transpires. They are traveling to Ravensbrück. Ravensbrück. In Germany, not in Poland. A long journey west, to the heart of the Reich, less than seventy miles from Berlin. Ahasuerus oscillates between relaxation and anger.

Grandpa Yosef comes back with a cup of coffee.

"I feared for my life. This Ahasuerus, there was no telling what he would do when he was angry. Again I found myself afraid to look up, trying to diminish myself. During my hours of rest, I thought up a job for myself: I would sweep the floor of the car and polish the windows and mirrors with my sleeve. That was my instinct—to be necessary. Learn it once, and it will never leave you. I tried out different ideas. I very much wanted to open the hood and glance at the engine, at the bird's hidden organs. I was innocent, I had hardly ever seen cars, and to see one exposed beneath its robes, I had not even imagined possible. I was so close, longing to get to know the mechanism, the technique, to reach out and touch it, to see where the power flowed.

"And so we drove on, swallowing up countries. And then finally we were close to Ravensbrück, where the Little Lover was—where, my heart fluttered, my Feiga might be. But just before the camp, Ahasuerus stopped, as if to gather his strength, to remind himself who he was, an omnipotent general—why should he fear one woman, a minor staff member? He got out of the car with great momentum and walked out into the cold air. He strode confidently, his SS boots creaking in the mud. He stood beside a bush, his hand hovering over the leaves, as if examining his fingers to see whether he was still capable of touching a delicate body. His hand flitted over the bush and I could see he liked the touch. His chin was turned down, his eyes shut tight. And suddenly I saw that Ahasuerus was crying. His hand made a fist around the tendrils of that poor bush. His entire body was trembling.

"Thoughts spun through my mind. *Nu*, such a general, a creature in love, and he was a murderer. How could these two things flow together in his blood? Hot and cold, poison and tenderness. How did his strength not run out? Every hour without her was worse than death and harder than hell.

"Ahasuerus walked away from the bush and came back. Upright, he opened the door and sat down regally. Only his face disclosed the shock, the annihilation to which he was leading himself, betraying his duties. This whole journey was just false hope, and there was no telling how it would end. A moment passed. Another moment. Ahasuerus sat without making a sound. I felt that time was running out, convinced that in Ravensbrück camp I would find Feiga. Ahasuerus would soon start the car and our hearts would be reunited. But Ahasuerus was lost in thought. His breathing was quiet, slow. I turned to look at him, thinking perhaps I could divine his intentions. Would he have the strength to start the car, to go as far as the camp gates? And then another thought ignited—what did he need me for? Once he found his Little Lover, what would he need me for? My fright increased. He will kill me. Why not here? What need is there for me? Two trees along, the side of the road grew large in my eyes. Perhaps he would shoot me beneath one of them, without the traditional escort, without a *kaddish* prayer, without a Jewish burial. *Nu*, Jews were dying in the thousands, and I wanted a Jewish burial. And where were my parents? I no longer believed, of course, that they had been taken East. The truths that had penetrated my ears in the Lodz ghetto, the killings, Chelmno, had slowly connected with my parents who had been sent away. What Chelmno had been for the Jews of Lodz, Belzec had been for my family. Lost, all my loved ones were lost, and there I was, dressed in fine clothing.

"I sighed. And my sigh drew a look from Ahasuerus. He quickly turned back to look at the road, removing me from his field of vision. I froze. I had reminded him of my existence, my unnecessary existence. A mistake.

"He turned and looked at me. 'It's hard...It's hard for everyone...'

"And silence. Emptiness around us. He had not spoken only to me. Around us were woods, and behind them camps, and somewhere in the distance the Lodz ghetto, and more camps, and the whole world was at war. It was hard, it was hard for everyone."

Grandpa Yosef stops talking. He gets up and goes to the window. He looks at the clouds. No rain, no rain. What will be the end? Clouds gather, the sky presses down to the earth, the cold deepens and still the rain does not come. Grandpa Yosef stays by the window but his story does not wait. Behind his back, details slip through, little pieces of morse code that he has already told me an era ago, and they take me through the rest of the story without him.

Ahasuerus starts the car and drives it up to the camp gates. In the women's camp of Ravensbrück there is hunger and disease. The inmates are exhausted. Those who do not join a group, die. Any woman who makes the mistake of standing out in front of the murderous female SS officers is killed. Death is a method, a solution. In the heart of the camp, the "bunker" provides a solution for those whose death the SS murderesses want to slow. But the main point for us—for Grandpa Yosef, for me, for Ahasuerus—is that the Little Lover is there, serving at Ravensbrück.

The car crosses through the gates. There is not even a moment's delay before the meeting. Ahasuerus walks into the staff building. Then he goes to one of the huts. A conversation takes place there for a moment or two. A fair young woman emerges and walks away with heavy, angry steps. He follows her, pleading. She pushes his hands away, speeding up. She is not tall. Pretty, let us say. Her face is flushed with anger. She disappears behind a hut.

"There, in the savagery, they were not bound by their rules of etiquette," Grandpa Yosef mumbles. "I had not imagined such a thin little thing. She wasn't huge or red-faced, like so many of the cruel SS female officers. And it was clear that she was unhappy with Ahasuerus's advances. Unaccustomed to such crudeness. She had been taught that a woman should be treated politely. Gently. And he, the villain, would not let her alone.

"In the car I could see little and hear nothing. The minutes passed and I felt a strong desire to get out and look for my Feiga. But it was good that I didn't, because here was Ahasuerus marching towards me, getting into the car, slamming its door. He started the engine in a fury, in a storm. His face was red, evil, as if nothing else mattered in the world. The car's tires screeched on the road, burst through the gates, the sentries barely had time to fling them open. Ahasuerus made the car gallop. Imposing the roar of his heart upon it, he strained the engine to its limits. His face was determined, as if there were great intent in his driving, but I sensed that our journey was over. He looked right and left, his driving seemed very purposeful, but I could sense the truth in the regal car. She acquiesced to having her pedals pressed, her wheel turned, but her senses had been weakened, and she was no longer searching for a route but rather she was fleeing. It was over and done with—the search for Feiga had failed.

"Again I believed he would kill me. But he did not. And what did he do with me? I will tell you the truth. All the horrors of the Shoah that I saw, everything that is best forgotten, lives on lucidly in my memory. The memories are clear and transparent, like a beautiful landscape. But the end of Ahasuerus is dim. When did we part ways? I vaguely remember someone walking me down a path of wet gravel. That was probably no longer Ahasuerus, but an officer, I think. And then the memory is swallowed up. Rain drenches the world and I am in a suffocating space. Figures around me, prisoners. I too am a prisoner. I awake in the men's camp of Ravensbrück. A merciful figure comes up to me, shoves at me some sort of thing which I shall call a blanket, although that is not what it was. A hard, cold sheet. It was barely flexible enough to be placed on one's body, it was useless for heat. The memories return. I am completely frozen, a cut on my head and a deep gash from ankle to knee. The merciful man, the head of the hut, whose name is Adler, whispers in my ear that I will feel better by morning. Although I had not yet been a prisoner in any camp, only ghettos and strange journeys, my voyage with Ahasuerus had taught me plenty about camp life. I would not feel better in the morning. In the morning there would be slave labor. I would starve. They would beat me ceaselessly. They would rob me of my bread, the other inmates too. It would not be better in the morning.

"Do you know what they called the camp system there, in the north? *Vernichtung durch Arbeit*. Extermination through work."

(He finds strange pleasure in rolling the German words off his tongue, tasting them on his lips. *Vernichtung durch Arbeit.*)

"But this man, Adler, tries to lift my sprits. From somewhere they bring hot soup, as if a restaurant is open not far away. The soup is a bland concoction, but I sip it, inhale the broth, and sense that without this Adler I will have no life.

"And indeed, I was right. Adler was one of the saints. My days of Ravensbrück had begun. *Vernichtung durch Arbeit.* Extermination through work. In the morning, still dark, roll-calls that last for hours. Shouting, beating, physical punishments. People murdered right beside you. The living go off to work. A moribund mass of prisoners sets off shoulder to shoulder. The work is exhausting, our brains dizzied from fear. The German supervisors do not spare the rod. One of them had fit a silver knob on the end of his whip. Everyone knew that all that whip needed was one thrash. Prisoners were murdered over mistakes, over nothing, over boredom that took hold of a German. The Ukrainian guards were not allowed to kill. Only the Germans had that right, and there was much jealousy. We, the prisoners, worked. All we did was work. At lunch there was a hard hunk of bread and soup. A stench rose from it, but the prisoners fought over one more spoonful and stole each other's slices of bread. Simple people, everyday Jews, became murderous and loathsome. They would rip a piece of bread away from you and laugh in your face, crazed. There are no depths of hell lower than that. And in the midst of it all was Adler.

"This man, Adler, revealed himself from the first as a sort of Judah the Maccabi. A courageous Jew, he did not fear the prisoners, and even found courage in front of the SS. He knew his limitations and exercised caution, but he guarded the prisoners like a Hasmonean. His work was exhausting. There was no shortage of villains among the prisoners, and even those who were not villainous had been driven mad by hunger and were capable of anything. Even in the heart of suffering, on the brink of death, the power-hungry still lust for power, the traitorous still hand over their brethren, and the informants still collaborate.

"Among all these, with infinite dedication, stood Adler. He

pronounced verdicts like King Solomon, separated the Jewish hawks from one another like Moses, and brandished a sword like David. He was as kind as—to whom can I compare his kindness? It was infinite. Incredibly, before the war he was a Doctor of Humanities at the university of Lvov. A scholar, a researcher of history, an author of books on theories of the soul. A Jew who had forgotten his Judaism, wrapped up in the world of the *goyim*, and that was how he liked it. He researched Jewish history too, but in the way that a geologist studies rocks or a geographer the patterns of streams. It was in the camp that his Jewish soul was revealed. By the time I, Yosef Ingberg, arrived at Ravensbrück men's camp, which was attached to the infamous women's camp, Adler was already positioned as a leader of the people, one to guide them through the desert for forty years. *Nu*, I am exaggerating a little…"

Grandpa Yosef stops. He breathes heavily, clearly searching for the right words. He wants to paint me an accurate picture of Adler, as great as the man himself, but not ordinarily great like memorial statues.

"The head of the prisoners in the camp was called Farkelstein. Adler, on his part, stayed away from him. He could easily have become head of the prisoners, but he avoided that role. The SS themselves, damn them, although they did not appoint Adler to Farkelstein's position, used to come to him, recognizing his authority over the prisoners. They let Farkelstein bear the official title, a sort of badge of respect invented in the camps, but much to Farkelstein's chagrin, they ignored him and his title. Farkelstein could have designated Adler for the hard jobs, the more injurious ones, or handed him over to the Germans with a wink, but more than he hated Adler, he feared him, and more than he feared him, he was trapped in a superstitious conviction that without Adler there would be no Farkelstein. Where did this belief come from? What was the logic? But then, where did places like Ravensbrück come from; what logic was behind them? There was none. Farkelstein dealt every day with his hatred and his envy and his fears. And it was into this river of flames that I slid. Because for some reason, Farkelstein immediately began to hate me and harass me. And harassment by the head of the prisoners was tantamount to a death sentence.

"A few days had passed since I arrived in the camps, and already I was half-dead. The work was grueling. My body, sensing death, suffered from dysentery. Inside the rags of my trousers the excrement dribbled over my body. The end was nearing. I no longer had the strength to work. There were moments, my mind dizzied, when I was drawn to the whip, especially the one with the silver knob. To offer my head, to kiss the whip. Shut off the whole world, no strength, no desires, only the whip, that whip, sharp and clear. That silver knob was like a *rimon*—like the finial that decorates a Torah scroll.

"How did I not die?

"Adler.

"Was there any other way?

"During work he protected me. When food was distributed he looked out for me. He got hold of clean clothing for me. At night, in the hut, he fed me the secret soup which a few prisoners cooked up somewhere in the distance every night. Only a few were lucky enough to get a few drops of it.

"Strange. So many were dying. *Vernichtung durch Arbeit.* Extermination through work. On every bed, every night, a Jew fought for his life. No justice and no mercy. Here died the son of a rabbi, there a tailor, a father of ten. Here was a boy dying, no one knew his name, there an elderly man—who knew how he had survived that long? Jews were dying everywhere and yet Adler took pity on me, visiting my bedside as if I alone were a patient among vacationers. A spoiled tourist with a bad stomach on a pleasure cruise, and the captain making himself personally responsible for his health, embarrassed by the regretful mishap. Because of such a trivial problem, the traveler might miss the best of the itinerary.

"Every night Adler sat on the edge of my bed, untouched by tiredness, by hunger. And do you know what Adler did before the dying body of Yosef Ingberg? He recited his studies. He told me about the theories he investigated, the matters on which he had almost completed a conclusion or two that were important for humanity, before the world had lost its mind. I lay at his feet, deathly ill, with only a spark remaining in my soul, a small candle's light not yet extinguished. And to that flame, it seems, Adler talked, night after night. What little remained of me was there in the core of the flame, and each night I had to regain strength for the next day, another day of *Vernichtung durch Arbeit*. During work too, between the trenches of dirt we dug only to fill up again—the purpose, after all, was extermination—Adler recited his studies softly, as if leafing through pages he had left only a moment ago on his desk at Lvov University. He was respectful of his only student, the dying Yosef Ingberg, as I lay on the side of the trench while he himself worked a double quota. The supervisor turned a blind eye, and against the background noise of the picks softly tapping, only Adler's voice could be heard. Every day he took a book off the shelf and taught me its content. The great Khans of Mongolia and the travels of Attila the Hun. The history of the Ancients and the mystery of the Danube. The ascendance of Jewish agriculture and the travels of Alexander the Great. He spread before me everything he had studied of the past and the present, until the war had snatched him away from his desk. And he revealed a new topic to me, which he had only just begun to explore, a study on the true nature of pirates. Every night when we returned from work, after he had fed me the extra soup, Adler told me of his preliminary conclusions, and in those moments it seemed that for him the Holocaust was merely a slight nuisance, as if he had been called away from his office to discuss a tedious memorandum with the faculty treasurer. He was not pained by the whip that cut through his flesh, nor by the hangings in the center of the camp, nor the bad food. His spirit fell because of the pirate Subatol Deul, who was waiting for him, unexplored, on the deck of the *Costa Negra*. There he stood, the skull-and-bones flag above him, while Adler carried baskets of dirt from the trenches to the mounds.

"What can I say? My soul was tiny, practically devoid of life, but Adler's words penetrated it and brought health. Slowly but surely, thanks to his lectures, I recovered. And Adler? From the moment it became clear that I would live, it was as if I had graduated to the next class, and he added advanced topics to the curriculum. Adler taught me—to survive. He taught me the ruses of existence and the customs of the camp and what was required if one wished to live. Every day one had to wage a careful war against the SS, against the Ukrainians, against the Jewish police—God help us—and do not forget Farkelstein and his gang. Among all these troubles and hardships, Adler roamed like a king, a lion, directing justice, obtaining here and giving there, and all in aid of the weak, the sick, to save one more soul from death. Not that Adler was able to help much. Prisoners died every day, and every day new ones came, and there was no clear law dictating what saved a man from death, what brought him to death. But Adler did not give up. His dealings were many and dangerous, always engaged in quick transactions intended to maintain human dignity.

"It is very difficult to describe the greatness of a man like Adler in such a place. Many prisoners ended up in the Ravensbrück men's camp, rabbis and intellectuals, community leaders and public figures. You cannot imagine how quickly one's soul declines in a place like that, and if it does not decline, the body withers. It is hard, hard to survive, to remain human. Many struggled to save their lives, to save a human soul, and some managed, but someone like Adler...*nu*, how can I describe him?

"One day I told him I would like to be like him. Adler smiled, waved his pick, and kept on digging the trench.

"He dug twice as many trenches as he needed to, completing quotas for the sick and the weary, in return for the supervisors' silence. His Jewish soul burst through like a young lion. Sometimes he said nothing, and I was enveloped by a silence of awe. I examined this marvelous man closely, wondering if bad memories tormented him, as they did me, or if perhaps he was plowing ahead, making inroads in his research. My eyes examined, my ears mined. And slowly I noticed a series of grumbles escaping silently from his lips, kind of furious mumbles, as if he were conducting a bitter negotiation with someone. The anger and mumbling did not go on for long. A short time later he taught me about the Pharaonic kings, the education of children in Sparta, the customs of the Greek Olympics. But I was intensely curious—what went on during those silences? What was the cause of Adler's bitterness? I had already learned that it was best to stay away from the truth, better not to know of peoples' wounds. Had he lost six children like Hirsch had? Had some other disaster befallen him? Curiosity has a way of triumphing, so one day I dared to ask about the meaning of his mumblings and anger.

"Adler, embarrassed, admitted that these murmurs of his were a theory he was trying out, a survival method, and he did not know if the theory was ripe for instruction yet. I demanded—teach me! And Adler began to teach me a simple theory. He explained that I had to contemplate the future that had been robbed from me and cry out in bitter resentment—how had they dared take the future that had been planned for me?! 'Grow bitter! Be furious!' he urged me. 'Imagine the future that was ready for you, and cry out against the reality trying to cancel it out!' And that was not all. I also had to outline before him the precise details of my robbed future, and complain, and rage, and wave my fists at reality.

"And so, every day, we both bitterly protested the theft of our futures, and threatened like lions—who would dare take this future from us? Adler was extremely fanatical about this future theory. The past was completely forbidden. He demanded that I rid myself of memories, throw them all out, shake out my pockets. When one day I began to tell him about Feiga and our good days in Bochnia, he grew enraged. 'The future! The future! If you wish to live, think about her and you in the future, only in the future!' He waved his pick in the air and the Ukrainian supervisor looked up in surprise and curiosity, thinking he might be lucky enough to witness one Jewish prisoner murdering another.

"There was no choice. From morning to evening the future preoccupied us. We were full of anger at all that had been stolen from us. Adler commanded the future to appear in all its details. At roll-calls, at food distribution, always we lived in the future. Day after day I left the splendid house I had built for my Feiga and myself in Bochnia, to study at a fine *yeshiva*. In the evenings we sat and dined and talked about life. And Adler, who held a chair at a university, labored over his book about pirates. He went to the Caribbean once or twice to expand his studies. He tasted pineapple, palm fruit, papaya. Studied the world of the pirates. And life in the future was simple and good.

"When we grew slightly tired of the future, we dwelled on Adler's research. I began to gain courage and ask questions, make comments, even construct a few hypotheses and semi-proposals of my own. Every single moment, from before sunrise until after sundown, waving our picks up and down, it was inexplicable how death had not yet taken us, but with Adler the hours passed pleasantly. Pleasantly, *nu*, perhaps that is an exaggeration. But it was tolerable. There was a hint of a reason to go on living in the trenches, in the stench of the hut, with the horrible punishments and the dead we no longer counted or thought of. Every morning I longed for the moment when we would be positioned alongside the pits after roll-call, after the interminable march, after the morning punishments, and there, in the pits, a few cigarettes for the supervisor, and then I could regale Adler with ideas built up overnight. My lust for knowledge impressed and amused Adler. He straightened up over his pick for a moment, giggling, 'As soon as you were brought here, I knew I could not lose my best student.'

"His compliment embarrassed me but filled me with pride. I wished I could be his student at the real university in Lvov. In Bochnia they had said I had the character of a scholar. One day I asked Adler, 'Why, why this extermination? Why is all this occurring?'

"Adler stopped working and stood bewildered, holding his pick up in mid-air. Then he slowly lowered it. 'Why the extermination?' He repeated my question, mulling it over. He went back to work. He hummed the sentence to himself one more time, 'Why the extermination?' Then he demanded, 'The future, we must think only of the future.'

"And so I told him of the future, of Feiga and me holding a son, the baby's lavish *briss* ceremony, rabbis gathering from all corners of the land to see the newborn, and blessing him, not explaining why they have convened, but with hints in their eyes. They huddle secretively every once in a while and sip the good wine, *khamra taba*, and they closely examine the baby's face in silence. I listed for Adler the names of the rabbis, gather them from all the dynasties of Poland and Lithuania, as if my eyes are passing over a wall of radiance.

"Adler listens, encouraging, and asks, 'What will you name your firstborn?'

"And my heart cries out, 'I will name him after you!'

"One day there was an outbreak of typhus in the camp and Adler fell ill. He was simply one among many. At first he kept his strength and tried to join the work group, but he quickly weakened. From then on our roles were reversed. I, the healthy one, took it upon myself to save Adler from the disease, from being finished off with a shot, from some connivance of damned Farkelstein. I called out to him, 'Be angry! Be bitter!' and begged our Creator to take pity on this man. I gave him food from my meager allowance, and he ate from my palm like a baby. His kind eyes thanked me, and that was the greatest gift I could have sought from *Hashem*, blessed be He. But Adler was dying. There was no choice but to take him to the *rivier*, the infirmary, a place that offered no great cures, only sadistic doctors and reduced food rations; at the end of every week, those who had not recovered were killed.

"For a day or two I was left on my own, and then a sudden boldness took hold of me. I stole an extra portion of bread for Adler and rushed to the *rivier* with some excuse to visit him. I handed him the bread, proud and embarrassed—but Adler needed food no longer. Instead of the bread he grasped my hand and pulled me to him. He began to mumble in my ears, words that I believed at first came from the shock of his waning mind, but slowly they began to make sense. Adler was trying to tell me about a portion of research he had not sufficiently delved into, a section he had found but had not been able to investigate. One day, he suggested, I might want to look into this line of research. From the force of his excitement he rose feverishly from his bed, attempting to sit up. I tried to hold him down with both hands, afraid he would make a commotion in that *rivier* of those cursed people, where both the healthy and the sick could find themselves dead. But Adler's strength was greater than mine, like Jacob our father battling the angel.

"'You know,' he said, 'Jews did not always allow themselves to be killed without taking revenge.' His voice grew bitter, as if he were practicing the future, not discussing the past. 'Jews fought. They formed groups to plot against the plunderers. They preferred death by the sword to a pathetic death like ours. And more than anyone, you must know about the Jewish pirates. Subatol Deul was Jewish, he wrote his secrets in Hebrew. And more wondrous than him were the rabbis that went out to sea to take revenge on the Spaniards who expelled the Jews from Spain. Pirate rabbis sailed the seven seas, kept the Sabbath, observed the mitzvahs, and on weekdays they rampaged against their enemies!' Then he told me, 'After you are freed, study them.' His body radiated with a strong force and he was actually shaking me. I could not listen to his words, horrified by his strength and his awful vacant face, which contained both the most beautiful of professorial looks, and the terror of a man about to die.

"The *rivier* physician, Doctor Gosen, damn him, had begun his evening rounds, God help us, and I grew frightened. I extricated myself from Adler and promised to visit him the next day, but both he and I knew it was a lie. The next day I was told to work in a new group, with the corpse burners, God help us. Adler's body was at the top of the heap, ready for us to burn in the pits. The Nazis, damn them, had not been able to kill him. Adler had returned his soul to the Creator and I said a *kaddish* prayer over him, so the Lord of the Universe would know that a Jew still mourned for a Jew. That even here, someone was still dear to someone else's heart.

"From that day forward I decided to take up my prayers again. Since being deported from Bochnia I had evaded all the duties of a Jew. I ate *treif*, I did not say the blessings, did not pray. But I made up my mind to pray every day for Adler's soul, and to go back to saying the three daily prayers: *shacharit, mincha* and *ma'ariv*."

Grandpa Yosef remembers it is time to pray now. He pauses the tale of his journey and is about to go to the end of the hallway, where he has found a corner for his prayers by the vending machine.

"What happened to Farkelstein?" I ask.

Grandpa Yosef stops in his tracks, annoyed. "What happened to

Farkelstein? How would I know what happened to Farkelstein? And what happened to every single Jew I met? There were thousands and thousands there—how should I know what happened to them?"

He walks out briskly and prays. Then he uses the coins Anat sent for him (sometimes the thermos isn't enough) for a cup of "Swiss coffee" from the machine. He comes back with a hesitant look on his face, slightly ashamed of his outburst, and says, "I don't know about Farkelstein. There's no way to know. But today I am Shoah-smart, you could say, and I know that people like Adler were marked men from the beginning. Who would live? Who would die? Was there any way to predict? That's not what I'm saying. But there were those whose fate was marked on them from the beginning. The brazen would live, the pure would die. Adler, there were no two ways about it, was fated to die, as if the Angel of Death himself had seen to it.

"I did not have much time to mourn for Adler. The typhus plague did not subside, the SS themselves began to fear infection, and they started with the transports. At the beginning of March I packed up my belongings again, as they say (*nu*, it's a joke, I had no belongings at all), and I was sent with a large group to Sachsenhausen camp. Documents have shown that the men's camp of Ravensbrück belonged to Sachsenhausen from the beginning. So once again we were transferred, probably to satisfy the cursed Nazis' quotas and regulations. Sachsenhausen is less than twenty miles northeast of Berlin.

"In Sachsenhausen I learned a profession for the first time in my life. I softened leather boots for German soldiers. How? By walking. Instead of a German soldier getting a pair of painful new leather boots, they used our infinite supply of spare feet. Under the supervision of orthopedic specialists, we marched back and forth through the camp in new army boots, without socks, without rest. We walked and walked. When a boot was worn in and the experts decreed it suitable for the noble foot of a soldier, we were rewarded with a new boot to teach us new pain.

"Is it possible to describe such a deathly nightmare? Worse than working in the trenches of Ravensbrück. Endless. The routine was disturbed only by the occasional shot—another stumbler giving in to his body. Usually there were no shots. The stumblers did their best not to stumble. The guards did their best to kick, whip, and arouse in the prisoner, if not energy, at least the fear of death. They whipped and whipped until he would start walking again. Only seldom did they shoot. And for us, how can I put this aptly, the shots were a slight reprieve from routine. One's mind, unwillingly, created a sort of anticipation of the shots. One side of your soul urges you to feel nothing, hear nothing, see nothing, think nothing—only march. The other side, secretly, with an inexplicable perversion, waits for the sound of the shot. Your head is stupefied and your body marches on, waiting. The shot rings out.

"We walked back and forth in straight lines. Every day we passed a wretched group of young Russian POWs, who for some reason had the letter 'T' imprinted on their foreheads. They were forced to march in a circle, handcuffed to one another in pairs, from morning to night. They did not march to wear in boots—only to die. They marched in an endless circle from which only one fate could remove them. Why did the Germans torture them so? Why not shoot them and be done with it? No way to know. German logic. But those poor wretches, they all met the same fate, and it was slow and hopeless. We never saw the same prisoner twice. And why only the Russians? Why did we walk in straight lines with army boots, people of many nations, Jews and non-Jews? German logic.

"Day after day I marched, and in Sachsenhausen too there were beatings, abuse, hunger, death. As we marched, at first our brains were in a daze. One could not think, could not do anything. We were forbidden to talk. Punishable by death. Later, just a little, I found myself thinking of Adler and his orphaned research. And wondrously, I found myself gaining strength from these thoughts, from the Jewish pirates on their glorious ships. I practiced my future, coming up with adventures for the pirates, inventing things from my soul, and also contemplating the halakhic problems posed by their profession. After all, this was no simple matter, the pirates and the 613 commandments! Every day I found myself embroiled in complex thoughts that reached dead-ends. It was beyond my Talmudic knowledge to solve such intricate issues. Not giving in, I scanned every aspect of a pirate's life, identified the problems, debated them with myself until all possibilities were exhausted, and then made notes of what I would ask the rabbis once I was free. At night in bed, exhausted and hungry, I forced myself to stick with the pirates, divvying up their loot according to the laws of Gemara, muddling through the thicket of laws concerning hostages and the allowance of trade in the fruits of plunder. I was excited to realize that I was asking questions, and they were not small. These were large questions!

"My questions were large, but life, diminished life, did not arise in their wake. Adler's theory was all well and good, but without food, without rest for one's body, life had no chance. And Adler had not only empowered the spirit, he had also added the nightly portion of soup. Without the soup, what good were thoughts? The soul, you should know, needs a body. Wise men philosophize, they separate the spirit from the body, aspire to do away with the corporeal for the sake of the spiritual. But those who know hunger have no questions. A person needs a body.

"In the meantime, in Sachsenhausen, I sensed death approaching in my bones. The dysentery was back. There were days when I ate no more than a turnip leaf from morning to night. And my feet began to refuse to move. They swelled and cracked. I was growing weak. Day after day, Asmodeus came to claim what was his. I knew I would not last long. At night, I exchanged not a single word with my neighbors to the left or the right, and did not know who they were. Our bodies were so shattered, our souls so crushed. Every so often, a neighbor disappeared. Died, shot, replaced. A new one was thrown onto the cot and I remained indifferent, not knowing who he was, not wanting to know, even though he was my brother in this trouble and his suffering was a brother to my own suffering. But there was emptiness. The soul was empty, everything was empty. Death was so close. In the twilight of life, memories invaded, overcoming Adler's prohibition, and my thoughts turned to the past. Even memories were too weak to go very far—the Lodz ghetto seemed as if it had happened many years ago. I could barely remember Bochnia. Only occasionally did childhood memories emerge, with the cheder, the tutor, and the stones we threw in the afternoon into the little Babica brook that flowed beneath the bridge.

"And where, you might ask, was Feiga in all of this? I did not have in me enough Yosef to contain Feiga. At the edge of the very edge, Yosef Ingberg ended. My soul made a decision: Tomorrow I will not get up from this cot. They may whip me to death, but I will not rise.

"That night, two of my neighbors died suddenly, one from beatings, taken from bed to be punished and never returned, and the other from exhaustion. The one who died of exhaustion would be removed in the morning with all the dead, but in place of the one who was beaten to death they tossed in a new neighbor, a diminutive Jew. And this Jew, as if he did not see how miserable my condition was, as if neither bothered by the body that separated us, nor deterred by the death sentence awarded to those who whispered in their cots, immediately began trying to get acquainted, asking questions, telling me about himself. I, in the twilight of death, was somewhat taken aback. It seemed strange that this little Jew was unafraid of Adler's command, talking freely about his past, his history. When morning came, I got up from the cot despite myself, rising to a new day of death, and I knew my Jewish neighbor's entire story by heart.

"Until the war started my new neighbor had been a tramp and a beggar. He ate in soup kitchens and at rich people's houses. In summers he played the violin at weddings, and in winters he was hungry for bread. He stole. A dangerous sort of Jew, he was. And indeed, I feared him, but I was also drawn to his companionship. How can I put it? I sensed that with him I might survive. When he told me his name, Rothschild, I did not know if he was joking or truthful. I dared not ask. I soon discovered that my intuition about Rothschild was correct. He always knew where they were secretly giving out another portion, where they were selling something, which work group was better off. I tell you this without shame: I put my trust in Rothschild. Incredibly, he put his in me. One day he caught me in the latrine, or, forgive me, the crapper, which served as a general market in the camps, and he stood up close to me. Whispering, he proposed a deal. He would keep me going, look out for me, and I would pray for him. He had seen me praying for Adler and he wanted me to pray for him too, so his sins would not be counted against him. I was taken aback.

Such a deal, *nu*. But he shoved a piece of cooked potato into my hand and I quickly stuffed it in my mouth. We had a deal.

"From that day on, Rothschild really did take care of me. He was cunning and seemed to be without conscience. He stole and tricked and cheated and lied. And he brought me half of his earnings, or so he assured me. Everything gained through his wheeling and dealing, I swallowed up; my body wanted it. Every evening he came to me and asked pragmatically, 'Have you prayed for me yet today, Rabbi?' As if we had not a general agreement, but a detailed contract.

"He insisted on calling me 'Rabbi.' No matter how many times I told him I was not a rabbi, Rothschild explained that for him I was. In any case, he said, he had seen the rabbi of his town being dragged through the snow by his beard. His entire congregation had already died in the crematoria. Only he was left. So he was a congregation, and I—a rabbi.

"So we remained, the pair of us. Every day I prayed for myself, for him, and for Israel. I dared to bring Feiga's name to my lips, pleading. He brought to me from his takings, and saved me twice from prisoners who wanted to slaughter me for my portion of soup. So small, he was, and so bold. A savage. At the end of every day he checked, making sure I hadn't forgotten to pray for him. I did not know what sort of a trap I had fallen into, and did not give it much thought because my body was surviving thanks to another radish, another bit of soup, another potato. Many times, when the food was in my stomach, I grew terrified of this partner, a thief and a robber—how had I joined up with this burglar? But hunger came and pierced through my thoughts, and when Rothschild passed me a potato I did not ask where it came from, whether from the prisoners' kitchen or the jailors' kitchen or the hoard of another miserable prisoner. I grabbed it and ate.

"One day there was a special roll-call. There were shouts, and a group of us was sent to work in the woods. There, we knew, death was waiting. You did not come back from working in the woods with those villains. I was to be annexed to the group, separated from fortunate Rothschild. I had already began marching with the rows of people, extremely frightened, when suddenly Rothschild slid into our group and squeezed in next to me. 'Right behind you, Rabbi!' I no longer knew who this Rothschild was—a villain or a righteous man. For he had sentenced himself to death.

"After many hours of walking, we were hurried into a wooded area and ordered to chop down the trees. Our hands grasped dull axes and broken saws, and the supervisors made sure the work was done according to certain rules and with the requisite energy. Every so often, one of the supervisors lost his patience, burst into the group, chose himself a victim, and that victim had no recourse. Why did they not shoot us and be done with it? Who can tell. For days, they worked us from morning to night. They themselves were bored. The woods made them irritable and we paid the price. We bowed our heads and continued to work. There was no Adler to come to my help here. Rothschild, in the woods, was also waning. We were both losing our strength. Around us people collapsed, unresponsive to thrashes, beatings. Anything was better than another hour of work. Each one who gave up his life, we regretted, because we would have to carry his body back to the camp. The Germans could not tolerate inaccurate numbers or a discrepancy between the number that set off and the number that returned.

"Rothschild, it turns out, was not idling. Every night when we were brought back to the camp, shattered, he did not lie down on his bed as I did, one foot in the grave. He ran around stirring things up, investigating, lobbying. A few days later he found himself a job in the kitchen and was also able to get me out of the woods group and back to the boot-marchers. One night he woke me up and dragged me out of the hut, unafraid of the supervisor and the SS outside. He stealthily gave me a piece of meat, a real piece of meat, which if not for the freezing cold would have probably sent a stench throughout the entire camp. I swallowed it. My stomach ached for two days, having forgotten the taste of meat. And the pain, well. *Nu*, like a new baby that keeps you from sleeping. Like Yariv, your Yariv, when he was born. He wouldn't let you sleep, but the joy, the joy!"

(Suddenly, my Yariv, in the middle of the camps.)

"And of course, he said, 'Don't forget to pray for me, Rabbi.'

263

He took me back to the hut but did not go in. For Rothschild, night was the time for doing business. He was always busy with intrigues and commerce. As if he meant to get rich in this place. For one whole month he tormented himself with a major secret transaction. He twitched on his cot at night, hitting and kicking the planks. He hit me too, thrashing this way and that. He was seeking reprieve from the calculations he labored over all day, skipping among his confidants, hiding, helping, bribing, slipping away. I was not let in on the secret and had no idea what kind of transaction could be so worthy of these torments. Apart from life, what asset could he gain here? Perhaps that was his business. Life. Saving his own life in some way. Escaping was not his intention. Not a simple escape. He was derisive of escape plans, and often mocked some poor garrulous rookie boasting of his idea. He would tell him dismissively, '*Nu*, so you escape. What then? What afterwards?' Perhaps Rothschild was plotting a large-scale plan. What he was scheming, I do not know. But one day it was all over. His strength suddenly ran out. He went back to the little transactions, a stub of salami here, a potato there, cigarettes. At night his sleep was restful again.

"More than anything, Rothschild looked to Cell Block 18, where the Germans had built a sophisticated printing house to print counterfeit bills in other currencies. The printing house ignited a flame in Rothschild's eyes. All his instincts fired up for the chance to get himself a job there. He talked with this one, debated with the other. Walked alongside the fence at night, returned excitedly from hasty meetings. He waited expectantly for a conversation, just a few words, a partner to arrive. Truly like a suitor and a lover. Yes, even in a creature such as Rothschild there was a manifestation of love.

"But before he managed to establish a role for himself in Cell Block 18, he had already jumped on another opportunity. A rumor was going around that soon a group of prisoners would be evacuated from Sachsenhausen. Where to? That was unclear. Perhaps, like other times, to the nearby woods to be shot in the head. But perhaps elsewhere. Rothschild considered the opportunity from all points of view, and decided to get himself into the transport. He informed me that he had put my name down for this corrupt business too. As if he could not imagine leaving for a new place without the man who prayed for him.

"I was terrified. What was I doing with a murderous character like this? How had I gotten mixed up with him? But when the rumor turned into an actual transport, and the list was real, and both of our names were on it, I joined him without a word—what life did I have without Rothschild? And that was how we arrived at Dora-Mittelbau camp.

"We were in that hell for only a few weeks. Rothschild soon realized he had struck a foul bargain. After our welcome, which included roll-call, lashings and punishments, we were thrown into rock caves. That was the camp. Entirely made of dark, stifling tunnels. There we had to dig tunnels for the Germans to store their secret missiles. Not that we knew that. We only knew that we were digging from morning till evening, no food, horrendous conditions, without any light. They did not let us see the light of day. We worked and slept and ate in the tunnels. For our intestinal needs, the Germans built for us, in their mercy, a wonderful kind of facility. Fuel barrels cut in half, which we were invited to fill up to our hearts' content. Apparently there was no shortage of empty barrels throughout the German Reich, but we were given only a few, so as not to spoil us. As if they were saying, you're not getting fed anyway—how could you have any excrement? There were very few barrels and they were always overflowing. We stepped in human waste. People gave up all remnants of human dignity and left their waste wherever they happened to crouch. The aqueducts filled with the smell of excrement and a strong odor of grease and dust.

"You know, there are almost no accounts of Dora-Mittelbau camp. Why is that? Because there are so few survivors fortunate enough to be able to tell what happened there. Every day people dropped dead by the dozens and the hundreds. You cannot imagine how murderous and terrible that place was. Rothschild realized immediately that he had made a bad move, and, incredibly, he discovered that in a nearby camp they needed metal workers. Right there and then he became a metal artisan, pushing himself under the kapo's nose just in time so some other prisoner wouldn't be taken instead.

They took ten prisoners, including the metal artisan Yosef Ingberg of Bochnia. There is no way of knowing what Rothschild did to get me onto that list, but he did not forget me, he did not leave me in that awful cemetery Dora-Mittelbau. Cursed is the world in which camps such as Dora-Mittelbau are created to kill human beings.

"In the nameless new camp we were welcomed by a huge German prisoner, a criminal, who tested our knowledge of frames and metal. In the dark, Rothschild asked me, 'What do you know about metal work?' I answered in a panic, 'Tubal-cain, the forger of every cutting instrument of brass and iron...' Rothschild did not comprehend my scriptural quote, and I whispered, 'Genesis, chapter four, verse twenty-two. The first metal cutter, Tubal-cain.' Rothschild sighed and said, 'In that case, you know slightly more than I do.'

"I was seized by fear—what would we answer to the German? But Rothschild remained calm, his eyes already investigating in the dark, finding out where there might be a chance to do good business. As if he himself were orchestrating things, just as we stood before the German, a siren pierced the camp, the lights went off and we were thrown into a dark hut without any orders and with no questions asked. It turned out the Allied planes were attacking. It was already September of 1943, and the Germans were no longer so sure of themselves. Every siren sent them into a panic. When calm was restored, we were miraculously led to a large cauldron, which held our dinner, and were given pieces of soft, grey bread. At the end of the meal Rothschild was already part of the kitchen crew—don't ask how—and I was his assistant. It turned out they needed no more than two or three metal workers in the camp, and apart from the ones the huge German chose, and apart from Rothschild and me, the others were nonchalantly taken to a nearby clearing in the woods and shot in the back of their heads.

"We were saved from Dora-Mittelbau, saved too from the fate of the metal cutters, and a few days later the camp was shut down. Again we were rolled along, this time south, to Buchenwald."

Grandpa Yosef says the word 'Buchenwald' and into the room comes the nurse. Behind her, the doctor. He examines Grandpa Lolek, gives the nurse some instructions, and tells us Grandpa Lolek is out of danger and has in fact begun to recover. He can be discharged, he should be in a nursing home of some sort, like Flieman Hospital, where he can complete his little journey until he goes home. Grandpa Yosef objects with a stony face—supervision is essential. But he lets it slide. He will wait for Effi's shift. She's a doctor, he can recruit her to his battle and do away with their plan. In the meantime he lets it slide, protesting with an angry mumble. The doctor answers, trying to explain that the treatment in a convalescence home will be better than what he'll get here, and in any case, he doesn't belong in this ward. All he needs is rest. Rest and observation. Grandpa Yosef decides to ignore him, as if the argument is over. He sits down carelessly in his chair, gives the doctor a defiant look, ready for battle. He has in him a courage he did not have on the train going to Buchenwald, rattling in the dark, burnt with thirst, singed from the nights of waiting, frozen on the tracks without moving, waiting for the devil knows what, perhaps for a torture that will grow, burst forth, assail these people who are desperate anyway and starving anyway in the darkness of the train car. The doctor thinks the better of any further argument. He leaves the room and the nurse follows him. The train ride goes on for days, in the depths of darkness, Grandpa Yosef and Rothschild cast into a darkness deeper than the one Grandpa Lolek is now resting in. Outside sirens rip through villages. They cross bridges, the rain slams down, and inside the arid darkness the water bucket is empty, the windows are closed, there is no air. Finally, the screeching of tracks announces the end. The train doors are flung open. Light. Buchenwald.

Buchenwald is a vast camp. First thing in the morning, the kapo is already harassing Grandpa Yosef, two shots of the whip on his face, and screams. Grandpa Yosef does not understand what he wants, the kapo kicks him in the ribs. But then Rothschild, risking his life, jumps boldly in front of the kapo and the incident is over. In some way that is beyond normal comprehension, the kapo immediately realizes that people like Rothschild should be avoided. He screams for another moment or two, kicks and fumes, but then leaves. Rothschild drags Grandpa Yosef to his cot. Grandpa Yosef is stunned, still not understanding why the kapo fell on him, but knowing that

Rothschild had saved his life. Over the next few days he learns what kind of lowly murderer the kapo is, how he amuses himself with the prisoners, but Grandpa Yosef has Rothschild's protection.

Grandpa Yosef regulates his breath a little.

"In Buchenwald, finally, I had a little rest from my travels. I spent a whole year there, from November '43 to November '44. First we were sent to work in the quarry. Every morning we marched in rows, pounded rocks for sixteen hours, then marched back to the camp, where we had roll-calls and more marches. I no longer had any strength anyway, I was no more than a skeleton, and if not for Rothschild... *nu*. He soon joined up with the Russian POWs and the criminals, hardened people who would murder over nothing. Thanks to them he found easy work for both of us in a nearby town. Every day we were actually taken out of the camp into a German town where citizens lived their lives. Children peered at us through windows, and on the streets we passed women with baskets and gentlemen going off to work. A town, simply a town. We repaired the water reservoirs. Hard work, but only as hard as any manual laborer's work.

"Rothschild cast his net here too, doing business, various corrupt transactions. Such a devil. He started to place his confidence in me, asked me questions, sought advice. He told me of his plans and deeds and secrets. His heart was completely unhesitant. He would do anything. He struck terror and fear in me—he could betray me at any moment, sell me for a potato.

"Only one thing did Rothschild ask of me, as ever. 'Pray for me, Rabbi.' His face would strain as he forced a smile, but he was entirely serious, and he took the trouble to make sure the prayer was being said.

"He grew tired of working at the water reservoirs very quickly. His business was not booming and the danger was too great, so he found himself a job in the kitchen. There, for those who dared, business was good. Rothschild traded, bribed, cheated, orchestrated transactions. In January there was snow and the ground was frozen, so they did not need us in the town. Rothschild tried to sneak me into kitchen duty, but was unable. Having no choice, we found ourselves the job of pushing the wagons that carried the dead. Throughout the camps, this job was done by the Ukrainian POWs, a hardened and frightening group. How Rothschild penetrated this evil band...*nu*, Rothschild. He was pleased with his accomplishment and could not understand the way my face fell when he told me. 'The work is easy, no? We'll survive. Gain some weight.'

"And so we took the dead out of the huts every morning. People I knew, the dying who had completed their process. One day I would look into the eyes of a dead man, *nu*, and the next day I piled his corpse onto the wagon. Worst of all was the inspection we had to do. Sometimes the man was not dead, but did not get up; he lay still, awaiting his fate—the hand that would put him to death. I was the wagon man. And then I had to deal with the corpses. I don't want to talk about that.

"The months in Buchenwald went by. I survived. Rothschild was with me. I prayed, he took care of the rest. Thoughts of Feiga returned. Thoughts of Adler. I worked with the dead wagon and imagined the future in all its details. We did not gain any weight, none at all. A great hunger fell on Buchenwald. Rations were cut. The black water known as 'soup' was taken from us, the gray mess known as 'bread' all but disappeared. The hunger brought death to the huts and we were always busy. Those who did not die sometimes lit up with a fever like torches and became crazed. They drank mud and ate their own clothing. God help us, we even found gnawed bodies on the cots. Yes, gnawed bodies. And the eyes, everyone's eyes, even those whose minds were still sound, were crazed and glimmering, their hearts wanted only a chance to nibble at some food, their souls ignited—when would the chance come? When would it come?

"One evening there was a commotion. We were crowded into the *Appellplatz* for a special roll-call. The officers surrounded us, there was shouting, dogs barking, something bad had happened. For a long time all we heard were paralyzing shouts. We were counted, then counted again, and the roll-call went on into the night and it was not clear what had happened, but we knew in our hearts that it would not end well. We slowly began to understand that we were being accused of stealing twenty candied apples. Twenty candied apples! They had been prepared in the kitchen for the birthday celebration of one of the senior SS men, and lo and behold, the apples were gone.

"We were left to freeze in the snow, tormented, and the SS did nothing, only walked among us shouting and threatening. It became evident that they would not be satisfied with killing someone. They needed the apples. They were frightened themselves—what would they do without the apples? They waited for someone to open his mouth and confess, or to turn in someone else. And we stood there, stupefied from cold and fear. But there was joy hiding in our hearts. Twenty candied apples! If it had been one apple, or one rotting potato, we would have been jealous, our empty stomachs would have demanded the *kartoshka*. We would have suspected one another, even hoped that a few would be shot, including the one who had stolen the apple, because then maybe later we would find the apple in his cot. But twenty candied apples! We had to whisper explanations to the villagers among us, stressing that this was not just an apple with sugar, but an apple dipped in boiling syrup bubbling in a cauldron, and the syrup is sweet like honey and it coats the apple and hardens like red glass. First the excess syrup drips down the apple, then the drops freeze as if ordered to stop and decorate the head of the apple like snow on a hilltop. Twenty such apples!

"Late at night the SS men gave up. This truly was a mystery, the thief was never discovered, even the informants couldn't say. The roll-call commander ordered his officers to take out every fifth man and shoot him. A rustle of terror stirred among us. Our bodies began to awaken from the cold, the nausea of fear crept inside us. An SS officer walked among the rows, pushing aside certain men with his whip, instructing them to join the condemned. He walked in front of me and his whip touched me. Yes, the whip touched me. And the sergeant marching behind him motioned at me with his head to leave the row. But to my right Rothschild jumped out. The sergeant glanced at this exchange for an instant. He didn't care, as long as the number added up nicely. I froze in my place without moving, and Rothschild was already standing at the edge of the condemned group. From the end of the line he gestured at me with his hands, mimicking a prayer stance, to remind me that I should continue to pray for him.

"They walked them to a clearing in the woods where the SS liked to execute people. As he passed me, with a real grin on his murderous face, Rothschild dared to call out loud to me, 'I am Leibel Rothschild. If you have a son, call him Leibel!'

"And the group was swallowed up in the darkness. I remained among the living, owing my life to another man. How did my legs plant me down at that moment of the switch? How did I allow it to happen? Why did I allow...*nu*...

"They shot Rothschild. Gone. That's all I can tell you. I don't remember much of the days that followed. A long period, months, and the memories are gone. I probably continued to work with the dead wagons, since I was not dead myself. I was not taken to work at the quarry. And what else did I do? I believe I was entirely submerged in the future. I imagined it beautifully, and my aim was not bad. The present was not all that agreeable to me, so I turned my thoughts to the future, where things were good. I made *aliya* with Feiga to Palestine, to build a new life. And even if I never imagined my home in Kiryat Haim, and Ben Gurion, still, I did picture Palestine. Feiga and I were most certainly alive. We sat on the beach at Jaffa, gobbling down oranges in the sunshine, our feet reaching out to touch the convoys of camels, the local Arabs admiring our culture, our religion. I did not envision wars and conflicts, not like this. But in dark Buchenwald we definitely gobbled down oranges and tangerines.

"I recall only one moment of the present. I leaned against a rod or a wagon shaft for a brief moment of contemplation. I suddenly thought about my journey with Ahasuerus. It was, after all, a journey to rescue Feiga, and I believed that the *Kadosh Baruch Hu* had given me this journey and the black car. I suddenly realized that I had not achieved a thing. Not Feiga, not anything. And in that moment, which memory is kind enough to illuminate to this day, I was filled with great desperation and confusion. I leaned hard against the wagon shaft. I remember the shaft well.

"At the end of 1944 the Germans decided it was time for me

271

to move on again, to Gross-Rosen camp. At that time, all the camp Jews were being sent west, mass transports going with the Germans as they retreated from the Russians. But for some reason, I was sent east. To Gross-Rosen.

"At Gross-Rosen I received the usual welcome. A shower in the nude, pushing, shouting, a long roll-call in the snow. The Germans wore fur coats, protecting their bodies from the wind, while we stood naked. Night came, the cold took its victims, and the Germans too were tired of the roll-calls. It was cold. We were taken into huts, a hundred people shoved into a space big enough for ten.

"At Gross-Rosen there was no work. They kept us in huts and took us out to be counted or punished. Then back to the hut. I do not remember many people dying in the daily routine of Gross-Rosen; not like at Sachsenhausen, not like at Buchenwald. But those who did die stand out in my memory. After Rothschild's death, I was lucidly aware of each and every subsequent man shot dead. To this day I think not only about Rothschild, who was not successful in all of his schemes and who ultimately died. I think about everyone who was executed in front of my eyes. In Ravensbrück, in Sachsenhausen, in Buchenwald, in Gross-Rosen. All those anonymous people drawn out from the end of their rows so a dog could tear through their flesh or they could be whipped to death. In their own eyes, these people were the whole wide world. They alone perceived the miracle of their salvation up until that moment, and at the instant before their death they surely thought in terror, 'I have been marked, God help me,' and they hoped for life, for one more miracle. They looked at our impenetrable faces, hoping salvation might come from us. Until the very last second they hoped, in their dying convulsions, in their memories, between the teeth of a dog, and could not imagine a world without themselves. Do you understand? They could not imagine a world without themselves in it. Every such person who knelt down to get a bullet in the back of his neck was a whole wide world. And not only because that is what the Scriptures say. Simply a whole wide world. Each man with his memories, his loves, his history. Just like me. And I am living, here, and they…

"In Gross-Rosen I came to see Rothschild and Adler and Rabbi

Hirsch as chaperones who knew that liberation was close, that it would take just one more little effort, a stroke of luck. And indeed, near the end of the war I was transferred from Gross-Rosen to an auxiliary camp. Then to another camp. And another. Towards their end, damn them, as if the Germans did not know what to do with me, they transferred me again and again. Finally they put me in a little camp near the Polish town of Walbrzych, which was not far from Waldenburg camp, where your father was with his father. In that camp, things were relatively comfortable. I worked at a sort of carpentry shop. It was work for work's sake, not for death's sake, and the foreman was an elderly German man. There was little food and I was ill, but survival was possible. I spent a month there, no more. The Russians came, the Germans fled, and I was set free. With me, everything happened simply. No last minute torture, no death march, no burning huts with inhabitants still inside, no being buried alive in a pit. I was simply set free.

"Then there was a difficult period of freedom. The world was in shambles, and I was all sickness and hunger. But we overcame. *Nu*, there was life, the *Kadosh Baruch Hu* gave life and commanded that we live, and you cannot imagine my joy when, in Bochnia, I met Feiga. But before that, in the last camp, I had another encounter, a unique one. Of all the people I met in my days, none was as important as this brief meeting.

"In our camp I found a prisoner who drew my attention for some reason. He was a sick man, lying silently on a cot, barely able to get up. He walked softly to the latrine, conversing with no one. He was fairly young, around thirty, but his face was drawn and old. For some reason I felt pity for him, as if I somehow still contained pity, and one day I went to him and gave him a piece of bread. I was deathly ill, my condition no better than his, and yet I offered him my bread. He thanked me with a limp wave of the hand and rejected my offer. He motioned with his fingers—perhaps I had a cigarette? For some reason I rushed around as if commanded by a great Admor. I searched the camp for someone who would trade food for a cigarette, and went back to the patient to give him the gift. Two real Eckstein cigarettes.

"He smoked one cigarette. Then the next one. I sat waiting at his feet for the devil knows what. But from that day we became connected. I would sit at his side, looking into his pale face as he smoked cigarettes. I noticed that he did not eat, and I tried to entreat him. But he dismissed my pleas completely. Strange, I had yet to hear his voice or learn his name, and yet I felt that I had found a friend. He too bowed his tired head, welcoming my arrival. I found myself sensing an increased desire to help, to encourage the man, to tell him about Rothschild, about Adler, about Hirsch. And indeed I began to tell him my stories, the entire past. From day to day I could see the man weakening, as if he did not want his life and was actually beckoning death to approach. I implored him to gain strength. 'Life is holy!' I told him.

"One day I heard from some people that the man came from the village of Kalow. I tried to engage him in conversation. 'His honor is from Kalow, so I hear? A long way his honor has traveled. *Nu*, these times... In Kalow, did you happen to know the 'Fledgling Tree,' the Rabbi of Kalow?'

"His lips whispered, 'I am the Rabbi of Kalow.'

"I was stunned into silence. Not just for a brief moment, but for whole days. I continued to tend to him, kneeling at his feet. What were my stories, all my worthless tales of Hirsch and Adler? Who knew what this man was engaged in during his moments of silence, in what secret and wonderful worlds the Rabbi of Kalow, the Fledgling Tree, roamed, he and none other, while I intruded on his visions with my Feiga here, and Ahasuerus there. With my idle talk I was putting spokes in the wheels of a true holy man, the Rabbi of Kalow! The author of important new interpretations of Torah that had sent shockwaves from the farthest corner of Galicia all the way to the land of Lithuania. I looked into his pale face, which now appeared clean and pure, and I was overcome. The Rabbi of Kalow!

"The next day I moved to the cot next to his. I would be quiet and would be an aid. I would save the Rabbi of Kalow from the claws of death. I would feed him, give him water, guard him. But my longing to talk, to regale him with what was in my heart, would not let go. I was quiet but full of questions—about pirates, about their mitzvahs, about the diminished questions. I wanted to ask the Rabbi of Kalow, 'Why, why the annihilation?'

"But the Rabbi was not there to be questioned. He silently smoked the cigarettes I brought him. Once in a while he posed a question and I responded as concisely as possible, so he would understand my answer correctly without a single superfluous word. He asked about Bochnia, about my family, my engagement. Then he surprised me by saying, 'My wife Rachel and I were not blessed with children. It was not His wish, *Hashem*, blessed be He.'

"I already knew this, having heard that the Rabbi of Kalow was not blessed by *Hashem* with offspring, and that hundreds of Jews used to come to him for fertility blessings. He was known as a curer of barrenness.

"And so we counted the days until liberation. Rumors abounded, and we could hear the Americans bombing. Echoes of cannons, rumors of Russian artillery. The prisoners were excited, the Germans anxious and tense. Only the Rabbi of Kalow was in his own world. He lay on his bed communing with other spheres. I introduced him to the other prisoners and promised he would be our savior. Here, this is the Fledgling Tree, the Rabbi of Kalow, our hope. People dismissed him with a mumble of indifference, perhaps contempt. What did they care about one more rabbi? In any case, they hinted, the pure rabbis had all been killed in the crematoria. Whoever was loyal to his people was gone now. These weary people did not understand, they missed the hidden intentions of the Rabbi of Kalow, and even if I myself did not entirely understand them, I did see their beauty, like the face of a bride through a veil.

"The Rabbi of Kalow was unaffected by the prisoners' opinions. Like us, he was imprisoned behind fences, but his soul danced freely wherever the good Lord took him. I was his servant, I fed him soup, found him cigarettes, while he tended the plains, measured the heavens.

"One day he put his hand to his tired face as if returning from an exhausting thought, and told me, 'When you have a son, name him Moshe.'

"'Moshe?'

"'Name him Moshe, and he will be the savior of Israel!'

"He turned away from me and sunk into his contemplations.

"I let him be and went to wander through the huts and latrines. I examined the fences and the buildings and the entire world. The future suddenly seemed solid and tangible. I saw Feiga and myself embracing a child. The hope for liberation that had remained in my heart through all the camp years in a shapeless, faceless form, suddenly took on a simple outline. Here was the future—not the future I had barely known how to sketch back in Ravensbrück, but a corporeal future, a future that would not be stolen from me! I was ill, hungry, and weak, but I had ceased doubting. I knew that I would live, that I would be free.

"Soon, time itself joined the flight of my soul: liberation day was approaching. The whole camp could hear the beat of freedom, the prisoners were growing anxious, trying to fortify themselves for one more day, one more hour. Only the Rabbi of Kalow remained outside the flow of time, still in his own world. He was no longer accepting the soup I brought him, he rejected bread, even cigarettes. He did not rise from his bed. He lay with his eyes open as if standing on guard, not here, but in some loftier world, and his hand weakly dismissed my words, my pleas, my attentions.

"Right on the verge of the great day, when we were counting the hours and the minutes, he called to me. I came and stood by him. The Rabbi of Kalow's face, although no more than skin and bones, filled with light, as if while still in this world he had been delivered to the angels. He asked to deposit his story with me. That was how he put it. Not 'I want to tell you,' but 'I wish to deposit.' In his angelic language, each word was carefully chosen. I sat alert, entirely prepared to hear his tale. And the Rabbi of Kalow deposited it:

"'In the Kalow ghetto, there, my wife Rachel died in the typhus plague. She was taken away, *baruch dayan ha'emet*—Blessed be the true judge. One day three young men came to my room. They announced: Tomorrow we must escape. The ghetto has been condemned. No one will live. They demanded that I keep the news a secret. I would leave alone, at dawn. Everyone else, may God protect them.

"'They took me to the forest. There, in advance, a hiding place had been prepared. From childhood until manhood, I had never been in the woods. Always among streets and houses, roads paved through fields on either side. Only from a distance would I gaze at the woods, contemplating their secrets, and here I was, called to a life in the forest, in a crowded hiding place with twenty men and their troubles. Bread was scarce, we never saw the light of day.

"'One day, someone must have informed. Germans and Poles surrounded the place, shots were fired, I heard shouts. I escaped. Bullets whistled around me, and they ordered: Stop! I ran. I did not know where my legs were taking me, whether towards or away from any town. In the heart of the woods there was no sunlight, no moonlight, and I had no strength left. But my body kept walking so the wolves would not eat me alive. I prayed, I called out from the depths, where shall I go? Anyone I meet will turn me in. The Germans promise two pounds of bread and half a salami for every Jew. And why should they not turn me in? For half a salami, I would give myself up.

"'Like a blind man I walked on. Stumbling, defeated. Suddenly the darkness was cleaved with a great light. Opposite me stood a house with the front door ajar, and a light shining from it. In the doorway, under the light, stood a huge peasant woman with white hair—she was *erva*, unchaste—and she called out to me, "Come, Jew, come...I will help..."

"'And so I found myself sitting in a crude room inside the crowded, warm peasants' house, and the *goya* served me. She gave me hot soup. Fed me potatoes and butter. All *treif*, all forbidden. But my mouth ate. The *goya* gave me a chicken wing and heaped a bounty of food onto my plate. She told me, "My husband is working...shhh! He must not know...I will hide you in the cellar. It will be fine." Then she caressed my hair with her thick fingers.'"

Grandpa Yosef stops his story for a moment. It is hard for him. He softens his words. He puts his mouth up close to my face so that only my ears will hear the story of the Rabbi of Kalow.

"Starting the next day, he told me, she forced him to do with her as a man does with a woman. Yes, his life was on the line and she made her demands, set her terms. What could he do? Day and night he hid in the cellar, and in the morning when the farmer went to work, she came down to him. Gave him food. Drink. Took care of his sanitation. And then he had to…with the peasant woman."

Grandpa Yosef is practically whispering. His modest voice seems unworthy of the Rabbi of Kalow. To heal this wound it will take a great roar.

"'I prayed to the heavens, I begged, Take away from me this Lilith of the woods! Leave me! From the depths I called out. Asmodeus! Demon woman! Lilith! Inhabitor of the corners of the world! But no redemption came.

"'In the cellar I was encased like a bird in the belly of a great fish, ensnared in a crevasse, embittered as wormwood. She came down every day to give me food and drink, and by the grace of the shadows she took her dues from me. There was no escape. Only prayer remained. So I offered prayers and did not give up. And indeed, on one of the days, the cellar door suddenly opened at noon and the farmer led a young Jewess down to the hiding place. He prepared a bed for her and assuaged her fears. He did not scheme like the peasant woman, not at all. Indeed he let his spouse in on the secret of the Jewess's existence. He entreated her with words that my ears could hear. A drunken Polish *goy*, persuading his spouse to show a measure of mercy towards all creatures of the world. He reassured her, the war will be over, no one will know, it is our duty. She consented to his demand and agreed to hide the survivor woman in the cellar. She did not divulge to him the secret of my existence.

"'Downstairs, in the dark, I revealed myself to the survivor. I calmed her spirits and told her my tale, omitting my deeds with the peasant woman. When I told her I was a rabbi in Kalow, she fell to her knees. Only three years ago she had come to ask for my blessing: she had asked for a son and been granted one. The son had died in the forest with her husband and mother. *Baruch dayan ha'emet*. She hid her face in her hands, thankful that fate had brought about our encounter, as if she was already saved. But we were both in the dark, residents of the cellar, like clods of clay, like valley denizens, and above us was life.

"'All the while the young woman was in the hiding place, the peasant woman stopped coming to me. She helped to care for the woman, bringing down double portions of food, but she did not give away a thing. The *Kadosh Baruch Hu* had granted me some respite from her. One day the farmer came down and sadly told the woman that the Germans would be searching all the village houses. Someone had informed. He had to try and take her elsewhere, perhaps he would find a friend who would agree to hide her. Having no choice, she left with him, and I never found out what happened to her. I stayed in the cellar. If the Germans came down, the farmer would be surprised to find me and would be killed with his wife and myself.

"'Indeed, over the next few days the village was visited by Germans. They came into the house and looked down into the cellar. The *Kadosh Baruch Hu* saved me from them and took mercy on the household. But then the peasant woman began to come down to the cellar every day once again, to feed me of her bounty. She did not impose upon me the terror of her urges. She was good natured, serving me with respect. My heart filled with fear, as if disaster was imminent. How long would I sit through dark days, meager of deeds and poor of feats, a captive in the dwellings of Midian? My soul cried out: Escape!

"'One day the peasant woman brought down a hearty meal for me. Eggs, fat, groats, cream and potatoes. Suddenly the *goya* said, "I will bear you a child." The taste of cream was still on my lips, and she explained, "It won't be long now. At winter's end we shall have a child."

"'A number of months, then, had passed since she had become pregnant. In six months she would have a son.'"

Grandpa Yosef weighs in. "Imagine to yourself. The Fledgling Tree, and his firstborn was conceived by a *goya*!"

"'Harlot!' The rabbi screamed, his limbs frozen in terror. The peasant woman's face turned red."

Grandpa Yosef gets up and walks quickly to the window. He points to the distance, his fingers trembling. The Rabbi of Kalow's deposit still unsettles him, a fifty year old pregnancy demanding to be solved. It is unclear what might placate Grandpa Yosef. Perhaps a little rain in the window coming in from the ocean—finally a November rain, offering surrender.

"The Rabbi of Kalow thinks. He must escape and save his soul from this Lilith. He will be better off if the Nazis catch him and he can join his Rachela. But how can he leave his firstborn? He is consumed with fright and distress. How can he leave? Trapped inside her body, his only son is growing."

Grandpa Yosef comes back from the window, hunched over as if bearing a heavy weight. He has been recounting the torments of the Rabbi of Kalow during Effi's shifts too, and during mine, and Dad's. As he retells the journey, from within his raging spirit comes the stormy soul of the rabbi, counting the passing days, shut in the cellar, agonizing. Grandpa Yosef spreads his hands out, explaining, "His firstborn was…with the *goya*!"

I nod understandingly. The months go by, and time is more powerful than the rabbi's supplications, than Grandpa Yosef's explanations, than my quiet nod.

"The peasant woman continues to bring the rabbi food and water, trim his beard, clip his nails. She cares for him generously and her stomach grows larger, a monstrous swelling in front of his eyes. Having no choice, he survives. In the hours between dawn and day, when the farmer is out, he goes up into the house to pray and soak up some light and air. The peasant woman watches him pray, sighing, and she too moves her great body about. 'I will call him Moises,' she says."

Grandpa Yosef grows agitated. "To use the name of Moshe our Teacher, she wants!"

"The Rabbi of Kalow says nothing. He finishes his prayers and goes down to the cellar. Most days he huddles there, sometimes hearing the farmer and his wife speaking above the floorboards of his prison. The farmer happily awaits the arrival of his child. He makes promises to his wife. He will work hard, make money, the newborn shall want for nothing."

I press him. "How does everyone know it's a boy? Are you telling me they did an ultrasound?"

Grandpa Yosef dismisses my question with a wave of his hand.

He hints at the world of holy rabbis, *goya* witches, and life at the edge of the woods on the margins of darkness. It would be a son.

"And indeed, it was a son. Her time to give birth had come. Over the head of the rabbi, on the floorboards, many pairs of boots and shoes creak. Farmers walk around the house, young neighbor women come and go. The peasant woman falls ill, grows weak, and is ordered not to leave her bed. The neighbor women care for her. Smells of cooking fill the house. And downstairs, the rabbi starves. He nibbles on onions and raw potatoes from a sack. And he prays. He offers up many prayers."

"What did he pray for?"

"Just prayers. The duties of a Jew." Grandpa Yosef stares at me, trying to comprehend what I am really asking. What do I mean? "Just prayers," he says.

"And then, one night, a great commotion. Elderly women in the house, *babas* dressed in cloaks, satanic midwives, they deliver a male child. A large, healthy boy, the farmer immediately falls in love with him. He repeats his promises to his ailing wife, tenderly caresses her head, promises support, good health, everything."

The rabbi can no longer contain himself. The conduit of Grandpa Yosef is not sufficient, and so he speaks up himself:

"No sooner had the farmer set off to work than the cellar door opened. The peasant woman, weakened, padded over to me, wrapped in many clothes. Alone she came, without my son. She brought me food. She asked my forgiveness in a soft, pained voice. She could barely leave her bed, the labor had weakened her greatly. Her face looked old and wrinkled, her body had barely any strength left. And so, how can I say this…I caressed her hair. One caress. After all, she too was created in His image."

"Caressing is permitted," Grandpa Yosef interjects.

"The peasant woman said, 'His name will be Mieczslaw, that is my husband's wish. But we will call him Moises.'

"And the boy was flesh and blood, and he had a name, he was a living creature, the deed could not be undone."

"Such an affair," Grandpa Yosef mumbles.

"I remained in the cellar while above me, day and night, I

could hear my son crying. I too wept. Seven days and seven nights. The next day the peasant woman came down. She waited for me to finish my meal and said, 'I have circumcised our son.'

"That night there was madness. The baby cried out in pain. The farmer was beside himself. He did not know what had happened, but his instincts were unsettled. Something was wrong and he did not know what. The peasant woman cared for the baby, secretly changing his bandages. The madness descended as far as the cellar. I had pain in my feet and burning in my heart. In the chambers of my soul the rebellion stirred—I would run away, take the boy and flee. And where would I bring the child? Where would I go? The urge, barely roused, was lost. It rose and fell. Born, then dead."

Grandpa Yosef sighs. "You must recall that he told me this story, he gave me the deposit, in the camp, by which I surmised that one day he had made a decision and committed an act. What did he do? There is no knowing. Where is the child? No telling. He ended up in our camp, and more than that he did not wish to tell. 'Here I am,' he said with a gray face, and looked away from me. He leaned back into the world of his ponderings, having completed his part in this world. He motioned to me to leave him alone. I was helpless. Soon the gates of liberation would open for the Jews, but the life of the Rabbi of Kalow was draining into the Next World like a leaking well.

"The next morning the gates of the camp opened. Liberation! Everyone ran to the gates and I rushed to check on the Rabbi of Kalow. He was still alive. I gave him the good news. The *Kadosh Baruch Hu* had provided for us. 'Liberation!' I told him. 'Liberation!'

"'Liberation,' he whispered. He was free to go. He breathed into the depths of his lungs, as if taking a final taste of this world, and his soul departed. The Rabbi of Kalow was dead. *Baruch dayan ha'emet.* I was not able to ask, 'Why, why the annihilation?' And he was the last to be annihilated. He brought the people to freedom but did not see it. He came to the brink of Israel, but remained on Mount Nebo.

"From outside I heard the prisoners celebrating, shouting, cheering. Feet pattered this way and that, storehouses were raided, people roamed outside the fences. I sat in the shadows of the hut at the feet of the dead rabbi. I could not share in the happiness. I whispered my vow: 'When I have a son, I will name him Moshe.' The rabbi's tortured face, now pure and bathed in the brilliance of the afterworld, seems to repeat his promise: 'And he will be the savior of Israel!'"

*

During Atalia and Effi's shift, Grandpa Lolek opened his eyes and lay facing the white ceiling, looking slightly bewildered, as if his deep blue eyes had left something behind. It soon became clear that it was his vision. Grandpa Lolek's sight had not yet come back, but his eyes had taught themselves how to open again. He remained a still, helpless figure. His eyes opened with great desire, but his body would not yet cooperate.

The doctors told us that Grandpa Lolek's body had made up its mind to get better, but there was a slight delay in the process. They still needed to remove the benign tumor pressing on his brain, although it was unclear if they should risk removing the entire tumor. In Switzerland there were experts on this kind of tumor. They may decide to remove only part of it. There were modern treatments that did not require surgery. They had to consider the risks, the dangers, the experts' recommendations. In any case, Grandpa Lolek no longer needed the ward.

Somehow a decision turned out to have been made: Grandpa Lolek would move in with Grandpa Yosef for now, so he could take care of him. He needed this supervisory transition period before anyone took a risk and rushed into wasting money on some Swiss treatment that might not be the best solution. When the decision had been made, or when there had been discussions and deliberations, was unclear. That was how it worked with them. The decision materialized out of thin air without requiring any sort of debate or concrete words. The situation set its own course, and from the hospital Grandpa Lolek went straight to Grandpa Yosef's house, for-a-supervisory-transition-period.

Grandpa Yosef put Grandpa Lolek in Feiga's room. He laid his clothes and suits on the closet shelves (where he found a forgotten tie belonging to Hans Oderman). He scattered towels and toiletries in the bathroom. Cleared space on the kitchen shelves. Then he began sending us to Grandpa Lolek's house on the Carmel to bring whatever he thought necessary for the recovering patient. He made us bring fine bed linen and fancy teacups, and the Leica camera. Each item we brought found its place, but did not satisfy Grandpa Yosef. He scanned the newly arranged room and found fault. Off he sent us for another item.

There seemed to be something overwrought about Grandpa Yosef's conduct, but we did not bother to question him. We assumed he was simply being accommodating, trying to introduce a certain amount of grandeur to his modest home. We thought he was trying to fill the house up for his patient's sake. We smiled and obeyed—it was unwise to refuse Grandpa Yosef's requests at a time when the Caribbeanism seemed to be rearing its head again.

Out in the world, the rain finally began to fall. December took its revenge in the form of storms, and we drove back and forth between Kiryat Haim and the Carmel, on the seat beside us a transistor radio, sometimes a scarf, sometimes a vase.

"He's emptying out my home!" Effi complained, already well entrenched in Grandpa Lolek's empty house. ("Just for a while," she explained, insinuating herself like a cuckoo.)

Grandpa Yosef would not rest. He declared his intent to vacate another shelf, the top one, which housed various useless antiques (an ivory elephant from Uncle Tulek, a backup menorah in case the regular one broke, a bag of Bonzo he hadn't had the fortitude to throw out). He climbed up a ladder and passed the little treasures down to us. He grinned awkwardly when he found a bottle of rum he had brought back on a Caribbean whim. "Well, now you know..." he mumbled. "The doctorate. I went there because of Adler, to research the Jewish pirates."

He seemed to feel the need to tie up loose ends and lift the veil off whatever still remained mysterious. We were struck by an odd sensation—a slight aversion to Grandpa Yosef. His life was suddenly deciphered, suddenly clear, all the way down to his most recent secret, the journey to the Caribbean, a dream dreamt by another. That, and Moshe's name, and the doctorate, were all spread out before us. It was hard to look at Grandpa Yosef without feeling uncomfortable. This Grandpa Yosef was too open, too broken down into factors. The bare facts of his life story had become just that—bare. Something had been exposed which should have remained hidden. A bright light had come and flooded with clarity what had thus far squirmed inside towers of clues, fractures of truth that had come together into the form we loved: mysterious Grandpa Yosef, who goes to university despite his age, who writes a doctoral thesis, who rises from sitting *shiva* and sets off for the Caribbean. Everything was exposed—everything. Even the fog tormenting his soul, his son Moshe and the names he was not given—demons which, according to his belief, had taken their revenge.

We had to fight to reconstruct a Grandpa Yosef free of this aversion. There commenced an era of clearing away shards. We fought. But the feelings grew more complicated, emerging in an opposite form to the one we had envisioned. We were unable to look lucidly at this man into whose house once again flowed the needy and the troubled, demanding that Grandpa Yosef give them solutions, assistance, shelter. His good deeds were depicted in a new light. Against our will we saw Grandpa Yosef having to persist, to do only good, without ceasing. If he stopped even for a moment, his old deeds would catch up with him and crush him under their wheels.

The world filled with rain and we fought inside it, against the mist, the dragons, the aversion. One day Grandpa Yosef sent me for Grandpa Lolek's files that contained his bills and the certificates for the land in Gedera and his other property. He thought the recovering patient needed the files to be present beside him on the bedside table. When I returned I found Green the Mechanic in the little parking lot, bringing the Vauxhall at Grandpa Yosef's demand. Then suddenly Hirsch emerged, the almost-deciphered Hirsch, but a chasm still stretched between the end of his story in Grandpa Yosef's voyage and the filthy old man now standing on Katznelson and enquiring theologically,

"Only saints were gassed?"

The root of evil had been revealed: Grandpa Yosef's unfinished voyage. From within the voyage, from one end to the other, questions erupted, movements stirred. What had happened to Hirsch after he left the Lodz ghetto? What happened to Farkelstein? What happened to Ahasuerus? Fragments had been born so that we could contemplate them and think of everything we had not had time to ponder during his hurtling voyage. And Grandpa Yosef's voyage began to roam inside me. All the days he had casually mentioned ("Sometimes I ate nothing but a turnip leaf for a whole day") sprawled out before me. Whole days depicting the events and suffering that had surrounded Grandpa Yosef. A tiny dot with a world around it. I had to fight. If not the dragon, at least its wings.

I came to Grandpa Yosef. "I want you to tell me your whole story again."

"What for?"

"So I can document it."

"What do you want to do that for?" Anat asked.

"What's the point of that?" Effi asked. She was sitting in Grandpa Lolek's house on a new couch she had bought "to make him happy when he comes home." She had placed it exactly above the opening of his secret cellar, opposite her newly purchased television; she had even paid for cable TV ("it's instead of men"). She would leave everything for Grandpa Lolek, to make him happy when he came home.

"We have to document, to understand," I reply.

Grandpa Yosef's voyage kept rambling, great bright landscapes around every small section of his story.

Grandpa Yosef acquiesced. "All right, if you think it's important."

We sat together night after night, him talking and me writing. Every so often he got up, leafed through what I had written, reviewed his own story on the pages, pleased with what he saw. As if every letter wore a little tie, and his duty was to walk among the rows and inspect them, correcting little imperfections in their appearance.

Night after night, I acquired Grandpa Yosef's memories.

Dad was also willing to talk. I was Old Enough.

This time, I was the emotional one. His style was short and simple, with no inexpedient words. His life, his memories. The lost world in which he had been left to wander among ruins, people-who-would-no-longer-be, places-that-were-gone, a culture that had left only pointy headstones in little cemeteries and monuments at the edges of train tracks, and now the whole world that had once convened at the edge of the tracks was gathering its memories into the monuments, enlarging them, and so my father turned the years back, slowly retelling.

His words were clear. Simple. He had the talent to remember, a talent I inherited. Sometimes he struggled, *"Nu…*what was the name of Einhorn's son from the furniture store?" But he did not give in to the fifty years. I tried to comprehend how deeply he was casting these moments of concentration as I sat beside him, unable to help. In the evenings I transcribed his story, documenting, without changing a single word. I left it just as Dad said.

I was born in Bochnia, Poland, in 1930. My father was a barber, my mother a housewife. Before the war I completed the third grade in a regular Polish school, the Jachowicza School. My family was middle class. My father was a Zionist. My mother had a Jewish National Fund collection box like all good Jewish women did. Father was very active in the Jewish community. He was involved in building a large synagogue in Bochnia. Until then there were many small synagogues, known as *stiebelech.* The Jews in Bochnia were divided. Some were very Orthodox, some traditional, and some were not religious. My grandfather on my father's side was traditional. On Mother's side I only knew Grandmother, and she was very religious. My mother was also very religious.

Our lives were ordinary. That was, until the war. I played with Polish kids and felt like a Polish patriot. I knew I was Jewish, and after school I went to the *cheder,* which I was a little bitter about, but I had no choice…[Dad tells me, "In the Cheder we studied the *Chumash* and translated from *loshen koidesh* (Hebrew) into Yiddish. I did not know Hebrew or Yiddish, so for me it was like translating Chinese into French. I didn't understand a word. One day I came home and told

my father proudly, *'doszedłem do shlishi!*—I reached the third!'
I had no idea what *'shlishi'* was, but I usually reached only
sheini—the second."] I was not in a youth movement myself,
I was too young, but Father used to take me sometimes to a
Zionist youth movement. I can't remember which one, but
since Father was a socialist and a Zionist, it must have been
a Zionist socialist youth movement.

In 1939 the war broke out. About a week later the Germans entered Bochnia. We saw the German might and had not
believed that such a thing existed. We lived on the main street,
and we saw the Germans coming in with tanks and artillery
and infantry riding on armored vehicles. Before the Germans
came, there was a battle with a small Polish force, which was
destroyed by air strikes in the morning. The Germans had no
difficulty getting in. The bombardments were not in the center of town, so we did not suffer from them.

When the Germans arrived, at first they paid no attention to the Jews. After a while, the first prohibition was that
Jews were not allowed to walk down the main street. When
they did anyway, they were beaten. Then they set up a sort of
Jewish police, the *Ordnungsdienst*, or OD. They posted guards
at the entries and exits of the street so Jews would not pass
through. After a while, we were instructed to put a sort of
band on our sleeves. Not a yellow patch, but white with light
blue. It was obligatory from age thirteen, but I also started to
wear one at some point. The summer break came to an end
and we went back to school. After about a week the teacher
called us to the front. There were five of us Jewish children in
the class, and he said to us, "Goodbye and not farewell." He
simply kicked us out. We left.

The Judenrat had already been established by then, and
they set up a Jewish school. There were no advanced studies,
it was mainly to keep the children busy. My father's shop was
not confiscated—on the contrary, he was instructed to open
the shop and make it available to the German army. At first
they paid well. The soldiers knew he was Jewish, and that

was fine. Father kept running the shop, but after a while the Germans went elsewhere. That was until '41. Of course, during that period there were all sorts of *Kontributionen*—levies. You had to give so many pounds of copper, lead, all sorts of materials. You would buy the material and hand it over. They would publish a notice that everyone had to bring a certain amount, and no one dared not to.

We kept on living in our apartment. In the same building, they set up a residence for German soldiers. I don't know if they knew we were Jews, but in any case they treated us fine. Some of them were anti-semites who spoke about Jews, and others took no notice. In fact our landlord, who was a Polish anti-Semite and wanted to inform on us, was treated badly by them because they had been taught that wealthy landlords were Jews. We actually developed good relationships with some of the soldiers. They would hang around when they were on duty, and once in a while they came to visit. Father spoke excellent German, and it was nice for them to have someone to talk to far from home. Once, I remember, it was a Jewish holiday, and we had a festive meal at home. Suddenly we heard their vehicle stop outside. They had come to visit. Father quickly gathered everything up from the table, with the tablecloth, and threw it all into the next room. The soldiers came in and saw us sitting at an empty table. They asked why. Father said times were hard, and we just couldn't afford anything. They were moved and wanted to help, so they drove off and brought us back lots of food and other things.

That was how it was with those soldiers. They were just people. During that time there was some activity going on, they say there were Polish Partisans or some sort of underground. There was shooting at night, and they killed two or three Germans. The Germans hanged the two men who had done it. Then they took everyone who was in prison, and "just to be sure," they added in a few Jews. They led them all the way through town, we watched it, and executed them in a spot near the woods, and that was in fact the first execution in Bochnia.

In 1941 we received an order to move to the ghetto. We left our home and found an apartment in the ghetto. Father was given a permit to transfer his business to the ghetto. Poles were taken out of the ghetto area. There was still a school then, to keep the children occupied. At that time we didn't think much about escaping. There were no thoughts of extermination. There was no talk about extermination. People knew there would be trouble, they knew the Germans did not like Jews, but they thought it would be like in Germany, where Jews were restricted and their freedom of movement was curtailed, but there was no talk of extermination. Even when they talked about transports to the East, they knew the Jews were being sent to work. No one knew it was to be killed. Everyone thought they would somehow get through. Jews were always optimistic. Germans reached as far as Moscow and still people said, "These are extraordinary circumstances." Perhaps that was what kept them going, because otherwise people might not have survived.

My father had a barbershop, and at some point there came orders that everyone had to work. The luxury of school came to an end and I was allowed to work with Father in the barbershop. I studied hairdressing, learned how to shave, lather, that sort of thing. I worked there for quite a long time. It was a kind of village life, where people traded with each other. There were some people who did business, made money, and there were still some connections outside the ghetto, but the economic situation really began to deteriorate. That was until the first *Aktion* in the summer of '42.

In the summer of 1942 all the Jews of Bochnia were ordered to appear at the military base, except those who were given stamps in their work cards permitting them to stay. Anyone who wanted to stay tried to find a respectable workplace, because they thought if they sent people away, it would be those who did not have work. In that *Aktion*, virtually all the Jews who were originally from Bochnia went to Belzec. Well, we didn't know that Belzec was a death camp. We thought they were being sent to work in the East. My sister did not get a stamp, and she was already prepared with a bag and everything to go east. But at the last minute she was able to get a stamp. I remember we were standing next to our home in the ghetto when the Gestapo head, Schomburg, walked by with my Uncle Yanek, who was in the Judenrat. Yanek pointed out my sister to Schomburg, and that was all she needed. After that she got a stamp. Yanek himself was not helped by his 'status'; he was sent with his wife and his son Sigmund, three years old, to Belzec, stamps and all.

There was a hospital in the ghetto, and the head of the hospital was my uncle, Anatol Gutfreund. Since they said patients would not be sent east but would stay in Bochnia, my uncle hospitalized his mother. People found ways. But the Germans, as usual, did not keep their word, and they took all the hospital patients to the Baczkow forest and shot them, all of them, including my grandmother. That was apparently not enough for the Germans, because afterwards all the people who had been given permits to stay in Bochnia were ordered to come to the Judenrat courtyard, and they took us to the military base and had another *Selektion*. They asked each person what he or she did. My father said he was a barber. They said, "Good, we need a barber." They let him go. Then my sister came up. She had two jobs, at the bakery and in the street sanitation department. Then my mother said she worked with Father, so somehow they let her go. My mother took me by the hand so we could pass through together, but the man stopped me with his *Peitsche*, his horsewhip, putting it between my hand and Mother's. I was a twelve-year-old boy. At that moment a commotion broke out over by the main transport, I don't know what it was about. He looked over to see what was going on, and Mother quickly pulled me away and I went over to the other side and joined the group of people permitted to stay. That was my first *Selektion* and, as in dozens of cases, it was a matter of a split second this way or that.

After the *Aktion* was over they took us to collect the

dead from the streets. I saw murdered rabbis lying there, and I asked Father, "Father, tell me, what is this? Rabbis...why? Where are they and where are we...?" So my father said something like, "Because of sins, for what has happened...penance for the People of Israel," and so forth. I said to him, "Yes, but there are children here too. What about these children?" Then Father started crying. What could he say?

In that *Aktion*, the main core of the Bochnia Jews disappeared. We went back to the ghetto. Then they started bringing Jews in from all sorts of towns and villages in the area, and concentrated them all in the ghetto. What happened was that all the people who had hidden during the *Aktion* and had been found, they shot them right on the spot. Those they didn't find stayed hidden in the ghetto, then they let them out. There was no problem, they came out, they got a stamp, and they stayed. Then they divided the ghetto into Ghetto A and Ghetto B. In Ghetto A were people who worked, in Ghetto B people who didn't work. The Germans had a long-term plan to liquidate Ghetto B.

The second *Aktion* was in the winter of 1942, in November. The Jews were fairly confused and did not know what to do. We got permits to stay again, but we were afraid by then, because we had seen that there were *Selektionen*. And we saw that all the people who had hidden the first time were still there. So my father decided we would hide. He set up a bunker in the attic of a storehouse in our back yard. There was another family there, the Marsends. They had a little girl of about four, Etinka. That little girl was not just educated, but really trained. They trained her to stay quiet, not to open her mouth, and she could sit for hours without making a sound. They taught her that if she was put into a backpack and someone hit the backpack, she mustn't open her mouth. She was well trained. She was also a very fearful girl, very frightened. I admit that I tormented her quite a bit. I was bigger than her, and I used to tease her. I would tell her scary stories and she would stare at me without saying a word for a long time, then suddenly burst into tears. Whatever you did to her she would stay very quiet, until she suddenly started crying. That poor little girl.

We hid with the Marsends, and Grandma was also with us, my mother's mother. We hid and the searches began. We heard that every time they found people in a house, they shot them. They went from house to house and we heard yelling and shots. They shot and shot and shot. The house next-door to us too, they found a family there who we knew, and they killed them. We heard all the shouts. Then they reached our house. I remember that on the front door it said 'Ordnungsdienst Hollander.' He was our neighbor. I remember that it was in the evening and they called his name out. They searched, turned things upside down, but they didn't find the storehouse where we were hiding. It must have been too dark for them to see. We were in a sort of attic, the entrance was through the storehouse. My father had put some heavy objects against the door, so it couldn't be opened from downstairs. At least we thought it couldn't. The next day we heard them starting the search all over again. They went through again and we heard shots fired. They were getting closer to us. They came right up to our storehouse. They looked at it and said, "There must be an attic here." They started searching. They pushed against the door with a pole and the things Father had put there started to shift. The German said, "There must be people here." They brought a ladder and sent people in through the roof. A Jewish man came in, a locksmith they had brought to open doors, and a Polish policeman.

Before the war we had lived in a building that belonged to the police, and all the policemen knew us. The policeman saw Father, and yelled, "Dear God, Mr. Gutfreund, what are you doing here?"

What are you doing here...

In any event, the policeman started trying to cover Father up, and the locksmith, who knew the Marsends, tried to cover them up. Then they opened the door. I was standing closest to the door, so they took me and threw me down. Mother screamed because she was afraid I would be hurt in the fall. She didn't consider that we were about to be shot. I came out of the warehouse and stood in the yard. The German called me over. There was one German there, and all the rest were Polish police. He told me to stand by the fence. He asked how many people were up there, but I didn't tell him. I knew they had covered up Father and the other family, so I said, "There's my mother, my sister, and my grandmother." I knew they had already been found, because they had been in the same place with me. Then he stood me up against the wall, took his rifle off his shoulder and put a bullet in it. And all I could think of was that I hoped it wouldn't hurt, because I knew it was the end. At that moment a messenger arrived on a motorcycle and shouted something at him in German. The German took the bullet out, put it back into the magazine, slung his rifle over his shoulder and went over to the messenger. They spoke in German, I couldn't hear what they were saying, and he signed an order for the messenger. In the meantime they had brought down Grandmother and Mother. And the German said, "Search, there are more people there. Search, there are more people up there." They searched and found the Marsends and Father.

What happened, we learned later, was that they didn't shoot me because an order came to stop all the shooting. In the military base that I mentioned before, there were German soldiers who had started asking questions about the shootings. The SS didn't want the soldiers to know what was going on, so they gave an order to stop shooting. So it was a stroke of luck that we weren't shot. It was my own private stroke of luck.

Father told the Polish officers, "Don't take us to the transport, we have a permit to stay in the ghetto. We hid here because we were late and we were afraid to go out during curfew. Take us to the Judenrat, they'll authorize it there."

They didn't care, the Polish officers. Terrible anti-semites.

Mother said, "Look, Grandmother isn't feeling well. Where is your conscience?"

One of the officers said, "My mother is already in her grave, why shouldn't yours be?"

Fortunately, a German citizen passed by, a Gestapo member. Father, who spoke excellent German because he had been in the Austrian Army in World War i, told him we had a permit to stay and that they should take us to the Judenrat. He took off a ring with gemstones. The German took the ring and said, "All right, take them to the Judenrat."

There at the Judenrat, they said, "Yes, they are on the list." But despite that, there was an instruction to put us in the transport, where everyone was gathered. After that, an order came from the Judenrat and we were taken back there. They left only my grandmother in the transport.

We sat in the Judenrat offices. I remember there was a baby boy there, a few months old, and they had given him sleeping pills so he wouldn't cry and give away the people hiding in his bunker. They must have given him too much, and he was dying. My uncle the doctor said, "Give him something, milk, I'll flush his stomach," but there was no milk. I think that boy died eventually, I don't know. In any case, we sat there until the afternoon, and saw how they moved all these people onto the train, all the ones who had to go, and those who couldn't walk were shot. Then we saw that they were taking the elderly people on wagons, and we saw my grandmother on one of the wagons. Where they took them to this day I do not know. Because all the ones on the train they took to Szebnie, a work camp. The elderly ones, I don't know. I have no idea. Either they took them somewhere and shot them, or to Belzec. We don't know.

By that time we already knew about the annihilation. Because in the same hospital where my uncle was a director, there was a nurse there, a medic, who had been taken in the first *Aktion*. After two or three weeks my uncle had received a letter from Belzec, with a stamp that said, 'Belzec.' In his letter, the man wrote, "Everyone is dead. I am the only one left alive. Everyone was gassed. [*zagazowani.*] I met an old school friend." (The man was from Bielsko-Biala, on the Czech border. The German he met was from Czechia, near the border, and he knew him and kept him alive.) But this Jew asked my uncle to send him poison because he didn't want to live. There was a problem of what to do with this postcard. They sensed panic, and were unsure whether or not to reveal it. Uncle and Father decided to give it to the Judenrat. They handed it over but the Judenrat also didn't know what to do with it. Then another postcard came, saying, "I am begging you, send me poison, I don't want to live." Then another postcard came, and that was it. Nothing more. So by then we already knew there was annihilation. That was the first time it was clear to us.

Now, after the second *Aktion*, they let us go back home. But first we had to collect all the dead bodies from bunkers and all that. They brought us to a kind of hilltop. First we put the dead into a wooden house, and they were going to set fire to the house and burn everything. That was the order. But there were too many, and they wouldn't fit in. So we were ordered to tear down the house and make a pile, a layer of wood and a layer of corpses, like that in layers. Just then three German soldiers came from the army base. They had heard the shots and wanted to know what was happening. They saw the pile of bodies and asked what was going on. My father, as I mentioned, spoke good German, and he said, "*Verbrecher.*" Criminals.

Criminals. All right.

But then they saw a heap of children over on the side, and asked, "Are those criminals too?"

Dad said, "Yes."

"What did they do?"

"Jews."

Then the soldiers realized what was happening. They said, "Those dogs, the SS, what they do in our name! And we will pay the price."

They went to the base and brought the whole division

back, and they were planning to fight the SS and kick up a storm about what was going on. We begged them not to do that because it would only hurt us and make things worse. And it wouldn't bring back the dead. We could see that the soldiers were really... They didn't know what was going on back then. They were horrified. They simply did not know what was going on. There may have been Wehrmacht units doing all sorts of things, but these soldiers did not know what was going on, clearly. [I ask Dad, "Your father was a little impudent, no? Saying things like that. They could have done something to him for talking back to them like that." Dad says, "Yes, but he was...at that moment I think he just didn't care. He also... there was another time, before the ghetto, when a German *Volksdeutsch* harassed him on the street, and Father wouldn't let it slide and he punched him. He didn't leave the house for three days after that, because they were looking for him, and his hand was injured. Sometimes he wouldn't give in, he did or said what he thought should be done or said. Maybe that's why he answered the soldiers like that, I think."]

We went back to our houses, and again they started bringing in Jews from the region. At some point they separated the men from the women and the place turned into a forced labor camp. Everyone worked. They set up a mess hall because there was no cooking at home. I remember once we were eating in the mess hall, and there was an execution across the way. Two brothers, Schentzer, they had a soap factory before the war. They tried to escape the ghetto and some Polish policemen caught them and beat them bloody. They threw them into the Babica, the brook. The next night, they tried again. They were, you know, macho, the two of them. The Germans caught them. I remember they shut them up in a cellar right across from the mess hall. They took out one of them and were about to shoot him, and he tried to resist. But the executioner, an older German, was quick as a fox. He grabbed the man quickly by the back of his neck, put the gun to his head, and shot. Then they took the second brother out.

He saw his brother on the ground and started struggling. Again the German grabbed him and shot him. Not that he had a chance—they were surrounded by SS men with guns. And the whole time this was happening, about twenty yards from us, we kept on eating.

Then they canceled the separation between men and women. That was probably because they wanted to concentrate as many Jews as possible into one place. They had their plans. We moved into a house again, all of us together, with my uncle the doctor, who was the hospital director. We lived on Solna Gora Street. That was when they divided the ghetto into Ghetto A and Ghetto B. There was a case where the ghetto commandant, the Lagerführer, found a woman from Ghetto A in Ghetto B. He warned her once. The second time he shot her dead.

The third *Aktion* was in the summer of 1943. One morning they started announcing, "Everybody out, everybody out, everybody to the *Appellplatz*," which was the roll-call square. "Everybody leave now, take small belongings with you." I had a stamp collection, and I went with my friend to hide it because we thought we would somehow get through it again. I went to the cellar with my friend and we hid the collection. We wrapped it up in some rags. When we came out, no one was there, they had taken everyone. We lived not far from the Judenrat, just a couple of hundred yards across the way. And next to the Judenrat a bunch of Germans were standing around. They saw us coming out and yelled, *"Stehen bleiben!"*— Stop! But I didn't really trust them and so we started running. My father had once taught me that if I was being shot at, I should run away in a zigzag. And so I did. My friend overtook me, he was about ten yards ahead of me. They opened fire on us and I suddenly saw a red spot spreading on his back. He fell down. I kept on running into an alleyway, then I ran to the *Appellplatz*, where everyone was gathered, and I found my family. The Germans chased me but they couldn't find me, there were a lot of people there. [I ask Dad, "Do you remem-

ber your friend's name?" (I wanted something of him to live
on.) Dad says, "No. He was one of the kids who came to the
ghetto from the outside, from somewhere else. I can't remember his name anymore." But a few days later he remembers. "I
think his name was Salek. Salek was a nickname for Shlomo.
I'm not certain. But I think so, Salek."]

Again we were left behind, among those who were supposed to stay for the ghetto liquidation. At the time we didn't
know it would be liquidated. Father got a permit to stay. We
all got permits to stay. They took us aside. All the others, they
started putting in the transport. Then we saw the family that
had lived with us, and the father was wearing a large backpack,
and we knew that inside that backpack was little Etinka. We
saw how the Germans hit the backpack with a stick. They hit
everyone. We saw them hitting and poking, and that little girl
kept quiet, didn't say a word. He managed to get her through
and they went to Szebnie.

I learned later that when they were in Szebnie, the work
camp, they found the girl and killed her. Etinka's father found
out who the German was who had killed her, and during one
of the roll-calls he broke out of line, attacked the German and
strangled him. They shot him on the spot, but I was told that
he managed to strangle the German who had killed his little
girl. [From the list we got when we visited the ghetto with
Dad on our trip to Poland, I copy his full name down: Noah
(Noe) Marsend. Even though he was murdered long ago, and
the details of his life have become insignificant, I document
everything I know. His date of birth, 8/31/1904. The name of
his wife, Manya. Her date of birth, 7/26/1904. And the name
of his only daughter, Beata, known as little Etinka, who was
born on 6/2/1938 and murdered in 1942 at Szebnie camp. She
was four, exactly the age of my Yariv, who was born in 1988,
and who now comes out of his room and sleepily asks me to
check his buttons. "My pj's are all twisted." He can't sleep.]

That was a bit of a digression. In any case, a whole group
of us sat and watched as they sent the other people to Szebnie.

299

Then we saw a Jew running away from the transport. We were sitting next to a Jewish slaughterhouse, a kosher one. The Jew broke in there and the Germans chased him. We heard shots, then we heard him shout, "*Shema Yisrael!*" And then everything went silent. After about ten minutes we heard him shout, "Water...water..." He was still alive. But no one could go to him. Then there was silence.

After that they took us to the house where the *Ordnungsdienst* lived. It was a house on Kraszewska Street. There were supposed to be a hundred and sixty Jews left out of all the ghetto, and what happened was that there were two hundred and sixty left. So they took everyone. They called it the 'bloody roll-call.' They decided they had to kill a hundred people. They told the Judenrat head, Simcha Weiss, to give them the list of everyone who was left. So he said, "I have no list." He was hoping, you see, that without a list they would be able to save more people. For some reason, the camp commandant, Müller, also said he didn't have the list. In that respect he was pretty decent. The *Aktion* commander, a colonel, said, "You don't have a list? All right. Shoot the whole pile of them!" He got into his car and started driving away. Then Weiss ran after the car like a puppy and started begging, "Listen...we'll do something." The colonel stopped and said, "You choose who goes." So Simcha Weiss said, "I cannot choose, but I will go first." I remember that.

The Germans had a discussion and they started taking out all sorts of people from the group. At first we were convinced they were choosing the ones who would stay, because they took out all sorts of people who had connections with the Germans. But it turned out that every German who had an account to settle with a Jew took him out to kill him.

Then they said, "All the children stand in the front row." So I ran out, but Father grabbed me and wouldn't let go. He lifted me up behind his back and stood in front of me, holding me, and someone from the row behind held me up by my pants so I would look taller. ["How long did he hold you like that?" "Oh, it was a roll-call that lasted several hours…" "And all that time he held you like that?" "Yes, with his hands behind his back, holding me by my belt."] They went back and forth, searching. They didn't notice that I was a kid. They picked out a hundred people, took them aside and shot them on the spot.

Then they took us to the *Appellplatz*, where they put us into these kinds of shacks. We were ordered to start liquidating the ghetto. But first they took us to cover all the…to get rid of all the dead people…and there were lots of them. Lots of dead people. I can't give a number, but there were hundreds. We were left to liquidate the ghetto. A lot of Jews had been hiding, and the way it went that time was, whenever they found anyone, they killed them. Before that, whenever they found people after an *Aktion* they had let them live. But not this time. Whoever they found, they killed. There were some that they threw into the Judenrat cellars, but mostly they killed them.

I remember once I was with Father and they found two children. The girl was maybe thirteen, and a boy of seven or eight, something like that. Father called me and showed me a tiny suitcase, and inside were a few carrots and radishes and potatoes, because there was nothing to eat. They must have been hiding for a long time. Father started crying when he saw that. Of course, they shot those children. They took us to light a fire. They put the children in a straw basket. In Poland they had these big straw baskets. They burned them in the basket, but the basket fell apart and I saw how their bodies spilled out onto the pile with their arms and legs to the sides. Then they scattered the ashes. ["Dad, how did you turn out so normal, Dad?"] My father was the head of a work group, and there was a woman who came out of her hiding place and joined his work group. She wasn't legal, but Father covered for her and helped her get in touch with the other side, the Aryan side, and she was able to escape.

At a certain point, they had another *Selektion* during

the ghetto liquidation. There were a hundred and sixty of us and there were only supposed to be a hundred left. The truth is we were in a bind, because at that stage Father was 'in a spat' with the Lagerführer, Müller. One day some Gestapo men had come from Krakow, and without asking any questions they burst into the ghetto hospital and seized a whole treasure of gold and silver from under the bed of a Jew who was lying there. There must have been an informant, because they went straight to his bed. Müller was very angry that the whole treasure went to someone else, and he blamed my uncle and my father, insisting they had known about the treasure and helped hide it. He didn't exactly accuse them—I shouldn't even use the word 'accuse' because it's not like he had to say anything. He simply gave an order that Father should stop coming to shave him every day, as he had done up to then. He was the ghetto barber, and that was his great 'privilege.' ["What sort of a character was he, this Müller?" "You know. Nothing special." "You once told me he used to shoot out of his office window." "At bottles, not at people. He had one obsession, about women with makeup. He would personally supervise, and if he caught a woman with makeup on he would force her to remove it. That was at the beginning of the ghetto. Later, he didn't have to do that anymore—who walked around with makeup? He collected stamps, and he kept a Jewish expert to get hold of whatever he could find for him in the ghetto. Apart from that, nothing special. He wasn't even an officer, he was a sergeant or a sergeant major, a Scharführer. I don't know what their ranks were."]

Anyway, the Lagerführer was in a 'spat' with our family, and then came the *Selektion* announcement. We were worried, of course. But something that had happened two or three days before saved our lives. My father was the head of a work group, and he was a hard-working man. It was in his character to get the job done, and for some reason Müller, who used to ride around on a horse, saw that he was working hard and he must have liked that a lot. He called Father over, took out a cigar and gave it to him. It was a Saturday, and my father didn't smoke on the Sabbath. Go tell a German that you don't smoke on the Sabbath. So Father said, "I don't smoke while I'm working. I'll smoke it after work." And he liked that even more. So when the *Selektion* came, two or three days later, he let us go again. Gave us a permit. Our whole family was part of the remaining hundred. My mother and sister too.

At the end of 1943 the Bochnia ghetto was basically done with, liquidated. They took everything that was still there to the trains. Everything went to Germany, all neatly packed up. During the ghetto liquidation there was a case where a Jewish policeman escaped from the ghetto. His mother lived there, Mrs. Rothkopf, a very elderly lady. And so the camp commandant, Müller, took her out and killed her. Oberstrumführer Müller. Those were the two incidents when he personally shot someone. That time, and the case of the woman who wasn't supposed to be in Ghetto A. ["That's not true, Dad." Müller, although he was a nothing, is well known to Attorney Perl. People testified that he shot lots of people. True, he wasn't as murderous as some others, he was just a minor and obedient SS man who did not take his own initiative or commit extraordinary acts, but he did his job. When necessary, he shot people.] It's fate, the way one person is saved just because someone else isn't. Since the son had run away and Müller had killed the mother, he was missing two people to make the numbers work, and numbers were important to the Germans. Just then they caught a woman I knew, Mrs. Schwimmer, and her daughter, who were hiding. They wanted to shoot them right then and there, but Müller added them to the group to replace the missing two, so it worked out all right for him. And that was how Mrs. Schwimmer was saved, and she lived in Israel with her daughter until she was a hundred and three. Fate, that's what it is. But another son of hers was killed back in the first *Aktion*. He was an ordained rabbi, and during the *Aktion* he ran to the Judenrat as if it were an embassy that could save him. They shot him on the steps, and his glasses broke and pierced his eyes. He lay there like that. On the steps, face up.

In any case, they liquidated the ghetto. They put us all into one big house. One fine day they said, "Everybody out." They put us into train cars and took us to the Plaszow concentration camp. That was at the beginning of 1944, the winter of '43–'44. When we arrived in Plaszow, they put me and my father to work in the paper mill, and my mother and sister worked as seamstresses. They separated the men from the women, and only occasionally would we see my mother and sister behind the fence. At some point they needed lots of tools on the front, like pickaxes and spades. So they transferred all the men from the paper mill to the carpentry shop. The food was indescribable. There was hardly any of it. There was constant turnover of people. Some they sent away, some they killed.

The camp commandant was Goeth, Amon Goeth, who had an 'illustrious' career. He was huge, almost six-five, a sadist and a murderer. They said he was even crazier before we arrived. By the time we got there at the end of '43, he had already calmed down. Not that it helped us—he put the fear of death in us. I was a boy and I couldn't look at him...I just couldn't. He was truly the Angel of Death. The minute we saw him walk outside, we knew it would end badly. He was... simple...and he had assistants who were no less cruel than him. Sometimes all sorts of senior officials would come to the camp, but they didn't pay any attention to us. They came and went. [Sometimes I think it is because he went through the Shoah that Dad finds it difficult to understand. He survived on instinct, not thought. Germans who shot were bad; Germans who didn't—didn't count. But he gave no thought to a German who passed by in his car for a moment, looked around and drove on without a word. Dad couldn't pay any attention to whoever wasn't shooting or abusing him. That

German in the car scanned the square and thought to himself something like, "There are two hundred more than the estimate here. The train cars won't be big enough. If Spauser had worked faster with the transport from Jeklowicze we could have added another car, but now it's too late. We'll have to knock off a hundred here and squeeze in the rest. We'll send another telegram to Spauser and a reminder to HQ. We can't have things held up here." My father was too close, too persecuted, and the evil that concerned him was the simple kind, the obvious kind. But my thoughts go to that other evil, the one sitting in the car wearing wire-rimmed glasses.]

We worked in the carpentry shop. The foreman, I don't know his name, but he was known as 'Mongol.' He was a character. When we worked the night shifts it was good because there were air-raid sirens. The Allies were already bombing, and we hardly worked at night because when they bombed the lights were turned off and we couldn't work. But the work was very hard and very high-pressure. Next to the carpentry shop there was an execution area. They used a very nasty word to refer to it, 'Chujowa Gorka,' which means "Dick Hill." And that's where they held executions. We saw a lot of them. At some point they started burning the corpses there. At first they buried them, but when the front got closer they started burning them because they wanted to hide that anything had happened there. They started taking the bodies out and there was an awful stench from the rotting corpses and the fire. We worked very nearby, about fifty yards away. Then they moved the execution place to a different area, on the other side of the carpentry shop.

One day I wanted to take a little rest and I hid in a pile of chopped wood. They used to put the logs out to dry and there was a gap inside the heap, where I sat. And then I saw that they were bringing...it must have been Germans. First, a German company in brown uniforms brought someone and shot him. A German in a brown uniform. Then came a company in black uniforms and shot someone in a black uniform. It was some sort of internal execution, but I almost died of fear, because if they had seen that I was watching it could have ended badly.

On May seventh, 1944, there was a big *Selektion*. We stood naked all day, and a doctor came, whose name I can't remember. [Attorney Perl remembers his name. He was Doctor Blancke, Hauptsturmführer Blancke.] He stood there in a huge fur coat and we stood naked all day, and it was raining, and he pointed with a little pencil and said, *"Links, Rechts, Links, Rechts"*—left, right, left, right. I, of course, went to the *Links* because I was a runt. The ones who went to the left were put on the list, and that was it, they were listed for the transport. The transport was a week later, and whoever was listed had to go. Somehow on that day they also wrote my mother down in the *Selektion* in the women's camp. And I got a cold that day. The Germans didn't mess around—if you had a cold, you went to the hospital. They were afraid of epidemics. After two or three days in the hospital, I felt better. I was just a kid, and one of the Germans, Doctor Kalfus, was building himself a fish pond next to his office. I came out and started bringing him cement and rocks. I later found out that he was the number one murderer in the hospital. He would inject kerosene into patients' veins to kill them. Yes, a real criminal.

The fifteenth of May arrived, a week after the *Selektion*, and everyone who had been listed was called to come to the transport. Of course my name was called out too, because I was on the list. They called and called and called but I was saved because I was in the hospital. Then they came and took the whole hospital away. When they came to get me, there was a Jewish doctor there who really liked me. Well, I was a kid, and he said something to Kalfus. Kalfus remembered that I had helped him, so he said, "He's still young, he can work," and they let me stay. Now, you see, if I had been healthy they would have taken me to begin with. If I had been sick they would have taken me from the hospital. There were about nine hundred people there, and out of all those people I was the only one who remained.

That was the day they took my mother away. It later turned out that the whole transport went to Auschwitz, straight to the crematoria, because they were sick and emaciated people who couldn't work. My mother had lost weight for a reason. She was very religious and she wouldn't eat *treif*. So she would exchange soup for bread and things like that. When Passover came, she wouldn't eat bread either. She lost a lot of weight and they took her...that was the end.

There were a few more *Selektionen*. Once they sent me to the left in the *Selektion* and they wrote me down for the transport, but something...they couldn't find me on the general list. There was a member of the Jewish police named Finkelstein. He was a criminal. Jewish. He looked through the lists and then he said in Yiddish, I don't know...something...his heart softened, and he said, "I hope I don't find you on this list." And suddenly I saw that all the people from my hut were going back to the hut, and I saw my father, and I didn't ask a lot of questions. I ran and joined that group of people and no one said anything. I got into the hut and was saved that time. [I've been counting, and that's the seventh time you've been saved, and me saved with you, thanks to resourcefulness, thanks to luck, thanks to your father, thanks to your mother. Every time you are saved, you save me. I was born easily, a normal child, without understanding what I understand now—the miracle of my existence. I am here thanks to the things that happened to you and did not happen to others, those whose children were not born, who do not exist. Sometimes, though, I think you can sense them in the air, maybe on holidays and large gatherings, you can sense the offspring of the man standing behind you, next to you, whose father did not hold him behind his back for three hours, for whom there was no order to stop shooting just in the nick of time, for whom no well-timed commotion arose just when the horse whip, the *Peitsche*, separated him from his mother.]

Life in Plaszow camp was very difficult because often, after work, they would make us do all sorts of things just to humiliate us and make our lives difficult. After a night shift, they would often take four people and load a wooden plank on their backs. There were these dismantled shacks that were made up of all sorts of pieces of wood and they would load a plank onto four people. The plank itself was heavy, and then they would load it up with anything we came across on the way. Rolls of barbed wire, stones, dirt. Until the people collapsed. He was simply a sadist, the officer who devised this game. I don't remember his name, some SS officer, this was his hobby. The four would collapse and he'd take another four. It was...almost every morning after the night shift. Living conditions were very harsh. We lived in shacks with beds...not exactly beds, triple bunks, and each section held three people, and there were lots of fleas. We called them 'paratroopers' because they were red and they would fall on us from above. It was impossible to sleep. We used to sleep outside, because inside it was impossible. Outside there was rain and cold and snow. But it was better to sleep outside in the rain and snow than inside, where it was impossible. We had a lot of lice. After work, people would sit and kill the lice. You couldn't wash or boil the linen.

Economically it was very difficult. There wasn't enough food. My father had left some money with a Polish man in Bochnia who used to work for him, Mieczslaw Kozek. This Pole, from time to time, would send sums of money to the concentration camp. It was possible to get it to Plaszow. How he did it, I do not know. There were Germans who helped him. They must have gotten ninety percent of the sums that went through, but the ten percent were enough for us to buy bread or something. After the war, the Polish assistant told us that one day he saw an SS officer coming up to his barbershop, and he thought they'd found out about him and so he ran. He spent a week away from Bochnia, afraid to go back. It turned out the officer he ran away from was actually the man who had come to transfer the money. But it was no laughing matter, they really could have killed him for that. It was a great help to us.

In any case, it was possible to get along for a while, but then it stopped. The economic situation was very difficult.

Then there was a time when Father was ill and had to be hospitalized. I also got ill. My joints were so inflamed I couldn't even walk. We used to pass twice a day through the gates, and they would count us. We walked in rows of five. So when we had to go through to be counted, they would pick me up and walk me through the gates so I would be counted. Then they would sit me on the side. I couldn't move. [Who would have cared if they had put a bullet through you? You lay there, unable to move, and for hundreds of miles around you there was no one who could help, no one to halt reality if a bullet shot out of the barrel. What did you think about? You say you didn't think about anything in particular. I understand why you are such a Zionist. That was when you realized something that is difficult for me to understand—what it is to be without your own country. Without independence. Without having someone with a gun on your side too. So many days, lying there without moving, people around you being murdered over nothing. It must be harder than standing against a wall in the Bochnia ghetto, harder than being sent to the left, to die, and waiting a week for the transport.] In the camp afterwards I just couldn't make it to the clinic. I couldn't. But somehow I made it, I don't remember how. They gave me some medicine. It helped me a little and I got better, but it was a very difficult time.

For a while they took us to work outside the camp and we built railroad tracks for Prokocim, a village near Krakow. Terrible conditions. The foremen were real murderers. They would beat us to death over any mistake, or not a mistake, just any little thing. And the walk was long, walking from Plaszow all the way to Prokocim and back. People collapsed, they couldn't do it. The one good thing was that we could buy things from the Poles and smuggle them back into the camp. At first there was no money, but then Father somehow organized some money to buy stuff and smuggle it in. But the Germans knew this, and every so often they conducted searches. One evening they started a search. Everyone who had anything would be beaten bloody. There were some cooking pots laid out on kind of wooden planks. I told someone, "Come on, let's take this plank and go." We took a plank and started walking away. A German saw us leaving so he chased us. He was certain we were hiding something in the pots. When he saw there was nothing, he hit me and we left. But I had lots of things on me, and then we were able to get money.

In Plaszow there were a few Jews who were no better than the Germans—and some that were worse. There was the Chilewicz, the 'head Jew.' This man was a criminal. There was also Finkelstein, the one I mentioned before, and the two of them were no less cruel than the Germans. Sometimes even worse. [I read in the testimonies about their fates. Just before the liquidation of the camp, the Germans took Finkelstein and Chilewicz and Chilewicz's wife, who was even worse than he was, to a hilltop and killed them. *Speak kindly of the dead.*] In that period there was nothing to eat. I always tried to find a way to sneak into the kitchen. I was a small, thin boy. I would burrow under the fences and steal soup and run with it to Father. On my shirt you could see the menu every week. There was no other way to survive. I also managed to get something through to my sister, in the women's camp. Mother, I already said, would not eat soup because it was *treif.* At the end of '44 they sent us in a transport to Gross-Rosen in Germany. At the same time they sent my sister to Auschwitz, and then to Ravensbrück. My father was already quite sick. We didn't know he was suffering from kidney problems. His legs swelled up horribly.

We came to Gross-Rosen. I remember at the station, we were met by Jewish prisoners in striped uniforms. They told us, "If you have anything, give it over quick, because you won't be needing it..." We thought they meant we were going to be gassed, but they must have meant that the Germans would take everything we had, and if we gave these people our things, at least the Germans couldn't take them. But we thought that was it, we were going to the gas chambers. We were ordered to strip. They put us in a little hall and we sat naked for three days and three nights, because Germans believed that people smuggled in gold and dollars in their bodies. Maybe there were people who did, I don't know. When someone needed to use the toilet they took him outside in the snow, naked, and he would have to do his business somewhere where they could search. There was a kind of container, and there were Jews who used sieves to find out if there was anything inside. We sat for three days and three nights without food or drink. Cold.

After three days they concluded that everyone had vacated themselves. They put us in cold showers and made us run in the snow for about a mile. We stood in a hut and they threw each of us a pair of pants, a shirt, a strange sort of wool hat, and shoes. Clothes with stripes. In the middle of winter, freezing cold, but those were the clothes they gave us. We slept in a little hall, if you can call it sleep. One man sat up against the wall and the next on his legs and the third on that one's legs, in rows and rows. If someone needed to go out to relieve himself, in the cold, he had to step on the other people's feet, because there was nowhere to walk. He had very little chance of reaching the door. On the way people held it in, they didn't want to go...but by the time they got to the door they didn't need to go out anymore. Whenever someone made a noise, a kapo would come in and make us exercise—up, down, up down, with murderous beatings. That's how the nights would go by. We worked in construction. The Germans were still building. Retreating on one end, building on the other. We were there for only two weeks. After that they sent us to Waldenburg.

In Waldenburg we lived in buildings. It wasn't a large camp. Most of the people worked. There was a chemical plant there, and some people worked in construction at all sorts of places where they walked on foot, over five miles, every day there and back. In Waldenburg we worked at peeling potatoes.

Next to the camp there was a bachelors' residence house. There were Italians and Frenchmen working at the plant because the Germans were all on the front. They were salaried civilians, and so they had this sort of bachelors' house where they lived, and whoever was able to get in there to work saw it as a boon, because the house matron was a Volksdeutsch, a Polish woman of German origin. Frau Paullina. She was very fair. Really, thanks to her my father was saved because his legs were very swollen, he was barely alive. She wasn't so strict about work. She was really all right. Once in a while people were beaten, but compared to other camps it was okay. The thing is, they were always preparing for an evacuation. They thought we would have to leave at any moment. [Dad was lucky. All the auxiliary camps of Gross-Rosen were ordered to go on Death Marches. Waldenburg was an auxiliary camp of Gross-Rosen, but there was no Death March, probably by personal order of the camp commandant. People went out on the marches from all the camps in the area, even from relatively comfortable camps like Waldenburg. People who believed they had gotten through it all, that they had been saved, went on the marches days and hours before the war was over. Cut off from the world. Around them was utter German defeat, the Russians were in Berlin, no more orders were coming through, but the lines marched on, a small disconnected world where there were still orders and shooting and an ostensible direction. On an endless course—a line of ants with no nest. Marching. No food, no water, no rest. The lines marched on and on. One step after the other. No questions asked. March on. Nazi Germany had surrendered, orders had stopped coming, and prisoners were being shot on the side of the road. The cruelty did not melt away—on the contrary, it grew harsher, more extreme. In the row of ants, the people with the guns clung to the familiar. Only if they kept on marching would the safe world, the good world, remain. If they stopped even for a moment it would all disappear. A row of ants with no nest, and I see those who falter shot immediately, and the shooters wipe the blood off a rifle butt held too close. I can actually see it. A row of ants with no nest, and Dad, because of an anonymous camp commandant, back on his cot in Waldenburg, while around him prisoners set off to march.] The camp commandant told us there were SS units going from camp to camp and killing whoever remained. I didn't hear it, but people told me that he said, "If they come here, everyone should run wherever they can." He was simply...well...he was all right.

The end of the war was getting closer. We saw German civilians gathering around our camp in increasing numbers because they were terribly frightened. They were already throwing food into the camp and trying to tell stories about how they weren't to blame, they didn't know and hadn't known. And then the eighth of May arrived. At two-thirty in the afternoon, the camp commandant closed the gates with a lock, threw the keys in and said, *"Jetzt seid Ihr frei"*—you're free now. And he fled. And that was that.

We didn't know what to do. People were frightened. We knew it was the end, but we didn't know what to do with our freedom. People didn't know what to do, they simply didn't know. They were afraid to go out in case the SS arrived after all. We didn't know what to do. So for a while we waited inside. After a couple of hours we broke open the gates and started running towards the main road. We got there at about four-thirty in the afternoon. That was when we saw the first Russian units. Russian troops rolled in on tanks. They had no food. They also had apparently not had much to eat. But people went into factories and houses and started eating. That was a disaster, because they got dysentery and food poisoning and had to be hospitalized. A lot of people died after that. Maybe it was my luck again that the Russians broke into a liquor factory—that's what they were after. I went in there and filled some bottles with all sorts of drinks. And for some reason I didn't think about food...I don't know why. I took it all back and brought it to Father. Father drank a little and I drank some, and we didn't have much strength left. We fell asleep. The next day we woke up and saw people vomiting, they were horribly sick. We realized that the little bit of drink had saved us.

Then we went to the German women. The German men were on the front, and the women wanted the people from the camps to come and protect them. We lived there for about two months. There were no trains, no means of transportation, so we couldn't get back. And we didn't know where to go back to. We lived there for about two months without doing anything. After two months we started to walk. We took a little wagon and loaded up a few things we had. At that time personal belongings had no value; when I needed a shirt I took one and threw away the old one. Who needed two shirts? In those circumstances, property had no value. So we took a wagon and loaded it with...I can't even remember what, and we started to walk. There were some stretches where there were trains and some where there weren't. When there were trains they were full. It wasn't well organized like it is today. Everywhere we went, we saw Poles standing around saying, "More Jews have come back."

I knew that my mother was not alive, because people who had been with me in Waldenburg, who had also been in Auschwitz, had told me. They said the transport that arrived on May 15th and 16th went straight to the gas chambers. I didn't tell my father anything. My sister went through very difficult things. She barely made it through alive. She was in Auschwitz, in Ravensbrück. In terrible conditions.

At Katowice there was a train to Krakow. In Krakow we caught a coal train to Bochnia, hoping someone would still be alive. We didn't know, but we hoped. We got to Bochnia. There was a horse and cart there, and the driver knew Father. He asked him in complete surprise, "You mean you're still alive? They said everyone was dead." He wasn't too happy, but he took us to the center of town, where we met a young man who had been in the concentration camp with us, and he said that my sister was in town. There were only a few Jews there, and my sister was among them. And so for a while we lived in Bochnia, but there was nothing to do there.

My father tried to rebuild the gravestones. The Germans had destroyed them all to pave roads. Mrs. Schwimmer was there. She was the elderly Jew who had been saved with her daughter because they shot the mother of the Jewish police- man who escaped. She was a serious woman. Together with my father they set up a lot of the gravestones they found. During the war, a Polish man had found my grandfather's gravestone in the road, and at night he came with his sons and took it and hid it in his barn. When we came back, he told Father that he couldn't allow himself to see the gravestone of Mr. Gutfreund on the road. He gave it back to Father and it still exists today.

I was basically illiterate. I had hardly had any schooling. Father sat me down and hired a private tutor who taught in the local high school, and within six months I finished elemen- tary school. I went through all the material. Then I took an exam at Jachowicza school, where I had gone before the war. The headmaster was the examiner. Amongst other things, he had me write about what I had been through during the war, in Polish. It was really the first time I sat down and thought about what had happened. He came into the class a few times, where I sat alone, and asked, "Haven't you finished yet?"

I wrote and wrote and wrote and wrote.

A few days later, I came to get my grade. He looked at me and said, "You wrote this?"

"Yes, I did."

"Are you sure?"

"No one was in the classroom, I was alone."

"And you went through all these things?"

"Yes," I said.

And then he said, *"biedny dziecko"*—poor boy. He patted my head and asked if I would be willing to leave the notebook with him. Stupidly, I left it. [I found out that the name of the headmaster was Witold Raganowitz.]

That's it. That was the end of the story in Bochnia. [After the war, Dad raised doves on the rooftops in Bochnia. Raising doves—that was good. A symbol of freedom. Something I will be proud to tell Yariv one day. He also sold contraband cigarettes. That's less good, but true. That's what happened. He used to go to Krakow to buy packs of cigarettes, then back to Bochnia to sell them in the market square. Competitors harassed him, policemen chased him down, but after the war they were no match for Dad. A man who had been blessed with so much cunningness and luck and survival skills—it took more than a Polish policeman to trip him up.] We moved to Krakow. In Krakow I went to high school, a Jewish school. And there we studied two classes every year to catch up. Then they demolished the Jewish school and I moved to a Polish school. At that time I was already active in the Shomer HaTzair movement, and my head was more in the movement and in making *aliya* to Israel than in my studies. But I studied because Father pressured me. He opened a barbershop in Krakow. He was always sick. He had uremia, a kidney disease, and he died in 1950. My sister left for Israel, leaving me on my own. I had an aunt and an uncle, but really I was alone. That was during the period when they didn't let people leave, it was a big problem. I went to Warsaw a few times, because the main *Shomer HaTzair* cell was there. Then they broke up the cell. Zionist movements were outlawed. My uncle was a captain in the Polish army, a dentist, and he was a first lieutenant in a military hospital. I lived in his apartment and I used to hold Shomer HaTzair cell meetings there. If he had known, he would have killed me. But it was a safe place, because a captain in the Polish army and all that...

The Israeli ambassador to Poland at that time was Barzilai, a member of Kibbutz Negba. He was very supportive, as much as he could be, of the Zionist issue, but we couldn't get exit visas. One day I decided to try. I went to the Ministry of the Interior in Warsaw. It was an office of the KGB and that sort of thing. Very secured. Guards everywhere. I searched for a way in, and managed somehow. There was a guard on every floor. When the guard was distracted by talking with someone I would sneak past. I got to the fourth or fifth floor, I can't remember, to the office of the Director General of the ministry. Getting there was...I myself don't know how I did it. Back then I could do those things.

When I walked into the office, the secretary started shouting, "Goodness gracious, how did you get in here?"

I said to her, "Listen, I'm Jewish, I have no one here, I want to go to Israel."

From all her yelling, because she was so afraid, the Director General came out. He asked, "What's going on here?"

So she said, "He snuck in."

He asked, "What are you doing here?"

I told him, "I'm Jewish, my father has died, my sister left, there's nothing for me here. I went through the whole war in the camps, I have nothing here."

He looked at me like this, put his arm around my shoulder, and said, "Go home, you'll get a travel permit."

So I said, "But you don't know my name."

"Give your name to the secretary."

I gave her my name and left the building legally. Two weeks later I received my passport. I believe to this day that he was Jewish. That's what I think. Because he...I could see that he...he was considerate. And the fact is, I got a passport.

So I made *aliya* to Israel. I went straight to Kibbutz Gan Shmuel. I came with a Shomer HaTzair group, part of a larger group. The Poles gave out exit permits, but only very few. We took trains through Czechia, Koshitza, Austria, Italy. In Venice we boarded the "Galila" ship, and that was how we arrived in Israel. Of course, they welcomed us by dousing us with DDT, but for some reason we did not complain. We understood. After Kibbutz Gan Shmuel, I went to Kibbutz Harel. Then I decided to join the army. I served for two and a half years, in the artillery. I finished my service. I was alone. My sister was in Israel, and there was an aunt, but...

Somehow I got a job at Ata. It was a big textile factory, one of the most famous in Israel. Getting a job there was a big deal, it was considered a good job. I worked there doing 'dirty work.' Before that I worked in construction and all sorts of other things. Slowly but surely, I made progress. I went through training, took courses, I was an instructor, a foreman, then a human resources manager. It took time. Thirty years. The factory closed down in 1985 and I got a job in the collections department at the municipality of Kiryat Bialik. Then I retired, and that was it.

1992: Yariv

*L*unch. Saturday. Yariv sits across from his grandfather—my father—contending with the revelation that Grandpa was once a little boy. A lovely crease ploughs its way across his forehead as he gazes at Dad suspiciously. Considering. Examining. Straining to find a place for this new truth. I watch as his mind processes the geology of knowledge. Effi watches too, still with an angry look on her face. Before lunch she had discovered that Yariv was unfamiliar with Little Red Riding Hood. She took him to his room to tell him the story, and emerged after a short while, announcing, "Your kid's a retard. He had no problems with the wolf, but he was afraid of Little Red Riding Hood!"

We eat in silence. What can we say? Our current life stories pale in comparison to the history evolving over at Grandpa Yosef's, where Grandpa Lolek's recuperation is rapidly progressing. Only two months have passed since Grandpa Yosef took him in, and Grandpa Lolek is already taking slow, probing steps around the neighborhood. He roams Katznelson Street, looks at his Vauxhall, even sits down in it for a furtive cigarette once in a while.

Except that doubt has seeped in. Something hasn't been sitting

321

right. Grandpa Lolek's rehabilitation process has begun to seem suspiciously marginal, as if its true tenor is in fact the advancement of the capricious protagonist, Grandpa Yosef. Something about him strikes us as odd. At first, when he insisted that Grandpa Lolek come to his home to recuperate, we thought he was simply trying to buy some more time before the inevitable loneliness set in (no-one-to-make-an-effort-for-no-one-to-make-an-effort-for.) He had escaped to the Caribbean, had then seized the opportunity to fill his home with the presence of Hans Oderman, and finally spent a heroic era at Grandpa Lolek's side in the hospital. We thought he was now attempting to acquire yet another stretch of time. But that was merely the outer layer of a disorganized thought.

We monitored the recuperating Grandpa Lolek as he slowly returned to us. We applauded the internal powers that redrew him without losing an iota of his former character. We were optimistic, despite the slight and perhaps typical oddness of the way his health was restored. His limbs and senses convened in separate units to regain their strength, each disconnected from the other. The first to recover were his legs, along with his vision and appetite. His hands remained rigid, almost paralyzed, and not a word left his lips. When his left hand recovered enough so that he could leaf through the obituary pages in *Yediot Aharonot*, an anonymous notice representing an opportunity to make a quick profit sufficed to extract a cry of excitement from his lips; thus his vocal capabilities were rebirthed. His right hand recovered along with his hearing. He slowly relocated his back pain and the urge to smoke. The lust for opportunity, the debtism—it all came back. He regained strength daily, limb by limb, sense by sense, character trait by character trait, as if he were healing himself according to an old blueprint he had kept hidden away somewhere. Eventually he came back to us completely, the old Grandpa Lolek we knew. He took an interest in the world, in what was different and new, in the dollar exchange rate and the family's well-being. He was somewhat alarmed by the rainfall, unaware of the drought that had raged while he was gone. He did not entirely comprehend his medical condition, utterly surprised to discover that he had been considered 'ailing' for some time now. He was very curious about the treatment options, the physician referrals, the types of surgery to choose from. He converted the proposals into a line of prices, options and costs, which clarified his situation with surgical precision.

We were impressed. We monitored him. With Grandpa Lolek—everything was fine. Coming along nicely. But with Grandpa Yosef there was a wild and indeterminate motion. From the moment Grandpa Lolek awoke and regained his senses, our suspicion increased. At all hours of the day and night, Grandpa Yosef hastened to pick up on Grandpa Lolek's every wish, fulfilling each and every desire as though it were a holy mission. Even when we considered his usual personality, together with the uniqueness of the situation, we were still far from understanding the power of his enthusiasm.

The devoted care-giving affected Grandpa Lolek in many ways. We found him usually vibrant and cheerful, well cared for, his face joyous. Even when the discussion revolved around surgery and the correlated risks, his face was full of surging optimism. Talk of the costs still did not diminish the lightness of his wrinkles. It seemed that Grandpa Lolek was not in complete control of a burning desire to smile, to rejoice, to enthuse. We could not understand the source of this happiness. We suspected it might be the delicacy that Grandpa Yosef cooked up for him every day, the inactive ingredients of which were pickled herring and onion, but which was in fact a potion con-cealing powers that sometimes took the form of dillweed. Grandpa Lolek ate it eagerly, asking for more every day, longing for the next helping to the point of total dependency. A light glow enveloped him, a constant light into which the dish was poured onwards and inwards.

Grandpa Yosef had become a complete savage in the kitchen. He turned his soups golden with turmeric and scattered cardamom pods in his fritters. Ginger and cilantro enhanced his meatballs, while the flavor of cinnamon took hold of rice pudding like a tyrant. When-ever we came, at any time of day, we would find the table covered with leftovers from their banquets, and over in the kitchen a new feast being concocted in the oven. Whenever we tasted anything, we recoiled. Grandpa Yosef was exploiting the temporary malfunction of his recu-perating guest's taste buds by embedding fiery spices in all his dishes, turning Grandpa Lolek's body into a refinery, a test-tube. Grandpa Lolek happily dined on the meatballs, the fritters and the dumplings, while mysterious reactions burned within his body. And Grandpa Yosef stood watching, concentrating, his eyes ablaze with purpose. "Stand back, stand back," he would urge, pushing us away.

Nutrition and digestion could not contain all of Grandpa Yosef's intentions. A fire was burning there, a great mystery. Perplexed, we watched as Grandpa Yosef rushed around and drained his energies. We asked ourselves what was going on. Effi was the first to understand: "Well, he's trying to turn back time."

We were amazed. No, not amazed, for this was an idea we had already considered—it had amazed us once and been rejected, but now it was clear. From the moment the idea was voiced, it seemed so obvious. How could it be otherwise? Grandpa Yosef was trying to turn back time. We looked at Grandpa Lolek, who had touched the brink of death and returned, rowing back into a life already lived. We looked at Grandpa Yosef staring longingly at him—if only Grandpa Lolek could recover and go back to the moment of the stroke. If only he could push and heal him a little more. Even the doctor had said, "Just give it time, take good care of him, and he'll be younger than he was before."

Grandpa Yosef was a realist, but he suffered from a mystical unconscious. His soul was preparing to create a miracle: to cure Grandpa Lolek with dizzying speed, to hasten the arrow of retreating time, and to use the momentum of his recuperation so that time would gallop backwards and restore Grandpa Lolek to his previous life, thereby also restoring Moshe. And by truly pushing reality to it limits, Feiga too would be restored. Grandpa Yosef's unconscious barely let him in on these plans. It only ran him around like a messenger boy, working towards the great purpose—to turn back time and demand that it give back Moshe and Feiga. To restore everything to the way it was.

Grandpa Yosef took in Grandpa Lolek like a beloved burden, a yoke worth its weight in gold. From his illness, from the regions of death he had touched, Grandpa Lolek was launched towards health, a load pulled back and released. Together with him, according to the laws of physics, and without disrupting the principle of inertia or the law of conservation, without transgressing the laws of this world, time was also supposed to be swept away, or at least to flutter and leave behind a twist, a fold, a dimple—that was enough.

We were concerned for his health. Grandpa-Yosef-against-time seemed like an unfair battle. We observed his desperation and endurance, and we fell in love anew. Matters were helped by the documentation of "Grandpa Yosef's Voyage." The pages, slowly accumulated, described a simple voyage that explained everything. I showed it to Effi and Dad. We fought off our aversion.

Grandpa Yosef's story was written down, as was Dad's. And then, in the spirit of the era, attention was turned to a more momentous task. I began to think about the other people in the family and in the neighborhood. Their stories. The Big Bang. I wanted to document it, to write everything down. Everything-that-had-happened-to-everyone-who-came-from-there. Everyone-I-knew. Everything-I-once-did-not-know. Everything-that-must-be-revealed-so-that-I-could-now-understand. Everything-that-must-be-written-so-it-was-not-lost.

Anat could not understand. "What do you need to deal with all this stuff for? It won't do them any good either."

During Grandpa Lolek's illness, she had joined forces with Grandpa Yosef. She could not contain herself for long while such an impressive nursing operation was taking place right in front of her eyes. She took over the domain of laundry and ironing, and contributed to the baking. We often met at the hospital, I with pages of documentation, she with piles of clothes on the Fiat seats.

"I don't want you to spend too much time with all that," she said.

"You're not letting it go, eh?" Effi said.

"It should be documented," Attorney Perl assured me.

I brought Yariv to see him in the store for the first time. He sat in the back room, in the corner at first, slightly frightened beneath the angular wall above him. He nervously kneaded the soles of his rain boots, a new acquisition, and examined the screws he had been given. He plucked up the courage to ask for a nut for each bolt, "So they won't be lonely."

Attorney Perl laughed and called out to his assistant in the front of the store, "Yakov, bring in a box with nuts for quarter-inches!"

He showed Yariv the photograph of his wife, Laura, and explained, "That was my wife."

"Whose mommy was she?" Yariv asked.

Attorney Perl rolled his eyes and sipped a cup of tea. Then he yelled, "Yakov?!"

Yakov came in with a box. It was a new Yakov, one we did not know. He scattered some nuts in front of Yariv and silently retreated to the front of the store.

The nuts bored Yariv. He started inspecting the little drawers along the back wall. He carefully pulled out one drawer, wondering if he would be rebuked, and revealed that the drawers did not contain the store inventory, as I had believed all those years, but rather notes of paper. The little drawers that filled the back room contained index cards bearing crowded notations.

"*Nu*, I've been collecting all these years." Attorney Perl took out a few cards and showed me his treasure trove of endless notations.

Franz Six. Head of the "ideological" branch at the Reich Security Main Office, responsible for disseminating material on the "Jewish question." Sentenced in 1948 to twenty years in prison, released four years later, in 1952.

Eduard Houdremont. A partner in the slave labor crimes at Krupp industries. Sentenced to ten years in prison in 1948, released in 1951.

Hermann Reinecke. Sentenced in the High Command trial to life imprisonment in 1948. Released in September 1954.

Walter Warlimont. Sentenced at the same trial to life imprisonment. His sentence was later commuted to eighteen years and he was released in 1957.

Endless lists. Crowded index cards with names and details, the stories of their lives after release from prison—the quiet lives, the little houses, the grandchildren, the longing for the good old days. Here, I realized, was where the treasure trove had always resided. Not in the memory of Attorney Perl, but in the little drawers.

"Could I read these?" I asked.

Attorney Perl gestured with his hand, putting all the drawers along the wall at my disposal. "Yes, yes. It would be interesting if someone finally did something with all this. You could write out all these notes nicely, with all the details. So if anyone in the world thinks the Nazi criminals were punished enough, they'll know."

Between my eyes and his there emerged a world in which I sat down immediately and began to toil. But Yariv pulled my hand, whispering, "I have a secret." He put his hand to my ear and explained gravely, "I have to go pee-pee." Then he announced, "Not here."

"Why not here?"

"Not here."

We went out to the street. Rain, as usual. A good time to try out his new boots. We found an old yard full of puddles glimmering under the street lamps.

"Here," Yariv chose.

And very quietly, like two bank robbers, we slipped into the yard "for a quick pee-pee." Later, at Yariv's demand, we went to "our" falafel stand, the one on Nevi'im Street. There, of course, came the memories. Dad used to take me to this stand, and I too had to be lifted up high so I could see over the counter laden with bowls of condiments. "Half a portion and juice," I used to say. The same place, so many years ago. Only the falafel guy is different—probably the son. "A ton of rain," he comments. "Yeah," I reply. I have no idea what his name is. So many years. This place has never been closed except for one week, when death notices covered the iron shutters, citing a name I have now forgotten. Then it opened up again. Same falafel, same flavor, only a different guy, but with the same features. He asks Yariv what he wants. Yariv does not speak, only points, cautious around strangers. But he stomps his feet in a puddle so everyone will see his new boots.

Lightning bolts through the sky, followed by thunder. Yariv is not scared, he likes it. He says, "rain," and his fingers mimic drops falling. "Lightning," he says, and one finger cuts through the air. He says, "thunder," and makes a tight fist, then opens it up as befitting thunder. Little Red Riding Hood scares him. Not thunder. At nights he gets out of bed and sings songs with the rain. They spent the whole fall at kindergarten looking forward to the rain, and when it was delayed, they sang the songs anyway and applauded. Now they're onto Chanukah songs, but Yariv happily wakes up at night, puts his nose against the window and sings for the rain. He thinks this is how it will be all year round. Rain and rain and rain and rain. He has no idea that something has happened this year, because of Grandpa Yosef and his war against time, and that the rain has already taken on the qualities of a deluge.

After the falafel, it's too late to go back to Attorney Perl's store. But over the next few days I go every day and stand in front of the great wall of drawers. (When Anat has to go out, I leave Yariv with the upstairs neighbor, the one who's always-happy-to-look-after-him-for-a-few-hours.) Attorney Perl lets me poke around and read, while on the other side of the wall he slowly climbs the ladder to take down bolts and nails for his customers.

Attorney Perl starts to bring me books from his home, endless volumes and pamphlets on the Holocaust. The Nazi trials are documented in thick brown volumes, testimonies bound in thin notebooks, anthologies of articles, the literature of Nazi laws, the speeches and verdicts of German leaders. "*Nu*, I've been collecting and buying for many years." Little notes and pencil markings indicate sections he finds particularly noteworthy. I read everything he has marked, and everything in-between.

He also starts sending me to Jerusalem, to the Yad Vashem library and archives. He gives me precise lists, citations in books, reports I have to read. He names documents, testimonies, protocols. The order and clarity in his ninety-two year old memory conflicts starkly with the labyrinthine archives. Energetic librarians do their best to search for my requests. Am I sure that's the name of the report? Being a well-briefed emissary, I insist. Sometimes Attorney Perl is vindicated, the report located. Other times—nothing, the report is missing. I go back to his store to peruse the documents with him, to hear explanations, opinions, further instructions.

"And don't forget," he says, supervising my work, "that you wanted to document testimonies from your family too."

I set up meetings with family members and come to demand

their recollections. I bring Yariv, the representative of sweetness and charm. We work as a team. His role—to extort wonder, excitement, attention. To soften them up. As soon as we arrive he makes himself comfortable on the rug, takes out two balls, a motorized car, an old plastic car, a water pistol. He never turns down a cup of juice, cookies, more juice. He rejects biographical questions, like "How are you doing?" "Do you like your teacher?" "What's your girlfriend's name at kindergarten?" In the meantime, his accomplice begins asking questions, listening, encouraging. The people acquiesce and their memories begin to pour out. First, happy memories. Always childhood. Always a town or a village, always with a market square (*rynek*, in their language). Mother. Father. Family. Sometimes the memories skip around, suddenly it is the post-war years. Pieces of family and fragments of encounters and life forces. At some undecipherable cue, the photo albums come out and great wings are spread. As the pages are turned, the storytellers are inspired to voice near-prophetic visions, although they are unable to belie the triviality of the photograph subjects—family displays and smiles in a row on chairs.

I let them talk. They roam through their memories, not always masters of their domain. Sometimes the storyline crosses the 1948 line, reaching the years of *aliya* to Israel and even as far as the Six Day War, in IDF uniforms with stories-you-wouldn't-believe, and yet it always reverts in the end, retreating back to 1939, the year of truth, the Big Bang.

On the rug, Yariv concocts battle and chase scenes, staging accomplishments for an imaginary enemy soon to be cowed by his own great victory. In the meantime, they reminisce. Sometimes in a flow, a series, an effortful sprint. Sometimes there are breaks and jumps and refusals and darkness. They cry too. Real tears. Yariv cranes his neck to see, one hand clutching a plastic car, the other on the table top as he stares.

Sometimes they say, "You know what, why do you need all these stories?"

"Documentation," I reply.

They ponder the word. It appeases them. Documentation. And they continue talking. Immortalized. Existing. Validated. Uncle

Lunkish and Aunt Frieda and Aunt Riesel and Aunt Zusa and Uncle Antek and Mrs. Kopel and Uncle Menashe. Darkness and ignorance and physical adjustments and escape and terror and trees and huts and people who once were and prayers and children and market squares and shooters and fear and quiet and silence.

In the evening I sit down to put it all into some sort of order. To document. I also copy down details from Attorney Perl's little cards. How do you form a coherent shape out of all this chaos?

Anat hovers around me, dissatisfied. "I'm telling you, you shouldn't be spending too much time with this."

Glowing embers.

"There's no such thing as too much!"

Because Walter Haensch, an Einsatzgruppe leader, was sentenced to death, but his sentence was commuted to fifteen years and in the end he was released after serving seven years in prison.

Because Heinz Schubert, another Einsatzgruppen leader, was sentenced to death, but his sentence was commuted to ten years and he was eventually released after three years in prison.

Because of their beautiful little houses in the newly formed Germany. Because of the gardens, the red roofs, the lawns to mow. The children, the grandchildren. The long weekends in the cold winters of Saxony, the autumns bursting through in the Erz mountains and painting the forests of Bavaria. And I am welcomed with open arms into a closed world of hands reaching out from the tiny windows of train cars, and Yariv's toothache, or maybe it was Anat's, fade away in my mind. I have to go down, down into that world, to repair it— that will repair the world above. Uncle Lunkish, in the world down there, promises to talk on condition I don't write it down, but in the end he doesn't tell me anything. "With my family in Tarnow..." he begins, and can't go any further. Mrs. Kopel went before Dr. Mengele's with her sister. Her sister died, Mrs. Kopel survived. Strange, he only tested her eyes, and she had no trouble with her vision, she could see perfectly—it was her womb that didn't work. Twice she got married, and twice went back to using Kopel, her maiden name, the name of her father, who died in the ghetto of a heart attack. Uncle Antek is surprised by my visit. Why don't we come more often? He asks about

Yariv, about Anat. And will there be another child? And how is Dad doing? He talks breezily about recent weddings, and remembers my *briss*, and Grandma Eva dancing. About Auschwitz he speaks slowly, not so lucid. "The winter in Auschwitz is hard, people don't know, in summer harder, diseases, people will die." I try to ask questions, to carefully turn back Uncle Antek's arrow of time, to get him to say one sentence about Auschwitz in the past tense. I touch ancient shards as I speak. All he can do is scatter his sentences around. "The head of our block, Prucher, thinks he'll survive because of his cruelty, but he'll go too. In Auschwitz you go, no matter how you behave. I'll end up going too, in the smoke. How long can you survive?" He warns me, "In the camps, even if you survive whole on the outside, thin as a skeleton, on the inside everything is finished. No dignity, no heart, no nothing."

Uncle Menashe doesn't want to talk in the evenings, before bed. He'll talk in the morning. He closes up the butcher shop for me again. "I was a five-year-old kid, what did you think, how could a five-year-old kid live?" He tells me about days spent hidden among kindly farmers—hidden not only from the Nazis, but from his current self. To this day he can't remember them, but he emphasizes, "The farmers were kind." He talks about his father, who paid a farmer he knew, and later, he remembers, he was moved to a different farm, a quiet place. As Uncle Menashe talks, Mom's story sneaks in. Her father also hid her with farmers, giving them all his money, and Uncle Menashe tells his story and I think about my mother, the prayers they made her learn in case the Germans interrogated her, the Hail Marys she kept on saying even when the war was over, even though they told her there was no need, and Uncle Menashe talks about the searches and the shootings in the village houses, he can't remember anything else, just that the farmers were kind, they gave him tasty bread with fat, and Mom walked barefoot for a whole winter, she remembered that, and that she was afraid of something, Dad told us that. She used to flee to the fields because something scared her, and Uncle Menashe says, "The farmers were kind. Once the farmer said, 'There's going to be trouble,' and he took me to another village for a few days, and there I saw a day-old lamb in a pen." That, he remembers; most everything else is gone. There was a light on in the pen. The lamb was almost white. That's all he can remember, and he apologizes for making me come all the way from Haifa to hear nothing. He says, "The main thing is that I turned out normal, right?" I smile. In our family, Uncle Menashe is one of the most normal people. He laughs, "Now, for thirty years, I'm the one who slaughters animals..."

Their stories collect and grow sharper. They tie into one another. I write and go back to ask questions, and write some more. Not infrequently, their memory betrays me. Something is related, but when I ask a question about it the next day, it's no longer clear—did it happen or didn't it? And when? With every passing day something is lost. Memory is like plaster—when you touch it, it crumbles. I struggle to leave as much as possible intact. Every evening at home the documentation continues like a stubborn battle. Grandpa Yosef's rains knock on the windows to remind me that somewhere out there another battle is raging. Grandpa Yosef fights against time. I pore over the testimonies, sometimes only understanding what I've written when I reread it at night. Then, sometimes, I understand their happiness—yes, it is happiness that I see erupting from them. They sit with me, unburdening themselves of massive gourds of memory, the gourds lying at an angle on the earth (thin stalks, unbelievably thin, nourish the huge resting bodies through connections forged among the leaves, into the earth, all the way far down and deep). They tell their stories, transferring their words to my notes, and stand back, leaving me to fight alone, to find order, to find the way, to document. (I combat memory while Grandpa Yosef battles time. We are both about to lose, but both as happy as victors.)

In Grandpa Yosef's house, meanwhile, the battle has intensified and reached a critical stage. Time will either turn back or not—the next few days will tell.

Pots simmer on the stove, the aromas of spices are absorbed into the walls. Grandpa Lolek has been cured despite himself; with food, with rest, with soft walks to the end of Katznelson, with the renewal of debtism, with slow appearances at court, with futile debates consisting mostly of the clerks' affection for him, pats on his shoulder and good wishes. Grandpa Yosef, constantly at Grandpa Lolek's side, manages the patient, guards him, and keeps a curious watch on events at the courthouse, consoling the neglected plaintiff. Sometimes, for Grandpa Lolek's and the car's sake, I take them for a spin in the 1970 Vauxhall. We circle the neighborhood, driving in rings of streets that grow longer and wider, the Vauxhall like a great centrifuge, accelerating more and more, producing power, until Grandpa Yosef is finally satisfied and announces, "Home, now."

On the surface, there is tranquility and responsibility in all his deeds. But the battle is raging. Every day he phones, and phones again, and forgets he has already phoned. He talks with me about Grandpa Lolek, boasting about the pounds he's gained. He invites Effi to give Grandpa Lolek a medical examination, demanding— "Come, weigh him." He talks with relatives, with friends, with all sorts of people he summons in no particular order, again and again, and it's no wonder that when the phone bill arrives, he is astounded and angry. Anger also erupts over the electricity and water bills (the flames fanned by Grandpa Lolek's objective estimation, "You're being robbed") and Grandpa Yosef, in a Caribbean mood, goes to enquire. The clerks welcome him warmly, who has he come for this time? But instead they are assailed by his wrath, lasting bitterness and furious demands, at the end of which Grandpa Yosef leaves with a slight look of shame on his face.

We believed he was losing. There were still only twenty-four hours in a day, and the hours were still only sixty minutes long. January proceeded at its dreary rate. Most of the time, the weather was still, but sometimes, especially at night, there would be a quick flash of lightning and a bolt of thunder that made the windows shudder and woke us, and we would wonder for a moment if perhaps Time was trying to overcompensate for its disgrace. November seemed to have returned, and even October. This downpour wasn't only January rain—everything that had been held back in November was now finally being added to the quota. In the mornings we would smile sheepishly. And then one day at the market, there was a sudden whiff of guavas. Sammy shrugged his shoulders. "I don't know how this is possible. Guavas in January? I heard they already have melons in the West Bank, and that shouldn't even happen in March."

Time's prophesying began to bother us. We noticed that lightning would strike, and only the next day would any thunder roll through the sky, born simply from itself.

The battle had reached its height. We were afraid for the loser's health—be it Grandpa Yosef's or Time's. We expressed our concern. Wasn't the care-giving exhausting him? Grandpa Yosef brushed off our worries. Artless and calm, entirely devoted to expediting the recovery, he found our questions mystifying. He used Anat as an alibi—she was doing half the work, after all, and besides, Grandpa Lolek was getting easier every day. He was already independent, self-sufficient. Why would it be difficult?

Inside, his subconscious forced him to keep working. Don't stop. There are things to do, plans to make, food to cook. Later—it will be heaven, with Feiga and Moshe. Grandpa Yosef toiled from morning to night (as if there were no Grandpa Lolek at the tail-end of his recovery, silently gaining weight; as if he was in fact fighting for his life), and from time to time, with triple and quadruple measures of cunning, he would remember his brief tourist days and start talking. Completely relaxed, chatting agreeably, lost in the sweet forests of his memory.

"They have, in the Caribbean, houses with pink shutters and lovely red roof-tops, and everything there is modest, and there are luscious plants. The children run around the streets with no worries, and the ocean is so clear. At sundown, red painted boats cast blue nets and the fishermen tug this way and that, pulling out stingrays and crabs from the sea, and shrimp and moonfish. The wooden doors are left ajar, and fine artisans engage in their labors for all to see. Women in pure white dresses patiently embroider, and their stores are so bright that it's blinding. In the market, everything is bustling, all the wares are out on display. Spotted fish and quivering seafood. Lemon-yellow bananas and other, nameless fruits. Strike them with your knife and their juice drips out, the aroma hitting your nostrils."

Grandpa Yosef furtively crawled towards his destination, outflanking time, ablaze, and out in the open he fried and cooked and rolled and whipped. Excited by the exotically named "Princess of the Nile"—which was in fact a simple Nile perch—he served it on fancy platters and fine dishes, garnished with chopped cilantro and nuts. Scattering slivered almonds as Grandpa Lolek looked on, he would comment, "Of course, I would prefer to fry it in palm oil."

He offered us a taste of the fish, dreamily reminiscing about the Caribbean as he handed out dishes. "There are restaurants scattered everywhere there, and cheerfully blazing fires. Fires in pits and fires under pots, and food wrapped in leaves and baked on coals. And I have not yet spoken of the little forests, and the lakes, and the light blue bays, and the coral reefs. The whole place is a Garden of Eden. As if there is not and never has been any suffering there."

We reminded him that much of the Caribbean population was descended from slaves led shackled onto ships, and that the islands' indigenous peoples had been completely eradicated. There was suffering there too. Grandpa Yosef mumbled, "Still…The quiet, the fruit," and continued his secret struggle. He and his adversary squeezed into a little arena, grasped each other's arms and pushed.

The decisive moment came unexpectedly on a simple February evening. Grandpa Lolek was sitting in the living room after dinner. He wiped his lips with the napkin Grandpa Yosef handed him, sighed a satisfied sigh and declared, "I think, time is for me to go home."

And for one tiny moment that was multiplied to the power of eternity, composed entirely of fragments of the present and fragments of the past and fragments of the future, standing ever-so-briefly on the scales of time to become present tense, the world froze. The second passed and it was followed by a new one. Everything continued as usual. Time went on its way. Grandpa Yosef had lost. He carefully packed up Grandpa Lolek's belongings. He emptied the closets, the drawers, the shelves. He left his home suitable for a single inhabitant.

Two days passed from the moment Grandpa Lolek made his pronouncement until we drove him in my car to his house. The hours of those two days lined up on either side of Grandpa Yosef and he walked between them, hour after hour, not so that they could whip him, but so that he could scan the hours as if they were a parade of honor. He walked towards the end of days, seeing us all the way to Katznelson. He respectfully bade farewell to Grandpa Lolek and turned back, erect, towards time, which was waiting for him at home. His look pierced us wildly, combatively. *Do you think I've forgotten Adler's philosophy? The future, that is what I am thinking of. The future. And I shall win.*

We left him there dolefully. Grandpa Yosef, without Moshe, without Feiga. How would he manage?

It soon turned out that the magical era had not come to an end without incident. From all the commotion, the fluttering of days, the prophetic time, the oscillating eras, the minutes pushed back like the poles of a magnet, a single distortion of time blossomed into a deed: Brandy came back. But not in her familiar canine form. Grandpa Yosef's neighborhood became filled with a plethora of dogs, passing transients of different breeds and different sizes. Each of them looked clearly like a particular aspect of Brandy—a rib of hers, something extracted from her wholeness and presented independently, developed into a whole dog, a barking puppy or a bitch pulled along on a leash.

We would see them and remember Brandy—because of a leg, because of an ear, because of a bark. It did not occur to us that the dogs were somehow related. Who was thinking of mysticism? We were thinking of what we missed. Even before Grandpa Yosef started battling the direction of time, if our thoughts went to Moshe, Brandy also waddled along and sat down to keep watch at his feet. Even in our thoughts, even after death, if Moshe was here, Brandy would come too, to make sure no harm came to him. Sometimes she turned up in our thoughts just like that, and we quickly conjured up a big lawn, butterflies, moles tunneling, even rabbits. Anything to make her happy. To excite her. To make her reach out with her ugly paws as she lunged, to make her run and jump, gaining full compensation for a life bound at Moshe's feet.

But now her appearance was clearly real. We could not ignore the dogs surrounding the house as if by chance. Effi was the first to say, "That dog has a nose exactly like Brandy's," and from that moment the silence was broken. Brandy's appearances were publicly discussed. It was Brandy—that much was clear. She was back. We simply had to explain how it could be that one dog could make such an exaggerated reappearance. We didn't have to try very hard: in that period, thanks to Grandpa Yosef, the reason for anything odd was easily hovering within arm's reach. The air disgorged explanations for any wonderment, logic defended even that which diverged from reason. For Brandy too, explanations gathered, and we could choose among them. We were persuaded by a particularly sobering explanation—Brandy was never a dog, but rather something intended to protect Moshe, which had taken on the form of a dog (probably so as not to raise any eyebrows). Now that Moshe was dead, the substance, which had planned on lasting for many more years of Moshe, was left uselessly out there somewhere, and had been summoned by the call of Grandpa Yosef. It had not found peace in the past, in the place where we had said goodbye to Brandy. All it needed was the moderate rocking which Grandpa Yosef gave time, to extract it from its unsuitable surroundings and fling it into our present-day, where it could re-embody Brandy. The new Brandy was only a drop of time splashed in our way, dismantled and multiplied into a host of dogs. And yet—it was Brandy.

We made do with Brandy in her reincarnated form, mystical and implausible, so long as she eased Grandpa Yosef's loneliness. From our point of view, all was clear. But explanations kept following us, waiting for us to adopt them despite their dwarfish appearance and unfounded claims. In their unfortunate ownerless state, the explanations united into a theory that charged our thoughts with wild speculations: the dramatic loss of Brandy during Moshe's *shiva* had been interpreted as death, but we had been mistaken. Brandy had disbanded into separate states. Her disappearance was not the result of death, but an act from the political sphere. Everything that had been held together, despite a genetic aversion, in order to serve the superpower that was Moshe, had been completely dismantled, eradicated, lost. The silent sitting at Moshe's feet turned out to have been quite the opposite of restful. Rather, it had been a concerted and desperate effort to keep herself united against internal factionalism, against the divisions made greater by micro-politicians. (Only after her death did we comprehend the concept of being *at Moshe's feet* to its full, cruel extent, a bound state of being, so difficult, so impossible.)

Brandy's dismantled existence, which surrounded the house with a cloud of damp tongues, wagging tails and loud barks, made it easier for Grandpa Yosef to accept the total failure of his plan to reverse time. Grandpa Lolek went back home, the grandiose attempt was concluded, without Feiga and without Moshe. But Grandpa Yosef began to come to terms with his new life—the desert in which only Brandy accompanied him, there to protect strips of existence from the past. Trickles of hidden possibilities nourished Grandpa Yosef's vacant hours and settled in as reality, as a restrained rendition of Feiga and Moshe. This was the garden in which Grandpa Yosef agreed to live.

There was no more tragedy.

*

From a speech given by Himmler, the Reichsführer, in October of 1943, to a group of senior officers:

"Most of you here know what it means when a hundred corpses lie next to each other, when five-hundred lie there or when a thousand are lined up. To have endured this and at the same time to have remained a decent person—with exceptions due to human weaknesses—has made us tough."

I wrote down Himmler's words on a white sheet of paper. I looked at them. The words were nothing new—I had copied them from one of Attorney Perl's little index cards, and they have been recorded in books. But I wanted to write them down. To write them myself. As I read the words, they approached one by one like customers going up to a counter with tense and hesitant steps, each preparing to present itself.

"Yes," said Attorney Perl, "the Nazi ideal was to create a human being who does his job without moral defects, without cruelty or harassment of his victims. In terms of the ideal, people like Kurt Franz, 'Doll,' or Amon Goeth, were utter failures, examples of the weakness of human beings engaged in an endeavor that is beyond their strength."

Himmler's speech continues:

"We have taken away the riches that they had…we have taken nothing from them for ourselves. A few, who have offended against this, will be judged in accordance with an order that I gave at the beginning: He who takes even one mark of this is a dead man…we have the moral right, we had the duty to our people to do it, to kill this people who wanted to kill us. But we do not have the right to enrich ourselves with even one fur, with one mark, with one cigarette, with one watch, with anything. That we do not have. Because at the end of this, we don't want, because we exterminated the bacillus, to become sick and die from the same bacillus."

Yes, Heinrich Himmler belonged to the genus of SS officers who fell in love with the persona of the clean, superior, moral man. His fellow senior leaders, particularly Goering, did not hesitate to plunder whatever property they could get their hands on. They did not care for Himmler's theories. But countless SS officers viewed his ideas as a gold standard.

Attorney Perl's cards contained quotes, speeches, orders, decisions made by the Nazi party. I dedicated a white sheet of paper to each sentence that caught my eye.

From an order issued by Generalfeldmarschall Erich von Manstein, dated November 20, 1941:

"Jewry constitutes the middleman between the enemy in the rear and the remainder of the Red Army Forces which is still fighting, and the Red leadership…. The Jewish-Bolshevik system must be exterminated once and for all…. The soldier must appreciate the necessity for the harsh punishment of Jewry." Von Manstein oversaw the operations of the Einsatzgruppe D task force, commanded by Otto Ohlendorf. After the war, he claimed to have had no knowledge of the exterminations.

In his speech at the Wannsee Conference, Reinhard Heydrich stated that "the evacuation of the Jews to the east has now emerged, after the appropriate prior approval of the Führer, as a further possible solution." The Jews would be utilized for labor in the east, Heydrich explained, and continued: "…a large part will doubtless fall away through natural diminution. The remnant that finally survives all this, because here it is undoubtedly a question of the part with the greatest resistance, will have to be treated accordingly, because this remnant, representing a natural selection, can be regarded as the germ cell of a new Jewish reconstruction if released."

"It was only thanks to the awareness of the personal responsibility of each one of the officers and the men that it was possible to get this plague under control in the shortest possible time," read the concluding remarks of the "Katzmann Report," authored by SS Gruppenführer Fritz Katzmann, a unit commander in the Galicia region. The report concerned the extermination of half a million Galician Jews. After the war, Katzmann lived under an assumed name. Only in 1960, three years after his death, was his true identity revealed.

At the bottom of the card devoted to Fritz Katzmann, Attorney Perl had noted, "Died in great agony from stomach cancer."

On the other side of the wall, in the front of the store, he calls out from the top of the ladder, "I've only got three-quarter inch nails with the plastic head, is that okay?"

An incredible man. Ninety-two years old in ninety-two. Ninety-three years old in ninety-three. An easily calculable miracle. He'll be ninety-four in ninety-four. Ninety-five in ninety-five. As his life progresses, another man also grows old: Edmund Veesenmeyer, born in 1904. Attorney Perl writes on his index cards every year:

"1981. Still alive."

"1982. Still alive."

"1983. Still alive."

He sounds almost apologetic when he tells me, "He's still alive, but I'm sick of checking, tired of the disappointment. I've checked every year since 1951. Here, it's all written down, his family and everything. Instead of shrinking, it's growing. What can you do? It's a shame."

The miracle of Attorney Perl's continuing life contends with the unending life of Edmund Veesenmeyer, a diplomat, Adolf Eichmann's partner in the implementation of the Final Solution in Hungary. In 1949 he was sentenced to twenty years in prison, but he was pardoned and released two years later. After that, he led a small, good life. Family, work.

On his little index cards, Attorney Perl tracks the war criminals. "My debtors," he calls them. He keeps track of what happens instead of hangings. Their punishments—the big ones, the little ones. The pardons. The commutations. The appeals, the retrials. The waiting.

The years that pass without any notes on the cards. Waiting, waiting. Sometimes the debtor moves to a different city, buys an apartment, starts up a business. And there are families, little European families that emerge as if from mazes, sending out offshoots that get further and further away from the center. The debtor integrates into society, gets appointed to positions where his talents are appreciated.

Siegfried Ruff, a superior of Dr. Rascher, who conducted gruesome medical experiments. Acquitted. Appointed head of the Institute for Aeronautical Medicine at the German Air Navigational Experiment Center, and later a professor at the University of Bonn.

Hermann Schmitz, senior member of I.G. Farben, the manufacturer of Zyklon B gas. Sentenced to four years, appointed honorary chairman of Rhein steel plants.

Friedrich Jaehne, senior member of I.G. Farben, manufacturer of Zyklon B gas. Sentenced to eighteen months detention. Awarded the Distinguished Service Cross of the Federal Republic of Germany.

Attorney Perl is not satisfied with general outlines. He carefully sketches the lack of revenge, assiduously noting every detail: First grandson; second marriage; promotion; date of death. Everything. He explains, "I thought, well, if I'm going to go mad, then I may as well do it like this, in this chair. Writing everything down." Then he goes back to the storefront to sell plaster and nails.

In the evening I go home. Anat is out, busy donating her time for the greater good. The neighbor from upstairs is watching Yariv. I think she just likes sleeping on our couch. Yariv comes out of his room and recites a well-rehearsed line: "Mom said there's rice in the pot and soup in the fridge." He stands watchfully opposite me and examines my face, wondering if he has conveyed the message successfully. It's important for him to do well.

I ask, "Have you eaten?"

"Yes."

"Where's Mom?"

"She went to help children who don't have a mommy and daddy."

Small, almost orphaned, he locates my wife in a place she will come home from late and tired. On the way to bed she'll pass by Yariv's room, the shower, the pots and pans, the things she needs to get ready for tomorrow, me. She'll look at the pages, at the memories I am acquiring. I show her the criminals, the families, the offspring carrying on their names. They love their grandpas. Nice children, well-bred. They support democracy, reject discrimination against foreigners. Sometimes they come to Israel and plant trees. They send postcards to Granddad and to Grandma Wilma, who waited five years for Granddad to get back from his missions in the East. She didn't give up on him, even though officers fell in love with her and offered her heaven and earth.

Anat goes to sleep, saying, "Yes, it's important, if you want to delve into it. But tomorrow don't forget to pick up Yariv from kindergarten early. He's not used to being the last one picked up. It makes him anxious."

We hardly see each other. She has her business, I have my index cards and the family testimonies. Yariv stands between us like a well to which we come at the end of the day.

From kindergarten I take him to Attorney Perl's. Instead of going home for lunch, we have "our" falafel. This makes Yariv happy; he thinks we're big-time criminals, although he is very worried about the pots of rice, *schnitzel* and fries that we're supposed to be heating up for lunch. He is buoyed by the thought of not having to eat the peas, but every so often, on the floor in the shop, among his soldier-screws, he is troubled by the uneaten rice. "What will we tell Mom?" he asks, his teeth glistening as he smiles. He knows we're committing a sin. Anat went to all that trouble to make us lunch, and besides, falafel-is-no-sort-of-food-for-a-growing-boy. Together, we come up with a solution—a different excuse each time, always successful. (In any case, I'm the one who spinelessly wolfs down two portions at home so Anat won't notice.)

He's already grown accustomed to Attorney Perl's store, and finds the front part more enchanting. He stands on a stool behind the counter like an extra salesman, in between Yakov the assistant and Attorney Perl, and watches the commerce in action. At the back, I sit among the cards. Everything is scattered around me, unprocessed, infinite. From day to day I gain insight—how quickly they forgave. If they weren't hanged immediately, their sentences simply melted away. Even the ones sentenced to long prison terms for crimes against humanity were released sooner than petty larcenists. We have already agreed, Attorney Perl and I, that the Nazis and their aids were not punished enough. Our disagreement concerns the appropriate punishment, if it had been up to us.

Attorney Perl clings to his fifty-year-old idea. "We should have kept them all alive, but in prison. Should have heard them. Even Eichmann. Should have marched him every morning from Ramleh prison to Latrun outside Jerusalem. There, we should have heard his story. Given him some water, not much. And in the evening, but only if he got there on time, a little 'soup,' like the kind they gave us."

I say, "No, they should have executed them. At least all the ones who were in SS units, not just the commanders. They should have executed everyone who took part in operations by army units and police. The Jewish collaborators too. No mercy. And all the clerks, the diplomats, the mayors, the volunteers. Everyone who knew that genocide was occurring and took an active part, even a small one. If they had executed all of them, we wouldn't need to 'understand' now."

Attorney Perl objects and grows slightly angry. He eagerly outlines a plan that will never come to fruition, things he tried to explain at the end of the war to ambassadors into whose offices he was able to sneak, to consuls who listened as they looked fearfully at this ghost of a man orating before them. When he talks about his plan, the thundering, lucid voice of Attorney Perl from before the war reawakens, recalling the way he sounded in the courts of Lvov and in his city of Stanislaw. Some time before 1939 he was sent to Bochnia for work and was trapped there when the war broke out. He was sent with his wife to the ghetto, to our house at 7 Leonarda. In the third *Aktion* he was sent to Szebnie camp, then transferred to Dora-Mittelbau. Between the lines, his own story emerges too. Sometimes he just starts talking about himself unprompted, then changes the subject. He mentions "Dora-Mittelbau" or "trains" and sighs, swept up in his own story again. He deposits his words at stops along the route, leaving me a sliver here and a morsel there, and they multiply and meld, as if Attorney Perl is challenging me to put the pieces of his story together.

At home, later, I edit the family stories and attempt to assemble his tale too. But in the shop, the story is the criminals, their restored lives after the war, the false identities, the borrowed personas. The lives dispersed among refuge countries—Argentina, Chile, Brazil, Canada, Syria. The irony of the diasporic dispersion of those who tried to destroy the diasporic nation. Their own Diaspora in Mexico, South Africa, Spain, Portugal, Bolivia. *The germ cell of a new reconstruction.* In the jungles of Brazil and in fenced suburbs of Buenos Aires, in wealthy South African homes and quiet villages in the heart of Germany. They were not killed and they continue to exist. *The germ cell of a new reconstruction.* We could have given them the great poet Yehuda Halevi's poems of yearning, the lamentations, the nostalgic liturgies. They had sent themselves to the Second World War, after all, to achieve *Lebensraum*—living space—for the German people, and now there they were, scattered around the world, absorbed in faraway diasporas. Two thousand years from now the Germans will look proudly at their accomplishment—a small German community in every remote spot, conducting its German life, maintaining a little German culture in foreign surroundings, its children longing for the homeland from which their parents were exiled. How did they get there? Ah, such a wonderful story. And some day, one of the curious young people will set off on a journey to trace his roots, and will expose the amazing adventure that led his founding fathers to Brazil, to South Africa, to the remote regions of Australia.

Is that their punishment? Living under false identities in humid jungles and faraway villages—is that the punishment? No. Too many of them were not exiled and did not escape, but continued to live under their real names in Germany. Sometimes they were pestered by the courts, more often left alone. Sometimes they were imprisoned and then released, assimilating nicely into their reconstructed lives. The worst criminals, the architects of the extermination, were sometimes not even investigated—these were the smart ones, the far-sighted ones, those whose fingerprints disappeared from all incriminating documents and deeds.

"Especially the legalists," Attorney Perl said.

The talks with Attorney Perl do not finish when I leave his shop. I recreate them with Effi, with Dad, with Anat. Sometimes I come up against opposing opinions, reservations. Waving my papers and reading out lines, I explain what the people did, what they said, what they declared. I contend that they only tried the ones they could prove had committed murder or torture, or had been guards. But what about the ones who drafted laws? Recruited for the SS? Directed movies propagandizing the extermination of handicapped people? Testified to a trace of Jewish origin in a neighbor's blood? They did not murder, torture, or lock anyone up in gas chambers, but without them? Who will judge the faceless masses, the ones who will never be convicted because between them and what they deserve there will always be the graceful giants of the law: "lack of evidence," "reasonable doubt," "lack of public interest."

"Not everyone who spoke against the Jews is a Nazi who should be hanged," Effi said.

"Don't forget, there were and still are good Germans," said Grandpa Yosef. And of course, the example soon follows. "Take Hans Oderman, for example."

Faced with the kindheartedness of the orphan researcher Hans Oderman, accusations must bow. We cannot embrace opinions that do not consider the existence of the good German. Yes, I know, Hans Oderman is coming to Israel. The good German is coming back to serve as an example. Grandpa Yosef has already phoned me twice. "Hans said he's coming!" And Effi called too, "Hans is coming!" I count the days until the volcanic eruption.

The existence of the Hans Odermans of the world seems to be attempting to erase the non-erasable—Attorney Perl's index cards, every single one of them, and the declaration of Obersturmführer Moeser, Dora-Mittelbau's commandant, while on trial for his acts: *With the same pleasure as you shoot deer, I shoot a human being.* Attorney Perl recalls, "There, in Dora-Mittelbau, in the tunnels, people dropped like flies. Bad food and beatings, and everything covered with dust and the smell of excrement. We weren't allowed to use water. We had to pee on our hands and rub our faces just to get the dust off. That was forbidden too, but we did it anyway. If I had stayed there any longer, I wouldn't have made it. No chance. Fortunately, I was moved. They took me to a camp not far from Dora-Mittelbau. There we dug pits, God knows why, and we sawed wood, maybe for heat.

"The commandant at that camp was Obersturmführer Sahl, but one day he was removed from the camp, literally taken away by the SS military police, and in front of us stood our Angel of Death, the new camp Commandant, Obersturmführer Jürgen Licht."

I ask, "Did he kill lots of prisoners, this Licht?"

Attorney Perl is taken aback. "Obersturmführer Jürgen Licht," he corrects me. Even from a distance of fifty years he stands on ceremony, noting the rank and name. But he replies, "Indeed he did. But he was always very quiet, as if the whole business of war had nothing to do with him. As if managing the camp was a necessary duty, beneath his true aspirations. He would shoot prisoners without losing his temper, and never gave punishments that took up time, like rollcalls in the snow all night. The Ukrainian and German staff members were afraid of him, but us prisoners…we trembled at the thought of him showing up. It would mean death. His eyes, oh the eyes! Quiet, almost bored. If you had been allowed to look into them, you would have seen grayness, but we couldn't look. The Angel of Death!"

Attorney Perl is animated, his voice changes as he talks about SS-Obersturmführer Jürgen Licht, who killed people with his pistols, of which he was extremely fond, without a second thought. But more than his pistols, he was enamored with puppet theater, and every time he was transferred to a new camp he would bring a little truck lined with shelves of marionettes. Puppet theaters were officially banned by the Nazi party, and Obersturmführer Licht never considered disobeying the law, but a lengthy correspondence with indifferent supervisors finally resulted in a personal authorization to engage in his beloved hobby, and so at every camp he set up a small but active puppet theater. He never took harsh measures upon arriving at a new camp before enquiring whether any of the prisoners might be of use. Carpenters, engravers, arts and craftsmen, tailors, painters, and perhaps even a rare gem—a puppet maker. Attorney Perl was none of these, which meant that by rights he should have

joined the grey herd destined to die, the herd at which Obersturmführer Licht shot on its way to work, often out of mere curiosity, to
see who would fall. Would it be the tall man he was aiming at, or the
yellowing one hunched next to him? Or someone else? Pistol bullets
were so unpredictable at times. Attorney Perl should have waited his
turn to be hanged from the gallows in the center of the camp; they
were painted red, and the rope that hung from them swayed constantly like a live snake. Or else he should have crouched down and
knelt on the muddy ground. Or perhaps he should have survived by
simply working day after day in the trenches, with a pick, without
dying, without making any noise, without meeting the fate of being
shot and having his body dumped into cold water. Except that during the first inspection, he lifted a trembling hand—a hand stronger
than he himself—and whispered right in Obersturmführer Licht's face
that yes, he too could be of use. Of use? Yes. He offered his singular
contribution, which was his voice. The clear, sometimes thunderous
tone that he had used to great advantage when representing his clients
in court. Even if in his private life his voice was soft, withdrawn, in
the courthouse he was taken over by some sort of spirit, a devil that
gave him tremendous oration skills. As his words were barely whispered to Obersturmführer Licht through the lips of a skeleton, in
fluent German, the devil grabbed hold of him and awoke his voice,
which grew clear and loud. He boldly proposed to be the voice of
the marionettes in the puppet theater.

From the front of the shop, Yariv's voice reaches me in a wail.
One of the customers was joking around and told Yariv he would buy
him along with his bag of nails. Yakov the assistant played along and
together they staged a complex negotiation. *How-much-for-the-sweet-
little-mama's-boy?* At first Yariv sat quietly, following the negotiations
in awe. But suddenly his sorrow broke through and he was washed
over with great self-pity. He cried, "Where's my daddy?" and shouted,
and the customer apologized, red-faced, looking left and right to enlist
other customers to attest to his innocence; he hadn't meant any harm.
There was no one on the right, and the two on the left nodded, trying to reassure Yariv, not knowing how difficult a task that would
be. I arrive on the scene to find my son standing frozen on a bench,

waiting for me helplessly. We have no choice but to leave the store. Off we go. Where to? Where do you want to go? To the lawn. We go to the big lawn at Memorial Park, with the white pillars. Yariv finds a line of ants and kneels down, enchanted. With a little twig he tries to pose dilemmas to the ants. I sit facing the sea. The bay of Haifa is spread out before us. I think about the beach, where *they* never go. Just over half a mile as the crow flies and yet never, never do they take their cheery flip-flops and varicose-veined legs onto the sandy shores. Only Grandpa Yosef, thanks to his righteousness and with the help of his bicycle (especially since returning from the Caribbean), dares to go that far. Later, he comes home from an idle hour at the beach with shells in his pockets.

One ant climbs onto Yariv's twig. He shakes it, but the ant clings. Yariv lets go in a fright. He comes over to me, ready to go home. Already? Yes. Don't you want to sit a little longer? No. We leave. People pass us by. They are happy here. The park assuages troubles, slows down the pace of life. People can come from downtown, from doing errands at City Hall across the way, from the army induction center, from the courthouse. Such a Haifa park, close to errands and shopping. You can walk around without feeling as if you're wasting time, opposite Haifa's round bay. You can sit on the benches, looking at the dirty pool and the swings that someone insists on constantly re-painting to make them look nice. (There's always a patch of wet paint or a glossy new layer, and people know to check carefully before they put a kid down). Dad used to bring us here on Saturday afternoons in our good shoes, in the sixties. Thirty years apparently had to go by for me to notice the park's name, "Memorial Park." A strange name. I never paid attention to it before. We used to come here without thinking about names, to play and walk around. Once a year the park justified its name when the official memorial services were held here. First for Holocaust Remembrance Day, then for the IDF soldiers on Memorial Day. Then there would be fireworks set off for Independence Day. I remember people dancing in circles, and lots of people coming up to Dad, excited, shaking his hand as if they had won the Nobel prize together.

On Attorney Perl's little cards there is mention of the *Aktion* in the small town of Koretz, on the holiday of Shavuot. When the *Aktion* was over, the Gestapo officer addressed the Jews whose family members had just been sent away in transports, saying, "The *Aktion* is over. Tomorrow morning all remaining Jews must arrive at their workplaces." I think about the unbelievable passivity. To be a human being whose family has been sent to extermination and to be asked to show up to work on time the next day. Here, in Memorial Park, I think about the *Aktion* in Koretz and realize what it was that Dad was celebrating with us. The fireworks, the dances, the Nobel winners. The Independence Day I take Yariv to is not the Independence Day I went to with Dad. With us there is happiness, and wheeling and dealing among the various stalls—Yariv is only allowed to pick two things. But with Dad we would walk among the Nobel winners, everyone strolling happily, and a wild cry of joy—I-N-D-E-P-E-N-D-E-N-C-E—rose up from peoples' bones to the stars, just like the fireworks. Green, red and yellow trails bursting like little thoughts that run out on their way down, making way for a new idea that erupts and is soon forgotten. Six million prosecutors in our Memorial Park, and young people dancing in circles, and Dad watching with us, buying falafel and little flags, and a Bedouin man from the Negev selling rides on his camel, and eating pita with spicy humus. I-N-D-E-P-E-N-D-E-N-C-E, I-N-D-E-P-E-N-D-E-N-C-E. Nobel prizes bursting through the holes in flimsy pitas, pickles dying like heroes, pale-pale green, I take them out and very quietly drop them to the ground. Food is Not Thrown Out.

Even in Grandpa Yosef's neighborhood they celebrated Independence Day. It was quiet, with only the state flags sneaking out of the windows. But Grandpa Yosef assured us, "Oh, believe me, it's very joyous here." To prove that something exciting was hiding beneath the surface, on the morning of Independence Day he would walk to synagogue and pray loudly for Israel. He would come back from prayers sparkling and festive, and tell us how he had gone to see the celebrations in the center of Kiryat Haim the night before. He had watched the fireworks that were set off from where we live, from Memorial Park.

*

I finish writing, editing and typing the testimonies. I send each member of the family their testimony so they can make comments and corrections.

Uncle Lunkish phones. "Will you be sending me what you wrote about me too?"

"But you didn't really say much..."

"But what I did say, will you send it?" And on second thought he adds, "Could you perhaps come again? I think I can talk now." He voice grows stronger. "What's the worst that could happen?"

The next day, with Yariv, we sit in his little home. Uncle Lunkish talks. First the childhood, the village, the square. Then the war. The hardships, the ghetto, the concentration camp. And finally, Hermann Dunevitz.

"That was the worst. He made me his helper, that bastard. He forced me. I had to write down on lists the people he named. He was Jewish, but he did not have the heart of a Jew. The Nazis liked him, and as soon as he got to the camp they made him half-prisoner half-officer. They didn't give him a uniform but they let him walk around the camp wherever he wanted and be their detective. He wrote down punishments, gave out punishments himself, and issued all sorts of orders. I wore glasses before the war, but he took them away from me and I couldn't see a thing. Everything I did with him afterwards, I didn't see. I could still write. He made sure of that before he took them. He showed me a pile of glasses and laughed, and explained where the glasses came from, and then he threw mine onto the pile and said it was a great privilege for me that my glasses were on that pile but I was still standing. From that day on I was his assistant. He got me off work duty, and that's why I'm still alive today, because my strength had already run out and I knew I would not make it through the next *Selektion*, that they would send me where they had sent the people with the glasses. I don't know why he needed me. Maybe because they wouldn't let him be a real officer with rank, because he was Jewish, so he wanted to at least have an assistant. I would walk around with him, seeing everything blurred, and when he stopped in front of someone to decide whether or not to punish them, I had to write down his decision. People would stand across from me, I could barely see them, and they would tell me their number and block number and the name of their block leader, who was the only one who had a name. I would hold the notebook up to my eyes and write everything down, afraid he would kill me if I made a mistake or changed their punishments, because for him, killing was nothing. I may have written down people I knew, who I used to know before they took my glasses. Once someone whispered to me, 'Naftali, it's me, Gotleib, get him to let me off.' I wasn't entirely sure who Gotleib was, as if for a brief moment the glasses of my memory had also been removed. I wrote down his number and the other stuff, and I wrote down thirty lashings, and in the evening he must have got them.

"That was how it went, from the moment he made up his mind to make me his assistant. I ate well and rested and didn't see a thing. He used to hold roll-calls too, after the regular roll-calls were over and people were about ready to die of exhaustion. But the Germans allowed him to have them, and I remember, before he took me as his assistant, I would also stand in the cold without food, tired. Now his roll-calls were after the regular ones, and people used to collapse. I would stand opposite the group without seeing anything, and he would walk among them and tell me what to write. He was always looking for Jews from his hometown, to write them down for deportations or kill them himself. During work, if he caught a Jew who wasn't working properly and discovered he was from his town, he would beat him to death just like that, right in front of me. I couldn't see anything, but if they were from his town, that was the end. It was as if he had decided to be like the Nazis, but instead of going after all the Jews, he wanted only the Jews from his town. I don't know why he wanted revenge, it was his obsession. And anytime he issued a punishment for some Jew, he would offer him the option of turning in Jews from his town, if he knew any, and then the punishment would be eased. People snitched on each other, and Dunevitz would interrogate them and get the truth out.

"Finally, the camps came to an end, and the Germans took out everyone who was left and sent them on the Death March. Hermann Dunevitz was convinced he would be allowed to go with the Germans, but they laughed and whipped him, and threw him out to walk with all the other prisoners. I walked too, and I was glad that the nightmare of being with Dunevitz and his notebook was finally over. We walked for a few days, and anyone who no longer had the strength to walk was shot immediately. We didn't get any food or drink. The Nazis took turns riding a wagon, they ate and drank, and they wouldn't let us stop walking. I still had some flesh left on my bones, so I had more energy, but even I almost collapsed. You cannot believe what torture it is to keep walking without any rest, for no reason, just so we would die. We were saved by the airplanes that bombed us. From the sky they thought we were soldiers, and they shot at us. All the Germans ran away, it was a day or two before the war was over. Dunevitz also ran, because he knew the Jews would kill him even if it was the last thing they did. I stayed with the Jews and at first they didn't touch me. People simply lay down on the ground with no strength left. There were some who died that way, and others who started walking and looking for food in the wagon the Germans left. After two days some soldiers found us and took us to a camp, where they took care of us. And it was there that people started harassing me, saying, 'That's the partner of Dunevitz, the animal.' They wanted to kill me. I wouldn't have resisted, I no longer had the strength to live, even though I couldn't see anything. But one guy said, 'Leave him alone,' and they did. They didn't have the strength in them either. After a few days I got hold of a pair of glasses, and I met a friend from my hometown who had heard stories about me, but he believed me when I told him I hadn't been able to see, and together we made our way back to our town. That's it. I didn't hear anything more about Dunevitz. Some said he was killed, some said he escaped to America, but I don't know, goddamn him. Because of him, people have been saying I did bad things my whole life. But I couldn't see anything."

Dunevitz. Hermann Dunevitz. Something in the name rings a bell in my memory, trying to come through. Hermann Dunevitz. I ask Attorney Perl.

"Dunevitz? No, I don't know him. But there were quite a few of those characters; the war gave them an opportunity. You can read in my cards about Yakov Honigman, the kapo from the Gräditz and Faulbruck camps. I also have Hanoch Bayski, who was a Jewish policeman. When the Nazis hanged a Jew he would run after them to report if the hanged man was not dead and should be hanged again. And there was Moshe Puczich from the Ostrowiec ghetto, who was charged with many acts of cruelty, including burying a Jew alive, but he was acquitted in an Israeli court. He probably did the things attributed to him, but the testimonies got complicated because of unreliable witnesses. People testified against him, and it turned out that after the war they had sent him friendly letters, asking him to help them buy a pair of shoes. You see, not all the victims stopped being victims when the war was over. That complicated the testimonies. There were other issues too. People informed on each other because of petty grievances. They took advantage of the circumstances to get back at each other over little quarrels, even conflicts from before the war. But there were some whom they didn't need to do much investigating to convict. Yehezkel Ingster was also a kapo at Gräditz and Faulbruck, the only person in Israel ever sentenced to death at the time he was tried. A Jew, and he was sentenced to death, even before Eichmann. They didn't implement the sentence because at the time of the trial he was already very ill, a broken man. They incarcerated him for a short while and he died later."

"And Dunevitz? Don't you have anything on Dunevitz?" I can't get rid of the impression, a plea served up from the depths, something in me knows the name—Hermann Dunevitz.

"No, I told you I don't. But we had one in our camp too. Oh, if I could get my hands on him…but in our camp we were mainly afraid of Obersturmführer Jürgen Licht himself. He was our Angel of Death. I had to be close to him most of the time because I was the voice of the puppet theater. Every evening we put on a show for him. He built himself the theater on a little hill overlooking the *Appellplatz*, and the entire hill was covered with lovely rugs like a Persian palace; he put an armchair in the middle of all the rugs. We put on classical plays, adapted to fit the times, and plays that a German political prisoner wrote for Licht on topics he commissioned. I remember we put on a dramatization of *Wenn ich der Kaiser Wär*—If I Were the Emperor—which I knew from before the war. We did other plays too, it doesn't matter now. It was all for Obersturmführer Licht. Sometimes he would invent a protagonist and we had to make the puppet and give it a part in the play. It didn't matter, because he was the only spectator anyway, and if he was happy the evening finished without trouble. He especially liked a knight character he had invented, called Zibrus the Knight. We had to build ugly puppets with defects, in our own images, so that Zibrus the Knight could heroically save young German girls from us.

"One evening there was a disaster. Obersturmführer Licht invited the regional commander, Sturmbanführer Hes, to the play. Hes did not like puppet theater, and all throughout the play I could see him glaring at the carpeted ground. At the end of the play he politely refused to accept the Zibrus puppet and gave Obersturmführer Licht an odd look. I was at the front and I saw everything. I knew there would be trouble, I just didn't know what kind. The next day all the puppets were ordered burned, the stage too, and the wooden frame; everything. All the theater workers were called for roll-call, and Obersturmführer Licht walked among us. I was first in line, and he walked past without looking at me, and for a moment we thought nothing would happen. But the man next to me was a puppet maker and he shot a bullet into his head without even hesitating. Then he kept walking and stood by different people. Sometimes he lingered, standing pensively. When he finally made up his mind he either shot the man or kept going. And it went on that way. He shot the expendable ones. That was it. In the morning, the kapos came and took all the remaining theater workers to regular jobs with the rest of the prisoners, and for almost a week we didn't hear from Obersturmführer Licht. There were no plays and we didn't see him. The hunger came back, the beatings, the desperation, and once again I thought I would not survive. Every evening we would go back to the camp and see his empty armchair up on the hill. We hoped something would happen, that the theater would be revived. After all, there must have been a reason why he had left some of us alive—we had a use.

"Day after day went by and not much hope was left. But late one night after a week, the head of my hut told me to go to Obersturmführer Licht's office. My heart sensed disaster. He had already summoned someone to his office once, a typist, and had dictated an entire letter to him and then shot him in the head. What did Obersturmführer Licht want of me? They took me into his room. It was warm in there. A nice fire was burning, and there were dogs lying on a rug. My body was stiff as a rock. In front of the desk where Obersturmführer Licht sat was an empty chair. Was I supposed to sit down? Greet him? Salute? His adjutant handed me some papers. Obersturmführer Licht had written a play about his childhood, and my job was to read the pages out loud for him.

"His play was called *Verbrecher*—Criminals—and it recounted the story of an affair from his school days—some incident where he was assigned the duty of carrying the flag on a holiday parade, but something happened and the teacher let another boy carry it. Obersturmführer Licht gave precise instructions for making the puppet that would represent the teacher. It had to have small, Communist, Jewish eyes. He spent half a page on how to make the puppet of the other boy. And the kids who laughed at little Obersturmführer Licht. And the Jewish headmaster. And the priest. All of them. Lots of instructions in German. How the puppet makers managed to finally build the marionettes the way he instructed, God only knows. Perhaps they were helped by the fear of death. After the teacher and the headmaster and the priest, on a fresh new page, there were instructions on how to portray his beloved mother's voice; there was to be no puppet representing her body. Then there was Zibrus the Knight, who in Obersturmführer Licht's play had to appear and put a stop to the parade, take the flag away from the other boy and give it to Obersturmführer Licht.

"Obersturmführer Licht had poured many words onto paper, and I was required to read the lines aloud, to pleasure his ears with his own composition. I did the best I could, acting the parts out as I read. I cackled evilly when the teacher—who was a traitor, a Jew and a Communist—tripped up Obersturmführer Licht in class. I was emotional when the flag was given to the other child. And then Obersturmführer Licht the boy got up from his seat in class to make a speech. That was how it went in the play. He had written himself

355

a long speech and as I tried to deliver it expertly, Obersturmführer Licht the commandant sat at his desk and, with his eyes shut and his hands beneath his chin holding a little pencil like a baton, instructed me to repeat my lines, make corrections, slow down the pace."

"How did you understand what he wanted?"

"I understood. Believe me, I understood. I was so scared, I almost went in my pants. I followed the pencil beneath his chin and understood everything Obersturmführer Licht wanted."

"And what happened in the end?"

"I got to the point where the voice of little Obersturmführer Licht's mother was supposed to come from behind a screen. She was to try and persuade the Jewish headmaster to reverse his terrible decision. I recited her noble pleas, some of which he had found, I believe, in party propaganda, and some of which were the sorts of things mothers really would say. The headmaster refused to listen to the mother's reasoning because little Obersturmführer Licht had a mark for misbehavior on the class roll, because he had thrown a spitball. I remember the headmaster's response to her: 'In our regime, as it is designed at present, in the year 1922, I am the one who decides which pupil shall march with the flag in the parade, and I am the one who decides that your son is not worthy of this great honor because he threw a spitball!'"

Attorney Perl does not need to recite the play for me. The tearful voice of a wronged child comes through amply in the space of the room: "But it was Heinrich who threw the spitball!" The mother's response is also superfluous. It is obvious that the headmaster, for whose puppet the prisoners will have to find a thick log of wood, will throw her out of his office. Obersturmführer Licht's lines need not continue either.

"He held up his hand: 'Stop!' and the play recitation ceased. The dogs perked up their ears and looked at me. The adjutant gave a brisk order and two guards came to take me away and deliver me back to the head of the hut. From the next day onwards, the whole camp was busy setting up the new theater and producing Obersturmführer Licht's play, *Verbrecher*."

Attorney Perl gets up to make us some more tea. With his

back turned to me he looks small and hunched. His feet still give him the strength to work. His hands tremble slightly, but he carries the tea confidently, cautiously, without spilling a drop. He sits down opposite me with a lucid mind—mercilessly lucid. I thank him, and from some troubled region of my memory I insist on murmuring, "I would still like to find out about Hermann Dunevitz."

Attorney Perl sighs. "You know, I think that maybe, somehow, with all my cards, you've gotten yourself headed in a bad direction. For every *dreck* like that Hermann Dunevitz or Yehezkel Ingster, there was a wonderful man who did more than you could imagine. Think about Mordecai Anielewicz, the leader of the Warsaw ghetto uprising—what a leader this country could have had if only he hadn't stayed in a bunker with the last of the insurgents. And think about Adam Czerniaków, head of the Warsaw Judenrat. Read about him. Such a wonderful man. And Robert Stricker, who could have used his connections to stay out of Auschwitz, but he insisted on going with his congregation precisely because 'that was where he was needed.' You have surely heard of Janusz Korczak. And just think of all the people whose names we don't even know but who gave morsels of bread to people who had no strength to get to the food because they were pushed away by the strong ones. Think of all the rabbis who did not flee but went with their people to death. Some of them carried Torah books in their hands, to give people courage in the train cars. And the people who sung *Hatikvah*, the national anthem, on the way to the crematoria. So many were killed in this Shoah—if only I had the courage and the strength to behave as they did. What happened there, in the Shoah, is more complex than what you can derive from my cards. All the educated people who committed acts of betrayal, and the simple Polish peasants who saved lives and were sometimes killed with their whole families because they hid a Jewish child. All the monks who were exterminated because they were caught hiding Jewish children. The people who informed on Jews, the people, even within the SS, who turned a blind eye and gave a prisoner one more chance to live. I told you, there were SS camp commandants who did their jobs without hating Jews. It didn't stop them from carrying out all their orders, and they killed prisoners to maintain discipline, but they tried to provide the Jews with the calorie quota dictated by their regulations, even during shortages. Then there were the Hanoch Bayskis, the Jews who hurried after hangmen to let them know a victim needed to be hanged again. Complicated, very complicated. Think of the Polish monk, Maximilian Kolbe, who volunteered at Auschwitz to go to his death in place of another prisoner. He knew his punishment would be death by starvation in a locked cellar beneath Cell Block 10, the hut of death. He knew he would lie in a dark hut until he died, but still he volunteered. It turns out that he was an anti-Semite and had published articles against Jews before the war. So what was he, this man? And what do we understand?"

We drink our tea.

But on the way home, Hermann Dunevitz floats to the surface like a strange dream trying to get out. Black markers are scattered through Memorial park. The kaleidoscope of memories is overturned, trying to record something. Upside down, it cannot find rest. On the pillow at night, troubled sleep, the kaleidoscope tries to emit a voice. There is something down there. Something down there.

The next day I ask Grandpa Yosef if he happens to know a Hermann Dunevitz. Grandpa Yosef struggles. His memory digs deep and enquires. Nothing. "Hermann Dunevitz, who is that?" He takes me into his house, although I have only come to pick up Grandpa Lolek's Vauxhall. It's Friday, Shabbat is almost here, and everyone has lots to get done. Grandpa Yosef pleads, "Come in, eat something, help me out. My pots and pans are bursting with food already. I don't know how it happened, the whole house is full of food." He takes my hand; the Vauxhall can wait, as well as my other errands. He sits me down in the kitchen and serves me plates of food. He chops, slices and waits for my reaction. Last night he insisted the Vauxhall had to go back to Grandpa Lolek's so it wouldn't be in the way here in his parking lot. Now the urgency is drowned out in steaming soup on the stovetop, in hot fritters he serves with grated fresh horseradish and ginger on top. "Taste these please." From the window I can see the edge of the parking lot. How is the Vauxhall in anyone's way? (Perhaps he wishes to erase all traces of the former tenant before he can host Hans Oderman wholeheartedly.)

Grandpa Yosef rushes off to his pots and in the window between the bushes, crazy Hirsch pops up. Motionless, he watches, looking straight at me. The man from the Lodz ghetto, the beadle of the Admor of Tipow, still dwelling on his question, "Only saints were gassed?" Perhaps he will come right up to the windowsill and scream his impenetrable question, shattering the days of my childhood. Yet the question is becoming clearer and clearer to me—I even have an answer. If he comes up to the window I will simply reply: Regular people were gassed. Righteous and evil people too, but mainly regular people, just like the ones who walk past me on the streets. If they were tossed into a reality of concentration camps, they would quickly settle into their roles—the attempts, the failures, the loss of sanity, the revelation of greatness. Hirsch knew this all along, and he questioned it. Ever since he began to ask in the Lodz ghetto, "Why, why the annihilation?" and to reply, "Because of the diminishment of life," all the way through the day he began asking his new question in the neighborhood, many thoughts must have passed through his mind, a theological debate beneath a cloak of filth and madness. Perhaps the debate continues still in secret, under cover of insanity. Perhaps he has found his role, to wander an entire lifetime on the path to one single conclusion—*the* conclusion, the essence of all contemplation.

I look at Hirsch in a new light. Perhaps he truly is the servant of a theological journey. But Hirsch simply disappears, going off to his daily routine in the bushes, and Grandpa Yosef comes back with a dish of sausage and cooked sauerkraut.

"Did you see Mr. Hirsch?" I ask.

Grandpa Yosef is daydreaming, not listening to my question, answering instead a question that was not asked at all. "Hans Oderman will stay with me, of course. He'll sit here and finish his research." He waits to see what I think about the dish. "Delicious, isn't it?"

Delicious.

"The Germans call it '*Bratwurst mit sauerkraut.*' Except of course, my sausage is kosher!"

I have trouble starting the Vauxhall. It would be better if Green the Mechanic took it to Grandpa Lolek's, but Grandpa Yosef called me last night urgently, as if the Vauxhall had to disappear at once.

"What's so urgent?" I angrily ask out loud. It's not as if Hans is arriving tomorrow. But the Vauxhall comes to Grandpa Yosef's assistance and wakes up. We can go, no answers needed.

On the way up to the Carmel neighborhood I pass by lights, intersections, a busy Friday coming to life. In the cars I see glum faces calculating lost time, trying to imagine a burst of salvation, a long wave of green lights rushing like a river all the way along their route. I have time. I only have to pick Yariv up from kindergarten at twelve. I need to talk to Grandpa Lolek and find out when he's planning to have the surgery—the tumor is still there and the doctors have urged him to get it treated.

"He's waiting for brain surgery to go on sale," Effi said.

She doesn't know why the name 'Hermann Dunevitz' sounds familiar to me either. I ask her when she comes over to talk with Anat. Anat is trying to recruit her to her army of volunteer women, to help them give out gift baskets to the poor on Purim. They sit talking in the kitchen, and before Effi leaves she comes by my desk.

"What's the deal with all the stuff you're documenting? Everyone's talking in the family. When will you show me?"

"Most of it's already finished, but not everything. There's so much material, you have no idea."

"Then show me what's ready, come on, the Shoah isn't a secret."

"You have no idea how much material there is." (My desperation grows right in front of her eyes.)

"Another reason why it's good the Shoah ended in '45. And oh yes, talking of Germans, I told you, didn't I? Hans Oderman is coming!"

"Yes, you told me already."

"Show me what you've finished."

She examines the pages, amazed at the length of the testimonies. She didn't know that Uncle Antek and Aunt Frieda and Aunt Zusa could remember so much, that there was so much unknown inside them.

"You know, I saw Hirsch today."

"So?"

"Hirsch…who we used to see around the neighborhood."

"Yeah, I know. So what happened?"

"Oh, nothing. But I was thinking about him. And you know, I dreamt about him a few days ago."

"About Hirsch? Nice choice."

"Well, never mind…"

She looks at me sitting among the pages, the drafts, the index cards. "You're going a little crazy," she opines.

"A little," I agree.

"It's only out of politeness that I still love you."

"Thanks."

"I really love you."

"Thanks again."

She leaves.

I really did have a dream about Hirsch, and my encounter with him has summoned up a fragmented memory of the extremely vivid dream. Hirsch was sitting in his hut in the woods. I came to him to ask for something. Something I'd been wanting for a long time, that everyone used to want, and now only the two of us had, except I didn't know where mine was. Hirsch's hut was surrounded by stray dogs, limping, exhausted. Tortured dogs with runny eyes, bald dogs. Old dogs thrown out of moving cars, resting with broken legs among bowls of bread and meat. Hirsch came out to me in his incarnation as the upright beadle of the Admor of Tipow, and said, "This is my penance. To right in dogs what I could not right in humans."

Crazy or not, that's what I dreamed. Crazy or not, I continue to document. It must be documented, the criminals and the victims. I must try and understand what is understandable. Crazy Hirsch struggles in his own way, Attorney Perl in his, and I in mine. Effi doesn't understand that something greater than the individual stories is emerging. Out of the chaos, a logic is transpiring. Everything can finally be combined, the framework comprehended. We can understand the clear process of the Nazi plan. Combine my father's story, random from his point of view, with the despotic framework of the plan around him, the simple cold calculation that declared *Aktionen* on certain dates in Bochnia, declared Bochnia "clean of Jews" on

October 1, 1943, performed a liquidation *Selektion* in Plaszow camp towards the middle of May, 1944, and sent his mother—Dad was saved—to a transport where no *Selektion* was held at all; they went straight from the train cars to the ovens, because in the organized formal procedure, the massive shipments from Hungary were supposed to have arrived at Auschwitz, according to the destruction plan drafted by Adolf Eichmann and Franz Novak. Orders, reports and commands were issued, postal trains passed by trains transporting Jews, Dad included, and documents containing action plans, dates, quotas—all of these together could explain each day in Dad's Shoah. They could also explain the transfer of Grandpa Yosef from one camp to the next and clarify why Attorney Perl was transferred to Dora-Mittelbau and why he was transferred again. Everything was in the documents, even answers to questions the family members asked themselves, sometimes out loud, sometimes silently, over and over and over again.

"I escaped in the middle of the Death March from Stutthof. Where did they end up taking the ones who didn't escape? How far did they get?" (Mrs. Kopel.)

"Why didn't they make allowances for our work permits in the Vilna ghetto? Why did they take my family away even though they had permits?" (Uncle Antek.)

"What was the end of SS Landau, Goddamn him, who was with us in Drohobicz?" (Aunt Frieda.)

"Perhaps you know what happened to the Greenspans from Koretz? Adella, Adella Greenspan, she was a friend of mine." (Aunt Zusa.)

And Dad, always practical. "Why did they want to send us to be gassed anyway?"

I should have shown Effi the Nazis' words too, the speeches, the declarations. So she would read and understand, so she would know that we mustn't stop thinking about the people who didn't hate Jews. The people who were just doing their jobs. The ones who did not derive pleasure from torture, from murder. The camp commandants who tried to give Jews the regulated calorie quotas even during shortages. The commandants who punished officers who cheated and withheld the prisoners' codified rights. The original SS people who enlisted in the purest of armies and swore not to lie or cheat or drink or curse. The people who saw themselves as exemplary human beings, whose enlistment in the SS was supposed to personify the oath they had taken towards all that was noble in the human soul. Even when they ruled over the lives of thousands and tens of thousands of people willing to do anything for a chance to live, they did not harm a single prisoner unless it was required for proper order in the camp. Pedantically and gravely, they continued to do their jobs. Effective, fair, non-murderous murderers. In the heart of a world gone mad they were not tempted to sin by enjoying the suffering of others. They squeezed, yes, they squeezed the gold out of Jews, out of their vessels, their teeth, out of what they tried to hide in their bodies. But for themselves they took not a crumb of loot. They produced raw materials—hair, teeth—for a Germany at war. They managed the annihilation efficiently. They shot anyone who hindered the process—the elderly, children—without enjoyment, without evil. Non-murderous murderers. Around them raged sadists, some in SS uniforms, uncurbed plunderers of property, rapists, demented minds, psychopaths—the war gave them a boundless cushion for their actions. Around them raged SS people who, at the beginning, did not demonstrate sadism or greed, but who slowly discovered in the camps a simple, supreme fact—that everything was allowed. The righteous purity of these paragons was vanquished by the intoxicating feeling that everything was allowed. Torture and murder and beatings and pranks—everything was allowed. Rape and plundering and a good laugh or two—everything was allowed. Simple souls who gradually comprehended that there was no one to punish them, no one to reprimand them. Sadism opened up like a fan and the temptation drew them on—how much further could they go? Without balance, without boundaries, these simple souls were dragged along in amazement—they still hadn't reached the limit, everything was still allowed. We-are-doing-the-unthinkable-and-still-it-is-allowed. We-are-doing-everything-we-want-to-and-no-one-is-punishing-us. Allowed! Like creatures erupting into a vacuum with nothing to hold them back and prevent them from bursting forth, out came the unstoppable urges. Everything was allowed, everything allowed. After the war it would all go back inside neat boxes. Twenty years later, judges and prosecutors would ask in astonishment—is this the man accused of the charges?

Those sadists, I understand. It is not them that I fear. People like them are hiding everywhere around me today. I can guess who they will be and where they will come from if-what-happened-there-happens-here-too. What frightens me is the ones who maintained their integrity. The-people-who-did-not-hate-Jews. The-people-who-were-only-doing-their-job. Those people, I cannot understand, and I have no idea where they will come from.

I pick Yariv up from kindergarten and we walk through his world together. No one will be shot here. Pregnant women need not worry—no one will stab them in the stomach. Women pushing strollers can keep peeking at their babies to make sure they're not too warm, not too cold. No one will throw a baby in the air, wish the first shot had hit it in flight, and try again. But I know. The monsters are here. The only thing missing is the circumstances, and when the circumstances arise it will all happen here, and it will be directed against me because I will not collaborate. They will emerge, all of them, even the people-who-did-not-hate—although where they will come from I do not know—and the camp-commandants-who-tried-to-supply-the-regulated-calorie-quotas-even-during-shortages. In the midst of it all, like a sailboat stuck in the mud of Lake Tiberias, waiting for the tide to go out, waiting for a drought to spread its smooth mantle, Hermann Dunevitz's name rises up, more than half of him now exposed. I must remember.

In the evening, Grandpa Yosef calls to report cheerfully, "I kept thinking about Hermann Dunevitz all day, and I remembered. Anat's mother's maiden name was Dunevitz. Maybe that's why the name stuck in your mind?"

Anat is making our dinner, Yariv is already asleep in bed. (Anat thinks he's getting an ear infection again.) I go up and ask her.

"Yes, before she was married my mother's name was Dunevitz. Why?"

My memory already knows, but still it questions—perhaps it is wrong, perhaps the certainty is a mistake.

"What was your grandfather's name?"

"My grandfather? Hermann. What are all these questions for?"

Hermann Dunevitz.

First there is a trickle of blood, not a rushing feeling. At first it goes, "So what? So what if it's her grandfather?" But the "so what" loses out, trampled, and newly disorganized thoughts take its place. She says, "My grandfather? Hermann." And this is Anat, and I gave him a great-grandson, and it is with me, and what am I going to do? I gave him a great-grandson who is sleeping now and he might have an ear infection and I'm married to his granddaughter. His granddaughter. Who is his granddaughter? Why, it's Anat! It's Anat and it's Yariv, and what difference does it make?

But like a necessary torture, it does make a difference, and I am a breathless, silent volcano. I wait silently for the next emotion, the next thought, an uncontrollable internal torrent. In the accompanying transparent light everything comes out, bursts through from within fantastical treasure boxes and locked dowry chests. Gustav Richter, one of Eichmann's senior aids, a primary implementer of deportation plans and the organizer of a failed attempt to transfer Rumanian Jewry to the concentration camps, was tried only in 1981 and sentenced to four years. Franz Novak, Eichmann's assistant, particularly active in the deportation of Hungary's Jews, hid after the war under an assumed name. In 1957 he began using his real name again, but was not tried. He continued to live his life. Only in 1961, after his name came up repeatedly during the Eichmann trial, was he incarcerated and tried; he was sentenced to eight years. He was retried after an appeal and released in 1966. Anton Streitwieser, commandant of Melk camp, was captured at the end of the war but escaped and lived under an assumed identity. He was caught in 1956. He was free until his trial, which began only in 1967. He was given a life sentence and died in prison in 1972. Alfred Nossig, a Jewish collaborator in the Warsaw ghetto, was assassinated by ZOB, the Jewish Fighting Organization (*Zydowska Organizacja Bojowa*). Herta Bothe, a female camp guard at Bergen-Belsen, was sentenced for her acts in the camp to ten years in prison in 1945, but released in 1951. George Eliot said, "Cruelty, like every

other vice, requires no motive outside of itself; it only requires opportunity." On one of the transports to Sobibor, some clown decided
to spill chlorine into the moving train cars. The chlorine coated the
people in the trains. By the time it arrived at Sobibor, the car was filled
with pale green bodies whose skin peeled away when touched. Anat
calls me for dinner. How can I eat dinner when Gottlieb Muzikant,
SS-Sanitätsdienstgrad at the hospital in Melk camp, admitted at his
trial, held only in 1960, that he had killed over ninety prisoners by
injecting phenol into their hearts and had strangled at least one hundred patients to death? He was sentenced to life in prison, not death.
Anat asks where I am and my thoughts need to stop, they must stop,
they do stop. I can exist for now in the form of a breathing volcano.
I can get up, eat dinner, keep going through the dark memory. I'll sit
next to her, we'll eat, we'll think. "So what? So what? So what? Why
did I even get mixed up in all this?"

Dinner. The volcano breathes heavily, absorbing little relief
from the air, the omelet, the salad.

"Is everything all right?" Anat asks. She wants to talk. It's Purim
soon and she'll be busy preparing the gift baskets.

The volcano asks, "What do you know about your grandfather,
Hermann Dunevitz?"

"Grandpa Hermann?"

"Yes."

"Not much. He died in Canada, a long time ago. My mother
was five."

"He came from the Lvov region, didn't he?"

"Maybe, yes, one of those towns. I don't know. Why? What
have you found out?"

"What have I found out? I'll tell you what I've found out. Your
grandfather was a murderer. He murdered Jews in the camps."

Her expression turns grave. "Really?"

I look at her face. Where will this go?

Anat wonders, "But he was Jewish, wasn't he?"

I tell her almost gleefully, "Yes, but he was a sadist, he was
crazy. He hung around the camps and murdered Jews like the worst
of the Nazis."

Silence. She spreads margarine on a slice of bread. The knife moves over the bread. Salt. Pepper. That's how she eats. "All right, well what do you want now?"

"Nothing."

I'm not accusing her, it's not her fault, is it? There's nothing to accuse her of. And if what came of Hermann Dunevitz is Anat, then everything must be all right, and the theories don't hold up. Except that now we have to forgive them too, the grandchildren of Nazis, who come here to plant forests.

Anat won't let it go. "It doesn't seem like nothing by the look on your face. Come on, tell me, what do you want?"

"Nothing, really nothing. It's not your fault."

We eat in silence. Pass the salt. I spread margarine on a slice of bread. I add salt, pepper. The flammable air above us—will it ignite or not?

"Just don't say anything to my mother! Even if it's true!"

"Okay."

We sit quietly. Drink coffee. Read the paper. We hear a noise and sigh. It's just Yariv stirring in his bed. We toss and turn on our bed until morning comes. Hermann Dunevitz is Anat's grandfather.

Grandpa Lolek's surgery became an urgent matter, something to busy ourselves with, because Grandpa Lolek was beginning to behave oddly. Whether it was old age or the tumor was unclear, but it became apparent that he had to have the surgery, and soon. Little defects flowed through his memory and thoughts. He announced that he was leaving the lands in Gedera to me—me and Joyce the dancer, jointly, as long as we didn't fight. He asked us all to give her the news when she arrived for her usual evening visit, and hoped she wouldn't be late this time. He was clearly going senile.

We gathered around him with suggestions and data. We took him to the doctor, and together consulted and recommended having the surgery here in Israel, at Hadassah Hospital—the best department. Grandpa Lolek looked frightened as he sat on his chair trying to understand our franticness and the urgent need to undergo surgery. He closed his light blue eyes for a moment, weighing the important decision. Then he opened them and said, "All right. You can have operation." And so we had to explain everything again, reintroduce the doctor, the room, the Sick Fund, and that the surgery was for *his* head, not anyone else's, and that it would be cheap and successful. The doctor would explain everything, here he was. Anat was among us, urging Grandpa Lolek, reassuring him, introducing him to the doctor. We all encouraged him and the doctor encouraged us, saying we should leave Grandpa Lolek in the room with him and let him explain. And Anat was among us, and we were living a quiet married life, kind to each other (shoving reasons to fight into the abyss). The panic over Grandpa Lolek's confusion was good for us, it softened our dormant troubles. Besides, I had convinced myself that everything was fine. At first I was angry, unable to tolerate the thought that she was the granddaughter of Hermann Dunevitz. But it all passed and I managed to say, "So what?" and to really feel, "So what?" So what if she's his granddaughter? We've been married for six years and I know everything about her, her love, her capacity to truly love people, to help them. She has a love of humankind. ("She has an ego that lives on the back porch," Effi said). I said, "So what?" and I felt, "So what?" I had simply been alarmed for a moment by the sound of shattering glass. I wasn't prepared for it. But nothing was broken, nothing had shattered.

Life got back on track. Documenting, talking with Attorney Perl, reading his books. Everything attested to routine. Grandpa Lolek broke an appliance and asked that my friend "who fixes things cheap" repair it. Effi found a new boyfriend. Anat said she'd be busy on Purim. Grandpa Yosef asked if I could bring back the Vauxhall, which Grandpa Lolek couldn't use anyway, because Hans might want to use it (for some time, his entire life had been dedicated to paving roads for Hans). I told him I had finished documenting most of the family stories, everything was ready, and he asked me to come over. He served me a dish of okra and banana. (Did I think Hans would like these sorts of exotic flavors?) I put down a neatly bound copy of everything I had documented. My documentary, on Grandpa Yosef's brown wooden table.

Grandpa Yosef left the bound pages where they were and did not even reach out a curious hand. He talked about how things were going in the neighborhood. Everything was the same as usual. Gershon Klima had decided he needed a rest and had found himself a suitable place near Tel Aviv. They were thinking of renting out his house here, but weren't sure they'd be able to. Not long ago, the Meretz party had rented the late Orgenstern's house and set up a local branch, but they had to leave after visiting dignitaries were bitten by dogs on two separate occasions, for no apparent reason. (Grandpa Yosef and I knew it was Brandy, who had become an extreme right-winger after her death.) Mr. Pepperman had stopped getting his mail, which alarmed him. They had to have a search. At the post office they said everything was in order. In the end they found all his mail lying in a puddle and no one knew who had done it. There was also a strange affair with the poet, Asher Schwimmer. He no longer lived with his brother; the brother had passed away. They took him to a place near Nazareth, a quiet place, so he'd be happy. But he suddenly started slapping people for no reason—the staff, the doctors, the caregivers. He yelled and made accusations and hit. Here in the neighborhood, Uncle Antek was losing his hearing, he couldn't hear at all in his right ear. The doctors were looking into it, and so was Effi. In the meantime she suggested he turn up the volume on his radio. Uncle Mendel was also losing his hearing, but he never listened to anyone anyway so it didn't matter.

"And how's Mr. Levertov?"

Mr. Levertov was absolutely fine. Ever since Effi had become his primary physician, he'd been truly exceptional. Like a young boy. People were envious; they wanted Effi to be their doctor too. Even Mrs. Tsanz. (And we both knew, because Effi had told us confidentially, that she was probably going to leave the clinic soon. A position had opened up for her at Hadassah Hospital in Jerusalem.)

The conversation naturally shifted to Grandpa Lolek. We agreed that he had to have the surgery—what was he waiting for? Grandpa Yosef asked about Yariv and how Anat was. We didn't talk about Hermann Dunevitz. As long as we didn't talk and didn't ask, everything would be fine. If-we-shut-our-eyes-the-monster-would-leave. Everything was fine. Simply fine. And really, I thought, it's no fault of hers. Everything is fine, I thought. Simply fine.

But at nights, our glaciers floated on as we slept.

Around the time Grandpa Lolek decided to leave me the lands in Gedera, I started feeling that I couldn't, I just couldn't. Not because of Anat, but because of Hermann Dunevitz. He had cunningly found a way to live on through me. To give himself a great-grandson, an eighth of himself, through me. Not only Hermann Dunevitz, but all the traitors, the murderers, the sadists. The people who made Hirsch wander the streets and gave Rachela Kempler that *look*. And Gershon Klima and Mr. Pepperman and Itcha Dinitz and Mr. Bergman and Linow Community and everyone.

In Effi's kangaroo court, I declared, "It won't leave me alone. You see, he's her grandfather, and Yariv is one eighth of him. One eighth. His blood is living on through her, through Yariv, through everyone who will come in the future. Precisely what shouldn't happen. Do you see?"

Effi bristled. "Are you listening to yourself? That's exactly what the Nazis said. They also looked for people with one eighth Jewish blood in them. They also said it coursed through one's blood and could not be helped. You've really lost your mind."

Attorney Perl said, "You have a wife, you mustn't do anything. Give it time. Trust me, don't do anything." He caressed the cover of a book, *The Protocols of the Nazi Trials, Volume IV*, printed in 1950. These were the protocols that should have explained, should have told us what the grandfathers did in Germany. They all kept telling me, "So what?" They told me to forget. But something stronger than "so what" had to come, it had to. I would give anything to be told how to go on, what to do. They told me, "So what?" and "Forget it," as if they were selling shiny objects to savages. As if I were incapable of understanding on my own that Anat was not to blame and neither were the German grandchildren who come here every summer to plant forests. Every summer, so I heard, they came to plant trees. Where were all these forests? Maybe you couldn't see them from the roads, but after a few more years of apologies, their trees would suddenly shoot up over the bald, white shoulders of the highways, and the roads would have to be paved through wooded fields. It wasn't her fault. I wished it was, so I could grasp at something. There wasn't even the edge of a thread, nothing to point to, to imagine, to locate the pain, to know what to heal. There was nothing to do, no way to go on. Still they disembarked on my island to sell me shiny objects. (My suffering could not be traded for simple glass beads.)

"You have a major problem," Effi said. "Everywhere you go, you take your hatred with you, like a dung beetle rolling a ball along. You need to stop. Get it in your head that there isn't as much black and white in the world as we would like. Just stop it."

"I don't want to stop it."

"I understand why it's bothering you, but enough, stop it. You're a grown man, you need to resolve this."

"How?"

"Well, think of a bridge, for example."

"A bridge?"

"Yes. When there's a river you can't cross, you build a bridge over it. It doesn't mean the river is gone, it just means now you can cross it. See?"

"Yes." I get the analogy. I get what she means. But Effi is enthusiastic about the idea and wants to keep explaining it. So what if I get it.

"That's what people do. They need bridges. See, no one is telling you to stop feeling what you're feeling. Just build a bridge. So you can cross over. You can even stand on the bridge and look down at the river, just without being inside it. Do you know how many bridges I've built?"

A bridge. I'm already taking measurements for the first supports, and Effi says, "Or maybe you could punish her."

"Punish?"

"Punish Anat, you know, maybe that's what you need."

"What do you mean, punish?"

"It has to be something you choose. Like you do with kids."

Punish Anat. Why should I punish Anat?

Effi comes to life. "For instance, another woman. Yes, something like that, so it won't be easy. Another woman, at least once, yes." (She is falling in love with the idea. She talks quickly, thinking, another woman, that's what will help.)

"What are you talking about?"

"Then think of something else."

"But why would I be with another woman?"

She gets annoyed. "Okay, you find something then. You're the child. Figure out what will make you feel that it's over and done with."

Another woman? Where did she get that peculiar idea? Anat is the only one, I'm not attracted to other women. Why would I be with another woman?

(There is one, oddly. We met not long ago at Yariv's kindergarten. I went to pick him up and it started raining. We stood beneath a small cornice that leaked; we were the last people in the kindergarten except for one of the teaching assistants, who jingled a large bunch of keys, put it in her bag, and stood next to us. She asked if I was Yariv's dad. I said, no, I was the infamous child-kidnapper, Heinrik Chapinski. She laughed and said, "Why didn't you say so? We give top honors to child-kidnappers around here!" I looked at her and wondered when kindergarten assistants got so pretty. Mine, Chana, was a half-mad dwarf who only liked quiet children, but she didn't like me even though I was quiet. I plucked up the courage to ask if she really was the teaching assistant. She laughed again and said actually she wasn't the assistant, she was also a child-kidnapper. In fact, Yariv was in her sights too because he was the cutest kid, but I, Heinrik Chapinski, had got to him first. I was surprised at how she had picked up the name and repeated it correctly. She didn't even know that Heinrik Chapinski was tried after the war for the sadistic extermination of Jews in the Bochnia ghetto. She smiled and said that if we were both child-kidnappers then we should get together some time to discuss professional hazards. I told her I was married. Happily, I stressed. I pointed to Yariv: "That's the result." She looked hurt and said she hadn't meant anything, she was just being nice. I wanted to say something friendly, to take it back, but Yariv started crying and tugged my hand. He wailed as only he knows how, without sentences, only words, leaving me responsible for the syntax. Half the words he was saying were "Itzik." Itzik was a daunting entity in Yariv's world, a kid who hit other kids and lorded over the sandbox and told all the other kids what to do. A kapo. Ever since that day, every time I come to pick Yariv up, I'm the embarrassed one. She seems quite cheerful. ("Hello, Heinrik!" She smiles prettily.)

Nothing will happen. There is love between Anat and me, six years of ever-growing love. I have no friends. Only Anat. I can't understand how other people keep up with their friends from the army. Effi is family. There are no other friends. Why would I punish her?

Just before Purim I come home to find Anat sitting with gift baskets for the poor scattered all over the living room. She conducts her campaigns from our little headquarters, all the rooms filled with cardboard boxes, items and notes. Everything has to fit in the packages and be sent off. Not everything is straightforward. There are different types of recipients, three sizes of boxes (the size of the package corresponds to the extent of the recipient's misfortune). She sits exhausted among the items. Yariv sits with her, curled up, obedient. He is as big as one of the packages. He doesn't try to reach into the gifts and sabotage them. A well bred and polite child.

I stand in the doorway and say, "Over there, just so you don't get mixed up, is our son. Should I mark him for you?"

She laughs, exhausted.

(Deep inside us our married life continues. Caution and apology and fragile affection. "Forget it" and "So what?" and "Go on.")

She smiles at me so that I will smile back at her. (How angry I was when she bought a German washing machine. For months I lay in wait, hoping for it to break, hoping for one non-German instant to penetrate the mechanism, the wrong kind of soap to tear up its innards—even if it meant our clothes would be ruined. I was angry at the machine, not at Anat, and I waited for a short, a blockage, knitwear washed too hot, even an electrical fire right here in my home. But that died down too, and the machine kept working quietly, became something that simply washed our clothes.) I have to smile, this needs to be over, this thing between us that slowly slinks and does not rest. Someone has to bridge the banks and I am the only one who can, I am the one who has to stop thinking it's important. But I was the one who saw Eva Lanczer on the lawn outside 12 Katznelson, and I saw Mr. Pepperman coming to Grandpa Yosef with his old bills to make sure his name was listed only to make sure he paid his bills. And I remember Finkelstein's gold, Finkelstein who knew everything back in 1939 and whose letter is still hidden in Grandpa Lolek's basement. I am the one who asks, why did Asher Schwimmer start slapping people? What did they do to him *there*, that made him forget all his Hebrew? Attorney Perl tries to calm me, to cancel out the affair, saying, "You have a good wife." Yet at the same time he stokes the engine with hot coals, saying, "Here, read this."

Orders issued by Reichsführer Heinrich Himmler concerning retaliation for the murder of six SS officers by Partisans near Kiev:

"I order that in the district of Kiev, ten thousand Jews shall die without regard to sex and age, for each of the six officers. Even a babe in the cradle must be trampled down like a poisonous toad.... We are living in an iron age, and there is no escape from using an iron broom."

Karl Jäger, commanding officer of Einsatzkommando 3, from a report summarizing his activities in Lithuania, dated December 1, 1941:

"I can confirm today that Einsatzkommando 3 has achieved the goal of solving the Jewish problem in Lithuania. There are no more Jews in Lithuania, apart from working Jews and their families.... I am of the opinion that the male working Jews should be sterilized immediately to prevent reproduction. Should any Jewess nevertheless become pregnant, she is to be liquidated."

I take the Karl Jäger index cards out of the drawers. What was his fate? The cards say nothing.

"Don't worry about him. I don't know how I could have forgotten to put it on the cards. After the war he hid, posing as a farmer. He was only exposed in 1959 and he committed suicide before his trial."

Don't worry about him. But there are others, and they cover the earth like weeds.

*

We finally took Grandpa Lolek to Hadassah Hospital. They promised he would only remain for a short while after the surgery, and then he could go home and be watched by Effi. The Lion of Life recited the terms to us and reminded me about the broken blender—what about my friend who fixed things for cheap? His blue eyes hinted at how lovely it would be if the repaired blender was waiting for him when he got back from his dangerous surgery.

Dangerous?

No.

They explained that the location of the tumor made Grandpa Lolek's surgery a fairly easy case. Very easy. They had to operate so there wouldn't be any more unpleasant surprises. Still, during evening phone calls, little drops of concern were voiced, fears for his well-being. We spoke our fears out loud so our hearts could make it through them. Here and there an explicit question was posed: Was there a chance he wouldn't make it?

Effi did not allow anyone to go too far. "Don't worry, he won't die. Before he goes under, we'll tell him the price of gravestones has gone up, and that will be that. No danger."

She greeted us in a white coat when we got to Hadassah, not yet a staff member, and in any case brain surgery was not her field. But for Grandpa Lolek, Effi in a white cloak was a good sign, evidence that someone was looking out for him. He agreed to be hospitalized without protest, saving us several hours we had planned to waste on a sudden refusal in the parking lot. Grandpa Lolek dismissed us, asked Dad to stay, and agreed to send me back to Haifa. (Behind the glass window in the door, far away, he turned back to me and twirled his finger around fast, to remind me about the blender. I nodded.)

Two days later, with his head bandaged, everything was behind him. As promised, it had been very simple. Grandpa Lolek was convinced we had come to release him from the doctors, he was sick-of-doctors, there-is-life-outside, there-is-business-outside, and he believed we would devise an impressive rescue operation, a kidnapping, something that would conclude at his home with a cup of tea and news from the neighbor's radio. His question for me was, "What about the blender?" He had been anesthetized for brain surgery, knives had sliced open his skull, blood infusions had been pumped into his veins, a tumor that had been pressing on a primary blood vessel had been cut out of him, and yet when he awoke, his desire to fix the blender on the cheap was still intact, having survived the procedure like a tightrope walker who tiptoes from one end to the other without losing his balance.

I looked at him and knew he would never die. He was the strength, the power. He had never come down from the peaks of Monte Cassino, and so he had no need for memories. He was the tree of life, and not only did he have no memories, he also had no hatred. No ball of loathing to roll around, only a large world full of profits and cups of tea, cigarettes to be smoked, and debts to accumulate. From him, from him I should be learning. Not bridges and not punishments. All I needed to do was ask, how do you get rid of the thoughts?

I did not forget his wish, and the next morning I turned up at his apartment to pick up the blender. (I was also there to move the Vauxhall back to Grandpa Yosef's parking lot. Twice he had called. "Hans is coming. Where's the Vauxhall?") I opened the darkened house and instead of going to the kitchen, where the blender was, I walked into the living room. Just to sit for a while on the couch, above the rug that covered the opening to the cellar and the box of letters to Joyce the dancer, and the letter from Finkelstein who knew everything back in 1939. The house of wonders was at my disposal. I could have opened the cellar door and found, with adult eyes, what we had not found as children, when Grandpa Lolek had walked in with the Leica camera. But the magic of the cellar had been dampened. We had grown up. On the couch at Grandpa Lolek's I could only rest and think, Yariv is an eighth of *him*. Who knew how many eighths like Yariv were running around in some kindergarten? Those eighths also had parents who, like me, had sat through Holocaust Remembrance Day ceremonies at school and recited words from black placards, and had learned to understand that we were the victims and that was it. Easy. We were the victims. We were. And that was that. Now life. Once a year our hearts would be sad, once a year we would remember what happened, and we would never look around us and realize that everything existed now too, here too. They did not see Mr. Pepperman checking his bills, they did not see Rachela Kempler. Itcha Dinitz, between the blinds, in the dark, living there; they did not see him either. They say I should build bridges, forget. But before the bridge-erectors came the abyss-builders. I am not willing to forget the abyss-builders. On Holocaust Day everyone stands for a moment of silence when the siren goes off, and everyone feels moved, and they all raise their children and do not know, and are sure of themselves, and do not understand. 1939, every year anew. 1939, and they do not know.

I went to check the blender. The only thing wrong with it was that it was unplugged. The power chord was lying cunningly on the counter, disconnected from the socket. When I plugged it in the blender started whirring loudly, ready to blend and mix. I took it with me anyway, for some reason, and placed it on the back seat of the Vauxhall. (There was a reddish-brown stain on the upholstery, as if right there was where the battle of Monte Cassino had ended, when Grandpa Lolek had spun around and stabbed a German on the back seat with his bayonet).

At Grandpa Yosef's house I opened the door to find him wearing an apron, holding a steaming pie fresh from the oven.

"I brought the Vauxhall."

"*Nu*, welcome, welcome. Come in please." He put the pie down and wiped his hands on the apron. On the brown wooden table was my documentation, bound and neat. Grandpa Yosef hadn't touched it.

"Haven't you read what I wrote?" I ask. Eighty well-written pages.

Grandpa Yosef squirmed. "*Nu*, no time. I didn't get to it. Hans is coming tomorrow morning, and the house...no time...." He sliced a piece of pie and served it to me, then continued to cut more slices for an invisible guest.

"All right. When you have time, read it."

"*Nu*, taste it, taste it. I'm a little...I'll read it, I'll read it all. I just haven't had time." He wouldn't leave the pie alone. He sliced and sliced, sinking the knife into the dough, attacking it nervously. He got up and asked, "Would you like some sugar for the pie?" Without waiting for an answer, he reached out and leafed through the pages. Then suddenly he said, "*Nu*, documentation. Naked in the snow for ten hours, can you know what that is? Hunger like there was in Buchenwald, can you know what that is? No, no. You cannot know what that is…" He darted into the kitchen.

I cautiously tasted the pie, another of Grandpa Yosef's strange concoctions. The sparks of his soul. He came back with sugar and scattered some on my pie without asking. I tasted it—cardamom and sugar.

"So, how are things?" I asked.

"Good, good. Just that there's no time for anything. Hans is coming and look, look at the state of the house."

"The house looks fine."

"Effi volunteered to pick him up at the airport. It's a good thing it worked out for her, and she's coming from Jerusalem. You're busy, I know, with Grandpa Lolek's operation. You can't do it, *nu*. It's a good thing Effi volunteered."

("Wherever Hans Oderman is concerned, I'm the first to volunteer," Effi said.)

I looked at Grandpa Yosef. In a white undershirt, his shoulders looked soft. His tiredness suddenly seemed very pronounced. A whole life of charity, of nerve-wracking righteousness, and one visit from Hans Oderman of Germany, of all things, was wearing him out to the point of exhaustion. (I suddenly understood and was seized by panic: He was not like Grandpa Lolek; he would die one day. There was a day waiting for us, a funeral, rain, umbrellas, a rabbi praying.)

"Aren't you a little tired?"

"Tired? Gracious no. I enjoy the work."

"Isn't it difficult for you like this here? Alone?"

"Difficult? No, not difficult. I get along fine, thank God."

Something strange in our conversation. Like forcing a puzzle piece that doesn't fit. Something wrong, but you ignore it.

Grandpa Yosef went into the kitchen again and reemerged with his pride and joy, a cake that looked like a hat with a battered rim. He declared, "Finally the *lekach* cake came out right! All those years my Feiga tried to teach me the recipe, and finally..." He placed the cake on the table to slice it. His pride was real, glowing. (Success, after years of failure, and there was no one to give him a prize.)

We both sat and ate. Grandpa Yosef wandered through his desert of life without Feiga, without Moshe. I pushed along a ball of hatred and they asked me to build bridges. To forget, to forgive. Hans Oderman was arriving soon, the orphan researcher.

"*Nu*, how's the cake?"

"Delicious."

"When my Feiga was still alive, she always knew how long to mix the batter, when to take it out of the oven. She would always remind me. Without her, sometimes strange things come out of the oven."

"It's still a little hard for you without Feiga, isn't it?"

"Oh...*nu*. When my Feiga was still alive, there was always someone to talk with, someone I could discuss an interesting Gemara page I had read with, or things they were saying in the neighborhood. Now there's no one to talk to, and my thoughts roll around inside and keep going. *Nu*, not to worry."

"It will be all right. Time heals, they say."

Grandpa Yosef looked up. "Time heals?" His face relaxed for a moment, gathering up a thought like a river collecting rivulets. Suddenly he shouted, "Time heals?! I still haven't healed from the people I lost long ago, and time heals? A little hard without Feiga? How about it's still a little hard without my brothers and my mother and father, who went in Belzec, and I still can't accept that? Maybe that's still a little hard?" He carved thick, moist slices of cake that fell on their sides, one on top of the other, on the dish.

I looked at him quietly. I had never heard Grandpa Yosef shout before.

He hummed and huffed as if to still himself. He moved his head from side to side, trying to understand. "*Nu*, I.... Well. You know...."

"It's all right."

"I'm actually a little...after I told you everything...things haven't been sitting well inside. *Nu*, the memories...."

He went to the kitchen and dragged some pots around. Opened and closed the oven door. Did what he knew best, putting himself into order. He pulled something off a shelf. Opened the fridge. Closed it. Came back and apologized again. I did too.

"Anat said it wasn't good of me to remind people of what happened."

"*Nu*, well, Anat. She knows how to feel things. Is everything okay with you two? With the issue?"

A ball of hatred rolled along. The dung beetle lost its ball.

"Everything's fine," I said.

"Yes…."

"There's nothing to be done."

"*Nu*, everybody has problems."

We spoke quietly, breaking down the previous exchange into small words, letters, tiny signs that meant nothing. Grandpa Yosef tried to find something to do with his hands. He started slicing the cake again. "You know, I still have trouble with Rothschild too. Since we spoke, it's been harder. I can't get rid of the thought that he somehow stayed there, for evermore in Buchenwald. That's where my last memory of him is, and apart from what is in my memory, what other existence does Rothschild have? Sometimes I think, if only I could get him out of there and have one memory of life after Buchenwald. For example, Rothschild managing a store here on Herzl Street, doing business. But how? That's where he stayed." He paused for a thought. "And Mr. Hirsch walking around the neighborhood, that's not easy for me, it reminds me of things. But you accept it. You live your life. With all sorts of things, you live."

Grandpa Yosef, our sleigh-dog, still pulling the corpse wagons.

We ate the cake silently. Grandpa Yosef pulled the pie towards himself and cut a slice. He tasted it. "I might have put too much cardamom in this," he mumbled. "Maybe it doesn't need any cardamom at all." He fell silent.

(He cannot be helped. Grandpa Yosef pulls the corpse wagons. Everyone here in the neighborhood, that's what they do. Pull wagons. White figures looking for things at night, sitting like tubers in warm homes, saying, "How are things?" and answering, "Life goes on," like a frightened lie, like something that redeems. Grandpa Yosef at least has the strength to live. Most of the people here have never lived after the camps. Even though they were liberated and sent to Israel on boats and given houses to live in, nothing truly alive came out from behind those fences. A massive fraud. Eating and drinking and sleeping for fifty years, with remarriages and new children—all a fraud. All that survived are shells with memories. Empty shells listening to the radio, walking to the grocery store, going to visit relatives. Fifty years, and in Germany the war is long over. The guard soldiers and the train conductors and the propaganda clerks have already forgotten. The foremen, the gas manufacturers, and the transport supervisors have already forgotten. The engine operators and the experimenters and the order-givers have already forgotten. Those who were not hanged have already forgotten. Those who were not shot by avengers—forgotten. Only here, in the neighborhood, shells with memories.)

I cut myself another slice of cake. To cheer him up. A cake he made from Feiga's recipe. Where did Feiga have recipes from? From her home, most likely, there, in Bochnia. We eat cake made from a recipe from a world destroyed. Grandpa Yosef, lost in thought, digs his fork into the crumbs. We don't know what to talk about. We try. There is always a way.

"*Nu*, what's new in the neighborhood?"

Littman from the grocery store may be closing down. His son might take over, or he might sell it to someone else. Adella Greuner has started singing. She's really disturbing the neighbors. They went to talk to her, and she promised, but nothing. (We both remember her brother who came from America in a taxi to slap her and go back home). Gershon Klima's bombax has started creaking in the wind, the branches must be old. Someone said it should be chopped down, but they won't let that happen.

"And Asher Schwimmer?"

"Asher Schwimmer. I really should go see him one of these days, poor man. I heard he's still slapping people. They don't know what to do with him."

"And Gershon?"

"Klima is all right. He asks about you and Effi. He's at home for now. *Nu*, things move slowly with him."

Before we say goodbye, Grandpa Yosef presents me with a twin brother of the *lekach* cake and a pie wrapped in foil ("In this one, thank God, I forgot to put cardamom"). He offers some home-made jam ("a little sour, but it's energizing"). He is back to his old self, our Grandpa Yosef. What happened to him before must have just been nerves. The preparations for Hans Oderman's arrival are exhausting him, and we all have bad days. He sends regards to Anat. "You have a wonderful wife," he says as he walks me down Katznel-son. I mustn't forget that I have a wonderful wife. He stops when a bark comes from the direction of his house. "Well, I have to go back to put out food. I'm sorry."

Of everything that happened at Grandpa Yosef's, his yelling, and our conversation, and the documentation that didn't affect him, and the corpse wagons, I suddenly think of Asher Schwimmer. I have to go and see him. He is the final riddle, the place where the marvel might be hiding, a true splinter from the Big Bang. I must go to his new place near Nazareth and talk to him, no matter in which language, whatever enables us to talk, to find some gem of King Solomon's wis-dom that will bring us together. Why did he forget his Hebrew? Why did he start slapping people? Grandpa Yosef spoke of him with worry, but I know that the slaps are in fact a sign that something has awoken. A blossoming of sorts. For fifty years he was quiet, his Hebrew lost (*The Carmel peaks shall I ascend / in His forest shall I prophesize. / The rivers of Levy shall be mine / a nest for the crow and a bed for the brambles*), but now he is returning, his powers are being restored and he has the courage to accuse. Something inside him is sprouting those slaps like brave flowers in a desert. I must see Asher Schwimmer. Whatever he says, I will use—kindling for everything I need.

I run after Grandpa Yosef, shouting, "Grandpa Yosef! Grandpa Yosef!" I explain to him, almost begging, and yet also commanding: "I'm taking the Vauxhall, I'll bring it back in a few hours." I run with the cake, the pie and the jam. I put them on the back seat next to the blender (I almost forgot about it, almost left it as prey for Hans Oderman). Forget about bridges and punishments. I'm going to Asher

Schwimmer, a dung beetle rolling a ball of hatred, but I already know: everything's all right with Anat, and with Yariv. An eighth of him—so what? That, I can forget. But I cannot rest inside. I have to keep going, to understand. To read everything I can about the Nazi criminals, the ideas, the acts committed by people who realized that everything-was-allowed-everything-was-allowed-no-one-would-punish-them. I have time. On the inside, I have time. But I must go on. Get help from Attorney Perl and investigate until I reach all the dead-ends. That is the goal, to reach every dead-end, to stop and realize that from there onwards only people like Hirsch can continue. Attorney Perl and I will stop at the dead-ends, we have no half-century-long theological journey, we do not have the strength not to die, to walk around Katznelson ill and injured, to be Mr. Hirsch-Who-Yells.

I drive the grumbling Vauxhall, lagging behind passing cars. I feel out of place—not spectacular enough, not as wonderful as Grandpa Lolek. Like an unwanted guest at the wheel. The Vauxhall carries me on and I try to imagine how it looks. (When Grandpa Lolek drove the Vauxhall it was always enveloped in velvety clouds and rings of cigarette smoke. The Vauxhall was a stormy tropical island. Something you could see only in the *Tarbut* encyclopedia and in Grandpa Yosef's parking lot. When Grandpa Lolek drove the Vauxhall, cigarette butts rolled around on the floor, sometimes still lit, under the seats too, embers scheming with red eyes. Every time he took a sharp turn, sparks flew, a substitute for the bulbs of the turn signal lights which had burned out in 1976 and could not be repaired because Green the Mechanic could not figure out what the matter was with the electrical wires.) The Vauxhall greets me with a restrained grumble and drives on. I am a grayish figure, propelled towards the convalescence home.

It was afternoon when I arrived. A pleasant corridor of large windows stretched from the entryway to the wards, displaying lawns and shrubs on either side. A bright, clear, beautiful light shone in. You could see almost the entire valley, but it was doubtful that anyone here looked at it. I passed elderly people wearing morbid looking robes, strolling along to somewhere. Elderly people sat on armchairs. They looked at me.

383

I did not have to search for long. I saw him in the hallway, standing opposite a doctor. He was waving his hands and shouting something and a frail group of old people surrounded him, talking excitedly. Only when I got closer did I realize they were translating. Asher Schwimmer was making accusations in Polish, and they were doing their best to interpret into old-fashioned Hebrew while the doctor listened. The slap came, not hard, but the doctor did not lose his attentive look, as if both the translated words and the slap itself contained a hint. Asher Schwimmer turned around, walked feebly to a bench and sat down. A friend wearing a faded suit hurried to his side, supporting Asher Schwimmer and sitting down beside him. I went up to him, wondering if he would recognize me. I scanned him as he sat with his eyes closed.

"Oh, oh! He once had a head of hair! Wild hair!" said his friend, as if, having noticed my look, he had assumed I was not doing justice to Asher Schwimmer in my thoughts. He held out his hand. "Nice to meet you. Dov Ber."

"Nice to meet you, Mr. Ber. I'm Amir. How is Mr. Schwimmer?" I addressed Mr. Ber as if he were Asher Schwimmer's spokesman, a position that he clearly aspired to. He accepted my greeting for both of them, and his look seemed to indicate that he would, at the very first opportunity, convey my good wishes to Asher Schwimmer himself (and for a moment it seemed that the transmission of the greeting would be delayed due to the infinite distance of Asher Schwimmer, rather than his sealed, extinguished face here on the bench beside us). "Not many people come here. One could say we've been forgotten. And your honor is...?"

I told him about Grandpa Yosef, about the little poetry book in his library, Asher Schwimmer's poems from the days when he knew Hebrew. I also sent warm regards from Grandpa Yosef to Asher Schwimmer. Asher Schwimmer opened his eyes. "Hello, Mr. Schwimmer. I said that Yosef Ingberg sends his warm regards!"

Asher Schwimmer replied, "*Todah*." Thank you. In Hebrew. In Hebrew! I must have looked astonished.

Mr. Ber beamed. "I'm teaching him Hebrew." Teaching him Hebrew! Asher Schwimmer closed his eyes again, but Mr. Ber would not let his prodigy disappear from our conversation. "Just like he taught me Hebrew! From him I learned! Everything!"

"Did you know him *there*?" I emphasized the last word and Mr. Ber nodded, confirming, but he did not understand what I meant. As far as he was concerned, *there* was Warsaw, before the war, where Asher Schwimmer had ruled the eager poetry circles, the lovers of the Hebrew language.

Mr. Ber called out, "He was born for great things! Tremendous! At nineteen, we all surrounded him! Worshipped him!" He pointed to Asher Schwimmer, whose eyes were shut tightly as if the memories that gripped him were too strong, as if the Hebrew he was learning was illuminating difficult things. Mr. Ber continued excitedly. "The Romantic style, that was his style. A Byronist! Roses! Pallor! Affairs of the heart! Then he began to take an interest in *Eretz Yisrael* and all his poetry became filled with carobs and sunshine! We loved the carobs and the sunshine too! He was not like us. We ran around trying to find someone who would agree to publish our verses. But him, they chased after him. And he? He only allowed the very best to publish him. If only you had been fortunate enough, such verses!"

"Yes, I know. My grandfather has a copy of his book at home."

Mr. Ber ignored me. "A Zionist, he became! A Zionist! I was a Zionist too, but to go to Palestine? Being a Zionist was talking! Arguing! Proving a point! Big meetings! Good for the soul! But Asher Schwimmer? He was really bitten! He decided to go to *Eretz Yisrael*, to Palestine. To see with his own eyes the Carmel, and Jerusalem. *Nu*, such a young man! And where did he end up? The war broke out, and who knows? Neither in Polish nor in Hebrew, about that matter, he will not talk. But they said he was in Gräditz. Suffering! That's what they said!"

(I pulled out the information easily. Gräditz. Yehezkel Ingster was there. The Jewish kapo who was tried in Israel and sentenced to death. Was it possible that Asher Schwimmer had lost his Hebrew in Gräditz? Did he know Yehezkel Ingster? Could I find out about Yehezkel Ingster from him? But no, I did not want to ask. I had to stop. Enough. Stop right now.)

But I asked Mr. Ber, "You weren't with him?"

"Me? No! No! In Israel too, I didn't see him for fifty years. Here, I found him. Right here, suddenly standing in front of me, Asher Schwimmer! Hebrew I teach him! And take care of him! I serve him gladly! If only you had seen him in Warsaw!"

Asher Schwimmer opened his eyes. I smiled at him.

(Leave. Leave now. There is nothing for me here. It doesn't matter if he slaps people. It doesn't matter what happened in Gräditz. Leave. The bridge is starting to crumble.)

I gently shook Asher Schwimmer's hand. "I'll come and visit again. Grandpa Yosef will come too."

"Pass the salt, please," said Asher Schwimmer, his mouth slowly plucking out the letters.

And his teacher, Mr. Ber, beamed. "See? He's learning! We'll bring back all the Hebrew! All the Hebrew!" He pats Asher Schwimmer's shoulder. "God willing, before we die we'll be reading new verses! Poems by Asher Schwimmer! Here! In Zion! Begone with your feeble poets—long live Asher Schwimmer! Rage on!" He grabbed my hand as it held Asher Schwimmer's. I gently disengaged my hand and turned to leave. As I said goodbye to them both, Mr. Ber helped Asher Schwimmer stand up. "We'll go and sit in the sun. He likes the sun very much!"

(*Roaming opposite your fields / fading / opposite the houses of wine and bread, from evil departing. / She alone yields crops—my soul implored / stalks of grain for her alone / Make golden my maternal sky—wheat of radiance*).

In the Vauxhall, the blender still sat on the back seat. I took it out and ran back. I found Mr. Ber and Asher Schwimmer on their way to the sun. "Here, a little gift. I almost forgot," I said, out of breath.

Mr. Ber was moved. "A blender! A food processor!" He grasped Grandpa Lolek's gift (I would have to come up with an excuse and buy something else for him), waving it at Asher Schwimmer. "A food processor! A food processor!"

We both waited silently to see if the drooping mouth would form the necessary words. But no. Mr. Ber covered for his silence, instantly trampling the failure with his words. "He's tired today. He's just tired!"

Asher Schwimmer stood up—perhaps about to slap me. But no. He ambled over to the shade, fleeing the sun, and Mr. Ber hurried after him to correct his error. I walked back to the Vauxhall. I had to tell Grandpa Yosef to visit.

When I got home, Anat said, "Yakov the assistant called. Attorney Perl passed away."

The next day they carried him on a black stretcher, wrapped in burial shrouds.

1900–1993.

They put his body down in front of us, beneath a sheet. As if this were the proper way to explain, to make us understand. I thought, with us, the ones we need don't die (like Brandy, like Linow Community, who some say has already died, it's just Sarkow Community who makes her keep walking to the grocery every day.) With us people last. But Attorney Perl died.

His body was covered with earth, and I realized that despite the gathered crowds, he was a solitary man. I never asked him about children. Why weren't there any? His life with Laura was not talked of much. Everything that, in his memory, had contained the beautiful days of their married life, shrunk in my memory to a wife led away to Belzec, living ever after in the house at 7 Leonarda Street. Now there was only me, and the remainder of her life would be shut up in train cars, on a slow voyage that would continue on with me. And children? Why weren't there any children? Hadn't he talked once about the eternity of procreation? He had glorified fertility. Like an elaborate agricultural plan in which he was not to participate, only to admire. Why didn't he have any children? I considered infertility, random happenstance, or perhaps a joint decision, or simply the fruits of bad luck. Reasons. Then I thought, And if he had had children? If they had grown up to be Dad's age during the Shoah, would they have survived? They would have been around ten in 1939, and would have fallen into the hands of Hermine Braunsteiner, "the Stomping Mare," or Kurt Franz, "Doll," or all the hands that had waited unknowingly from the moment the children of the thirties were conceived. Anat and I had Yariv. Eternity was ours. And Attorney Perl? His eternity was broken down on little index cards, and I could already envision them as crumbling shreds in a crate stored in a faraway basement. Seventy years on, someone nosy would find the swollen box and investigate the round handwriting. Hermine Braunsteiner, "the Stomping Mare," was charged with the sadistic murder of children and infants at Majdanek. She shot children at close range and whipped their eyes. She managed to immigrate to the United States, was exposed in the early seventies, extradited to Germany and sentenced to life imprisonment. Attorney Perl's eternity was assigned by topic, separated in drawers, hopeless. Why did he not have children?

Anat and I had already discussed having more children, and we probably would (the castles they convince us to build). I thought about the madness of procreation. The families who at the beginning of the century raised children who would become inmates of concentration camps. The families who raised children who would become SS officers. Pitted against one another. At the beginning of the century, on both sides, families feared for the fates of their loved ones on the front of the First World War. My family sent four sons to the war. Four sons who fought for Germany, shoulder to shoulder with people who would one day join the SS and participate in the extermination. Dad's father, Ze'ev, marched all the way to the Italian front. His brother, Dr. Anatol, served in a military hospital. Moshe Gutfreund, aged nineteen, was killed on the Carpathian front, and Leon Gutfreund was taken hostage by the Russians and came home after many years; in World War II he was taken to Belzec. Among those who guarded them, among the jailors, the commanders, the shooters, were the war veterans who-could-be-trusted, the people who didn't flinch at a few heaps of women and children.

When I documented *them*, I recalled, sometimes they looked at me as if to say, "We are documented. Now we are eternalized. And you? Your child, is that your eternity? We had children too, but it was not enough." I thought and thought. Behind the thoughts lurked a fear of sorts; it did not move, but it threatened to cave in, held together only by the thoughts.

The rabbi prayed. A lot of people came to Attorney Perl's

funeral. The many assistants he had employed over the years came, including predecessors of the predecessors. A trail of Yakovs scattered throughout the crowd, prominent in name, visible to strangers. The rabbi had apparently been expecting a quick funeral for a solitary man, and was surprised by the crowds. He prolonged and drew out and glorified the ceremony, trying to catch the relatives' eyes, surprised again, and somewhat vexed, when he invited an orphan to recite the *kaddish* and there was none. Nor was there a brother, or any relatives at all. He looked around sharply to show he wasn't joking around, and Grandpa Yosef came to his rescue. The outcome of their quiet convening was an appropriate *kaddish* prayer.

For a moment it seemed that a true lamentation erupted from the rabbi. The deceased man described in his notes as "a solitary man with no relatives," who had surprised him with a large, grieving crowd, wrung sorrow from his heart. Something stole into his prayers and nested in the routine words and took hold. His voice changed. He recited the letters of the deceased's name, adding a small prayer for each letter, and his anxiety was perceptible (he looked into my eyes—if there was no orphan, he would make do with me). At the end of the ceremony, the mourners filed past me is if I were a relative. They sweltered on the April asphalt (talking about Attorney Perl, about Bochnia, about the city of Stanislaw, about yesterday's news, about the new couch, which had cost a fortune, about a new immigrant technician who repairs televisions, good and cheap, about the uncomfortable shoes, they said it would take a week to wear them in but it's been two weeks and they still hurt). The rabbi shook my hand and bid me farewell. The Yakovs passed me by, their faces familiar. Memories, like a breeze, blew all the way to the deep days of the past. At the end of the row, like a uniter of them all, Yakov the current assistant came up to me. He said he would take care of "all the necessary payments," but he needed to talk to me about something. He asked me to come to the store. Then a figure appeared on the edge of the landscape like a ghostly apparition, six-foot-three-sapphire-blue-eyes-golden-locks. Effi and Hans Oderman had come straight from the airport to meet Grandpa Yosef. What could they do, who could plan on a funeral? Hans Oderman, the artiste of awkwardness, marched behind Effi, passing cautiously among the tombstones. He came up and shook my hand heartily. He pressed Dad's hand too, and Grandpa Yosef's, but our handshake was resonant—the other shakes could not push away a truly gloomy impression. Hans Oderman came back to me and shook my hand again, as if to close the circle of all his impressions of the moment. He stood tensely above the mounds of earth, looking down. The irony could not be ignored: Six-foot-three-sapphire-blue-eyes-golden-locks standing above the lonesome grave of Attorney Perl.

*

We came to the store, Anat and I. (She was the one who asked to come. We're building bridges.) Yakov the assistant welcomed us.

"Mr. Perl, of blessed memory, left the store to me and to Yakov Zimra, who used to work here, on condition that we help the people he always helped. He left a list. He asked that everything behind the wall be given to you. That means the kettle, the towel, the picture of his wife, of blessed memory, and everything in the drawers."

He listed all the things lacking from his inheritance with a cautious look of authority on his face, not yet knowing how far he would take it, what was permitted and what was not. He sized me up, somehow believing I had the power to revoke everything, his share too, and waited for me to say something.

"All right," I said.

I took Anat to the back room. The kettle. The cups. The photograph.

She opened a drawer and took out a little index card. She read it and took out another. "Why was this Hermann Michel called 'the Preacher of Sobibor'?"

"He was responsible for receiving the new transports of Jews. His job was to gather all the Jews as they stepped off the trains and give them a speech about the rosy future waiting for them in the East, and about the importance of work and all sorts of values. It reassured the Jews, and from the Germans' point of view it made the process more efficient. It was easier to lead them to the gas chambers.

Hermann Michel gave speeches to shipment after shipment, twenty minutes before they started shoving them into the gas chambers."

"It says here that he disappeared."

"Yes, they couldn't find him after the war, in the big land of the Germans."

She looked at some more cards, taking an interest.

"You know," I tell her, "they tried out different methods in Sobibor. They suspected the Jews were managing to code warnings into the letters they were forced to write just before being gassed. So in Sobibor they changed the system. When the Jews arrived, they were welcomed at the train platform with light refreshments, cigarettes, hot drinks. They apologized for the difficult transport conditions, explained that the state of war prevented them from using more humane means. They chatted with the Jews, took an interest in their problems and requests. Then they casually encouraged them to go and write postcards to their relatives, for free, before continuing their journey to the East. After the postcards were written, the extermination began."

Anat sighed. "There's no limit to what people can come up with."

"Yes, think of how they looked at the Jews while they wrote their postcards. How they waited for them to finish. Impatiently, but with a gracious expression. They knew they had to restrain themselves just a little longer, just another few moments."

I'm on fire now—she thinks she has an inkling of what the limit is. *There's no limit*, she says, still imagining she knows, more or less, what the limit in fact was.

"You asked about Hermann Michel from Sobibor. Well, I'll tell you about Sobibor. One day the gas chamber engines broke down in Majdanek. There were dying prisoners there, who were supposed to be gassed that day, but because of the break-down they couldn't do it. They found a solution. They transferred them on a special shipment to Sobibor. It was already getting dark when they arrived and the camp staff were resting in their rooms. So they just threw them in a heap in the rain and mud, and left them there until the next morning. You know, survivors of Sobibor testified about that night. They thought they'd seen everything in Sobibor. That's what they thought, but they were wrong. The dying people wailed and sobbed. They were skeletal, ill, without much life left in them, but the rain and cold brought even more suffering. At some point the SS people lost their patience. They went out to the dying people and whipped and whipped and whipped them, until the last whimper died down. Do you still think you have any idea what the limit is?"

"Okay, enough," Anat says.

But I persist, cruelly struggling on—I want her to understand the drawers. Bridges are built from two sides.

"You know, there were Jews who cleaned out the transport trains, to get rid of everything left by those who died or were dying on the way. They were also used to everything by that time. But one day they were forced to open the doors to some train cars and they found them full of greenish corpses. Piles of bodies whose skin peeled away as soon they touched it. Someone had poured chlorine into the cars while the train was in motion. Try to imagine now, the people who had chlorine poured on them, inside moving train cars…"

"Okay, stop, enough."

I have to go on, so she understands. (This is our lust for the abyss). So she realizes that she thinks she knows what went on in the concentration camps, but she doesn't. That only these drawers can bring the truth out. That only through these drawers will she know that Dr. Gohrbandt, in Dachau, investigated how inmates would behave when forced to stand naked for fourteen hours in sub-zero temperatures. She needs to know that because of their screams they could not continue the experiment in Dachau; it was too close to civilian residential areas. And she needs to know that inmates were infected with epidemics and pus was injected under their skin, to see how they would handle the infection. She needs to know that Dr. Mengele pierced the eyes out of little children and he was never caught. She needs to know.

I keep quiet and Anat shuts the drawers, looking pale. "What are you planning to do with all this?"

(Meaning, how far are you intending to go—where are you thinking of arriving?)

"I'm planning to leave it, to quit. I'll put it all in a sealed box in Grandpa Lolek's basement."

(Seventy years from now, someone nosy will find the bloated box and investigate the round handwriting. Hermine Braunsteiner, "the Stomping Mare" of Majdanek.)

She understands—I am quitting for her. Building a bridge. She hugs me.

"Okay…All right, well…" I say. Not only my words are mumbled, but my thoughts too. (We embrace, everything seemingly back to the elemental materials. We will have to refurnish our emotions. Refurnish what is now empty and hard. And the documentation? Should I betray it? Betray Attorney Perl? Should I really quit?)

Anat picks up the photograph of Laura Perl, who was killed in the gas chambers at Belzec, and whose husband taught himself what she had been through in her final moments, and was sad because she had always been so conscientious about cleanliness, even in the harsh ghetto conditions. From the day they took his wife from the house at 7 Leonarda Street, he had launched himself on a route of investigation, pierced a pinhole in the atmosphere and shot off into the distance to watch the ongoing world from high above.

Anat asks, "And the things Attorney Perl went through in the war, did you document them?"

No.

I didn't have time.

*

Obersturmführer Licht mobilized the whole camp to work on *Verbrecher.* But then what? I had no idea. But I had read so much, so many survivor testimonies, that from that endless mass I learned that in fact there were not that many stories, only a multitude of versions of one story, versions that duplicated themselves and were distinguishable only by minute details. I realized I could tell Anat the rest of the story without making too many mistakes. Only trivial details would differentiate what I told her from the truth. The main thing was not to say "Licht," but "Obersturmführer Licht." It could have been another part of the bridge, and the bridge itself was more important than the little details. I would tell her about Obersturm-führer Jürgen Licht, about his deadly gray eyes and his love of guns and puppet theater. After all, here in the store I was taking revenge on her for Attorney Perl's death, and again—what fault was it of hers? Instead of taking revenge, better to tell her about Obersturmführer Licht's play, *Verbercher*, and convince her that a grown man had actu-ally written these things. Explain to her how in the camp that was at his disposal, where everything was allowed, where nothing-can-stop-us-when-we-want-something, a seed of insult planted in his child-hood sprouted, and he used his prisoners to produce the play. Yes, that madness too was allowed in the world of the camps, something as innocent and colorful as a puppet theater, among guard towers and fences. Yes, a world in which they could say, "The *Aktion* is over, be at work on time tomorrow," was a world of fairytales, and from what Attorney Perl had started to tell me about the true existence of the puppet theater, anything could have happened.

In order to tell her, one would have to imagine that the pup-pet theater had become the main facet of life in the camp, and to guess that even so, routine was not abandoned. Every morning rows of prisoners were taken out to dig pits and chop wood. Only those involved in the theater in some way were treated well. It is easy to imagine how work on the theater progressed, and how Obersturm-führer Licht treated Attorney Perl like a personal assistant in a striped uniform. The adjutant was cast aside—his reports and documents were uninteresting. Obersturmführer Jürgen Licht avoided almost any interference in the camp life—that work had always bored him. He devoted all his attention to the play, ignoring orders that came from the outside, until one of his officers, the adjutant for example, complained to senior officers. Then Sturmbanführer Hes came to conduct an inspection visit and Obersturmführer Licht gave him an SS officer's word of honor that everything was as it should be in the camp. In the meantime, the inmates on their way to work began to see refugees on the streets. German civilians. They traveled in long lines with wagons, and the looks on their faces told the inmates that the war was coming to an end. Then the rumors sprung up: all the inmates would be marched on long walks whose purpose was death.

In the camp things were no longer in order. Roll-call was held later and later in the day. Work was stopped before dark and the SS officers hurried back behind the fences. The skies were now the domain of the Americans, and almost every day there were planes dropping bombs, engines always roaring in the distance. Obersturm-führer Licht's camp did not constitute a target, but stray bombs found their way inside every so often. The officers were nervous, looking up at the sky even when it was empty. Some of them simply left, and Obersturmführer Licht did not object. Some inmates escaped too. I can already picture the final scene, in which Obersturmführer Licht and Attorney Perl remain on their own on the theater hilltop. Yes, that will be the scene. I will use all the adventure stories I used to read in Mrs. Gottmartz's library, all the Karl May books about the Wild West, to imagine the finale. Anat will believe it, she has to. Anyone who says "there is no limit" and thinks they are capable of imagining the limit, must believe. Because if Sobibor happened and Majdanek happened, anything could happen between Obersturmführer Licht and Attorney Perl, even a duel. No one could protest even if that was the final scene, even if I decide right now that Obersturmführer Licht's black pistol has a twin, a silver pistol on his right hip.

Up until the final duel, everything was devoted to the play. That was the new order of the camp. The production of *Verbercher* had to go on. Some of the Ukrainian policemen, perhaps because they liked working with wood, were assigned to work on the puppets. Whips and guns were laid down, and guards and inmates began convers-ing with one another. Everything revolved around the theater, while planes flew through the skies and a stream of refugees filed past the camp. Obersturmführer Licht's officers had already decided to wrest the reins of power from him, but he outsmarted them by quickly ordering a rapid organization of death marches. Three rows left the camp, all of his officers and soldiers leading lines of those inmates who were not essential to the theater. Most of the puppet makers were sent off too, and the carvers and tailors—anyone who's work was already done. Obersturmführer Licht instructed that the camp gates be locked and guard posts reinforced. He summoned his adjutant and shot him. The Ukrainian guards were ordered not to allow anyone in, not even SS. The camp became Obersturmführer Licht's fortress. There would be a puppet theater.

American planes kept bombing, and their shattering trail of bombardments fell inside the camp too. The Ukrainian guards began to flee. Obersturmführer Licht did not stop them. He remained alone with his two pistols among the inmates still at work on his play, at his side only two Ukrainians who chose to continue their puppet-building work.

On April 6th everything was ready. Obersturmführer Licht set curtain time for six in the evening. Planes had been attacking in the distance as early as noon, sounds of artillery reverberating through the air. The distant noise grew closer and closer, as if the planes were about to blindly assail the camp. Two Ukrainians tried to escape. From over forty yards away, with only two bullets, Obersturmführer Licht shot them. There were whispers among the inmates, some conjectured that he had no bullets left, but no one dared attack him. Alone among twenty-one inmates and three Ukrainians, Obersturmführer Licht annihilated any intentions of rebellion, any hopes of liberation, any lust for revenge; the play would go on at six.

At six in the evening he sat down in his armchair on the rugs. The rectangular stage was lit up and the play began. Attorney Perl stood on the little wooden stage and began the opening speech in his lucidly thundering voice, just as a pulverizing barrage of artillery landed between the fences. Obersturmführer Licht drew his pistol and placed it on his lap. "Continue!"

The artillery was merciless. A battle was raging in the distance. When the puppet of the Communist teacher appeared in the window, about to confiscate little Obersturmführer Licht's flag, a shell exploded at the foot of the hill and shrapnel sparked through the night sky. The puppeteers ran away. Behind the curtain they fled on their hands and knees and ran down the hill as Obersturmführer Licht's bullets whistled around them. The remaining inmates burst out of the camp and disappeared into the dark. The dim thundering of plane engines could be heard, and after a few moments there were bombardments that set a nearby hill ablaze. The only figures remaining on the theater hilltop were Obersturmführer Licht and Attorney Perl.

Anyone who says, *There is no limit*, and thinks they can imagine the limit, must believe.

Obersturmführer Licht looked at Attorney Perl as he stood thundering on the wooden stage. The Commandant approached his prisoner. He thrust his silver pistol into Attorney Perl's hand and set the terms. "Ten steps, then turn and shoot!" He turned and began walking.

And I have no idea if the Jew Attorney Perl will fight the Nazi officer, like the Jew Grandpa Lolek did, or if he will wisely escape, like the Jew Grandpa Yosef did. Or whether he might do something unexpected, like the Jew Hirsch, something that will transcend logic and imagination.

Anat will ask me, "So, what happened?"

And I will smile at her and say something like, "He ran away." I have to say something. After all, we know he survived. "Attorney Perl lived, as you know."

*

All the wonders, all the treasures, all the miracles. All the secrets, all the riddles, all the questions. It all spun into a gleaming cloud whose center hung over the brown wooden table in Grandpa Yosef's house.

For three days he asked, and finally I came to meet Hans Oderman at his house. Effi said, "Come this evening, I'll be there too." So I did.

We sit within circles of pleasant conversation, bringing each other up to date on what's new, telling stories, reporting how we're doing. But over the circles looms a pulsating cloud, its vapors dripping down and baptizing us—the end is near. The childhood riddles, Gershon Klima's sewage, the letter from Finkelstein, the battle at Monte Cassino, Grandpa Hainek's sons, the questions I asked Attorney Perl, Grandpa Yosef's journey, Adler's philosophy, Hirsch's theological inquiries, a ray of light from the Rabbi of Kalow, and the memory of Rothschild—all come together like clouds at the edge of a landscape. We sit at the table and talk comfortably, and I am certain: There will be closure here.

Grandpa Yosef serves us dinner. He brings out more and more dishes of increasingly peculiar concoctions. Effi helps him, leaving me and Hans to face one another. Six-foot-three-sapphire-blue-eyes-golden-locks and I converse. Every so often she comes in to interfere:

"I told Hans about your documentation. Talk to him, he's very interested."

She has an agenda; she's promoting a scheme.

Hans smiles awkwardly, having partially understood what Effi said in Hebrew.

"They told me that you have documented what happened to your family in the war. I'm very interested in this."

"Interested?"

"Yes, Mr. Ingberg said he would translate what you wrote into German for me, if you would agree." Hans looks at me with a certain discomfort on his face. As if things are about to float to the surface and he can already sense them erupting. "Effi said you found out some unpleasant things about your wife's grandfather."

(What else did she tell him? She looks like she's plotting something. She seems too directed, too arrow-like. As if she is assassinating the life I have now. But she walks past us innocently and asks, "Coffee, anyone?")

"Umm…yes. He was a sort of Jewish collaborator," I tell Hans. That's enough.

"You know, something similar happened to me."

Similar?

Tribal stories unfold around the campfire, and Grandpa Yosef arrives from somewhere and sits down, and Effi comes, with the coffee miraculously already brewed. We linger over our mugs for a while. Add sugar cubes. Stir politely. More milk?

"When I was here last year and you asked me what my family did during the war, you could say that I lied. Actually, I did not lie. Everything I said was the truth, but it was the truth that I am comfortable with. My father really was an orphan, and he was adopted by a family when he was ten. Everything I told you was about that family. I did not tell you about the real family, not because of lies, but because I have no idea who my family is."

(All of us are sitting at the table, yet Hans Oderman is talking to me.)

"My father grew up an orphan. As a child, he was moved around from one orphanage to another. He told me very little about that period. It was an unspoken matter in our home. I'm sure you understand..."

(All the secrets, all the riddles, all the questions.)

"It was as though his orphanhood concealed a great secret. Perhaps because of how little he told and how much I tried to fill in with my imagination, I began to take an interest in orphanages. That was how I got to my academic research. And when I was writing my dissertation, I read one day something about the "Fountain of Life" project, *Lebensborn* in German. This is not something that is talked about very much. There I was, an academic researcher in the field, and I had never even heard of *Lebensborn*. Much less a layman. The *Lebensborn* was part of a plan devised by Himmler to encourage the procreation of the Aryan race. That word, *Lebensborn*, would not leave my thoughts. I felt that it had some connection to my father. I had a clear intuition. Something you cannot understand, but still you sense. I'm sure you understand...

"I began to make calculations, you see. My father never mentioned any details, and in Germany it was not so customary to investigate what had happened during the war years. But I began asking Father about his early years and, as if he had been waiting all that time for me to uncover his secret on my own, he said, 'Yes, I am a *Lebensborn* child, and I have no idea where I come from.'"

"What do you mean, 'no idea where he comes from'?" I ask.

But Hans Oderman heatedly continues a flow of talk that has long been welling inside of him. Questions can be answered later. He tells me about Heinrich Himmler—Reichsführer Himmler—who, more than all the other Nazi leaders, had the appearance of a modest clerk, shy and withdrawn. Behind his small glasses hid a disturbed personality bound by hallucinations, aspiring to fame, unfeeling. He constructed ideals of an eternal Reich and tried to make them come true; he failed, but the remnants of his ideas were left in the world to suffer. He had his scientists calculate the rate of exterminating unwanted peoples and the rate of building the German Aryan race, and they indicated a discrepancy between the required number and the expected outcome. Riechsführer Himmler hatched a scheme. He promised his Führer a hundred and twenty million Aryan Germans by 1980. He came up with a plan that would, in the future, produce half a billion Aryan Germans if everything went according to his calculations. First he began a campaign to encourage higher birthrates, supporting every German child-bearing woman through any possible circumstances of childbirth—every child was adopted by the Reich. Even children born from relations between German soldiers and suitable women in the occupied lands were adopted by the Reich. Heinrich Himmler instructed that not even a drop of German seed should be lost. Still, that was not enough. The population growth was too small and too slow. Himmler ordered that children and babies in occupied countries with potentially Aryan qualities be either kidnapped or purchased. Children were taken from their parents by bribery or by force. In problematic cases, the parents were liquidated, labeled as partisans or outlaws or enemy agents. The children, from all over Europe, were educated in special boarding schools. Those who grew up to be disappointments, lacking in Aryan traits, were exterminated. Those who met expectations joined the Reich. The little girls were treated with hormones to expedite their sexual maturation—without the ability to quickly produce offspring, their annexation to the Reich would be fruitless.

Despite the kidnapping and adoption programs, the birthrate was not promising. And so Himmler declared a new program: *Lebensborn*, the Fountain of Life. Pure Aryan women were housed in convalescence homes in order to bear children for the Reich. The fathers were all SS men, the purest of the race. Each woman and her offspring were awarded the finest of conditions, in a world completely cut off from the hardships and hunger that were slowly descending upon the people of Germany. All that was required of these women was to give birth, to produce more and more babies for the Reich.

The essence of the *Lebensborn* scheme was to fill the wombs of German women with fetuses, to quickly manufacture rushed progeny and deliver them so the wombs would be available for the next batch of offspring.

Hans Oderman keeps talking without a pause, and I realize that the two polarities of the German Reich are coming to light simultaneously: On the one hand, a twisted enterprise of death is taking place, a burning urgency to shove more and more transports into the gas chambers, each transport making way for the next. On the other, an equally twisted enterprise of life, the chambers of female wombs being stuffed to capacity, one fetus making way for the next. This animalistic machine does not rest for a moment, so urgent are the needs of the Reich.

Within this wild, confused enterprise, born of the yearnings of Reichsführer Himmler, Hans Oderman's father is created. Born, perhaps, or possibly kidnapped and reeducated. Hans Oderman has no idea. Hans's father did not remember the *Lebensborn* years. The four-year-old's memories go back only to the post-war years, after German defeat. He told Hans very little about those blurred years of hunger. Huge orphanages, endless hours of enforced sleep. Facing the broken window of an abandoned house. A large hole behind a tree. For some reason, the hole becomes his friend, he likes to look at it, in the dark too, when he must sleep, sleep, sleep.

The war left thousands of infants, a master race that no one wanted, and there was no one to keep the promises that had created them.

"I began a tireless investigation. Most of the *Lebensborn* files were destroyed by the officials before the *Lebensborn* houses were occupied. A few papers were left, some memos, but there was no way to find my father. He was born a *Lebensborn*, that much he knew. An elderly childless couple had taken him in after the war, but they died and my father went back to the orphanages. He still had an aunt from his adoptive parents, and she told him everything she knew, which was very little. I searched through all the remaining files and documents. My father's father might have been an SS man, my father might have been a kidnapped child, perhaps Polish.

Hundreds of thousands of children were kidnapped in the war years, and who knows? I asked my dad what he thought, and he told me that sometimes he felt as if the Polish language sounded familiar. I would like to think that my father was kidnapped, rather than the planned child of an SS man, but look at me..."

Six-foot-three-sapphire-blue-eyes-golden-locks looks at me and I find myself convicting him against my own will. Then I think, "So what? So what if his father's father was in the SS?"

(All the wonders, all the treasures, all the miracles.)

"I would like to believe that my father was kidnapped. The children they kidnapped were usually a little older, but still. Or maybe my father was the offspring of a simple German army man. They usually only allowed party members to impregnate women in the *Lebensborn* houses, but sometimes, towards the end, regular soldiers were given the chance too."

We sit quietly. Grandpa Yosef remembers that we haven't eaten dessert yet. Something hovers over Hans and myself, the story of my documentation and the story of his research, the truth I did not want to reach and the truth Hans wished not to find. From that clashing of wings comes a deceitful sort of lesson that says loudly: Never enquire.

"When you asked me what my family did during the war, I told you what was convenient, I didn't exactly lie."

(Still making excuses, Hans Oderman the artiste of awkwardness.)

"My father built his life without complaints. He built a house. He built a family. He started from nothing and achieved everything. I respect him very much, admire him even. It's a shame I never had a grandfather like everyone else did. There was the aunt, and I called her Grandma, but it wasn't really...."

(All the wonders, all the treasures, all the miracles.)

As I look at Hans Oderman, I realize what his role is, what it has been from the first day I saw him. He is my reflection. That's it. I can no longer say *us* and *them*. Every move I make, every line I draw, there will be a line on my reflection too. Every thought of

mine will produce a thought on the other side too. There is no more
us and *them*.

"I want to write a book about the *Lebensborn*, about the kidnapping operation and the breeding farms. Today in Germany there
are hundreds of thousands of people who are assumed to be *Lebensborn* children. There were more. Some were returned to their parents,
if there were any. But there are many left without fathers, without
mothers, without memories. You know, no one ever punished the
Lebensborn directors, Dr. Gregor Ebner and Dr. Max Sollmann. And
they were the people who signed documents ordering that a disap-
pointing baby be liquidated. They allowed transports of kidnapped
children with unsatisfactory data to be left to die. No one even bothered to investigate them. Strange, isn't it?"

A reflection. A transparency. An unwanted world of mirrors, all
the lines between me and him are reflected, joined together, insepa-
rable. Since the day I let him carry his own suitcases, it was clear—he
was destined to finish my search. To show me that everything was
more complicated than I could even conceive.

A gleaming cloud whose center hung over the brown wooden
table in Grandpa Yosef's house opens up. All the wonders shower
down, all the treasures, all the miracles. All the secrets, all the riddles,
all the questions.

I did not go straight home that evening. After what Hans had
told me, after the *Lebensborn*, after what I had come to understand,
the reflection that trapped me and the realization that there was no
simple explanation, I just stayed there. I could not leave. In order
to be capable of being at home with Anat and Yariv, in order to be
capable of living my life, the world had to operate differently. Like
turning a sock inside out, the world simply spun around us, leaving us
in our place, in our time, but it came in closer, upside-down, joining
in. Time would have to figure out how to make things settle down—
with us everything continued as usual. Hans stayed at Grandpa Yosef's,
washing dishes I suppose, speaking German. Effi disappeared somewhere—probably home, or perhaps to another place in her life (she
too had bridges), and I found myself walking down Katznelson in

the direction of home. At the end of all days, I believe, I will be sitting on a couch opposite Hans Oderman in Grandpa Yosef's house. That will be the revenge of time. But that night, I walked down Katznelson without a thought in my head, and looked up at one of the tall poplar trees. Some of its bark was starting to shed, hanging limply as if I had caught it in the middle of an escape attempt. I stood and thought of those neighborhood trees for a long time. Who had planted them? Who had chosen poplars and poincianas and pepper trees and pink bauhinias and purple jacarandas and divided them up among the yards by some secret code? Who had taken the time? The people who lived here had never planted a tree, and I could not imagine a single one of them dropping everything to dig a hole for a sapling. Someone, perhaps a municipal clerk, must have picked out the trees when this neighborhood was designed. It was designed, after all, wasn't it? And the trees, to which I had never given much thought before, suddenly appeared before me: the poplar, the poinciana, Gershon Klima's Indian bombax. Hirsch emerged from the hibiscus shrubs, as if summoned for a purpose. Hirsch.

He looked at me with his lost gaze, seeming unsure of how he had come to be standing in front of me. The usual madness was gone from his face. He looked at me as if he knew me, as if I were doomed to be his audience, the first to hear the conclusion of a lifetime of enquiry, a theological exploration that, to the outside, had always appeared to be a frightening madness, but inside was profound erudition.

Hirsch stood facing me and found himself with no choice but to expose, precisely and terrifyingly, the final, definitive sentence, the conclusion of an irrevocably sealed life: Everything, the Shoah, had been an ordinary occurrence. Ordinary people made it happen and ordinary people were its victims.

I looked at him and answered silently, yes.

Afterword

Lolek and Hainek were my father's cousins, the sons of Gustava Gutfreund, who died of cancer at the age of thirty-one, before Dad was born. They lived in Kielce with their father, the educator Doctor Feuer, headmaster of the Hebrew Gymnasium in Kielce, and with his second wife. Dad never saw Hainek and Lolek. Only his sister, Aunt Anola, once saw Hainek, the younger brother. She was around twelve, he was thirteen or so, and to this day she carries the impression of their encounter. From their one conversation, as they walked down the streets of Bochnia, she remembers that he was handsome and had the aura of being a "man of the world." Fifty years later, she remembers exactly what he told her.

His older brother, Lolek, who was several years older than Hainek, was never seen. They know he had planned to go to *Eretz Yisrael* to study, but did not make it. The war broke out. As far as is known, Dr. Feuer and his sons, Hainek and Lolek, were killed in the region of Lvov, or perhaps somewhere else. The Kielce memorial book mentions Dr. Feuer and his second wife. Hainek and Lolek are not mentioned. We looked for the grave of their mother, Gustava, in the Bochnia cemetery, but it is gone too.

I continued the lives of Lolek and Hainek in their new, surviving, personas, two brothers from the generation of our grandfathers. Grandpa Lolek's service in the volunteer army of the Polish General Anders is based on the service of Avraham (Romek) Gutfreund, my father's uncle, in that same army.

Grandpa Yosef is a purely invented character. He is probably inspired by my true grandfather, Grandpa Shalom, who was tortured by the Gestapo. The tortures caused the onset of his disease, and I only knew him through the barriers of illness. When I grew up I heard stories of the man he had been before he became ill, and I recreated his character with a different name, far from the one and only persona of Grandpa Shalom I can imagine.

Attorney Perl from Stanislaw lived in the house at 7 Leonarda Street in the Bochnia ghetto, with my father's family. He and his wife, whose name I do not know, were killed in Belzec together. Dad remembers him as an educated and dignified attorney, an imposing persona. He was born in 1872 and his full name was Solomon (Shlomo) Perl. During the course of writing this book I discovered that the couple had a daughter, Genya, and a granddaughter, Danusha, of whom the Perls spoke incessantly. I have no information about their fates. I recreated him so that he could expose a little of the truth about that period. The names, quotes and other details from Attorney Perl's index card are true, to the extent I was able to verify through publicly available sources.

Only a fraction of the Nazi criminals were tried or served any significant sentences. Contrary to popular belief, the vast majority of those who committed or collaborated in atrocities accepted no responsibility for their actions. Formal pardons, shady deals, and a conspiracy of forgiveness and silence enabled the committers of atrocities to live out their lives in freedom.

Characters who are part of the plot, such as Ahasuerus and Obersturmführer Licht, never existed, but were forged out of a mosaic of the extreme figures who most certainly did exist in the mad world of the Nazi regime.

Persons mentioned in the plot such as Kurt Franz, 'Doll,' of Treblinka, or the Jewish kapo Yehezkel Ingster, absolutely existed. One can read of their misdeeds and those of hundreds and thousands like them, in the Yad Vashem library and archives.

The mad enterprise of the *Lebensborn*, the "Fountain of Life," is chronicled in *Of Pure Blood*, by Mark Hillel and Clarissa Henry.

About the Author

Amir Gutfreund

Amir Gutfreund was born in Haifa in 1963. After studying applied mathematics at the Technion, he joined the Israeli Air Force and became a Lieutenant Colonel. *Our Holocaust* was his first novel. It was awarded the Buchman Prize by the Yad Vashem Holocaust Remembrance Institute. His second novel, *Shoreline Mansions*, won the prestigious Sapir Prize in 2003, and is forthcoming from *the* Toby Press. His third novel, *The World, a Little Later*, was recently published in Israel. Gutfreund lives in the Galilee with his wife, Netta, a clinical psychologist, and their two children, Romi and Nimrod.

The fonts used in this book are from the Garamond family